RADIO STARR

A NOVEL

LISA LEHMANN

First edition, 2025

ISBN Number: 979-8-9912318-8-6
Library of Congress Number: 2025938990

Author photo ~ Erika Humke, Humke Group
"Takin' Me Too Soon" and "Love Knot" lyrics ~ Lisa Lehmann
Cover design ~ Vagabond Creative Studio

The story, all names, characters, and incidents portrayed in this production are fictitious. No identification with actual persons (living or deceased), places, buildings, and products are intended or should be inferred.

Content warning: This book explores mature content including cigarette smoking, drug use, sexual assault, and other adult situations. Additional scenes include death.

Dedication

For anyone who worked in radio—from spinning vinyl during a semester in college to those who made it a career.

And for anyone who loved radio growing up and wondered what's going on when the microphone is off.

"I couldn't be myself . . . that just never works.

You have to be yourself on the radio."

~ Bob Edwards
Long-time host of Morning Edition
as told to Terry Gross on the NPR show Fresh Air

```
********************************
*   EVA'S TOP 50 COUNTDOWN SHOW   *
********************************
```

1	SWEET DREAMS	YES	:18	3:45	FADE
2	TO PLAY SOME MUSIC	JOURNEY	:17	3:13	COLD
3	HAD TO FALL IN LOVE	THE MOODY BLUES	:25	3:54	COLD
4	EVERYTHING'S COMING OUR WAY	SANTANA	:16	3:14	FADE
5	FEARLESS	PINK FLOYD	:44	6:08	FADE
6	TURN IT ON AGAIN	GENESIS	:35	3:27	FADE
7	JUST GOT PAID	ZZ TOP	:27	3:48	FADE
8	CHANGES	LOGGINS AND MESSINA	:14	3:45	COLD
9	MIDNIGHT RIDER	ALLMAN BROTHERS	:14	2:56	FADE
10	SOMETHING'S HAPPENING LIVE	PETER FRAMPTON	:17	5:29	COLD
11	RAPTURE	BLONDIE	:27	4:55	FADE
12	IN THE DARK	BILLY SQUIRE	:24	4:08	COLD
13	IT DOESN'T MATTER	FIREFALL	:15	3:26	FADE
14	DO THEY KNOW IT'S CHRISTMAS	BAND AID	:07	3:40	FADE
15	BLOWIN' FREE	WISHBONE ASH	:42	5:17	COLD

16	LIKE A HURRICANE	NEIL YOUNG	:15	8:20	COLD
17	EASY LIVIN'	URIAH HEEP	:12	2:35	COLD
18	TILL IT SHINES	BOB SEGER	:16	3:47	FADE
19	STAND BACK	STEVIE NICKS	:20	4:44	FADE
20	(I KNOW) I'M LOSING YOU	ROD STEWART	:39	5:19	COLD
21	CHAIN OF FOOLS	ARETHA FRANKLIN	:03	2:34	FADE
22	PICTURE BOOK	THE KINKS	:07	2:33	COLD
23	WORKING MAN	RUSH	:14	7:08	COLD

24	TELL MAMA	SAVOY BROWN	:31	5:16	COLD
25	PHOENIX	DAN FOGELBERG	:17	7:07	COLD
26	TOO LATE FOR GOODBYES	JULIAN LENNON	:07	3:26	FADE
27	MORE THAN THIS	ROXY MUSIC	:13	4:11	FADE
28	HEARD IT IN A LOVE SONG	MARSHALL TUCKER	:12	3:26	COLD
29	THE RAIN SONG	LED ZEPPELIN	:30	7:35	COLD
30	LIVING IN AMERICA	JAMES BROWN	:01	5:55	COLD
31	HONEY BEE	TOM PETTY & HEARTBREAKERS	:00	4:55	COLD
32	WILL THE WOLF SURVIVE?	LOS LOBOS	:29	3:38	COLD
33	FEELIN' BLUE	CCR	:25	4:58	FADE
34	DON'T DO IT	THE BAND	:23	4:21	COLD
35	YOU'RE NO GOOD	LINDA RONSTADT	:08	3:34	FADE
36	DON'T GET ME WRONG	PRETENDERS	:18	3:47	COLD
37	IT'S TOO LATE	CAROLE KING	:09	3:50	COLD
38	LUCKY STAR	MADONNA	:23	3:33	FADE
39	SPARE ME A LITTLE OF YOUR LOVE	FLEETWOOD MAC	:23	3:36	FADE
40	WHAT'S ON MY MIND	KANSAS	:15	3:25	COLD
41	A DREAM GOES ON FOREVER	TODD RUNDGREN	:10	2:20	COLD
42	DON'T SHED A TEAR	PAUL CARRACK	:26	4:55	FADE
43	FROM THE BEGINNING	EMERSON, LAKE & PALMER	:32	4:13	FADE
44	TAKIN' THE TIME TO FIND	DAVE MASON	:32	4:27	FADE

45	HEADING FOR THE LIGHT	TRAVELING WILBURYS	:05	3:34	COLD
46	ROAD TO NOWHERE	TALKING HEADS	:00	4:02	COLD
47	WALK AWAY	JAMES GANG	:09	3:30	FADE
48	SLOW TURNING	JOHN HIATT	:12	3:28	FADE
49	DON'T CHANGE	INXS	:47	4:25	FADE
50	RIGHT HERE RIGHT NOW	JESUS JONES	:23	3:06	COLD

PART ONE

1. SWEET DREAMS ~ YES

The dream swirled in Eva's head all day, a nightmare really, of opening the microphone and not knowing her name.

Sitting cross-legged on the floor at her mother's apartment, she tried to stay present, but her mind kept fast-forwarding to her first gig at the campus radio station. Would her voice be good enough? Would she even find her voice?

All afternoon, they had sifted through boxes of curled photos and faded memorabilia, a delicate dance between getting rid of stuff and overwhelming her mother. A rhythm emerged: *Keep. Sell. Chuck.* A picture of Eva and her mom dressed like sisters: petite frames, dark hair, matching dimples—*Keep.* A Jimi Hendrix concert ticket from the Dane County Coliseum—*Sell.* A wrinkled Brewers bumper sticker—*Chuck.*

With their heads close, they studied a Polaroid of Eva's father under a bright spotlight on stage wearing his red beret, eyes closed, his face blissful. The smoke from a cigarette tucked into the head of his electric bass surrounded him in a blue swirl. Everything in the photo was now gone. The guitar. The hat. The charming man who adored her.

Eva read the caption, written in her mom's artistic longhand. "Dean 'Pop' Chastine. Mississippi River Blues Fest, July '71." Eva *tsk*ed. "That was ten years ago."

"That was the summer you stayed with Grandma Chastine, and I traveled with your pop," her mom said, sadness in her eyes. "You may have gotten your height from me, but you're lucky you got your musical talent from him. Your pop was one cool cat."

Eva stared at the picture of her father. He would sing in her ear, his voice rumbly, his face rough against hers. She tugged on her lower lip, wishing Artie could have met him.

The first time she'd laid eyes on her husband *he'd* been on stage wielding a guitar with his band, Artie LaVette & the Inverted

1

Paradiddles. "I could get lost in those big brown eyes," he'd said to her after the show, a well-used line, but it worked. Oblivious to the cold October rain, they had made out in a dark alley behind the Starlight Lounge, which led to a short period of infatuation. A whirlwind of dating, shows, and feverish sex. *That was two years ago.* She frowned. Artie hadn't been the same since the band broke up and everything else went to hell.

Eva kissed her pop's photo before tucking it into her backpack. She wanted to have her dad near her that night.

"Oh wow," her mom said. "Here's a note he left before the Heartland tour with Steve Miller."

> *Honeybunch,*
> *Didn't want to wake you, but the bus is here.*
> *Don't worry, the time will slip by as fast as a bebop solo.*
> *Tell Little Eva I'll be home for her recital. Make her hit*
> *those keys like a pro! You're my girls, the heartbeat in*
> *every note I play.*
> *XOXO, Dean*

"Keep," Eva said.

From a shoebox, she retrieved a bundled stack of Polaroids, all closeups: peeling paint on a gas pump, a cracked headlamp, rusty rivets on a steel girder.

"Once upon a time, I dreamed of being an artist," her mom said. She yanked Eva's long braid and smiled. "Chuck."

Eva stood. She tossed the packet into an overflowing wicker basket. With her hands on her hips, she observed her mom's cramped basement efficiency. Rust-colored shag carpet, a mini oven, a fondue set on the counter, the small icebox. How many times had she offered to help clear out Pop's stuff? At least some progress had been made. The money from selling his Rickenbacker guitar and his standup bass would cover her mom's rent for a few years. Near the door, stacks of boxes sat waiting for a ride to the thrift store. Yet size XL jackets hung in the closet, and crammed in a nook by the bed, the family piano suffocated under piles of men's clothes: jeans, wool sweaters, his scarf collection.

Her mom opened a flat shirt box, unraveling an object from layers of tissue paper. "Oh my gosh! Check it out."

Pop's raspberry-red beret.

Eva pulled the hat on, lowering it to one side. "How do I look?"

"Like daddy's little girl again." Her mom laughed and tweaked Eva's nose. "He thought you'd be famous, you know. His 'Little Liberace.'"

Eva had forgotten he called her that. She wondered how he'd feel if he knew his daughter was about to play music—not on stage—but on the radio. "I'm Billie Soul," she whispered.

"Why don't you use your real name? Eva LaVette has a nice ring to it." She rubbed Eva's back.

"I don't want anyone to know it's me. Not at first. What if I sound awful?"

Her mom got up from the floor and slipped an arm around her waist. "You'll be great. Just be yourself."

I don't need to be myself. I just need to be a star. For Pop.

"What's Artie doing tonight? Will he be listening?"

"He's at Faye and Dwayne's. The guys are going over their weekly fantasy football roster and then they're going shopping for the party tonight. The annual Christmas bash."

"And you'll be missing out on the fun? Come here. I've got an idea," her mom said while she dug through a drawer in her vanity.

Eva adjusted the beret in the mirror, conjuring Billie Soul: *Born in Memphis and named after Billie Holiday, Ms. Soul is the daughter of a record producer and a sheep farmer. A piano virtuoso from the age of five, Billie shares her vast knowledge of rock and roll on her late-night radio show,* Vinyl Grooves. *She's married to Mark Hamill, Luke from* Star Wars.

"Try these on," her mom said, passing her a pair of tinted granny glasses.

My disguise. Eva smiled as she curled the wire stems behind her ears. The spectacles looked more hippie than jazz, but the pink tint matched the beret. She spoke into a perfume bottle. "Good evening, cool cats and kittens. I'm Billie Soul and here's a little number from the Mississippi Blues Collaborative with 'Pop' Chastine on bass." She knew the campus station had the recording. The listeners would eat it up—a DJ playing her own father's music.

From across the room, Grandma Chastine's old cuckoo clock chimed, the mechanical bird emerging five times.

"Crap! I'm supposed to pull records before my shift." Coco Nix, the student mentor, would be miffed if she came in late. Eva cleaned the pink glasses using the tail of her flannel shirt. "I have to split. The bus will be here soon." She zipped up her navy parka, a coat she'd had since freshman year of high school.

"I'll be listening," her mom said, smiling.

She kissed her mother before racing out the door.

Oh, man. Here goes nothing.

Eva liked being a passenger. She peered out the bus window into homes glowing with incandescent light, catching glimpses of people at their kitchen sink or watching TV, their blinds still open in the twilight. She pressed her face against the cold glass, thinking how nice it would be to have a beard like Artie's.

The bus passed La Crosse South, her old high school, home of the Tigers. Shaking her head, she thought of the unofficial class motto: *Sex, drugs, and rock 'n' roll, baby!* The school's clock tower was still standing. She wrung her hands; she was on in twenty minutes!

Most students had done the required air shift early in the semester, and now they were the cool kids on campus. Instead, Eva chose to practice until she was perfect. She hoped it had been enough, as an idea had been growing all semester: if her voice

4

sounded good, she could change her career path and switch her major from teaching to broadcasting. It was now or never.

The bus passed the "World's Largest Six-Pack" and lumbered down Front Street. Along Riverside Park, illuminated by streetlights in fog, the lonesome La Crosse Queen paddleboat sat on blocks. Eva's inner DJ kicked in. *From the summer of '75 and the LP* What Were Once Vices are Now Habits, *the Doobie Brothers with "Black Water," their first number one single.* The summer before last, she and Artie stood at the stern on a balmy night, watching the paddlewheel churn foam into the black river as it glided between bluffs. Under the stars, Artie took her by the hand and called her "pretty mama"—just like the song—while Dixieland music tinkled up from the lower deck. It had been the most romantic evening of her life. *Life.* When the baby kicked for the first time, Artie was behind her with his hands on her stomach. As the paddlewheel turned, she'd felt the first inkling of love for him.

With a squeal of the brakes, the bus stopped in front of the J. Wayne Communications building. She hustled out the door, her boots sloshing in a pile of slush at the curb, her backpack flying as she sprinted up the three flights to the radio department. Just as she approached master control, the on-air light blinked on.

2. TO PLAY SOME MUSIC ~ JOURNEY

Eva waited outside the studio for the red on-air light to go off. Bending down, she quietly unzipped her backpack to retrieve her brand-new radio operator's license, a manila-colored ticket to a golden career, and an expensive pair of Koss headphones, a purchase she hadn't disclosed to Artie.

Her breathing became quick and shallow; her first time on the air would be in minutes. What if she stammered or accidentally swore on a hot mic, like Coco's cousin Dustin had?

The light blinked off. She took a deep breath and squared her narrow shoulders. Inside the dark, cozy studio, music throbbed low on the monitors, subdued by black foam walls. Familiar smells surrounded her: the scent of vinyl and audio tape, the grease used to lubricate warm equipment like turntables and reel-to-reel decks, the lingering trace of cigarettes and coffee. A U-shaped workstation, encircling a control board packed with sliders and switches, dominated the room. A gooseneck lamp illuminated the board. On the right sat two turntables, one spinning at a lazy 33⅓ revolutions per minute. Above the board, a shiny microphone hung from a suspension boom.

The mic! Eva's heart drummed a syncopated beat against her ribs. She dropped her backpack on the counter near the guest mic and shook melted snow from her parka before draping it on a chair to dry.

Coco Nix, a senior and Eva's mentor for the evening, burst in from a door in the back, holding a stack of records in front of her like a birthday cake.

"Hey, LaVette. You should have been here an hour ago. I had to pull your records."

Eva adjusted the beret and ran a hand down her long braid, wet with snow. "I'm sorry, Coco. I was stuck helping my mom." At the board, she plugged in her headphones and sat.

6

Coco leaned the albums on the floor against a cabinet. "Hey, are you okay? I like your getup, but you look shook."

"I'm petrified. Look. My hands are shaking. What if I blow it?"

"You'll be great! Just relax."

"How many people will be listening?"

Coco put a finger on her chin. "Listenership peaks during Morning Edition but by nighttime, five thousand or so."

"Five *thousand?*"

"Don't worry, LaVette. They're not listening to critique you. They want to know the name of a song or hear the forecast. Speaking of, I'll go clear the wire." As Coco swung through the door to the news department, the Teletype dinged. "Something's up!"

"Really?" *Holy crap.* Eva hoped it wasn't a big story, something to throw off her game. The format at night was supposed to be all music: blues, bebop, fusion, smooth jazz. Announcers were to break in only for a tornado warning or an emergency alert. Like when Mount St. Helens exploded or President Reagan was shot.

Coco returned, waving paper ripped from the Teletype. "A winter storm warning." She handed the bulletin to Eva, who had been cuing and re-cuing a record.

"Whew. Thanks." Eva rehearsed the weather alert out loud, then practiced hand movements from the mic's volume knob to the turntable switch and back to the mic.

"Are you using your real name?" Coco asked.

"Oh, no! I'm going incognito." Eva lowered her voice, peering over the tops of her granny glasses. "*I'm Billie Soul.*"

"Ooh. Sexy."

"Yeah? That's what I'm going for—a jazz siren. The opposite of me." What would people say when they found out rock-and-roll Eva was playing jazz?

"Just be careful."

Eva turned to look at Coco, who had taken a seat behind her. "Of what? Stalkers?"

"No. I mean, it takes a big ego to work in this business." She held her arms out wide and bowed over her knees. "It's like theater. You've got to be larger than life. Just don't get lost in your on-air personality."

Eva laughed. "There's no chance of that." She'd always been an underdog: undersized and understated. The rolling chair squeaked as she turned to the board.

Coco stood behind her. "Keep the cart machines loaded, just in case. Pull the mic a little closer to your chest; you want it to pick up the low tones in your voice. Or just raise the chair."

The adjustable chair whooshed when Eva pulled the lever. Her platform boots dangled. *Carts.* She selected a few prerecorded announcements from a rack under the counter and pushed the rectangular plastic cartridges into the small, square players. Carts looked like 8-track tapes, just a little smaller. She remembered cruising around town with Faye in her dad's car listening to the only two 8-track tapes Eva owned—Head East and Styx.

"There's so much to remember."

"Practice makes perfect," Coco said.

"That's what my pop used to say!" Eva touched her wrist.

No doubt, her pop would have sat by the radio all night. He'd been her biggest fan, the loudest in the crowd at her piano recitals and spelling bees. Middle school flew in her face, the time she flubbed an easy word at the state spelling bee, and the kids had a good laugh at her expense.

"Feeling nervous isn't just a sign of anxiety, LaVette. Channel that excitement," Coco said. "Pretend you're with friends smoking a spliff, playing music. Imagine someone you love across the mic."

Eva fished her pop's Polaroid out of her backpack and placed it behind the microphone. When "The In Crowd" by Ramsey Lewis started to fade, she segued into a record by Pat Metheny. "How do you pronounce his name? I took Fundamentals of Jazz last semester, but it was mostly the early stuff."

"Metheny. Rhymes with weenie." Coco giggled.

"You're funny."

They leaned back and listened. Coco had a cool way of nodding to the music.

"Is Coco Nix your real n—?"

Suddenly, the record skipped. A clipped guitar riff stuttered over and over. Eva's hands locked onto the arms of the chair. Time suspended. Her mind blanked.

Coco dove forward, knocking an ashtray off the counter and somehow wedged her hefty body between Eva and the board. She dumped the skipping song and started a public service announcement. "It's okay. The PSA will buy you sixty seconds. Now hurry. Cue up another record."

"Ugh. I can't believe this," Eva said. Her hand shook as she gave the scratched record to Coco. "I haven't even gone on the air yet. I feel so stupid. Should I apologize?"

"No. It's not your fault. Anyone who just tuned in doesn't know the record skipped, so don't tell them. Put your mistakes behind you. It's not like dead air—that'll get you fired. Radio is ephemeral; stay in the moment." As Coco monitored the PSA, she laughed. "You should have seen your face. Your eyes bugged out like you were sitting in the electric chair."

"*Me?*" Eva grinned, despite how dumb she felt. "You should have seen yourself fly across the room."

"It's good to see you smile, LaVette. Smiling affects the shape of your voice. It's contagious, like yawning. Even a fake radio smile makes people engage their 'zygomaticus major' muscles and smile with you."

Coco pointed to a yellow smiley-face poster taped to the window in between the format clock and a hand-drawn *No Food - No Drinks - No Smoking* sign.

Eva took a sip of her Tab.

"You've got thirty seconds," Coco said, glancing at the clock. She bent to scrape up the spilled cigarette butts.

Eva donned her headphones. She locked eyes with her pop and smiled a genuine smile.

###

Sound waves generated by Eva's voice were transformed by a transducer into acoustic energy. The signal surged through copper coils and gained amplification before being transmitted into the night, and in an instant, reached the cars and kitchens of the Coulee Region.

> BILLIE SOUL: Good evening. This is 90.7 FM, La Crosse Public Radio. I'm, er, Billie Soul. Um, more music is coming up. Jazz and blues to fuel your soul. First, here's a special statement from the National Weather Service.

Despite gargling her words, her voice resonated inside the headphones like a shot of smooth Wisconsin brandy. Thousands of people were listening, waiting to hear the weather warning. Deep in her soul, Eva experienced the buoyant emotions of every young announcer who had sat in the same squeaky chair breaking their chops at the same daunting control board, their hearts in their mouths, their fear betrayed only by a crack in their voice. *I'm doing this. I'm really doing this.* She filled her chest with air and spoke with authority.

> BILLIE SOUL: A winter storm warning is in effect until midnight. As the temperatures drop, freezing rain will be followed by heavy snow, making roadways dangerous. Travel is not advised, so stay in, get comfy, and turn up this groovy track by Stanley Turrentine. From the album *Salt Song*, here's "Storm."

Eva untangled her braid from the headphones' curly cord and took a slow, long breath, savoring the adrenalin high. Reflected multiple times in the fishbowl of a studio, red and green audio equipment lights glittered around her. She spun in the chair, craving more of the heady feeling.

"What a rush, Coco. I feel ecstatic."

"You just got bit by the radio bug. It's addicting." Coco reached over and squeezed her shoulder. "Love at first mic."

"I feel it in my bones—I want to be a DJ. Hard rock, blues, funk, heavy metal. Any of those would be cool."

An hour later, after taking the transmitter reading, Coco returned with two PowerHouse candy bars. "Want one?"

"Temping, but no, thanks."

The phone line blinked. Eva's first call. She smiled and pressed Line 1.

"La Crosse Public Radio."

She took a request for John Coltrane. *People are listening. To me.*

"'Giant Steps' is a good cut. Short though. Under three minutes," Coco said. She dug out the album, handing it over. "God, it stinks in here."

"Dumping that grody ashtray didn't help." Eva set the record on the turntable.

"Professor Holt says smoking adds grit to the voice. Usually, he's a real square—but I'm glad I never tried it." Coco bit into a candy bar, talking with her mouth full. "Nicotine is ten times more addictive than heroin."

Eva was glad she'd never smoked, either. The phone lit again.

"La Crosse Public Radio."

"Hey, runt!" Artie yelled above the party crowd.

Tightness gripped her shoulders. "Artie, you're on the speaker."

"We're listening on the stereo," he said, sounding trashed.

Eva supposed he deserved to have fun; he'd been working hard to pay the rent while she finished school, two more years, at least.

"Dwayne says you sound tall."

"I do?" she asked. "Artie. Listen. I've been thinking about something for a while, and tonight, well, now I'm sure." She drew in a deep breath. "I want to be a DJ. I'd still be teaching music—but on the radio."

11

"Hold your horses, Eva." His voice shifted into annoyance. "Teachers make good money. We need to save for a house."

"Coco said I could make big bucks in Chicago or LA."

"We're sure as hell not moving to Los Angeles, Eva."

"Well. How about Madison?" That would appeal to him. He loved the Wisconsin Badgers. She glanced at her record.

"I don't know. I like the idea of you teaching."

After she had to give up her dream of being a performance major, Artie had pressed her into teaching, extolling the perks: summers off (to take care of future kids), paid holidays, long breaks at Christmas and Easter, state benefits, a decent pension.

"I get it, Artie. Your mom's a teacher." *A chain-smoking gym teacher.* Eva envisioned his mother with her cropped gray hair and an ever-present whistle hanging on her saggy chest. *Maybe I need a whistle to get him to hear me.* "But you're not listening."

"Let's talk about it tomorrow. I gotta tap the keg."

"It's slippery out. Tell everyone to be careful—"

He had hung up.

"Was that your old man?" Coco asked.

"Yeah. Damn it." Eva slapped the counter and turned to Coco. "I'm sick of everyone telling me what to do."

"You need to do a break," Coco said, deadpan. She picked up the stack of played records and headed into the library.

Eva leaned back, contemplating her decision. To hell with Artie. Nothing could be better than a job playing records all day, especially at an album-oriented rock station. And finishing school on time would sweeten the soundtrack that was her life.

She adjusted her beret, tucking a loose strand of hair behind her ear. In just a few hours, she had transformed from a nobody into a real-life disc jockey, a cool cat, and brave, too. She glanced at the picture of her pop propped behind the mic and wondered how her father would feel if he knew she was trading her dream of being a performer for the airwaves, her fingers no longer dancing over the keys but reaching for a microphone.

How many people would want a job where every mistake is broadcast to the world? Being live felt vastly different from playing radio in the practice studio with its forgiving foam walls. If she flubbed a name or stumbled, she imagined, people listening in their cars or kitchens would mock her. Maybe even call in and say nasty things. Like in fifth grade, when she was chosen to recite the morning Pledge of Allegiance and she froze over the intercom, forgetting the memorized words. She'd hid in a bathroom stall until the principal sent for her mother. Her asshole classmates had taunted her for weeks. *Lamebrain. Moron. Runt.*

No. She did not want to teach bratty kids. How would someone as short as her have authority over them? And enrolling in the teaching program—which she had already signed up for—tacked on another year to her studies, time not earning a salary. Thousands more on tuition. *Hmm.* Saving money would get Artie's attention.

Coco came in with more albums. She glanced at the clock. "Did you give the legal ID? You have to say the call letters and city, in that order, within five minutes of the top of the hour."

Amused at Coco's serious tone, Eva said, "Yes, I know. Every hour on the hour. I did."

"Hey, now." Coco smiled as she handed over the records. Her stomach growled. "These should last until midnight."

"Thanks," Eva said. "Hey, if you're hungry, I've got a peanut butter sandwich."

"I've got the other candy bar."

The studio door swung open. Dustin, Coco's cousin, breezed in, his face flushed from the cold, his wire-rimmed aviator glasses fogged along the bridge. He yanked off his leather cowboy hat and with his fingers, combed his mussed hair. The long layers fell into place from his middle part. He stomped his boots. "Cripes, my feet are fuckin' freezing. Why are the lights off?"

"It's called atmosphere," Coco said. "What are you doing here?"

"I came to see who that sexy-sounding woman Billie Soul is."
He winked at Eva. "Oh, it's *you*. The girl with the dimples."

They had seen each other around campus. A coy smile played on her lips. Beware of the guys with bedroom eyes, her mom always said.

"I'm here to redo my final project. Professor Holt could hear the splices on my tape. *Tk–tk–tk*." He laughed. "I'd better get cuttin'. Don't forget to catch my show tomorrow afternoon."

Dustin's warm, rich voice reminded Eva of melted chocolate. He breezed out, leaving behind the provocative scent of Jovan Musk Oil.

"Dusty's a brat," Coco said.

Dustin was the opposite of Artie, who rarely flirted or joked. Eva's eyes narrowed. Artie the spoilsport. *And he wants to dictate my career?* Dustin seemed so cool.

"So. Radio runs in your family," Eva said.

"Yes, and Dustin's dad worked in radio, too. I fell in love with it when I was little. My parental units are both psychiatrists and they bicker constantly. Psychoanalysis or behavioral treatment? Cognitive or humanist therapy? Blah-de-blah-blah. I'd curl up in the back seat of the car with my transistor radio. The DJs felt like my best friends." Coco rolled her neck, working out the cricks. "I love my parents, but I couldn't wait to get away—that's why I came to La Crosse for school."

Eva pictured a round-faced little girl with straight black bangs and piercing green eyes, ignored by her intellectual parents. "You're a baby shrink!"

Then, Eva remembered the folded envelope from her backpack. "I made this for you."

Coco gasped as she opened the envelope. "Love beads? Cool, man. Great colors. Thank you." She stretched the choker over her head, patting her neck with her fingers. "You'd better get a song ready."

The microscopic diamond in Eva's wedding ring winked as she picked up a Chick Corea album. She read the jacket. "Interesting.

14

Chick started playing piano when he was four, then he started the drums."

"That's why his keyboard technique is so percussive," Coco said. "Talking about the artists is way better than babbling on about celebrities or pop culture. It drives me nuts when announcers lean on that drivel—it's a crutch. I mean, who gives a crap about Elizabeth Taylor, or Billy Beer, or Kristy McNichol?"

At midnight, they shut down the transmitter, filed the program log, and locked the doors.

Outside the J. Wayne Communications building, the young women lingered. Fluffy snowflakes filtered down, blanketing the deserted campus with quiet. After the noisy studio, the world seemed muted, as if pressed by a damper pedal on a piano.

Coco pulled a stocking hat over her boyish haircut. "It's surreal out here," she said, hushed. Her frozen breath floated in the night air.

"Good snowman snow," Eva said, making tracks in it with her boots. "So, what's your plan, for after college?"

"Ultimately, I'll be a music director at a rock station in a big market. Like KIIS-FM in Los Angeles. I'll discover new bands. *Rolling Stone* will write about me."

"You have it all worked out! With my background, I'd be a shoo-in for music director," Eva said.

"You would. When I'm famous, I'm going to live in a high-rise with a rooftop pool surrounded by palm trees. I'll fly to my morning gig in a helicopter."

"So glamorous. Will you pick me up?" Eva imagined commuting over a cityscape, coffee and newspaper in hand, so accustomed to the view she no longer looked.

Coco gave her a mittened high-five. "Yeah, baby! Sounds like a plan. We'll be the first all-girl morning show."

"You think my voice is good enough?" Eva asked.

"Definitely. You sound fabulous. You have everything you need to succeed," Coco said. "I *guar-an-tee* it."

Eva sighed in relief, forgetting to let the compliment sink in. "Hey, man. Why don't you come to the party with me? It's only a few blocks."

"Nah, I've got to get truckin'. I need my beauty sleep. I'm doing the morning shift."

"Aren't you going home to Madison for Christmas?"

"No. Professor Holt is giving me extra credit by working during the break." Coco turned away, sliding her untied high-tops through the snow, leaving skid marks on the slippery sidewalk. She lifted a fist. "Radio sisters, forever!"

"Far out!"

As an only child, Eva had always wanted a sister.

She ducked her head into the falling snow, hurrying toward Faye and Dwayne's apartment. After a few steps, she hesitated. The way Artie cut her off and dismissed her idea about radio had created a shadow over her first experience on the air. This was her career, not his. Like her pop said, life was like a barge on the Mississippi. The direction she took at this moment—at twenty years old—if she went off course by just one degree, she'd end up mired on the banks of the river.

"Screw Artie. I'm Billie Soul."

3. HAD TO FALL IN LOVE ~ MOODY BLUES

As graduation day approached, Eva and Dustin worked in the windowless production booth between the main studio and the news department. Their final assignment: writing and producing two hypothetical commercials. She wound blank tape onto a reel. He filled out the label: *Bill's Car Wash, :60, Dustin Nixon and Billie Soul, April 5, 1984*. If anyone asked what her favorite area of radio was now, she'd say production, a class more fun than news reporting, which she also loved.

While Eva ran the board, she stole glances at Dustin over at Mic 2. What a fortuitous stroke of luck, she thought, to be partnered with him again. Over the last few years, they'd gotten to know each other in a chummy, supportive manner. But she knew of his reputation. The girls called him "Hotrod," not just because of his '73 Barracuda.

"Let's do one more take, Billie," he said from across the counter.

He set down his pen, brushing feathered bangs away from his forehead. Behind his aviator glasses, his steady gaze made Eva giddy. She told herself it was simply their infectious passion for radio.

At the control board, she hit Record on Reel 1. They made it to the last lines of the sixty-second script without any screw ups.

> DUSTIN: The torrid days of summer are coming! So, get your jalopy to Bill's Hippie Dippy Car Wash!
> BILLIE: Bring your pickup, your Pacer, your Corvette or convertible.
> DUSTIN: Mention this ad for a dollar off.
> TOGETHER: And don't forget to put the top up!

They held their breath until Eva hit the Stop button, then laughed themselves silly.

"That was a really good call to action if I say so myself," she said after settling down. "And you. Way to work a word like 'torrid' into a car wash commercial."

"Thanks. I have an affection for words," Dustin said. He placed the reel into the box. "You know why we catalog the masters, right?"

"Yes. No dubs from dubs. Always start with the master, because the original is best."

Professor Holt poked his wizened head into the studio. "I'm on my way out. Did you reorganize the library, son? I can't give you the extra credit until it's done."

"Yup," Dustin said. He waved an arm toward a shelving unit. "The reel-to-reels are now filed by date. I alphabetized the sound effects library."

Holt left. Dustin leaned into the black foam wall, his body long and slim.

"Have you checked out these sound effects?" he asked. "There's everything from a baby crying and car crashes to dishes breaking and comical *boings*." He wiggled his head and made his eyes big.

"Outta sight! I don't suppose we should add a car crash to the car wash spot," Eva said, laughing. "Professor Holt should give you an A for all the organizing you've done in here."

"He'll give you an A just for your 'torrid' voice, Billie Soul."

She let out a nervous giggle. *He likes my voice.* "Do you really think so? I haven't had one bite on my tape and resume. You're lucky; you don't have to worry."

"Right-o." Dustin nodded. He was bound for an NPR station in Minneapolis after graduation.

In fact, many of the students had gigs lined up. Like everyone else, Eva sent her tapes and resumes to every station around. To no avail. After a tip, both she and Coco had applied at Z100, the local Top 40 powerhouse as they were looking to hire their first woman DJ.

18

"I'm *jonesing* for a smoke. Let's take a break," Dustin said. He slapped on his leather cowboy hat and drew a pack of Camels from the breast pocket of his suede jacket. With an unlit cigarette between his lips, he sang Cheech & Chong's "Basketball Jones."

Eva put on her pop's beret and her jean jacket, laughing at his falsetto. They headed down the hall past the main studio window, where they pulled goofy faces at the student on the air.

"There's a secret passageway to the rooftop." Dusty propped the door with a folded piece of paper. Outside, the sun hung low in the sky. They moved to the edge of the roof and looked out at the sprawling campus. Eva's mind wandered through the countless days she had spent navigating these grounds, her shoulders weighed down by her backpack full of books and more recently, reels of audio tape.

The cool spring air lifted Dusty's long layered hair. She was a little envious; his tawny locks were thick and full, yet smooth and shiny, not frizzy like hers.

"Want one?" he mumbled, cupping his hand to light the cigarette. "Everyone in commercial radio smokes. It makes your voice deep and sexy."

"I heard that, too. Can't hurt, I guess," Eva removed the cigarette from between his fingers, noting how clean and square he kept his nails. The filter was moist with his saliva. She sucked the smoke deep into her lungs as if it were a joint and began to hack.

"You'll kill yourself doing that!" Dustin smacked her on the back. He lit one for himself. "Slow down, lady."

A buzz rushed from her lungs to the top of her head. "Whoa," she said, reaching for the wall. Something about the way the smoke streamed from her mouth and through her teeth felt powerful, like a fire-breathing tiger.

With his lips making an "O," Dustin puffed out perfect smoke rings. "So, Billie. What brought you here to this moment in time, pursuing your radio dreams?"

A loaded question. "I was going to be a concert pianist, but . . ." With the toe of her boot, Eva scuffed at pea gravel. "My father was a performer. He was a session musician, but sometimes he toured. I was daddy's little girl. His star." Her throat caught. She waved her hand. "Forgive me for getting emotional. He passed away when I was fourteen."

"Jeepers. I'm sorry."

Dustin blew smoke from his nostrils. Eva copied him. The smoke burned her nose, a good distraction.

"Thank you. Radio just crept up on me." The advisor in charge of the teaching program had recommended Radio 101 for Eva instead of Public Speaking due to her diminutive stature and demure nature, adding it would be more fun, too. "I didn't expect it to hook me. Take news reporting. Professor Holt really pushes us. There's nothing like the thrill of doing a phone interview, banging out the story, carting up the sound bites—er, actualities—and rushing into the studio just as the news sounder plays."

"Your face lights up when you talk about radio. I dig it. My dad, Coco's uncle, was a newsman." A pained look came over his face. "I lost my mom when I was little. Brain cancer."

"Oh, god, I'm so sorry. Pop was killed in a car accident."

Her fingers looped around her wrist. Stinging hot tears welled up, catching her by surprise. Bouts of grief always hit like a wave: a nauseous feeling in her gut that rolled through her like a black cloud. She sniffed back tears.

Facing her, Dustin shifted his weight. At five feet ten, he seemed so much taller than Artie. For a second, she thought he was going to lean in for a kiss. Instead, he tweaked the edge of her beret.

"You have cute dimples."

She stepped back and took a gentler puff from the cigarette. Smoke curled into a question mark in the air. What was she doing out there with Dustin? But what did it matter? Artie was at his bookkeeping job at Penzle's School Supply.

They stared out over the campus, smoking in compatible silence. The cigarette made her feel bad, as in badass, like she should be wearing leather. She glanced at the rooftop door. They should get back inside.

"Dad told me this story about an announcer who locked himself out of the station," Dustin said, laughing. "It's a radio urban legend."

"Really? Tell me."

He moved in close, lowering his voice. "Radio stations used to air church programs on Sunday mornings, recorded on vinyl."

"Vinyl? Not tape?"

"Yup. During the first part of the service, a guy running the board ran out of cigarettes. After one side played, he flipped the record, which gave him twenty minutes to drive to the filling station down the street. After buying his smokes and a jumbo soda, he jumped into his car and on the radio, heard the preacher saying, '. . . and you will go to Hell . . . *zrrppp!* . . . and you will go to Hell . . . *zrrppp!*' Over and over."

"The record was skipping the whole time? Holy shit." Eva tapped ash from her cigarette onto the raised concrete edge of the roof.

"As he got back to the station, the program director tore into the lot, tires screeching."

"I bet his ass was grass."

They laughed hysterically, bending and holding their stomachs.

He tugged the end of her braid. "It's getting late. We need to write a second spot."

Eva closed her eyes. "How about one for the cineplex about a zombie movie. It could feature Three Mile Island survivors."

"Funny. I really wanted to use one of my impersonations. *Ayyyy!*" he said, holding his palms out like Fonzie from *Happy Days*.

They ground out their cigarettes, brainstorming as they left the rooftop. Back in production, they recorded Dustin's spot, laughing so hard at his impression that it took a dozen takes.

After he left, she gathered scripts and put the splicing tape and block back in the box. It was almost six o'clock; she sure hoped there was a message from Z100 on her home answering machine. Was there even a remote possibility she could beat Coco for the job? Working in Top 40 would be fun and super-high energy. But playing the same forty songs, week after week, day after day, though? B93, the AOR station, would suit her better. Album-oriented rock: sophisticated, few ads, deep tracks. *Billie Soul would dig it.*

###

The only message on Eva's machine that night was from Coco, who wanted to meet for a drink. At the student union, the girls slid onto tall stools. With his back to them, the lone bartender scooped popcorn from a butter-shiny glass machine. Only one other customer sat at the long bar, a guy with a scruffy beard, his nose in a book.

Coco wrapped her knuckles on the rail and ordered two Old Styles. She pulled a twenty from a stack in her billfold. "My treat."

"When we first met, you called Dustin a brat. I think he's nice."

"You didn't grow up with him. One time, he bet me five bucks I couldn't chug a glass of milk. Little did I know he'd put a worm in it." She gagged, pressing her hand to her throat.

Eva laughed. "Sorry, I think it's funny."

"I got the job at Z100," Coco blurted.

Eva put her hands to the sides of her head, her mind totally blown. The radio station hadn't bothered to let her know. *Like a shitty boyfriend who breaks up with you but never tells you.* The bartender slid overflowing mugs between the women, a cold buffer. Eva took a swallow of her beer—and her pride.

"Congratulations, Coco. When do you start?"

"Right after spring break. I'm spending it with my folks in Madison." She looked Eva in the eye. "I know you wanted it, too."

"No, I'm happy for you. You *should* be celebrating."

Coco's eyes sparkled. "I'm gonna get paid to be a DJ!"

"I hope I will, too," Eva said. "And I won't just live in a high-rise with a pool, I'm also going to have a personal chef."

"Don't worry, LaVette. We both know radio is a tough gig to get, especially for us women. Something will happen. I guarantee it."

"Well, I can't wait to listen to you," Eva said. She elbowed her friend. "You're taking me out to dinner, though."

The crack of a cue hitting balls drew their attention to pool tables in the back room. A young man bent behind a girl as she leaned over the pool table, helping her guide the cue, one hand on her bum.

"Let's talk about something else."

"Okay," Coco said, playing with the love beads around her neck. "Not many college kids are married—were you and Artie high school sweethearts?"

"No, he's older. I met him here at school. He's from Sheboygan. We had just started dating when—" She huffed. "I got pregnant."

A look of shock appeared on Coco's face. The bartender brought them a basket of popcorn.

"Artie's mother said I should drop out of college. Behind my back, she called me a Protestant tramp. Even though he's the only guy I've been with."

"You had a shotgun wedding."

"The shotgun wedding that backfired. Don't get me wrong, Artie is a good guy, he works hard, and he's a killer guitar player." Who really had wanted the child.

Coco's eyes widened. "Who's watching your kid tonight?"

"The baby was born premature. He only lived a few days."

Eva covered her mouth with the back of her hand. The frail infant spent his brief life in an incubator. They'd sat with him day and night, singing and talking, telling him he could grow up to be anything. A pitcher for the Brewers, Artie had said. Discouraged by the doctors, they never named him. She heaved a terrible sigh. Normally, she didn't allow herself to think of the baby. *Pop is rocking him in his strong arms up in heaven, under a rainbow.* She wiped her nose with a bar napkin, then knocked back her beer, tapping the bottom to drain every drop from her glass.

Coco signaled to the bartender.

"I'm sorry, Eva. That's really sad. How did Artie take it?"

"As much as he wanted to be a dad, he's a baby at home." A harsh statement: she recapitulated. "Maybe I've watched too many romantic movies where the man sweeps a woman off her feet. Ever since I was little, I wanted to fall madly in love—to make beautiful music with someone. Or at least play it."

On their wedding night, they made love on pure-white sheets and through the open screens, a churning, loud Lake Michigan provided the soundtrack. She whispered "I love you"—wishful words that hadn't come true. Not once had Artie said the word "love," not for her or her cooking or the way she looked.

"I know it's stupid. I'm just a small-town girl looking for love."

"Okay, Cinderella."

The bartender set down two glasses of beer with nice heads. Coco sipped, giving herself a foam moustache.

"My parents say when people fall in love, it's for a version of someone that exists more in their heads than reality," she said. "After a while, Mr. Perfect isn't so perfect anymore. You give away your power when you believe someone else is responsible for your happiness. You've got to love yourself first."

Eva played with her braid. She hated it when people said that. What did "love yourself" mean? Taking bubble baths? Eating healthy? Fame and success would go a long way in building her self-esteem and confidence. Was that self-love?

"I'll never let a lover define who I am," Coco said. "I just want to be a DJ and have fun. No kids for me."

Eva laughed. No woman she knew talked like that. It seemed verboten to say the words. "My friend Faye can't wait to be a mom. I'd rather have a cat than a kid, for now anyway."

The bartender approached with two shots, compliments of Scruffy Beard Guy who nodded at them from down the bar.

"Here's to you and your radio lover. May you have many happy years together." Eva raised her shot glass.

Coco clinked, then gave her a sisterly punch on the arm.

Eva's song ended abruptly. In the middle of the console, the twin VU meter needles—stereo left and right—lay limp. What song was only twenty seconds? Why hadn't she cued another? Dead air stretched on as she searched the studio, but the shelves were devoid of a single record. Her heart pounded. Where was the emergency PSA?

Panicking, she called out to Coco. "Cocoorrgle graahhgle . . ."

Her eyes flew open. The dead-air dream faded like the end of a sad song. Next to her in bed, Artie snored.

Despite the nightmare, she wanted to fall back asleep, to be on the radio once again, to watch the audio meters dance as the music played. But the bright morning sun squinted through their skewed mini-blinds and, like reality, glared in her face. Was her dream of being on the radio truly as dead as the airwaves in her nightmare?

A tear splotched onto her pillowcase. It wasn't fair. After Coco landed the coveted job at Z100 in April, Eva found a job in telemarketing, selling roadside assistance policies over the dinner hour. Once she began using her Billie Soul voice, sales increased, and when the boss learned she'd be graduating, he offered her a full-time position. Artie said it was too good to turn down; in a few years they could buy a house and focus on starting a family. She buried her head under the pillow and groaned.

When Artie stirred, she wiped her eyes. He yawned and scratched his beard.

"*Blech.* My mouth tastes terrible. I was over-served last night."

"You were here at home, silly. No one over-served you but yourself." She laughed at the hair sticking out from his head before smoothing it down. "How'd the Brewers do?"

"They won. Molitor hit a homer in the bottom of the ninth." He hauled his compact body out of bed. "Well, it's moving day."

Eva got up and dressed in old clothes. She made Artie a cup of coffee and leaned against the counter. "I made a list of everything we need to do."

"You and your lists." He studied her with his deep brown eyes. "Next, you'll have to consult your horoscope."

"I already did." She flicked open the *La Crosse Tribune*. "It says 'Change is in the air and with the summer equinox, there will be an unexpected event.'" She wiggled an eyebrow.

"I can predict the future," he said, smirking. "We're moving. Then at 2:30 I'm leaving for work. Can you get this place cleaned up? We really need the security deposit."

Their absentee landlord would find an excuse to keep every penny. The place literally had holes in the walls. During winter, their feet froze in the drafty house. Worse, the gauge on the oil furnace was broken and it ran out of fuel multiple times, leaving them to use space heaters and scrambling to get it refilled.

"Since you have to work, yes, I'll clean." She looked for supplies underneath the sink. "Should we drive our stuff over or walk?"

At the front window, Artie peeked through the blinds. The new apartment was just around the corner. Their rusty 1974 Chrysler Imperial sat at the curb, a beast that occupied almost two spaces.

"By the time we put boxes in the car, load and unload, it's six of one and a half-dozen of the other. Let's just carry everything."

After breakfast, the couple began the move with their heavy queen-sized mattress that had lost its hand straps. The hot sun beat on their bent necks as they struggled down the sidewalk. Halfway there, Eva dropped her end, stopping to coil her thick braid and stuff it under her baseball cap.

"C'mon, Eva. Shake a leg," he said, sweat dripping from his brow.

She put her fists on her hips. "Your hands are bigger than mine. I can't grab it." Huffing and puffing, they finally pushed the mattress up and over the battered stoop into the living room, leaving the door propped open. The front room, paneled in dark wood, was large enough to accommodate Artie's old couch and her cheap, TV-stereo-plant stand, but not a piano. Its only redeeming feature was a window seat that caught the morning sun.

"The band director said I could use the practice rooms at Marion Hall this summer."

Artie grunted instead of commenting as he ripped tape from a box, removed a tangle of patch cords, and began to hook up the stereo system.

"I don't know what I'll do come fall." Eva's fingers twitched.

She sighed as she evaluated the claustrophobic apartment. Beyond the living room, the closet-size kitchen was more like a hallway; it led to a small bathroom with a disappointing narrow shower, not big enough for two. Their dingy bedroom had barely enough space to fit a dresser. The back hallway led to an alley and a one-car garage. But the rent was more affordable. For Artie, it was all about saving money.

Out of nowhere, a mangy orange tabby cat with striking gold eyes sauntered in and plopped down in a patch of sun on the thin carpet.

"Artie. Look."

He bent to scratch the cat's head and in a high voice said, "Hey, kitty. Where'd you come from?"

It meowed and rolled over, purring and stretching in the beam of light. Eva picked it up, cradling it like a baby.

"That's how you can tell it's a good cat, if you can hold it upside down," she said, rocking the purring kitty.

When the bell rang, the cat jumped from her arms. Their new landlord stood in the doorway. The stylish widow who lived next door wore a neck scarf and reeked of perfume.

"Hello, hello!" she said, shoving an Avon catalog into Eva's hand. "We're having a sale. The order form is in the back."

"Thanks." Eva rubbed her nose. *But no, thanks.* She found her purse and retrieved the security deposit. Meanwhile, the tiger cat licked its paws in the sun. "This cat just waltzed in. It's not ours."

"*Hmph.* Unfortunately, people leave pets behind." The landlord peered over her glasses. "Well, here's your lease. Sign here."

After the landlord left, they pushed the mattress into the bedroom. Eva found a water bowl for the cat. They walked back to the old apartment, where, in the kitchen, she opened and closed drawers to see if they'd left anything behind.

"Let's go shopping. I've got to pick up some L'eggs. Every pair of pantyhose I own has runs." The thought of having to wear nylons and dresses at the new job turned her stomach. She paused, tapping a finger on her chin. "I need a new dress for Faye and Dwayne's wedding. Did you schedule your tux fitting?"

"I did. But we can't afford to go shopping, Eva." He lifted a cardboard box.

"Yes, we can. I have $500 from graduation. And I get my first paycheck in two weeks."

"Oh, yeah. You start training on Monday."

"I'm relieved I found a job. I'm just super-bummed it's not radio."

All that time spent at the campus station, only to conclude she wasn't good enough. If she had stayed in the teaching program instead of putting all her eggs into the radio basket, she'd be student-teaching by now.

"Gateguard Insurance will be a good, steady job." He took the box into the living room, set it by the door, and came back to the kitchen. "Not like the radio rollercoaster. Like I say, you spent all week planning your shows. You didn't get paid, and now all that time you spent away from me was for nothing."

"But it was fun."

"Work isn't supposed to be fun. Holy mackerel, Eva, that's why they call it work."

He rinsed out the coffee pot and handed it to Eva, who dried it with a towel.

"Artie, you loved getting all those free hockey and basketball tickets. You said my radio friends were cool."

She placed the pot into the last of the boxes. He leaned against the wall, slipping a hand in his pocket.

"They're like a high school clique."

"You're just jealous," Eva said.

The gang was tight. The best part of radio was the camaraderie, the secret rapport, the shared stories of all the crazy things that happened behind the scenes, and mostly, being a member of the club—getting free tickets to shows, hanging out at an exclusive table at the student union. The kind of bond Artie had with his band. She smiled.

"Why don't you get the Paradiddles back together?"

"Because the bass player moved away, our singer is in grad school, and the drummer has twins now."

"Form a new band. I'll draw up flyers. We can post them at the music store. There must be bands looking for guitarists."

She unplugged the boombox on the counter. Artie took it from her. He set it on top of the box near the door.

"I don't want to be in a stupid cover band or play music I hate."

Then why had he stayed at Penzle's? A college job unloading boxes of school supplies had turned into a bookkeeping position, with the owner's unfulfilled promise to computerize their inventory and accounting systems. It made no sense to Eva why he remained in that job, not using his computer science degree. She followed him into the front room.

"I'll never forget the first time I saw you. The moment is pinned into my mind. You were on stage, shredding your guitar. Your eyes were closed. You were the most talented guy in the band. Maybe you could find some better musicians."

"I think we should focus on the future," Artie said. He turned to her. "We're not kids anymore, Eva."

"You'd be happier if you were playing," she said, and flung the dish towel over her shoulder. "I'm going to see if we missed anything."

That afternoon, Eva sat on the floor unpacking while an installer from the telephone company hooked up their phone, luckily, with the same number. Minutes after the workman gathered his tools and left, it rang, the standard call to test the line.

"Hello?"

"This is Yardley St. Martins from B93," a man with a booming bass voice said.

Eva's mouth dropped open.

"I've got a position available on overnights. Can you come in to talk about it?"

Her mind churned. "Please hold on a sec. I need to find my calendar."

Yes! Yes! Her voice *was* good enough! With one phone call, this man had awakened a dormant dream, sending waves of exhilaration throughout her body.

"Of course," he said.

She dug through the closest box. *Shit!* Overnights meant the graveyard shift: sleeping during the day, a messed-up schedule. Perhaps she could work both jobs until something full-time opened at the radio station. But that would be brutal, and she'd never see Artie. She tore the packing tape from another box. Why had she accepted the insurance job? She couldn't bail; that would be wrong. Gateguard had already set up six weeks of intense training for her to become a licensed auto agent. She had to tell Mr. St. Martins no. But what if this was her one and only chance to work in radio?

"Hello? Eva? Are you there? What do you think?" he asked. "We really like your voice."

5. FEARLESS ~ PINK FLOYD

Unpacking hadn't taken long. While Artie paced the room deep in conversation, phone pressed to his ear, Eva tapped a final nail into the wall and stepped back, squinting at the clock now hanging above the kitchen table. As she straightened it, Artie ended the call.

"That was Dwayne. Would you like to go to Sheboygan for the weekend? I can take a personal day."

"Why not?" Eva said.

She liked going to the pretty city on Lake Michigan, a three-and-a-half-hour drive across Wisconsin, where Artie had gone to North High with Faye and Dwayne and where Artie's mom lived.

"Road trip!" he yelled, waving his hands. "I'm going to pack."

Eva hadn't seen him that excited since he played in the band. As a bonus, taking a trip would help take her mind off the upcoming interview.

###

In Sheboygan on Friday night, they dropped their bags off at Artie's mother's and took her out for a fish fry. She'd come straight from school where she coached girls' volleyball and still wore her whistle.

On Saturday, they met Faye and Dwayne at Elkhart Lake, a nearby tourist town, home to a wonderful public beach on the small lake with its name. The women spread blankets in a sunny spot away from the concession stand while the guys set up a volleyball net. "Money" from Pink Floyd blared over loudspeakers. A kid holding a bright-green pail toddled across their blanket with carefree abandon on his way to the sandy beach.

Artie and Dwayne bumped the ball back and forth. Both men had medium-long sandy hair and similar builds—muscular shoulders and arms over slim waists and strong legs.

"They could be brothers," Eva said as she sat on her pink towel. "I'm so glad Artie suggested we get away."

Faye removed a bottle of coconut tanning oil from her beach bag and began to rub it on her arms. The following week, she would open the doors to her daycare center in the lower level of a Victorian two-flat in downtown La Crosse, not too far from Eva and Artie's. Dwayne's dad, owner of a shoe store, had gifted them with the down payment. Faye's future was in place; soon they'd try for a baby. Some women were meant to be mothers.

Closing her eyes, Eva took in the mingled summer scents of tanning oil, charcoal-grilled chicken, and algae.

"If I was home in La Crosse right now, I'd be obsessing about my job interview at B93," she said, although Coco noted they wouldn't have called her if they weren't serious. She pushed the straps of her bikini top down her arms. "Get my back for me?"

Oiled up, they settled on their stomachs. Faye turned the pages of a *Good Housekeeping* magazine. The sun baked into their skin. From the concession stand, the jukebox blared. Little kids screamed as they played in the shallows. Eva lit a cigarette. Faye took off her sunglasses and stood.

"I'm hot. I'm going for a swim. You coming?"

"I want an ice cream bar first."

Eva found a dollar bill in Artie's shorts pocket. Inside the concession stand, she stood in line behind a mom who was yelling at her little boy for swatting people with a plastic shovel. Outside, Artie and Dwayne splashed into the lake, knees pumping before they dove in. What was taking the ice cream scooper so long? She kept an eye on their stuff at the blanket.

"Eva? Is that you?"

The mom, wearing a frumpy swimsuit, looked vaguely familiar.

"Yeah. Hi, um. How are you doing?"

The woman's melodious voice rang a bell. Cinder from high school, the star of every musical and cabaret. The best dancer in their class. And now her legs were riddled with varicose veins, her once-magnificent, waist-length hair chopped short and lank, her eyes ringed with dark circles.

"You look great!" Cinder said.

"You, too. Wow. Is this your son?" He must be four years old, Eva thought. "Do you live around here now?"

"Mommy," the boy said while he tugged on the skirt of her suit. "I want a popsicle."

"You have to wait your turn, Dillon." Cinder addressed Eva. "No, but we needed a vacation. We're staying with my sister here in Elkhart Lake."

"I want to go to Wisconsin Dells," the kid whined.

"Maybe next year, honey," Cinder said, ruffling his hair. "He's my oldest. I've got a newborn, too. Remember Bruce? He works at the G. Heileman bottling plant now. He's got the baby."

The former La Crosse South High School Tigers linebacker sat on a blanket, sucking a bottle of beer and cradling a child in one arm. Everyone thought he'd play college football, maybe even turn pro. This was the guy Eva had a crush on in middle school, who had written in her autograph book, "Roses are red, violets are blue, sugar is sweet, and so are candy bars," a blow to her tender pubescent heart.

Eva could've been Cinder, her life consumed with raising children, her own dreams on hold—no exciting job, no freedom. Now, on the brink of venturing into the unknown, a vision of the future was becoming clear. *I'm going to live the radio dream!*

6. TURN IT ON ~ GENESIS

Dwarfed behind the wheel of the '74 Imperial, Eva sped down Losey Boulevard, her Head East 8-track tape cranked. She could hardly believe she might work at her favorite station, Album Rock B93. She pretended to announce a song.

"That's 'Since You've Been Gone.' I'm Billie Soul, rocking you from coast to coast—from the coulees of Wisconsin to the Minnesota bluffs. Thin Lizzy is up next with 'Cowboy Song.'"

While glancing at a scrap of paper clutched between her knuckles on the wheel, she scanned businesses and careworn homes as she flew past. Why didn't they put addresses where people could see them?

She tuned the radio dial to B93.

> YARDLEY ST. MARTINS: That's Phil Collins. Now, you all know I like reading the tabloids. It seems Elizabeth Taylor, the Queen of Hollywood, and Michael Jackson, the King of Pop, held a tea party. The guest of honor? Bubbles, his pet chimpanzee! Can you imagine? Crazy stuff. Stay tuned, a long music set is coming up, on B93 FM.

What had happened to the regular morning guy? A raucous ad for a used car dealer came on. At the Southside Plaza, she slowed for a yellow light, stopping behind a city bus. A placard featuring the Marlboro Man sparking a smoke beckoned: *Come to where the flavor is.* Now craving a cigarette, Eva lowered the volume and drummed her fingers on the wheel.

What if she'd lost her chops? Professor Holt made the students practice diction, pronunciation, pitch, and articulation by reading scripts with a cork between their teeth. She tried out a few. "Seventy-seven benevolent elephants. I saw a kitten eating chicken in the kitchen." And the one Coco could never get right, "Which witch switched the Swiss wristwatches?" *I still have it.*

If she got the job, or, better yet, *when* she got the job, she'd need a new name. Not Billie Soul, something more rock and roll. Thin Lizzy . . . Elizabeth Taylor . . . "I'm Lizzy Taylor on B93," she said in an upbeat announcer style. A reinvention of her own choosing. It felt delicious. Down the road, in another town or when she became famous, she'd use her real name. For now, in case she was terrible, there'd be nothing to lose if she used a fake name.

The traffic light changed to green, and Eva proceeded slowly, squinting at addresses. She turned up the volume in time to catch his sign-off.

YARDLEY: That does it for me. Jack Matthews is up next. This one came out three years ago, in 1981. It's Foreigner, "Waiting for a Girl Like You," on B93 FM.

Eva's breath caught in her throat. *He's waiting for me!* Directly across from South Towne Mall behind a neglected-looking motor lodge nestled into the base of the bluffs, she spotted the broadcast tower. Its lights blinked above the tree line. With only a minute to spare, she swerved into the driveway, spinning gravel onto the road. She parked between a shiny sable-black Cadillac and a souped-up lime-green Dodge Charger with racing stripes.

Before going out, she checked the mirror. The emerald eyeliner she'd applied accentuated her coppery-brown eyes. She refreshed her frosty lip gloss, smoothed her unruly hair, and adjusted her uncomfortable, itchy padded bra.

Along the uneven sidewalk, a hand-lettered B93 sign stuck out from overgrown evergreen bushes. The walkway continued in front of numerous motel room doors covered in plywood. A piece of electrical tape covered the doorbell. *Yikes.* Could they pay her enough to satisfy Artie? And why was Yardley doing the morning show? She knocked, waited, and entered the sunlit lobby. The smell of coffee permeated the air.

"Hello-o," she called. "Mr. St. Martins?"

A Tina Turner song streamed from speakers mounted in the ceiling. Eva nodded to the beat and surveyed the space, which must have been the lobby of the old motel. A table spread with magazines was surrounded by an avocado-green velvet couch and matching chairs. She took a closer look at the mottled shag carpet— it looked just like the rug at her mom's. In the distance, the clacking of a typewriter and the murmur of a man's voice mixed with the music.

Eva took a few steps forward then stopped, spellbound by a massive wall of electronics. She had never seen so much equipment in one place. The transmitter, four reel-to-reel decks, and various other units occupied a space where once upon a time, people may have checked into the motel. One ten-and-a-half-inch silver reel turned, making a faint metallic *swish-swish* as the tape threaded its way through a pinch roller, passed over the play heads, and spooled onto a take-up reel. A round carousel held numerous carts. The blinking lights and bouncing meters on the audio equipment made her think of NASA's mission control. She smiled. It felt like home.

Up a few stairs, in the back of the building, a man moved about a glassed-in booth. She waved. Not noticing her, he sat and put on headphones as the song began to fade.

JACK MATTHEWS: "What's Love Got to Do with It," that's Tina Turner. I'm Jack, saying thanks to Yardley St. Martins—our very own suave and debonair heartthrob of the Coulee Region—for a fantastic show this morning. I'll be taking you through the midday on your station for continuous Lite Hits, B93. We're the Lite you want to leave on. The amazing Chaka Khan is up next.

Lite Hits? Who was this midday guy with the kind, fatherly voice? Eva sat on the sofa, clutching her purse. Just the day before, they played Black Sabbath and David Bowie. She stared out the picture window as traffic whizzed by on the highway between the station and the mall. What if this was a trend? The Album Rock station out of Milwaukee that Artie worshipped during high school had recently switched to something called Classic Rock: a much narrower playlist featuring only familiar, commercially successful songs. Music already overplayed, in her opinion, with a heavier commercial load. What if she had missed the boat? *I'm a '70s girl caught in an '80s world.*

Footsteps sounded from down a hallway near the equipment. A tall, gangly man with a luxurious head of wavy, iron-gray hair appeared. He was dressed in a black suit with a crisp shirt, open at the collar, where Eva couldn't help but notice a large gold pendant. She blinked; he couldn't possibly be the young-sounding man with the charming "heartthrob" radio personality. Judging from his wrinkled neck and the deep creases around his eyes, she estimated him to be over sixty. The suit looked custom made; it fit perfectly.

"I'm Yardley St. Martins," he said with a toothy grin, "and you must be Eva." Towering over her, he extended a bony hand.

She stood and shook it. "It's nice to meet you."

He tipped his head. "You're not at all what I imagined from your tape," he said.

Before she knew it, Yardley began to sing "The Loco-motion," adding a few dance moves. Pretty smooth for an old guy. "Little Eva, a 1962 hit written by Carole King and—"

"I didn't know she wrote that. Grand Funk did a version, too."

"Little Eva Boyd babysat for Carole King's kids, and King wrote 'Loco-motion' with her husband, ah—" He snapped his fingers. "I've got it. Gerry Goffin."

His resonant laugh boomed around the room like a bass drum in a parade. His earlobe was pierced, but he wore no earring. Eva could never remember which side meant straight or gay. He composed himself and fixed his gaze on her with a scrutinizing eye.

"You're a little girl with a big voice!"

Eva nodded. Despite his age the man oozed with charisma. She'd never met anyone like him. The rotating reels drew her attention away.

"I'll give you the nickel tour in a bit," he said. "The station used to be a motel. We converted it a few years ago, back in '77. The studios are up there," he said, craning his eyes toward the glass windows. "The salesmen work out of the basement. Our offices are in the old motel rooms. There's still a bible in my desk drawer."

It sounded so silly she started to laugh. When he joined in, she saw that Yardley's front tooth was edged in gold and slightly crooked. She took a closer look at his necklace. He was a Leo: proud and fierce, a natural leader.

"You may have noticed the format change. Just this morning, we switched from Album Rock to Lite Hits."

What the hell? Aware of the disappointment shown on her face, Eva pulled her mouth into a fake radio smile. "I noticed."

"You'll never have to cue up a record again," he said as he swung a long, skinny arm toward the automation system. He spoke with such pride she debated whether to push it.

A man with the build of a rugby player came barreling down the hall, waving papers. He, too, wore a fancy suit and flashy jewelry.

"I finished the sponsorship packages for your show, Yardley."

He barged right up and stood close, jangling coins or keys in his pocket. Despite her two-inch clogs, the men towered over her.

"Catch me later." Yardley took the papers. "Eva, this our sales manager, Merv Harms."

The brawny man's eyes went straight to her padded bust. He grasped her small hand in his blonde paw, squeezing too hard. Before she knew it, Merv lifted her arm high in the air and spun her around as if they were on the dance floor.

"Aren't you a cute little number."

"Oh, my!" That was the last thing she had expected. She yanked her hand away and smoothed the back of her skirt.

"It's okay, I don't bite," Merv said and looked at Yardley. "I'll find you after lunch."

Merv disappeared into the dark hallway. It was all Eva could do to not point her middle finger at his broad back.

"Alright, kiddo," Yardley said. "Let's get started."

They sat on the couch. He explained the station's history, adding technical stuff that made her eyes glaze over. He carried on with *his* career, *his* fans, *his* show . . . making her uneasy. It didn't seem like an interview. Eva interrupted to tell him about her passion for music. Coached by Artie on how to interview, she stated she was a team player and a self-starter.

As she was about to ask how much the job paid, he asked, "You have any kids at home or any on the way?"

"Ah, not that I know of." She gave a nervous laugh.

"What goals do you have for yourself," he asked, leveling his gaze. "One year, five years—"

"Well, I'd like to move up to evenings and then middays here at B93. Someday, I'd like to be on a morning show, maybe in LA."

"Morning show, huh? If you keep your nose clean, you never know what might happen."

Were they grooming her for mornings?

He winked. "You shouldn't have to work overnights for too long. Radio is a business with high turnover. Just do what I say and play by the rules."

Like Professor Holt once said about commercial radio during an unguarded moment in class, if the man signing the checks tells you to say 'shit,' you say it. *Say it, play it.* Although technically, she thought, you can't say that word on the radio.

"So. What do you say?" he asked.

Although it had bothered her when earlier, he'd slipped and said all they needed for overnight shifts was a warm body, she grinned so hard she thought her face would crack. "Yes. I'll take it."

"Well, little darlin', be here for training at eleven tonight," he said. "Donn will show you the ropes."

Tonight? Eva's mind raced. She'd have to quit the insurance job without giving notice. She twisted the end of her braid. For radio, she would do that. But they only had one car.

"Is there a bus stop nearby?"

"Yes. Over at South Towne." He stood and clapped his hands. "Are you ready for the grand tour?

Eva followed Yardley as he cleared the steps from the lobby to the back of the station in one stride. To their left, in the industrial kitchen, two well-dressed young men lounged against the counter. She could feel their eyes on her from over their steaming mugs.

"I'll introduce you to Sales later," he said, as if "Sales" were a type of person. He waved toward the opposite side of the building. "The production studio is down there, past master control. We're standing in the bullpen where you can check the wire and do your show prep."

In what may have been the former continental breakfast area of the motel, separated from the kitchen by a counter and three stools, the bullpen held an easy chair, a coat rack, and the announcers' cubbies. Sliding glass doors led to an outdoor patio. The Associated Press Teletype sat against the wall next to the doors. Continuous roll paper wound into the back of the machine from a box underneath. Eva inhaled the familiar ink smell. *I can't believe I'm here. I get to work on the radio again!*

Suddenly, the printer made a racket, pumping out news bulletins. *Zip-zip. Clack-clack.* The news spilled into a pile on the floor. The ding of a bell indicated an urgent bulletin. She resisted the urge to tear off the story. Yardley knocked on the hazy window and stabbed his finger towards the Teletype. Jack, the midday guy, nodded before putting on his headphones. In his pastel yellow sweater vest, he looked as fatherly as he sounded on the air.

"Please keep up with the news feed," Yardley said. "It's my pet peeve to see no one's cleared the wire."

She nodded. "Mine, too. And announcers who say 'ray-road' and 'this-sour,' or 'em' instead of 'them.' Or worse, 'yer' and 'fer sher,' 'hice school,' 'hunnerd,' 'dubbya,' and 'Feb-you-ary.' And leaving the 'g' off '-ing' words."

"You've got strong opinions, missy. But I'm down with that."

Encouraged, she added, "Why do sports announcers always say 'git?' Drives me nuts." *Like men who call me baby names.*

Yardley smiled. "Alright, kiddo, simmer down. I get here before daybreak, so around four o'clock start compiling content for my show. Set aside local news, sports, and weather. Stack them over there." He pointed to the former breakfast bar.

"Got it."

"You've reported the news, so you know how to prioritize. Find some fun stuff, too, like human interest stories, the almanac, celebrity news, Hollywood rumors—that sort of crap."

One perk of overnights was that she'd be helping Yardley, the boss. She found a small reporter's notebook in her purse and dug around for a pen. He ripped the long scroll of paper from the AP wire. He couldn't resist seeing what the *ding* was about, either.

"I'll be damned," he said. "Walter Mondale has chosen Geraldine Ferraro for his running mate, the first woman vice president."

"That's totally rad!" Eva said. An historic moment she thought she'd never live to see. Her mom would love it.

"Not my bag." He bunched up the story, tossing it basketball-style into a green trash bin.

"Two points!"

Yardley burst out laughing and his crooked gold tooth sparkled. "You're funny, kiddo."

Catching up, Eva scribbled notes: *weather, celebrity, Hollywood, crap.* "So, how do you want me to sound?"

"Just be yourself. Play music, talk about the artists, read liners and PSAs, keep up with the AP, give the forecast. Look, I start everyone with an A. You've got to work hard to earn an F in my book."

"Got it." Striving for As was in Eva's DNA. "Will anyone be listening? My college station signed off at midnight."

"You bet your sweet bippy. You'll get a surge of calls when the bars close." He winked. "But, yeah, it might be dead at times. You can tidy up the place during the wee hours."

43

"Like, wipe down the board and put away albums?" she asked, wrinkling her forehead.

"We don't play albums anymore. All our music is on those big reels." He pointed at the wall in the lobby. "Vacuum, clean the kitchen and the bathroom."

Heat burned in her chest. He had not mentioned maid service. Would it have been a deal breaker? She thought those days were behind her, having to clean dorm bathrooms as part of her work-study job. And no more records? The automated system scared her.

Yardley continued, oblivious to her distress. "Flip the automation on while you're cleaning. Don't let it go too long, though."

He touched a hand to her back. It lingered over the hooks on her bra. When his hand dropped away, it brushed against her buns. She froze, feeling like a mouse in a trap. Whatever he was saying, she did not hear it. Was this normal? A stronger woman might slap him or at least say something. She twisted slightly away. Artie would lose it if she told him about the interaction. Keeping physical distance from Yardley might be the best strategy.

"Okay, little darlin', let's go see Dottie."

He led her through the kitchen, down the hall, and into an office that smelled of lilacs masking stale smoke. A petite prune-faced woman beamed as she tucked a strand of bobbed, jet-black hair behind her ear.

"Dottie, this is Eva LaVette. Do you have her W-4s?" He turned to Eva. "Dottie's the glue that holds this place together."

"Nice to meet you," Dottie said. Her voice was deep and scratchy, a smoker's voice. Dottie blushed as she peered at her boss through fluttering lashes.

Eva shook her dainty hand.

Dottie shuffled through papers on her desk. Adding to the mess, a postage stamp dispenser spewed a long strip of stamps. She came up with a folder of paperwork. "Just the Two of Us," a syrupy song from Grover Washington, Jr. played on her radio. Eva guessed this was their new target audience: a middle-aged office manager who listened to bland background music all day. Dottie handed over the employment forms.

Yardley tugged at Eva's elbow. "I'm at the end of the hall."

Mounted on his office door was a nameplate engraved ROLF MARKHAM, General Manager. *Rolf Markham?* Inside, behind his desk, a line of trophies boasted his awards: Station of the Year, Best Morning Show, Local Broadcast Legend—two of those. There were no pictures of kids making goofy faces, dogs with red Christmas bows, a smiling wife on a sailboat. But a framed gold record hung on the wall, Led Zeppelin IV, a relic from the station's prior format.

"Have a seat," he said, checking the gold watch hanging from his wrist. "Do you have any questions?"

"How many people listen to the station?"

"It depends. In the morning, our average quarter-hour is around 20,000. We expect that to double with the new format."

"40,000 people? Wow."

"Yes. The signal blankets La Crosse and travels out past the bluffs and into the coulees."

Eva squirmed in her chair. The news would travel fast; everyone from high school would soon learn she was Lizzy Taylor.

"Don't fret, kiddo. The numbers are much smaller on overnights. You'll see. You'll get a smattering of calls at bar time, or from mothers up with sick babies, people working third shift at the factory, stuff like that." Yardley ran a hand through his wavy hair. "We have high expectations for you, Eva. You're a rock star."

She winced. She wasn't a star, she was a novice, desperate to get her foot in the door. Even at a soft-hits station on overnights.

"Thank you, sir. Should I call you Yardley or Rolf?"

"Yardley." He paged through his day planner. "Good luck tonight."

"Thank you."

Eva wandered down the dark hall. Feeling lighter now that the interview was over, she stepped into the lobby. Temporarily blinded by the bright daylight, her senses kicked into a higher level of awareness. *Is this really happening?* The golden air seemingly shimmered with diamantine sparkles or maybe dust. She reached out a hand to catch the light. *Radio!*

Startling her into reality, a reel on the equipment wall clicked on. Another stopped as the automatic system segued into "Down Under" by Men At Work. Reeling and giddy, she bounced out the front door and down the sidewalk. No longer a student volunteer, she would receive a salary to be on the radio! She swelled with a fundamental sense of belonging. This was better than a dream.

Halfway into the front seat of the Chrysler, Eva paused. Artie was going to kill her. She'd forgotten to ask how much the job paid.

8. CHANGES ~ LOGGINS AND MESSINA

Eva rushed into the apartment. "Artie?"

A note on the counter in his jagged scrawl said he'd walked to the grocery store. Ludwig, the orange tabby who adopted them on their first day in the new apartment, bound out from the bedroom and rubbed against her nylons. She kicked off her clogs and dialed Gateguard. Taken aback by her abrupt resignation, the pointy-nosed Mr. Olson's anger came through the wire. Eva grinned as he ranted. Radio was dawning on her horizon, albeit on the midnight horizon.

She dialed her mom.

"Hello-o."

Eva loved the way her mother sang out the greeting.

"Hi, Mom. I've got big news . . . I got the job!"

"That's fantastic, honey. I'll get to hear your voice all the time now. When do you start?"

"Tonight, unfortunately on the graveyard shift. I'll move up as soon as there's an opening."

"That'll be rough on you and Artie. Your father would get so revved up from playing, I'd sit up with him for half the night."

Eva stretched the long phone cord over to the coffee table and sat on the couch. "But you and Pop were happy, right?"

"Of course. You know that. He was the love of my life."

And the love of Eva's life. It sounded like her mother was having one of her good days, the right time to bring up a worry that weighed on her since his death.

"Mom, sometimes I feel like it's my fault that he died."

"What? No!"

"But he wouldn't have if he hadn't been taking me to my piano lesson." She wound the cord around her fist. Helpless to stop it, the accident replayed in her mind. Her father at the wheel lighting a cigarette with his Zippo, giving her a pseudo lecture

47

about focus: she needed to prioritize her studies and the piano. The way the car in front of them had skidded on the ice, the back end sailing around smoothly like a figure skater going into a spin. Her pop wrestling with the steering wheel as they fishtailed. A blinding spray of snow hitting the windshield as they spun into the ditch. Her hand bleeding from the barrage of shattered glass. The shrieks from her own mouth. Her throat tightened. She missed him. He truly listened to her, while other adults believed children should be seen and not heard.

"Eva, your father loved nurturing your dreams. He was happy to drive you. He talked all the time about you being a famous pianist. He dreamed of seeing you on stage playing 'Clair de Lune,' his favorite."

Debussy. Her throat relaxed. "I'll have to get the music."

A memory triggered of her sitting at the piano, her pop's fingers resting over hers, the first time she had really looked at his hands: long strong fingers, patches of hair on his knuckles. He had been the most positive person in her life. *You can be anything you want, Eva. A female Arthur Rubinstein. A modern-day Mozart or Liszt.*

So that's why she felt like such a disappointment.

"It was his time to go," her mom said softly. "I'm thankful he didn't suffer and that you didn't get hurt worse."

Eva touched the scar that stretched from her little finger to her wrist, the fine, white, jagged wound she wore like a bracelet. She could still be famous, play his music on the radio, honor his legacy.

"So, come on now. I'm dying to hear about this new job. I sure wish I'd had career choices. I was only nineteen when I had you."

While she filled her mother in, someone thumped up the wooden porch stairs.

"I've got to go. Artie's home."

"Good luck tonight," her mom said. "Come over soon. I love you more than all the stars in the sky."

A warm smile filled Eva's face. "Me too."

Artie entered, set down his keys, and crossed the room, flip-flops slapping. He shuffled overflowing bags from one arm to the other. "How'd it go?"

"He was so rude."

Artie looked confused.

She laughed. "Oh, I quit Gateguard . . . I'm the new overnight girl at B93!"

Incredulous, he shook his head, eyes wide. "You took the job? You didn't think to talk it over with me? When do you start?"

He pulled a stalk of celery from the brown paper Quillins bag and put it into the refrigerator.

"Tonight." Eva got up to help him with the groceries.

"Tonight? What are the hours?"

"Eleven to five-thirty, Sunday through Thursday, and weekends."

"This means we'll no longer be sleeping together."

She hadn't thought of that.

"I swear to god, Eva. I can't believe you went and took the job. How much does it pay?"

"I forgot to ask, but I assume it's more than minimum. I mean, I have a college degree." She sat at their hand-me-down Formica table, tracing her finger along its chrome edge.

"You didn't ask? I'm telling ya', Eva. You have to negotiate."

"I was more worried about how I'd stay awake all night, honestly. It has to be more than minimum. I'll find out when I get my check."

"There's got to be a reason they didn't talk about the pay, Eva," he said as he handed her a bunch of bananas for the fruit bowl in the middle of the table. "What if it's only minimum? We need to start saving for a house, and college funds, even retirement."

"I can't drive to work in a house."

He always had to bring her down, harping about the future. College for their imaginary kids? Retirement? They had decades to think about that. She rolled her eyes, then tried to lighten the mood.

"But Artie, I have a face for radio."

He sat at the table, took a banana from the bunch, and shook it at her. "I've heard you say that before, Eva. You need to stop it. You look nice."

"I'll get paid for training," she said, brushing off his compliment.

Under the table, Ludwig rubbed against her shins. She bent down to scratch his head.

"What are the benefits? How much vacation?"

"I'll ask the guy I'm observing tonight. Donn, with two Ns."

The muscles in Artie's arms flexed as he scratched a grid onto the back of the grocery list, his head bent to the paper.

"I'm gone from two-thirty until midnight," he said. "If you sleep while I'm at work, we can spend mornings together."

She would have to take the bus during the week, as he needed the car for his second-shift job at Penzle's. While he talked, he stroked his beard, muffling his words. She wished he would shave it. Eva started making lunch. Artie ate his banana. At the table, they talked over grilled cheese and bowls of tomato soup.

"I should have given Gateguard two weeks' notice," Eva said as she cleared the dishes. "It's not like me. My parents taught me to do things right."

"There's a difference between making a career move and being a flake, although I wish you had waited. This affects me, too. I guess I'll always know where you are when you're on the air."

While she washed dishes, Eva whistled along to the kitchen radio. When her shirttail got wet from the spray, she realized she still wore her interview outfit. Tonight, she could probably throw on some jeans for training—it was the graveyard shift, no one would be there. Yet, Yardley came in for his morning show at five. She decided to wear her Steely Dan T-shirt with a denim skirt and bring a sweater in case the air conditioning was cold.

50

"It's nice having you home during the day," Artie said. After she finished drying dishes, in the living room, he picked up his twelve-string guitar and sat on the couch. "Let's write a song."

"What should we call it?" She followed him and sat on the arm of the couch.

"Here's a little ditty called 'Ode to Eva.' A one, an' a-two." He began strumming; he hummed until he found a melody. "*Eva the DJ, the talk of the town. She plays great music and never gets down.*"

"My turn," she said, picking up his phrasing. "*From Bowie to Boston, from Springsteen to the Stones, she plays them all and answers the phones.*"

Although, a Lite Hits station wouldn't include those artists.

Artie added a percussive beat, slapping his hand on the wood between strums. It was too bad his band, the Inverted Paradiddles, had broken up. She had loved watching him play, the way he banged his head to the beat, striped bell-bottoms swinging, teeth gnashing behind his bold, blonde Zappa mustache. At five-six, just a few inches taller than her, Artie stood tall onstage. How handsome he looked now in the filtered afternoon sunlight.

"*From free concert tickets to going backstage, she thinks it'll pay more than minimum wage.*" He laughed. "*She's on her way to fortune and fame. She's so cool. They all know her name.*"

Eva moved closer to Artie, lowering her voice. She removed the guitar and sat on his lap, thanking him for the song with a smooch.

"Hi there, handsome. I'm Lizzy Taylor. This song is dedicated to a fine guitar player—formerly of Sheboygan, it's Mr. Arthur B. LaVette of La Crosse!"

"I'm using my formal name?" Artie gave her waist a squeeze. "Hmm. I wonder how Lizzy Taylor makes love."

He scooped her up like a kitten and took her into the bedroom. Her body buzzed with desire. She wrapped her arms around his neck.

Later, as they lay entwined, Eva stared into the sunlight that filtered through their gauzy curtains. Artie hadn't been that amorous in ages. Playing the guitar always did excite him. Or maybe her being Lizzy Taylor had spiced things up. She closed her eyes and snuggled onto his shoulder, taking in the scent of his bare skin.

Who was Lizzy Taylor? *Known for her Lite Voice, in the early '70s Lizzy was an "it" girl in New York City who became known as the "Velvet Voice" of Soft Rock Radio. She moved to Wisconsin to start a hobby farm with her husband, Harrison Ford.*

9. MIDNIGHT RIDER ~ ALLMAN BROTHERS

Beholden to the bus schedule, Eva arrived at the station five minutes late. In the studio, Donn introduced himself as he moved a wine-colored leather briefcase from the guest chair, where she sat. Her objective that night was to observe and learn everything, to soak up as much as she could, because come Monday she'd be manning master control on her own. She inched the Naugahyde chair close, trying not to look astounded by his hair—an imitation of the singer from A Flock of Seagulls, brushed up on the sides and down in the middle. Apparently, Donn hadn't stepped into daylight the entire three years he'd been on the graveyard shift; vanilla pudding had more color. In contrast, he wore a black T-shirt and jeans. His large gut spilled over the waistband and bulged around his helpless Mork from Ork rainbow suspenders. Her eyes widened when she noticed white powder on his upper lip.

Donn held up a finger. He slipped on the headphones and cleared his throat before switching on the mic to do a break.

Eva eyed him quizzically, wondering what her impression of his voice would have been if she hadn't seen him first. Smooth and generic, it fit the Lite format. After his break, he removed his headphones. They had left a dent in his tall hair.

The station wasn't what Eva thought: Tina Turner had tricked her on that first day when she'd grooved to the music. Chaka Khan, too. It was now apparent those were the only good songs on the entire playlist. She worried that repetitive Lite Hits might drive her batty during the desolate late-night shifts.

Donn initialed recently played commercials on the log. He loaded the cart machines with spots for his next break. Eva talked to his back.

"What do you think about the sudden format change?"

"I don't care about the music. I'm just happy to be off overnights."

Eva was shocked. For her, it was all about the music. "Who comes up with the playlist, then?" she asked.

"Some corporate suits sitting around a conference table, I suppose. They send reels to stations across the country. Yardley said getting the format was a coup, 'cause only one station in a market can play Lite Hits."

Oh, what a pity. She cocked her head, struck by the fact there were no album covers to look at or quote from. "How do you know what songs are coming up?"

"They're listed on the music log. It's here somewhere."

Donn rummaged around the narrow counter under the board and slid the log from under a glossy magazine open to the centerfold, a spread-eagled naked woman. He slapped it closed—it was the issue with Vanessa Williams on the cover. Is that what he stored in his briefcase? Not sure what to do, Eva looked away while he stuffed the magazine under the log.

An hour later, after yawning three times in a row, Eva went into the bullpen where she stretched her arms up over her head. She bent down to touch her toes. Her head level with her cubby, she saw a stack of memos. She took the papers into the studio and sat. "It's a welcome memo from the engineer. *No smoking. No beverages allowed in the studio. No guests after hours.*"

"Yeah, you can ignore that," Donn said. "But don't be surprised to see him in the middle of the night. He takes the station off the air while he fixes equipment."

"What does he look like?"

"Hmm. Like Shaggy from *Scooby-Doo* but wearing overalls. His workshop is in the basement."

Donn checked the log and changed out the carts.

Eva poked a memo with her finger. "Did you see this? A radio announcer in St. Louis was electrocuted during a remote broadcast. The antenna tipped onto an overhead line."

"An arc of electricity can travel through the air. You don't need to touch a power line."

"Sheesh."

54

"If you ever do a remote, look up before raising the antenna. And for god's sake, put it down after. More than one numbskull has driven away with the antenna up."

"What a shock!" Eva joked, and for the first time, Donn laughed.

While consulting the log, he stacked carts on the side counter.

"We have an automated carousel system for commercials, but it's broken. It started playing the wrong spots. The sales scum bags get bent out of shape if you miss their ads. It's money from their pockets.

Eva knew little about sales—they dressed up, stood around drinking coffee, and drove nice cars.

Donn took a request for the Clash and told the caller that he'd play it.

"We don't play The Clash, do we?" she asked. It would literally clash to segue from punk rock into a Celine Dion ballad.

"Nope. Not with the M.O.R. format."

"Emmowar?"

"Middle of the road—music for dentist offices. Anyway, if people think their request is coming, they'll listen longer. It helps with the ratings. If you want to keep your job you've got to have good ratings." Donn leaned back in his chair. "I got fired once. In North Dakota. I was driving to work on a Monday morning, and I heard a promo for 'an exciting new show with your host So-and-So.' Not me. They told the entire city of Fargo before me. The program director was wearing a three-piece suit, of course. I couldn't believe he did that, but it's a rite of passage in this business. Kind of a ticking clock."

Eva was getting that impression.

He jabbed a thumb towards the production studio. "There are blank tapes in there. Start a master right away, because you never know when you'll need an audition tape."

Donn took another call. "B93."

"Am I the winner?"

Donn covered the receiver and whispered, "Listen and learn."

"Yes! What's your name?" he asked.

"Jeff."

"Congratulations, Jeff! Your prizes will be waiting at our office. What's your favorite station?"

"Z100!"

He hung up.

"Donn, now that guy will go over to Z100 to pick up his prize."

"Yup."

"You're bad."

It was funny, but Eva didn't think it was right. Tired of sitting, she went over to the cork bulletin board at the back of the studio and scanned the FCC licenses pinned into crooked rows. None of the names matched the air staff. Rolf Markham was Yardley. John R. Figgleston must be Jack. Donn's name was Donald Snelm.

The weekly DJ schedule hung next to the licenses. Everyone but Yardley was assigned shifts on the weekend. *Lucky for him.* Flipping the page to the following week, Lizzy Taylor was written across the bottom row. A thrill passed through her body. She dropped the pages; they swished into place.

Along the windowsill between studios, a Mister Potato Head presided over a row of neon troll dolls. Eva ran her finger through the dust. She rearranged the dolls by height.

"When do you clean?"

"Cleaning is women's work."

With a tight-lipped smile, she asked, "Who does it, then?"

"I don't know. Probably Dottie."

So much for women's lib. How infuriating.

Donn's carts were stacked haphazardly. As Eva smoothed the sides, her hand bumped into the tower. It leaned, then tipped. All the plastic carts tumbled to the floor, clattering loudly as they bounced.

"Son of a bitch!" Donn yelled. He wheeled away from the ruckus and rolled over a cart with his chair, cracking it in half.

"I am so sorry," she said, mortified, gathering them in her arms.

Donn grunted as he bent over his bulging stomach, his face as red as the on-air light. Eva blew dust off the carts while Donn re-stacked.

"It's okay. It's not the first time that's happened," he said. "I'll run into production and re-dub it. Peel off the label. I can reuse it."

Donn offered her the chair. "Back-announce the song, ID the station, introduce Joe Jackson."

"Me? Now?"

He left the studio. Eva put on his oily, funky headphones.

"*Yow!* You're going to wreck your hearing!" she yelled.

The song faded. Her mouth went dry. "Oh, my god, oh, my god, oh, my god," she whispered. She plastered a smile on her face and opened the mic.

10. SOMETHING'S HAPPENING ~ PETER FRAMPTON

On Sunday night, Eva entered the station, her guts as tangled as an unspooled cassette. There would be no one sitting by her side if something went wrong over the next six hours.

Donn left precisely at eleven. She ran to the front window and watched his red taillights fade down the highway, feeling like an astronaut floating in space after the tether broke.

Back in the studio, she plugged in her headphones. Yardley would be listening, and perhaps everyone else who worked there. *Check out the new girl!*

She set her pop's faded photo, now in a gilded frame, on the console behind the mic. After writing a few notes about the upcoming music, she practiced reading a Head Start PSA. Eva switched on the microphone.

> LIZZY: Ahh, heaven-sent love that lasts forever. Peaches and Herb with "I Pledge My Love to You," going out to Faye and Dwayne on their anniversary. We heard Sade before that. I'm Lizzy Taylor. The La Crosse Head Start program has openings for classroom assistants. The only qualification? A love of children. Apply in person during normal business hours. Up next on B93, it's "Sweet Dreams," a song Eurythmics recently made into a cool—and very weird—MTV video.

Eva started a commercial. It was indeed her friends' anniversary, but they wouldn't be listening to the radio; they'd gone bonkers for MTV. She wished Artie would let her get cable.

During the break, while glancing over her shoulder, she wrote talking points; there was nothing worse than a DJ who blathered on and on. She had ad-libbed herself into a corner more than once at the college jazz station.

58

In the bullpen, the glass patio doors reflected nothing but darkness. Anyone from a neighborhood kid to a peeping Tom could be lurking out there. She went out and checked the deadbolt. Misaligned, it wouldn't latch. As a quick fix, someone had wedged a thick dowel into the bottom rail. She yanked the door; it held.

The Teletype was out of paper. "Shit." She tore open a new box and threaded it into the machine. It quickly spit out a string of stories, but the ink was fading.

After changing the spooled ribbon, she checked her cubby. No messages, but there was an envelope with her name written on it in Donn's writing. A tiny baggie, wrapped in a note. *To help you get thru the night—I can get more.* She opened the baggie, touched her finger to the powder, and placed it on her tongue. It instantly numbed—it was cocaine, all right. *Holy crap. Does he run a drug ring here? Maybe that's why Yardley is so skinny.* Worried about fingerprints, she wiped the bag with her shirt and chucked it into the back of Donn's cubby. Addiction was the last thing she needed.

Later, after vacuuming—which really burned her butt—she stared at the phone. Unless someone called, radio was a one-way transmission. There had to be people out there. *That's the magic of radio. You never know who might be listening.* Maybe Dustin, her production partner from college, or the mayor of La Crosse, or even Rod Stewart, who was in town for a show. Whatever happened to Dustin and his aviator glasses and cowboy hat? Eva hadn't talked to Coco since she got the job at Z100. She wrote a reminder to tune in occasionally, even if she hated Top 40.

In the studio, she cranked up Bruce Springsteen's "I'm On Fire." Line one blinked. Her mother had already called. Her first fan? Eva turned down the monitors.

"B93, this is Lizzy. What's your name and where are you calling from?"

"Hi *Lizzy*, it's me. I just got home. How's it going?"

59

Was Artie coming on to her? With the phone under her ear, she pulled carts, speaking low, using her sultry Billie Soul voice. "Well, hello, you stud. Thanks for calling B93 FM."

"So, big news," he said, ignoring her come-on. "Van Halen is coming, and Dwayne's cousin is going to stand in line for tickets."

"Cool! When's the show?" she said in her everyday voice.

"The twenty-eighth. Can you take the night off?"

"There's no way. I just started."

"I'll go without you then."

"Hold on." While listening to a segue, she chewed her lower lip. "Did you have some of the chili I made?"

"Ah, no. Honestly, I like it the way Ma makes it."

Why had she believed marriage would be a radiant, glowing experience? Faye and Dwayne, her mom and dad—they'd had it. She was beginning to doubt if she and Artie would ever have it. Here was an opportunity to use a tip from the book about healthy marriages she'd been reading.

"Why don't you ask your mom for the recipe? It would be a nice bonding experience."

"She cooks. I eat. That's how we bond."

"Artie. Listen to yourself."

"Never mind." He sighed. "When you say Lite Hits it sounds like 'Lite Tits.'"

"Oh, god. I'll never un-hear that." *Enunciate, Eva.* She listened to the song playing over the studio monitor and glanced at the log. "The hotline is blinking. I need to go."

They said goodbye. She punched the hotline button.

"Hi Lizzy," Yardley said, sounding groggy.

He needs to snort a line, she thought. "I'm glad you called, Yardley. I was wondering, what happens if I miss a spot? The Timothy Jewelers cart broke."

"Put it aside with a note. Don't worry about it, the commercials overnight are freebies." He chuckled. "Not even a dollar a holler."

Before she could react to this shocking news, he jumped in.

"Just a note. Please don't talk about MTV. Video killed the— you-know-what. Even though we play the songs, it reminds people to turn off the radio. Don't talk about anything on television for that matter. And I heard you say 'Sade,' but her name is pronounced 'Shar-day.' Have you been listening to the other announcers?"

She slumped in the chair.

"And one more thing. I need you to take the evening shift on Wednesday night. It might be premature to put you in primetime, but I have no other option. The afternoon drive guy is taking his kids up north for the Fourth, so Donn's filling in."

As a new announcer, she was a baby; overnights were supposed to be her incubation period, with the hope that she'd emerge as a fully-fledged professional in no time. Already, he was giving her a chance to show what she could do during normal hours.

"Wow! Yes!"

"It's settled. Thanks, Lizzy. You're a lifesaver. A real team player."

But her excitement fizzled like a dud sparkler. Wednesday was the Fourth of July, her second favorite holiday. They planned to meet Faye and Dwayne at Riverside Park for volleyball, followed by a Sunblind Lion concert and the fireworks before her midnight shift.

It's just a small sacrifice on my journey to success.

11. RAPTURE ~ BLONDIE

Eva sang along to The Go-Go's with a full moon beaming into the studio. She tapped her toes as she twirled in the chair. A groovy lava lamp splashed the dark studio with psychedelic lights. Patchouli incense swirled in the air. As "Our Lips Are Sealed" began to wind down, she glanced at Turntable Two, but there was no record.

"Dang! I forgot to cue it up."

When she turned to the bins, she frowned—all the albums had vanished. Instead, shards of broken records covered the floor.

Just fifteen seconds remained on the song. She wheeled over the clattery debris to the board to make a Technical Difficulties announcement. With a tremendous lunge, Eva got to the mic. When she tried to talk, all that came out was a dry "Ack."

Her tongue had shrunk into a nubby pencil at the back of her parched throat. Panic erased her ability to think; she couldn't remember her air name, or the station call letters. The needle scraped into its final groove with a *ka-thunk, chhhhh.*

There had now been a minute of dead air; Mr. Carlson would be calling on the hotline any second to scream at her. If Eva didn't get something going it would be curtains for her career.

She spun the cart rack, fumbling for a PSA. Under her fingers, the carts cracked open, spilling their guts into ribbons of tape. With leaden feet, Eva backed away, stumbling. Mocking, floating faces appeared in a cloud of dust above her head.

"Dead air! Dead air!" they chanted.

Eva jerked awake, coughing and clutching the sheets. Mr. Carlson from WKRP? She peered around the bedroom—it was afternoon, and she was at home in bed, a fuzzy cat next to her face on the pillow. Outside, a stiff breeze stirred bare branches, casting shadows through the curtains and onto the ceiling. The dead-air nightmare retreated into the recesses of her brain like vapor.

She pulled the alarm clock close to her face.

"Ugh, only two o'clock. Your papa hasn't gone to work yet, kitty."

She kicked off the covers. Artie was on the couch reading *Sports Illustrated*.

"I tried to be quiet," he said.

"The wind woke me." That, or a flushing toilet upstairs.

At the stereo, she turned on Z100. Coco came on, speaking fast.

> COCO: "Whip It," Devo coming at you on your hit station, Z100! You all know someone who tries too hard, who's afraid to make a mistake. It's called imposter syndrome, folks. But Billy Joel? He loves you "Just the Way You Are." Z100 with the Hits!

Although Coco's overtone-rich, raspy voice sounded perfect for radio, Eva sure was happy she didn't have to sound so hyped. She'd have to ask Coco about imposter syndrome.

"It's supposed to rain tonight," Artie said.

"November rains are the worst," Eva said, yawning. "Man, I can't get adjusted to third shift and it's been four months. By five I'm so beat I need toothpicks to hold my eyes open. At least the callers were active yesterday. I got lots of love."

"You should have gone into teaching. You could have had summers off, and great benefits, too."

Eva ignored his comment and put a slice of whole wheat bread in the toaster and opened a jar of peanut butter. Since she'd started, no one had quit or gotten fired.

"It's strange. There are thousands of people listening, yet I feel so alone, like I'm in solitary confinement. I hope I can move up soon. A better shift would pay more."

Artie did not appear to be listening to her.

"Did you feed the cat?"

Ludwig's bowl was empty. She peeked at the litter box in the hallway near the back door. Full of lumps. In the kitchen, Eva added "clean kitty litter" to her list of chores. Her toast popped.

"Artie. Could you please help with Ludwig?"

"Quit being a nag," he said, rattling the pages of his magazine. "You wanted the cat as much as I did."

"It doesn't hurt if he runs out of food. Makes him appreciate us."

"Maybe. And we need to keep fresh water in the bowl. It's important for his kidneys." She wished he would help her more.

"You working again this weekend?"

"I traded shifts with Schmidty, that young kid, remember? I'm covering for him tonight. I'll have the weekend off."

She sat at the table with her meal—not quite breakfast, lunch, nor dinner. "We could go to the laundromat tomorrow. Or hike up Grandad Bluff."

"Either, or both," he said. "You know what? Faye and Dwayne are going back to Sheboygan. We could go, too. Let's leave tomorrow morning when you get home."

"That's a great idea! I'll sleep on the way," Eva said. She chewed her toast, covering her mouth, talking fast. "I haven't been anywhere since I started this job. We've hardly seen Faye and Dwayne. I'm a stranger in my own life."

Revived, she jumped up from the kitchen table to pack a suitcase. In the bedroom, the tortured sheets roused her nightmare. A snippet of The Dream came back: a translucent Coco, floating through the air outside the booth, turning a deaf ear, fading away.

"I'm a ghost. A ghost in my own life," Eva whispered.

12. IN THE DARK ~ BILLY SQUIRE

With her head ducked, Eva pinched the hood of her raincoat under her chin as she ran to the bus stop, dodging puddles lit only by streetlights. There, she huddled on the bench and, with wet fingers, struggled to light a cigarette. Once lit, she took a deep puff and exhaled smoke into the night air. When headlights approached, the pinpoints created bokeh in the multitude of raindrops coating the glass enclosure. Only a car. She leaned back, shaking her head. Every day, she woke up excited to go to work, but this wasn't what she had imagined when she chose a career in radio. Yes, she knew she'd have to pay her dues, but waiting alone on a street corner at ten o'clock on a cold, rainy November night? Then six hours of mind-numbing Lite music? The shine was starting to wear off the microphone.

At the station, with the studio door propped open, Donn sat at the board, humming along to Nena's "99 Luftballons" and wearing his headphones. Leaning to one side, he farted. When she shook out her wet coat, the motion startled him.

"You working for Schmidty?" he asked, blushing.

"Yeah. He's going to a dance. Important high school stuff."

She hung her coat in the bullpen.

"Prepare yourself," he yelled. "It's a double-whammy—a full moon *and* Friday the thirteenth. The wackos and telephone screamers are out in full force." He rushed into the bullpen and grabbed his sheepskin coat with the matted wooly collar. "You mind if I go? I'm meeting this chick who called in. She sounded nice."

Meeting a stranger? Eva's mom would say he needs to get his head examined. But men didn't have much to worry about, she supposed—it was Donn's groupies who should be afraid. Suddenly, Eva understood his motivation: radio was about meeting chicks. "Knock yourself out."

"If I don't show for my shift tomorrow, call the authorities."

"I won't be here. I'll be on a road trip."

Donn retrieved his wine-colored briefcase from the studio. Eva had yet to solve the mystery of what he carried in the posh leather case. His cocaine?

As the last song of the hour wound down, she wheeled up to the board, hit the legal ID, and flipped the switch to start "Wake Me Up Before You Go" by Wham, an upbeat poppy current on Reel A.

Through the studio window, Eva watched a shadowy Donn as he slipped out the front door. If women found him attractive, there was only one reason: celebrity. *Blech. I need another shower.* She wiped down the board with a floral disinfectant.

An hour later, the storm had cleared. While Lionel Richie sang "Hello," the saddest song she'd ever heard, Eva vacuumed, scrubbed the toilet, dusted, and washed mugs. She checked the safety stick in the patio door. Standing in front of the glass, she became captivated by the stark moon, its edges sharpened in the cold night air, the light illuminating the neighbor's clothesline and the fence under the tower. *Radio waves are light waves, too.*

"Ahem."

Eva wheeled around to see a young man dressed in grease-stained overalls, holding a knife at his side. Her hands flew to her throat; she wanted to scream but nothing came out.

"It's okay. I'm the engineer," he said as he lifted the knife. "Did you tape this under the board?"

"No. For crying out loud, man, I swear to god my heart just stopped."

"Sorry. I'm here to fix that wonky D reel. Don't switch the automation back on till I'm done. I'll be downstairs."

The song was fading out. Eva ran into the studio. Diving into the air chair, she plucked a station liner from the box.

LIZZY: The Thompson Twins, "Hold Me Now" on B93, home of Radio-opoly! Roll the dice and play along for a chance at $5,000 in fabulous prizes! Pick up your official game board at, um, participating sponsors. Listen and win with B93.

That's why you always pre-read stuff, you dumb-dumb. Eva found a Radio-opoly cheat sheet in the promos folder along with a list of sponsors the announcer was supposed to name. Prizes included pizzas, dinners, dry-cleaning certificates, *and much, much more!* Valuable items, too, including a snowblower, spa treatments, vacations, and gym memberships. In his excitement to meet his fan, Donn had forgotten to give her a heads up about the cheat sheet. Staff meetings were held during the day, while she slept.

"I'd like to win these prizes," she said, laughing at Yardley's atrocious spelling: "congradulate the winner" and "lables." She found the cart labeled "DICE SFX" and previewed five versions of rolling dice sound effects.

She listened while a promo played, the last stop in the set. All the guys had prerecorded bits—*Jack Matthews, taking you through middays on B93 FM!*—but none for her, because overnights weren't worth promoting. Out in the lobby, the row of framed eight-by-ten air staff photos confirmed her thoughts. Clean-cut daytime guys, with all-American smiles, posed with the same tilt to their heads, a catchlight in their eyes. Even Donn managed to look perky.

She back announced "Watching the Wheels" by John Lennon and, after, stared at the clock. On overnights, she had too much time to think about her shitty marriage. Line 1 lit up.

"Hi there, Lizzy Taylor," said a man with a provocative baritone voice. "Can I request 'I Would Die for You' by Prince?"

"Sure. What's your name?"

"Let's keep that a mystery. You busy?"

"Not really." She glanced at the clock above the board. Only 1:30 a.m.—four hours to go. Keeping him on the line would kill some time. "Okay, mystery man. What *can* you tell me?"

"I just wanted to let you know someone's listening. When I hear your voice . . . I don't know, I feel like you get me. The songs you pick are always what I need. Anyway, I thought maybe you're lonely too, all alone there."

Eva half-listened as she crossed off and initialed ads on the log. She *wished* she could choose the music.

Over the phone, something popped and fizzed. "I'm getting into bed with a beer." He spoke in a modulated, pleasant manner.

"Let me guess. You're a radio announcer. You have the voice."

"Guess again."

"A police dispatcher?"

"Nope."

"A dog catcher?"

He laughed. "How did you guess?"

Time flew as they pillow-talked. He seemed nice and asked a lot of questions. As Lizzy, Eva reverted to her young and flirty self. She felt a spark of attraction, and it wasn't static electricity from dragging her boots on the carpet as she twirled the chair while they talked. Hours and a few beers later, he became drowsy and begged off.

While Eva was putting away the cleaning supplies, headlights flashed into the lobby. She ran out and sidled beside the window, peeking out between the knobby fabric curtains. A station wagon had pulled into the lot. Its dome light went on—a woman with big hair applied lipstick using her rearview mirror. She got out and picked her way across the gravel. Eva turned on the porch light.

"Can I help you?"

"Where's Donn?"

"He left hours ago."

She teetered a little in her high-heeled, over-the-knee red suede boots. "That jackass bastard," she muttered.

The woman spun around and left. Eva locked the door, waiting to turn off the light until the tall-boots girl was safely in her car. What had Donn gotten himself into now?

Back in the studio, she consulted the music log. "Oh, cool." There was a new song by Genesis, one of her favorite bands from high school. It was about time the music reels were refreshed. A few bars in, however, it became apparent. "That's All" was another formulaic pop song with a repetitive riff, and now people would start requesting it. Two lines lit up at once.

"B93. Please hold." She punched Line 2.

A crazy-sounding caller screamed a torrent of obscenities. Eva hung up so fast she knocked her mug off the counter. Cold coffee spilled onto her lap. *Bweet! Bweet! Pepsi Syndrome*—just like the *Saturday Night Live* skit at a nuclear power plant. The mess dripped onto the carpet, where newer stains overlapped old. She mopped at it feebly with a wad of tissues while answering the other line.

"Is everything okay, kiddo? This is Yardley. I was on hold a long time."

"Everything's fine!" *Just reeking of coffee and dealing with the Teetering Tall Boots Girl.* She looked at the clock. "You're up early."

"I'm a bit of an insomniac. A couple of notes . . . please don't go into a commercial break saying we need to pay some bills."

"I'm sorry. Donn always says that."

"And regarding the Radio-opoly promo, next time, insert two sponsors from the list."

"I didn't know. But the contest sounds like a blast!" she said.

"The AEs have done a splendid job rounding up prizes on trade."

"Yardley, what's an AE?"

"Account executive. A classy name for salesman."

"Oh. Another question. Will you show me how to put the Radio-opoly callers on the air?"

He laughed. "The contest won't be played on your shift, darlin'. And another thing. Never play two female artists back-to-back. You segued from Madonna into Cyndi Lauper."

"Really?" She paged through the music log. "That's how they're scheduled. Why not?"

"You're still in your probationary period, kiddo."

Her head jerked back.

"I am? For how long?"

"I've got to go. I'll see you soon."

Yardley hadn't answered her question. Eva pinched her upper lip as she got up to consult the work calendar. She flipped forward to the week of Thanksgiving. He had conveniently forgotten to mention she was scheduled to work on the holiday. But she didn't dare ask off, not for Thanksgiving, Christmas, Easter, or even Valentine's, for that matter. There was no other option if she wanted to move up, except to be the most reliable, indispensable employee. She took a cigarette from her purse and went into the lobby.

While she smoked, the Teletype kicked into high gear with the first news of the day. She dragged herself off the couch. A long string of stories printed out. Astronauts aboard Discovery had removed a satellite from orbit. Ryne Sandberg won the baseball MVP. There was an updated forecast. And Eva found a nice, feel-good kicker, a bit she would normally set aside for Yardley. *Screw him and his chauvinistic rules.* It would sound good on her audition tape, a spliced-together reel with her best on-air bits. In the studio, she hit the record button on the reel player.

LIZZY: Michael Murphy on B93. Michael Bolton before that, and kicking off the set, Michael McDonald! Now here's a story about a guy named Michael. For a hundred days, he took pictures of himself in different places holding signs saying "I Love You," then gave his girlfriend a photo album on their first anniversary. So romantic! After this quick break, it's Quincy Ways, I mean, Quincy Jones, "Find One Hundred Ways."

Crap, I blew it. While the spots played, Eva rewound the tape and listened. Thank goodness she had enunciated—it'd be easy to splice out the flub. Before rewinding it, she bookmarked her audition tape with a tab of paper. Yardly was so prickly on the phone. Did he invent a probationary period because of her screw-ups? *I need a back-up plan.* She packed the small transparent plastic reel in its white box, kissing it for luck. Other stations might take a second look at her now that she had experience in commercial radio.

During the next music set, she roamed the station, feeling like the last person on the planet. In the lobby, she sat on the edge of the couch, watching the reels. The Police's "Wrapped Around My Finger" epitomized the soundtrack of automation: the song's swirling, rolling beat and percussive *ching-ching* seemed to power the rotating reels. Frankly, she never wanted to hear that song again, yet it came up every night, sometimes twice. Why couldn't she play "Can't Stand Losing You?" And why did B93 have to go and change the format? The timing was just her luck. She'd give anything to drop the needle on Robin Trower, Heart, The Outlaws, or Savoy Brown.

In the kitchen, she rummaged through cupboards. There was nothing edible but a box of stale Smurf-Berry Crunch and packets of cocoa with hard lumps. In the hallway, she peered down the narrow staircase to the basement. During her long and lonely overnights, she'd never explored the "sales pit," as the on-air guys called it. She shivered and turned away.

And there was Donn's briefcase sitting on the kitchen stool. In his hurry to meet his fan, he'd left it behind. She pressed one sticky brass lock. *Boing!* Then the other. *Boing!* With trepidation, she lifted the lid. His résumé sat on top, and underneath it, nerdy-looking books along with a Rubik's cube and a half-empty sleeve of powdered doughnuts, but no drugs. *Interesting résumé*: North Dakota, Iowa, Minnesota, and now Wisconsin.

She glanced over the back cover of "Spock Must Die" and admired pictures of old stamps in a guide from the American Philatelic Society. Of course, a *Hustler* magazine was hidden under the books. She paged through, looking at the beautiful women. What was it like to pose for the photographer? Was there an entire crew of ogling men? Looking flawless, they wore lipstick smiles, their bodies airbrushed to perfection—or did they have to starve themselves? *Those poor women, compromising their integrity, just for a job.* She hoped they were paid a ton of money.

When Eva closed the magazine, Polaroids cascaded out, scattering onto the floor. She scooped them up. Her jaw dropped. It was that poor, deluded girl who had stopped by, posing against the turntables in the production studio, legs apart, dressed only in her red boots—like the girls in *Hustler*.

What the . . . Eva wondered if this was something she should report; she'd encountered pornography in the workplace twice now. She stuffed everything back, shut the latches, and at the kitchen sink, washed her hands.

13. IT DOESN'T MATTER ~ FIREFALL

A tinge of light appeared over the bluffs behind South Towne Mall. After playing the legal ID, Eva gathered her belongings and waited for her replacement in the lobby, still stewing over Donn's Polaroids and Yardley's no-back-to-back-female-artists rule. She leaned against the couch cushions, arms crossed. It was after six. The bus would arrive at the mall in just a few minutes. Artie would be waiting for her to get home. "*Come on*, Schmidty."

She removed her coat and stomped back into the studio while Michael Jackson and Paul McCartney sang "The Doggone Girl is Mine," an insipid song from *Thriller*. The album had hit like a tornado and won a record-setting eight Grammys. Eddie Van Halen played a stellar guitar solo on "Beat It." But no, not on B93.

She laid her head on the counter.

A blinking phone line grabbed Eva's attention. Maybe the kid had car trouble.

"Lizzy, this is Yardley. Please answer the phone with 'B93, your station for continuous Lite Hits.'"

"Sorry. I will."

"So, how's it going?" he asked.

How's it going? A red flag popped like a tip-up.

"Truthfully, I'm wiped. Schmidty isn't here and I have to leave. Artie and I are taking a road trip."

"Here's the deal. The kid is sick and no one else is picking up."

"Oh, brother." *Whoops. Get it together, Eva.*

There'd be no road trip if she offered to help. Artie had been so excited. Then again, it was the morning show. She heaved a deep sigh.

"I'll stay until you find someone." She rifled through the log.

"Thank you, darlin.'"

"I see there's a remote at ten."

"Yeah. I can't relieve you—I've got to help Jack set up the Marti, that's our remote broadcast unit. He'll be calling the station a few times an hour. Until then, promote the hot dogs and soda. Free food brings in droves of listeners, more than a diamond pendant giveaway."

As he explained how to put the phone over the air, it became clear—he was counting on her to do the entire morning shift.

"There's a preview mode, so you and Jack can confer before you put him on. When you introduce him, say, 'And now we go to Jack Matthews, broadcasting live from Timothy Jewelers.'"

After he hung up, Eva galumphed into the kitchen where she made a pot of extra-strong coffee. In the back of the cupboard, she found a funny WKRP mug, the one listing all six of Johnny Fever's past on-air names.

Shit. She dreaded calling Artie. Faye said that men thrived on three things: admiration, sex, and recreational companionship. Since Artie quit the band, her admiration for him had waned. Because of their jobs, their sex life had dwindled. And regarding companionship, he'd been spending more time with Dwayne than her. But there wasn't time to think about that now. She had another show to do.

Back in the studio, she called Artie to tell him their plans were off. Boy, was he mad; he'd go without her. She hoped radio was worth the wedge it kept driving between them.

Running on pure caffeine, she did her best to sound lively, reminding the listeners to stop by Timothy's to register before noon. She decided to make the most of her predicament and accomplish something worthwhile. During a long song, she made copies of Donn's résumé. During another, she found his master reel, and throughout the morning, made dubs. Inside each tape box, she placed a folded résumé. On the outside, she addressed each box to the program directors listed in the employment section of *Radio & Records*. Dottie's stamp dispenser provided the postage.

After that little project, she entertained herself by mocking commercials.

Get mom what she really wants this year, a diamond pendant from Timothy Jewelers. "What mom *really* wants is for dad to honor date night."

Party season is coming, ladies, and Simm's Boutique has the perfect dress for your big night out. She spun in the chair. And a sleazy owner who pinches the salesclerks' bottoms. Faye's cousin worked at Simm's.

For all your automotive needs, the Auto Mill has you covered. Eva chuckled as she thought of Coco, who had coined the phrase "For all your roast beef needs" to poke fun at clichés in advertising. Lackadaisical copywriters used it to describe everything from hardware to healthcare, and cow breeders to bank loans.

She laughed herself silly during a car ad. "Hurry on down to Lemon's Ford Dodge Honda Plymouth BMW Pontiac Volkswagen, where we have a knowledgeable and friendly staff! You'll be glad you did! Everything must go!"

Just before ten, Yardley called in. "Jack's ready for a mic check."

Eva imagined them standing near the front of Timothy Jewelers at a table festooned with the station banner, the entry box between them.

"Go ahead, Jack!" he said.

"Testing 1-2-3. Testes. Testicles 1-2-3."

Yardley guffawed.

"Hey Jack, move those cords away from there," he yelled. "The last thing we need is for anyone to trip or get electrocuted."

As noon and the big drawing approached, Eva—who had consumed so much coffee she'd be up until Sunday—eavesdropped on Jack and Yardley as they conversed loudly over other excited voices, bursts of laughter, and clinking sounds.

"Thank goodness Lizzy could stay. She's a lifesaver."

In the studio, Eva beamed as if she'd won a Peabody.

"Hi, there!" Yardley said. (Muffled voice.) "Where are you from?" (More muffled voices.)

"Yes, we'll be drawing the name soon! Here. Fill out a ticket. Have you had a hot dog?" (Shuffling sounds.)

"OK, Jack," Yardley said, his voice lowered. "Let's pull the winning ticket now. Then we'll have a good one."

Eva heard the entry box being shaken, a bonk on the mic, and a low whistle and Jack say, "Wow, look at that stone fox! She'd look good in the pendant."

"And nothing else," Yardley said. "Okay. Here's a winner. Look, it's Jack Mehoff again."

"Jack Uhoff's cousin?" Jack chortled. "Throw that one out."

There were more rustling sounds.

"I can't make out the name. It looks like a first grader's writing. See? That's why we do this."

The box rattled as Yardley pulled another ticket.

"Oh, geez. This one's from Miami—the rules plainly state 'open to residents of Wisconsin only.'"

More box shaking sounds.

"Here's a good one. Lori Jo Smithers from Westby."

Eva rolled her eyes.

"Lizzy? Can you hear me? We're ready. Put us on after this song."

She leaned into the phone. "Aye aye, boss. Twenty seconds."

The following week, Eva and Faye made a date to go shopping while Artie and Dwayne were in the woods for the start of deer hunting season. Faye opened the door to Her-Story, a sexuality resource center that had just opened in downtown La Crosse. Eva pulled the hood of her Badgers sweatshirt around her face before stepping into the well-lit store unsure that Faye's idea of getting toys to spice things up was going to help her marriage.

"Her-Story is all about us. Oh, look!" She picked up a feather and tickled Eva's arm.

A feather would not enhance her marriage, Eva thought, taking it from Faye. It was turquoise blue, cheaply dyed. She ran it up her arm, feeling the soft edges against her skin. The marriage needed more than sex. Didn't it? But honestly, in contrast to her and Artie's relationship, Faye and Dwayne were always flirting, touching, whispering in each other's ears. Eva trusted her friend when she suggested they take a trip to the new store for something ridiculous, something fun. So here she was, standing in a soft-pink neon glow in a store smelling of latex and lavender, making an effort. *Marriage is work, they say.* This was good work.

Eva's eyes ballooned at the variety and amount of products on display, and she wasn't the only person wearing a hoodie or a hat pulled low. She had expected a small store with a few vibrators and edible panties. There were books and VHS videos—some erotic but most educational—shelved along one wall. What could she bring home that Artie would like? Her body became aroused while browsing the sex games, massage oils, and sexy lingerie. She laughed—it was already working.

"This is nothing like a typical porn shop," Faye said. "Places like that exist for men's pleasure."

"What did the book say about the top three needs of women?"

Faye counted on her fingers. "Affection, conversation, and honesty. And if I'm being honest, number four is foreplay. I don't know who taught Dwayne, but I sure would like to thank her."

"Now you're just showing off!"

Eva browsed the sensory items that made her insides feel strung taut, like a violin waiting to be played. She picked up a rainbow-colored vibrator. Even if Artie didn't want to use it, she could. On her way to the checkout, she picked up a package of ribbed condoms and a warming lubricant.

Eva couldn't wait to get home.

14. DO THEY KNOW IT'S CHRISTMAS ~ BAND AID

On a snowy evening, at the Bluffside Inn, the exclusive B93 staff Christmas party was in full swing. Dressed in a black velveteen dress and the strappy heels she'd bought for Faye and Dwayne's wedding, Eva stood at the U-shaped bar with Dottie and Candi Kane, a saleswoman who, rumor had it, DJed at a rock station in Milwaukee in her younger years.

Yardley approached. "Hi ladies. Can I talk to you, Lizzy?"

He ushered her over to a tall table where he set down his martini. Was he finally giving her a promotion?

"One of these days we're going to get a big snowstorm, and when that happens, I'll need you to help me out because we can't start calling the schools until five-thirty. It's too much for me to do while I'm on the air. Dottie will give you the phone list. Capisce?"

"Sure, I can do that."

"Thanks, kiddo."

He slapped her on the back and picked up his drink, leaving her standing alone at the table. If there were school closings maybe he'd put her on the guest mic during his show. She rejoined Candi and Dottie at the bar.

"Where are the announcers?" Eva asked, just as bawdy laughter erupted from a smoke-filled game room at the back.

"Let's go sit with the boys," Candi said.

Dottie declined, choosing to join Yardley, Merv Harms, and a silver-haired guy in a booth. In the game room, Donn was animated, telling a story, talking with his hands. Jack waved them over to the crowded leather sectional. Candi perched on the end. Eva squeezed next to Jack.

"Why couldn't we bring our spouses?" she whispered to him.

"Too expensive," Jack whispered. "Did you see the hors d'oeuvres? Dottie made them."

Artie had muttered a few choice words when he found out he wasn't invited, saying Yardley treated people poorly because he'd reached the end of his potential at a shitty, small-market station, and therefore had to exercise his dominance over people with more talent to feel superior. She consoled him, saying she'd bring home a dessert. But that wasn't happening because there was no dinner.

Donn kept talking, "On April Fool's, we announced a format change . . . to polka!" Everyone hooted. "The phones rang off the hook for a week."

"It *is* the Wisconsin state dance," Jack said.

A buxom waitress carrying a tray of cocktails appeared with drinks. The guys quieted as they watched her bend forward over the coffee table.

"After a week on the air in college, a listener told me I was saying the wrong call letters," Schmidty said.

Eva lowered her head and whispered to Jack. "At least they aren't telling horror stories of getting fired."

That jinxed it. Everyone began to talk at once.

"I got fired for telling a caller to fuck off." "I got fired for making long-distance calls from the studio." "I got canned for dedicating 'Take This Job and Shove It' to my PD."

Donn piped in. "I got fired after 'a friend' left a pair of lacy panties in the production studio."

Eva had heard enough. She picked up her purse and stood, just as Yardley entered the room wearing a Santa hat, carrying a stack of envelopes. He grinned from ear to ear. She turned to Candi.

"Cash bonuses?"

"Ho, ho, ho! Merry Christmas. But don't call me a ho! Wait until you get home to open these, okay? Keep up the great work, guys. Big things are happening. I'm proud of each and every one of you."

###

On Christmas Eve, while Chuck Berry sang "Run Rudolph Run," Eva wandered around the chilly radio station. After spending the afternoon with her mom, she felt especially alone. In retrospect, the brownie points she'd gain by working on Christmas weren't worth the sacrifice. And to think, six months earlier, she'd been over the moon at getting the job. This was not how she had pictured her career.

She pulled on an extra sweater and, in the kitchen, poured a cup of steaming coffee, warming her hands on the mug. In the bullpen, she flicked on the floodlights which lit up the backyard. Snowflakes the size of goose feathers floated down like the inside of a snow globe. When she was a kid, her pop would bundle her up in a snowmobile suit. They'd lay in the yard with the outdoor lights on, mesmerized as snow streaked in spirals from the night sky. She switched off the lights. Five-and-a-half hours until midnight.

Someone had left a plate of festive-looking gingerbread cookies on the kitchen counter, perhaps remnants from the weekly sales meeting. Eva took a couple into the studio. The rock-hard cookies were inedible. She picked at the Red Hots buttons, trying not to cry.

Right about then, Artie would be having Brandy eggnog with his mother, her house glowing with candles and delicious food baking in the oven, the tree sparkling with twinkly lights. They'd be schnockered for midnight Mass.

Damn Artie. She had put herself out there, playfully pulling the new vibrator out of the bedside drawer while he was running his first, second, third-base routine—a quick circuit of her body, cutting the corners. It had taken a lot of courage; she'd thought ahead on when to bring it out and what to say. But he wouldn't touch the sex toy; he almost recoiled. She didn't understand. Artie wasn't a prude. Did it have something to do with the Catholic mortal sin of masturbation?

Whatever it was, his visceral response felt like a personal rejection, a balk on future attempts to deepen their relationship. It wasn't just the idea he'd rejected, her hopes of a new and exciting love life deflated. She had made an error. He hadn't received her offering with care.

But Artie still scored. Before he fell asleep, she scraped every bit of courage from within to ask why he didn't want to experiment, to help them reconnect. When he wouldn't talk, she pressed him.

"We don't need that stuff, Eva," he had mumbled before rolling over. Another layer of resentment sprung between them, like an old-fashioned bundling board in the bed.

A lump formed in her throat. *What if he's not attracted to me anymore?* From her cubby, she grabbed a bottle of Chloraseptic labeled LIZZY, opened her mouth, and sprayed.

At the mic, as "The Christmas Song" wound down, she pulled her face into a mask of holiday warmth.

LIZZY: Nat King Cole, a yuletide classic on B93, your station for the holidays. This hour of Christmas music is being brought to you by your good friends at Willshire Funeral Home, for all your funeral needs. I'm Eva LaVette, pardon me, I'm Lizzy Taylor. Will we have a "White Christmas?" Stay tuned for the forecast and a Bing Crosby classic.

"Shit!" Eva slammed the counter. "What the fuck is wrong with me?" she asked her reflection in the studio window. How could she have said her real name on the air?

Out in the lobby, she crumpled onto the couch. "White Christmas" segued into "Happy Christmas." Hot tears came as she dug into her pocket for a lighter. *Happy Christmas, my ass.* The ashtray on the end table overflowed with butts. She leaned back and lit a cigarette, puffing deeply. When had she started to smoke so much? Artie had grown up in a smoky household and he hated it.

But cigarettes and radio went hand in hand. Everyone knew smoking made the voice sound deeper. The best compliment a man could get was to have "monster pipes" and for women, to be told they sound sexy. Smoking gave DJs something to do while waiting for a song or commercial to end. The small adrenaline rush from nicotine helped announcers stay awake. But film from the smoke and tar damaged sensitive electronics, thus the engineer's *No Smoking* signs that everyone ignored.

She got off the couch and ran to the studio for a quick break, then came back into the lobby to finish her cigarette, bringing along the station's Christmas music policy memo. Yardley had misspelled the word "lable" again. He'd signed the memo with his "slogen," "Keep up the great work, everyone! I'm proud of each and every one of you!" That was nice. But where was her cash bonus? Standing outside the coatroom after the holiday party, she'd overheard Jack and the afternoon drive guy as they ripped open their envelopes. Both received fifty-dollar Bluffside Inn gift certificates—a nice dinner for four—while in hers, she found coupons for twenty dollars off a massage and a free hearing test, proving, once more, overnights and the person working on the shift didn't matter.

Feeling invisible and not needed, she stubbed out her smoke and stared at the turning music reels.

After Thanksgiving, the station introduced a smattering of Christmas songs, and by mid-December they played the music twenty-four hours a day. The repetition drove her crazy. How many renditions of "Silent Night" could there possibly be? Ironically, she'd be thrilled to get back to the normal sappy playlist after the holidays.

When the phone lit up, she hurried into the studio. Maybe it was Mystery Man, who started to call almost every night.

"Hi *Lizzy*, it's Faye!"

"Merry Christmas," Dwayne said from in the background.

"Ditzy is here, too," Faye said as her cat meowed. "We thought you could use some holiday cheer."

Glasses clinked.

"Oh Faye. I'm so glad you called." She reached for a tissue.

"Did you talk to Artie tonight?"

"No. Why?" Eva asked.

"No reason. Do you guys have plans for New Year's? We're having a wapatuli!"

Eva glanced at the schedule on the wall behind her. "I have to work."

"Jeepers, Eva. We never see you anymore."

Eva scrunched the phone cord in her fist. "I'd love to come over and watch MTV with you again, though." She looked at the clock. None of her carts were pulled for the next hour. "Shoot. I should go."

"I'll call you tomorrow. We love you."

###

Later, Eva poked around the building, looking through cupboards and wiggling doorknobs, only to find Yardley's office door unlocked. A folder sat out, labeled KOEHNE. She shuffled through the contents.

"Holy shit!" Who was Koehne? A new salesgirl? "*Merv massaged my shoulders . . . made inappropriate comments . . . said I should wear shorter dresses and lower necklines on sales calls . . . scared I'll get fired.*"

Eva closed the folder and slammed Yardley's door behind her as she ran down the hall, through the kitchen, and into the studio. With seconds left in the song, she quickly cued "Away in a Manger" by John Denver. The phone blinked. She took a deep breath.

"Merry Christmas. Guess what? Ma is retiring," Artie said. "She says it's hard to blow her whistle anymore. Old age, I guess."

Eva frowned. His mother, only fifty-eight, smoked like a chimney.

"We're leaving for church soon. Anyway, thanks for the Swatch watch," he said. "I hid your Christmas present in the front closet."

"You did?" She smiled. "I can't wait. Oh, hang on a sec."

Eva set down the handset as "Grandma Got Run Over by a Reindeer" began to fade. The segue from the silly song into the solemn "Do You Hear What I Hear" was jolting to say the least.

"Thanks for giving me something to look forward to. I'm trying to think of it as just another day, but it's hard. I'm not even getting overtime."

"Look Eva, I get why you're working holidays for now, but I'm telling you, when I receive a promotion, you can stay home and take care of the kids."

Eva blinked, hard. "This is my career, Artie."

"I know, but Ma keeps pestering me. *'When are you going to give me some grandkids?'*" he mimicked. "I'd better go. This is long-distance, and she can't afford it now that's she's retiring. I'll be home the day after tomorrow."

Eva gulped. "I accidentally said my name on the air."

"Oh, man. Did anyone notice?"

"No one called."

"For cripes sake, Eva. You should just use your real name."

"Do you think it's safe? With all the weirdos out there?"

Line 2 lit up. It had better be Yardley calling to express his immense gratitude to her for working on the holiday.

"I need to go, Artie. Please wish your mom Merry Christmas."

Holding the phone between her ear and shoulder, she answered the other line. She flipped to the next page on the log.

"Hi, Lizzy. It's me, Mystery Man," he said in his deep voice.

"You're not working?"

"Nope, there are no dogs to catch on Christmas Eve," he joked.

Screw it, she thought, switching the system to complete automation. *Everyone else does it.* After turning down the volume, she put her feet up on the counter, glanced at the engineer's *No Smoking* sign, and lit a cigarette.

They talked for hours, arguing over which was better, cats or dogs. They talked about Ringo Starr and Herbie Hancock on *SNL*; a new game called Tetris played on some type of computer; music; shopping malls; and microphones. She said his voice was perfect for radio. They talked about fake smiling.

Out of the blue, he said, "Think of me when you blow into the mic."

"Blowing into the mic can damage it," she said, pulling carts.

"Eva, my dear, I want you to blow *me*."

She jerked the phone away. Another goddamn creep. "You pervert! Don't ever call here again."

She slammed down the receiver. She had slipped too far down the slippery slope. She lit her last cigarette, mulling over what she'd disclosed during their many conversations.

A chill tingled up her spine; had he heard her say her real name?

15. BLOWIN' FREE ~ WISHBONE ASH

It was a mild, moonless March evening. Eva whistled as she strolled to the bus stop. The constellation Orion hovered near the western horizon, ready to slip into the Southern Hemisphere, a sign of winter finally waning. Temperatures during the entire month of January had averaged below normal. Faye and Dwayne had canceled their New Year's Eve party when the wind chill reached a treacherous minus-forty-five. A blizzard hit on Eva's birthday. At least Yardley raised her pay up fifty cents an hour—a thousand dollars a year. Artie wanted to save it for a second car. Eva had already started saving for a portable electronic keyboard, but she wanted her MTV.

She zipped her coat up to her chin. A shooting star streaked the sky and with it came a wish: *I need to get off overnights.* The bus arrived; the door opened with a pneumatic hiss. The friendly driver no longer checked her pass.

At work, Donn rushed past her. "Check your cubby for an important memo."

Like a tag team in the night, he slapped her hand on his way out.

During her first music set, Eva set cleaning products and rags on the kitchen counter. In the studio, she crawled under the mixing board to plug in the vacuum.

After a break, she went to her cubby for the memo. The blood drained from her face. It really was big news. The station had changed its slogan—or "slogen" the way Yardley spelled it—to "Wrapping You in the Arms of Love." Letterhead, T-shirts, and a new banner were on order. The liners, sweepers, and promos had been replaced. *Dang.* How many breaks had she done without the syrupy new slogan?

As she red-penned Yardley's typos, Eva practiced saying "Wrapping You in the Arms of Love." Cheesy, but anything to do with love was okay. The old liners had driven her crazy. The listeners couldn't have known the word Lite was misspelled, but to her, light' and 'lite' felt different in her mouth.

LIZZY: Joe Cocker and Jennifer Warnes with a Grammy-winning duet from the movie *An Officer and A Gentleman*. I'm Lizzy Taylor. Stay tuned; I've got more free movie tickets! Duran Duran are coming up next with the title track from the LP "Rio," right here on B93, Wrapping Up, uh, the Arms of Love.

Flustered, Eva started the commercials. The hotline lit.

"I see you finally read the memo, kiddo." Yardley acted nice about the goof, but his words cut. "I need to talk to you when I get in."

They normally talked during their shift overlap—she always had time to kill while she waited for the first bus of the day. But something in his voice shook her. Was the guillotine about to come down? Her heart went thud. Everyone in radio talked about getting fired. She'd messed up the Radio-opoly contest and blown the new slogan. While she'd been vacuuming earlier in the week, he'd caught some dead air. It was obvious to her—she wasn't making the grade.

At five o'clock, Yardley St. Martins stepped inside the studio. Without a word, he dropped a *New York Times* and the *La Crosse Tribune* on the counter before going out to check the Teletype.

Eva started a song, sat back, and fiddled with her new Aquarius necklace, the hidden Christmas gift from Artie (which Faye had picked out—and wrapped). Was Yardley wearing a suit? Finally, he returned, carrying a doughnut on a paper plate. He sat across the counter at the guest mic. It relieved her somewhat to see he wore jeans and a sport coat.

"I'd have brought you coffee, but you're going home to sleep." He drum-rolled his fingers on the counter. "I need a sidekick on the morning show. Are you game?"

He wasn't firing her? Eva jumped out of the air chair, stopping short of reaching across to hug him. She had aspired to move up to evenings and only dreamed of middays but had never expected this.

"For real?"

"You bet your sweet bippy."

Her mind raced. No more overnights. No more cleaning. Artie wouldn't have to tiptoe around the house during the day while she slept. No more taking the bus—now they could share the car. The morning show had to mean big bucks—she could buy her own car! This was too good to be true. She twisted her necklace so hard she worried it might break.

"We'll be on from five-thirty until nine. You'll go solo from nine until ten. After that, do production and help Dottie in the office. What do you say, kiddo?" He got up and gave her shoulder a friendly shake.

"I'm flabbergasted. Yes! But won't the other DJs be mad?"

"No, by golly. You're not replacing anyone. Jack loves middays. The afternoon guy's shift works perfectly with his wife's schedule at the hospital. And we all know Donn's a night owl."

A *vampire*.

"We'll have lots of fun. I've been doing the show alone for—" He tugged on his earlobe. "Three years now."

"Wow," she said. There's no way she could have worked overnights that long.

At five-thirty they switched seats. Yardley cued up "Love to Love You Baby" by Donna Summer. Eva leaned on the door frame.

"You'll need a new name," he said, pulling a slip of paper from his breast pocket.

"But the audience knows me as Lizzy."

"That's true, but, you see, my schtick is celebrities. What if I did an Elizabeth Taylor bit and then you're Lizzy Taylor?" He consulted his list. "How about Ginger Cox?"

A wrinkle formed between her brows.

"Michelle Russell? Kim Pfeiffer?"

Yardley had no imagination. *How about Jennifer Derek or Bo Beals?* She buried her face in her hands. *Ugh.* To have a name imposed felt like a violation. She had taken LaVette, Artie's last name, willingly, because that's what everyone did. "I need time to think."

"Tanya Starr?"

She gave him a questioning look. "Like Ringo? Or the Packers coach?"

He laughed. "I was thinking Bart Starr—who not only *coached* but was the only quarterback in NFL history to lead a team to three consecutive league championships. But Ringo works for me, if that's what you like."

Eva tried the new name using a smoky voice. "I'm Tanya Starr."

"I love it! We'll start on Monday." Yardley plugged in his headphones. "Go into production and write up a promo. I'll run in and dub my part when you are done."

Eva grabbed a notepad. As she wrote, their names jumped off the page. *Tanya Starr.* Like magic, he had conjured a new person out of thin air. She gasped. *The shooting star at the bus stop!* A star that would not descend to vacuum, dust, or swab toilets. A star who would get more sleep and live a normal life.

PART TWO

```
867   SIMM'S BOUTIQUE                      :60
      2/1-2/28
      "...where everything must go!"

530   TIMOTHY JEWELERS                     :30
      1/1-tfn
      "...for all your jewelry needs."

986   LEMON'S FORD DODGE HONDA VW    :60
      2/28-3/15
      "...you'll be glad you did."

753   HOMETOWN BANK                        :30
      2/1-2/28
      "...Thats 555-1212."

098   FRIENDLY HARDWARE                    :30
      tfn
      "...and much, much more!"
```

16. LIKE A HURRICANE ~ NEIL YOUNG

On Monday morning, Eva entered the studio toting cups of rich, steaming coffee from their new sponsor, a local roaster. Yardley sat at the board, swapping out carts with the phone tucked under his ear. She felt the pressure to be a perfect sidekick; to prove he made the right decision. She ran a hand through her brand-new hairstyle, a wildly textured copy of MTV's Nina Blackwood's which came out a little more rock-and-roll than she'd expected, and the first time she had bangs since grade school. *I'm Tanya Starr.* This morning, there could be no gaffes, no blunders, no bloopers. She sat at the guest mic, pinching her thigh under the counter.

Yardley hung up the phone. "Jiminy Cricket! If we get one more obscene caller, I'm gonna have to sell Ivory soap sponsorships." He laughed at his joke while slipping on his headphones, his head tilted, his gold tooth glinting. "Alrighty. Strap in, Tanya."

She swooned. He called her Tanya. He looked so handsome to her in that moment. Charisma went a long way to enhance looks.

"Remember, I'm the star of this show," he said.

> YARDLEY: Cyndi Lauper, "Time After Time" on B93, Wrapping You in the Arms of Love. She'll be stopping by the studio in a few weeks, so make sure to stay tuned. Now, I want you all to give a warm welcome to the lovely and charming Tanya Starr, Bart's daughter!
> TANYA: Thanks Yardley. He's joking, everyone—I'm pretty sure Bart Starr only has sons. But I'm excited to join the show!
> YARDLEY: You've got an updated forecast?
> TANYA: Spring has arrived. Sunshine today, with a high of 50!
> YARDLEY: Dy-no-*mite!* What else is happening?

TANYA: This story just came over the wire. In the year 2000, Americans will live longer and healthier lives. Birth control may be available by—get this—nasal spray.
YARDLEY: Really? Hold on, sweetheart. (*Sniffs*) Ahh. Let's go. Hahaha!
TANYA: I'll be spritzing on some "No Baby" every night before bed!
YARDLEY: Okay. Well. I've got a Perfect Portion Pizza for the first caller to name the band from Minneapolis who scored this world-wide hit. Ooh, I like that cowbell! Call now, while we groove to "Funkytown" on B93.

"Did you like the birth control bit?" Eva asked. It had seemed effortless to slip into the persona of Tanya Starr.

"You need to let me have the punchline, but yeah, find more stories like that," he said.

The morning had flown by like a whirlwind. Over the course of three and a half hours, he ran the board and took calls while she read the news and giggled at his jokes. Despite not sleeping all weekend—she and Artie had another fight about money—and having to wake up at three-thirty so she could shower, drive to work, and put together a newscast, she'd been perky and cheerful. Her cheeks were sore from laughing. But Yardley clearly owned the show. When she suggested they do a "Name That Tune" segment, he poo-poohed it. When she suggested they read horoscopes—real ones—he made up his own, Yardleyscopes: Today, you will forget to put the top on your blender and will find blueberry milkshake on your ceiling for years to come. Over time, perhaps he would trust her.

Eva checked the commercial log where the name Tanya Starr topped the nine o'clock hour. *I've been reborn.* Tanya was real. Lizzy Taylor had been relegated to the radio graveyard, mourned by a handful of overnight fans: drooling drunks, crank-calling adolescents, weary mothers of newborns, and bleary-eyed third-shifters. Ben Dover, Anita Joint, and Dixie Normous would deliver her eulogy—*Here lies Lizzy Taylor, overnight girl with the beloved Lite voice.* Mystery Man would toss flowers on her grave.

Dottie snuck into the studio. She tapped a pencil on her pink Phone Message pad. "I can't get anything done, Tanya. The phones are ringing off the hook. People love the show. They like hearing local news without having to change stations. One guy asked if you're Yardley's wife."

"What? Too funny."

All three phone lines blinked. As soon as Dottie rushed out, the studio door swung open.

"Hi, Tanya. Merv Harms, sales manager." The big guy stuck out his hand. "Just stopping in to introduce myself."

"Yes, we met when I first took a tour."

According to Donn, Merv was the owner of the lime-green muscle car.

"Yardley sounded better than ever this morning. And I like that you've added sports reports—having a girl on the show should boost our ratings with men, so try to sound sexy." He looked her over and *tsked.* "It wouldn't hurt for you to wear something nice, Tanya. Anyway, welcome."

Her jaw dropped; she snapped it shut as he gave her a look.

"And don't forget," he added on his way out. "Sales is the reason you have a paycheck."

As if the announcers had nothing to do with the success of the station. As if her pay was a livable wage. She half expected to see a trail of slime in his wake. *What a dickhead.*

After a break and Eva turned off the mic, Candi Kane breezed into the studio, bringing with her a delicate floral fragrance. The jingle for Heaven Scent popped into Eva's head: *Suddenly, you are everything you were meant to be.*

"Hi, Tanya!"

Candi's shiny black bangs swept away from her face. She wore bright fuchsia lipstick. On her cheekbones, a sharp slash of orange blush was an unlikely companion to her tasteful eyeliner. Her classy black suit with its wide satin lapels put Eva's polyester track suit and messy braid to shame. Lizzy Taylor was the slob who wore old clothes to clean the station and stay comfortable during the dark nights. It was time to act the part of Tanya.

"Say, I've got a remote broadcast lined up for the Independent Electronics Anniversary Sale. They aren't paying a talent fee for this one, but you could pick out a microwave or a VCR. It's called trade. Are you interested?"

"Maybe. Hang on a second."

Eva checked the log and loaded carts into the machines for an upcoming break. Actual people, watching her while she worked? They could use a VCR—she and Artie hadn't yet seen their wedding video, made by one of his bandmates. She'd almost tripped over the guy, walking down the aisle on the arm of Dwayne, who'd stood in for her father. Watching the video might invigorate good vibes between her and Artie.

"Groovy. Sure, I'll do it."

"Fabulous! I'll run it by Yardley." Candi clapped her hands. Her charm bracelet rattled. "Another thing. I've been trying to get a nightclub down on 3rd Street on the air. If we did a remote for their Disco Happy Hour on Fridays, we could reach people on their way home from work. Seventy-five bucks for you. Cash."

The money turned Eva's head. She could buy a few new outfits. Surely, though, there was someone else on staff who would need it more.

"Why don't you ask Jack? He can use the dough. He's got a baby on the way."

Candi reached into her purse, taking out a tube of Dr. Pepper lip gloss. "I already asked him. Did you know he has another job after he leaves here?" She smeared the shiny balm over her full mouth.

"You're kidding," Eva said as she segued into a song.

"Yup. I do, too—I sell Avon. Hold on. I'll be right back."

A minute later, she returned, armed with tiny lipstick samples which she dumped in a pile on top of the log and a little mirror that folded flat.

94

"Wow, this is cool." Eva checked her eyeliner. She would look at the brochures after getting her first big, fat, juicy morning show paycheck.

Candi whisked out of the studio. Over her shoulder, she added, "Ask the engineer if the remote equipment is available on Friday."

As the hour wrapped up, the studio became quiet. Eva recalled her dead-of-the-night boredom from only a week earlier. It seemed as if eons had passed. Lizzy Taylor had evaporated into the thin airwaves. Or perhaps her voice was still being carried on a signal extending far into outer space. As Tanya, she'd rocketed from obscurity to the most coveted position—an "overnight" sensation.

Before he left the studio on Thursday, Yardley asked Eva to help with production.

"Candi's new client, Pfister Realty, is coming in at noon to cut some spots."

"Of course." Eva loved splicing tape and everything else about production: choosing music beds, recording voiceovers, mixing it all together. The result? A thirty- or sixty-second work of art.

He waggled a finger. "Pfister has the potential to become a major sponsor, so be on your best behavior."

There was a stack of dead carts next to the board. Eva checked the end dates on the labels before erasing them with the bulk-eraser, a powerful magnet inside a shiny black box. Holding in the red button, she picked up a cart, slid it across the smooth surface, then ran it back the other way, and with a flourish like Liberace, pulled the cart up and away from the magnet once again. While she degaussed the rest, through the window, she watched Jack in the main studio, laughing and talking on the phone. Did the other announcers have their own mystery callers? She stacked the erased carts under the windowsill by length.

Waiting for the client, she leaned back and rested her eyes. The hushed, dark atmosphere in the production studio brought back memories from college. She wondered if Dustin's hair was still long and feathered so perfectly away from his face. If he were here, she'd turn off the lights, slip off his cowboy hat and his aviator glasses, and push him up against the plush acoustic foam walls . . .

Dottie tapped at the door.

"Artie is holding on the business line."

Eva spun around, her face hot. "Thanks, Dottie."

Artie needed the car. Eva told him she'd be home by two o'clock, hanging up just as Dottie ushered the rotund realtor into the studio. She hoped the chair could support him. As he passed, Old Spice overwhelmed her senses.

"So, have you voiced spots before?" she asked.

"Yes," he said, picking up the script. "I normally produce them at Z100, but your saleslady convinced me to try it here. We'll see."

He placed a pair of slim reading glasses on the tip of his bulbous nose. Eva understood: Candi was after the income from producing the spots and making dubs for other stations.

He read a few sentences while Eva set the volume. She lowered it a little, because people always talked louder when the actual tape started to roll.

"Here we go," she said.

The singers sang. "*You belong at home. A home to call your own. Home Realty.*" With an exaggerated motion, she pointed.

"I'm Frank Pfister from Home Realty."

Eva winced. He'd pronounced Realty with three syllables.

At the end, he said, "Call Pfister Home Real-i-ty today because these homes will go fast." He shook the script with his fat fist. "That girl messed up the tagline. It should say 'Call today, because these homes won't last.'"

"Well, 'won't last' sounds like the houses might fall apart." Eva sniffed; her sinuses irritated by the strong cologne. "Did Candi run the copy by you?"

"I didn't notice the change." He scratched at the script with his pen.

The client is always right.

She hit the record button. Mr. Pfister read his ads about homes that wouldn't last.

After he left, Eva ventured down the creaky basement steps. The dank, cement-floored room accommodated a half-dozen workspaces separated by bland, tan partitions. She found Candi's cubicle. An under-cabinet light illuminated snapshots pinned to the fabric walls: college grads in caps and gowns, a Collie, a classic engagement pose—the ring on Candi's hand sparkling against the chest of a man with hair poking from his collar.

Raising a brow, Eva scrutinized Candi's desktop calendar. In neat handwriting, entries for sales meetings packed her days. Next to the phone, an open notebook displayed lists of sales goals and cold-call prospects. Eva left a note about Mr. Pfister and his self-destructing homes. She hurried upstairs to daylight and fresh air, hoping she hadn't wrecked Candi's chance of getting the production deal.

17. EASY LIVIN' ~ URIAH HEEP

The big day had arrived, the first payday since Eva joined the morning show. She rubbed her hands in anticipation as she sat at the guest mic. She couldn't wait to find out her raise.

> TANYA: The Fixx with "Saved By Zero" on B93.
> YARDLEY: You're listening to Yardley and Tanya. Say, what holiday dates all the way back to Roman and Greek times and honors the goddesses of fertility and Mother Earth?
> TANYA: Mother's Day?
> YARDLEY: Oh, for crying out loud, Tanya.
> TANYA: Were you asking a trivia question?
> YARDLEY: I sure was.
> TANYA: Do I get a Perfect Portion Pizza?
> YARDLEY: How about a perfect punch in the mouth!

"Do you have another trivia question?" she asked during commercials.

"I'll think of something you won't know the answer to."

Although Yardley had laughed on the air, he wore a sour look. He turned his back to her as he cued up a record.

Eva threw out an idea she'd been working on. "We have tons of those pizza gift certificates. Let's do a regular trivia bit. We could call it 'Let's Get Quizzical' or something. Maybe at the twenty-after break, before people get in their cars to drive to work."

"Maybe" was all he said as he shook his gray head. "Go look for an update on the fire at the cheese factory."

She dutifully followed his order and went to clear the AP wire. If she worked at a station with a real newsroom, she would have gone down to the plant with a cassette deck and hand-held mic or at least called the fire department for a statement.

At ten o'clock, when Jack took over, Eva had nothing to do but wait for her paycheck. She filled the kitchen sink and washed mugs, looking out the window. Outside, the engineer, wearing the brown overalls he never washed, mowed grass under the broadcast tower. Over on the next block, little kids rode Big Wheels down the sidewalk.

Sloshing her hands in the warm soapy water, Eva daydreamed, picturing herself announcing a big show at the La Crosse Center. As Tanya Starr, the most popular morning show celebrity in town, she'd leap from the curtains, breathless with excitement over Queen, or Yes, a golden spotlight following her. She'd look cool in leather pants and a sparkling sequin top. Or maybe a flowy dress with her hair long again, wearing an embroidered shawl and boots with five-inch heels. She'd whip the crowd into a frenzy, tossing station frisbees. Backstage in the green room, the musicians would pose with their arms around her. As she rinsed the last cup, she envisioned being handed a bouquet of roses and a large check for emceeing. She dried her hands on a raggedy towel and went to see about her pay.

Dottie was still typing. Not wanting to interfere, Eva tiptoed past her office, down the hall where Yardley's door was ajar.

His voice sounded strained. "I've got things under control with those two buffoons. I promise, there will be no more incidents."

This was an earful. Who could he be talking about? Yardley went silent for a minute.

"But we haven't seen the spring numbers yet," he finally said. "They're going to be good. The phones ring constantly. People are streaming in to collect prizes. I've got a bunch of remotes lined up for me and Tanya. She's an eager beaver." He gave a dirty laugh.

Silence again.

"The complaint? I'm just trying to avoid a lawsuit. She's one loopy broad, but for the most part, she loves working here. I'll give her a big automotive account."

When she heard his chair roll, Eva backed off. She slipped into Dottie's office.

"Yardley is under a ton of pressure. Who's he talking to?"

"Barry Snow, the owner. He was at the Christmas party."

"No one introduced me." Eva kicked at the shag carpet. "Does Barry want to cancel our show? Yardley was begging him to give it more time."

"It's a game. Barry makes threats then Yardley puts pressure on Merv to sell more ads."

"Oh." Eva's shoulders relaxed. "Yardley's not the owner?"

"No, dear. He's just a pawn like the rest of us. Barry lives in Chicago. We're one of the stations in his so-called portfolio."

"What's he like?" Eva asked.

"Just another silver-haired fella in a suit. Now go and fetch yourself a cup of coffee. Keep me company while I finish payroll."

When she returned, Eva sat with her hands folded while Dottie logged numbers into the payroll ledger and typed checks. The office was lined with posters. "Patience is a Virtue" hung next to a classic "Hang in There!" kitten, and above Dottie's desk, "Genius is 1% Inspiration and 99% Perspiration," the yellow words wrapped into the shape of a lightbulb.

Dottie loaded a blank check into her typewriter. *Crrk-crrrkkk.* Eva perched on the edge of her seat.

"Would you like to hand out prizes?" Dottie opened a drawer and drew out a large manila envelope closed with a piece of string wound between two cardboard buttons. Her phone rang. She covered the handset, miming "It's Barry."

Giving Dottie privacy for the call, Eva took the envelope, and in the lobby, sat in a sunshine-warmed spot on the velvet couch. How would she spend her morning show money? A new car, a waterbed, nice clothes, cable TV. Yardley said DJs made serious cash doing remotes. But the thought of speaking in front of people sent Eva's nerves to frazzle like a frayed patch cord. She preferred speaking to an invisible audience. She lit a cigarette and watched as traffic sped by.

A rusty Ford Pinto pulled into the driveway. A young couple got out and peeked in the window, confused as most people were by the station's abandoned motor-lodge exterior. Eva stubbed out her smoke and went to the door.

"I won a bottle of Hiney Wine," the guy said, removing his baseball cap. The girl stood behind him.

"I'll need your ID," Eva said.

"Are you Tanya from the radio?" he asked while getting out his wallet.

"Yes, I am." She gave him her brightest radio smile.

Lines formed on his forehead. "I thought you were blonde and busty."

As if Tanya Starr had no feelings. What could she say? *And I thought you were a gentleman.*

"Benny, that's not nice," the girl said. "Is Yardley here?"

"She's in love with him," the guy said, jabbing his thumb at her.

"Yardley's not here," Eva lied. "But we'll be at South Towne Mall next Saturday."

The girl lit up. "Far out. We'll be there."

Benny opened the prize envelope. A look of disappointment came over his face. "A $10 Speedy Liquor gift certificate? Where's my Hiney wine?"

"Sorry. It's just a gag. You can buy anything you want, though."

"I wanted some Hiney." As they turned to leave, he grumbled, "What a rip-off."

Eva wished Yardley would tire of the stupid wine bit.

Dottie came into the lobby, handing Eva her check. She scooted away. Eva tore open the envelope. To: Eva LaVette. In the amount of . . . *What?* She scanned the numbers and found the same hourly wage as overnights. In a flash, her heart dropped ten stories like an elevator with no brakes. There had to be a mistake. But the pay period matched the date she started on the morning show. She rubbed her forehead. Artie would tell her she should have been a teacher, where raises and benefits were negotiated annually by the statewide union. She wanted to tear the check into pieces, but they needed every cent.

18. TILL IT SHINES ~ BOB SEGER

At home, Eva sat at the kitchen table with a stack of bills and her pay stub. A groggy Artie emerged from the bedroom in his underwear, his gut protruding over the waistband. He didn't try to hold it in anymore. Too many beers and tailgate bratwursts. She got up to put bread in the toaster and a cup of coffee in the microwave for him, then sat down to write a list of her skills and strengths. Number one, she'd never missed a day of work.

"You get paid today?" he asked, standing close. He still hadn't commented on her hair.

"Yes. I did."

"How much was your raise?" When the microwave beeped, he removed his mug and sipped.

"That's the thing. I didn't get one. So much for fame and fortune." She stabbed her list with a pen. "Dang it. I really wanted to get cable so we can have MTV." And something for him. "And ESPN."

"We're not paying for TV. Television is free." He let out an exasperated sigh. "Gol' darn it, Eva. Radio sucks. They're paying you peanuts. You need to talk to Yardley."

Eva had been thinking about it since opening her check, thus the list. What would Tanya do? Charm the charmer? Or would she bust into his office making demands?

"We've got to give it time, Artie. Things will change. Yardley said advertisers will want to use my voice now. I can make ten bucks for each spot. And he's got another opportunity for me—a product endorsement deal. I'm not sure what it is."

She set down her pen. Good things *were* happening. She'd already met Sidney Moncrief and Cyndi Lauper, both guests on the show.

"We're barely making enough to pay our bills, Eva. God forbid the car breaks down or Ludwig gets sick," he said.

"Is there any chance you'll get promoted?"

"Old man Penzle says he wants to computerize our bookkeeping but when I bring it up, he won't spend the dough. Believe me, I suggest it all the time."

The toaster popped.

"Why don't you apply somewhere else?"

"For crying out loud, Eva. Will you quit nagging? I just woke up." He wolfed down his toast. "I need to build up my résumé to show I'm loyal. No one wants a job jumper."

He shuffled into the bathroom. She found his guitar in the closet and while he showered, she tuned it, and polished the wood. When he came out with his robe on, she held it out.

"Here, Artie. Why don't you play something for me? It might make you feel better."

"I don't feel like it." He sat next to her on the couch, put his hands behind his head, and looked at the ceiling.

Ludwig jumped into her lap. She stroked his soft body.

"We got another overdraft fee, Artie. You forgot to write in your ATM withdrawal."

"I did? Well. How much are you spending on those goddamn cigarettes? I know you're smoking in the house while I'm gone."

"I only smoke a half-pack a day." Enough to earn a free Camel lighter by saving coupons. "Faye and Dwayne go through two cartons a week. If we had more money, I could buy them in bulk and save."

"That's the stupidest thing I ever heard. Sounds like one of your dumb commercials. *The more you buy, the more you save!* What horseshit. You radio people are so—"

"What?" Her shoulders tightened.

"Fake. Like Tanya Starr. Where did that come from?"

"Yardley."

"*Yardley,*" he mocked. "I'm starting to hate that son of a bitch."

"Come on, Artie." Eva tapped her list. "Look, I wrote down what I bring to the table. I'll talk to him. Just promise that you'll look for jobs."

"Oh, all right. Where's the *Tribune?*"

He huffed off. Eva massaged the back of her neck. It seemed her hopes for a happy marriage kept diminishing. She wondered how low her expectations could go.

With her unsupportive husband snoring loudly, Eva spent Saturday morning fretting and pacing in their tiny apartment, her stomach unsettled. What if no one showed up at the mall? Or what if there was an enormous crowd, full of hecklers? To help make her case for a raise, she really had to impress Yardley.

Surely Coco had experience with remote broadcasts. After making a cup of tea and settling into the couch, Eva dialed her number. It had been months since she'd tuned in to Coco's show on Z100. When was the last time they talked? But Coco's phone had been disconnected. Eva listened to the operator on repeat. *The number you have called is no longer in service.* She felt like crying. God forbid she'd have red eyes for the remote. Back in the kitchen, she sat at the table and wrote Coco a letter, hoping it would get forwarded to wherever she was. *I've been a bad friend.*

Food didn't seem appealing at lunchtime. Eva took a seat at the table and re-examined the disappointing pay stub. Artie finally woke up. While she made him a cup of coffee, he situated himself on the couch with the newspaper. After a shower, she walked into the kitchen naked, wearing only a towel on her head. Artie never looked up from the sports page.

Nothing in her closet was groovy enough for a live appearance. She defaulted to her best outfit: gray wool pants, a matching vest with a silk back, and a silvery-blue blouse that tied at the throat. Not very cool, but presentable.

An hour later, the live broadcast was in full swing at the mall's main entrance near a Mexican restaurant. The enticing smell of tacos filled the air. Women of all ages and shapes streamed in for their free T-shirts and to enter drawings, fawning over a schmoozing Yardley St. Martins. Eva kept a low profile, running the equipment and handing out prizes. Lite Hits blared from speakers on either side of the table, upon which Yardley had hung the new station banner. An embarrassing misspelling stood out to Eva immediately: *Warping You in the Arms of Love*. She took a wild guess at who had approved it.

###

On Monday, Artie needed the car. Eva took the bus to work, like the old days.

"Big news!" Yardley crowed. "We did such a great job on Saturday, the mall is offering us a contract to broadcast live every Friday from Hacienda Mexico."

Free huevos rancheros for breakfast sounded good to Eva. He cued up an oldie, "You Should Be Dancing" by the Bee Gees.

Afraid of ruining his mood, smiling through clenched teeth, Eva waited until nine o'clock to ask for a meeting. She fingered the list of accomplishments and ideas in her pocket. Her anger burned low, just enough to fuel her courage.

A commotion arose in the lobby where Yardley and Merv were fussing over a willowy young woman. During a song set, Eva poked her head out of the studio. Yardley's booming voice contrasted with the girl's, but Eva couldn't make out what they were saying. From his tone, she could tell he was in show-off mode. Minutes later, the two came into the studio.

"Tanya, meet Sunny," Yardley said. "She's a senior at UW-L and works at the campus station. She wants to pick up a shift or two."

The lissome girl's sleek hair sashayed across her shoulders. Eva admired her polka-dot dress with its big shoulders, peplum, red belt, and *damn*—matching shoes. Sunny gazed at Yardley with reverence from under her Brooke Shields eyebrows. Eva frowned.

"It's nice to meet you," she said, gawping at Eva, her voice dulcet like a child's. There was no chance the girl could succeed;

106

she'd be a warm body for weekends or overnights. "Good luck, Sunny. I started at the campus station, too," Eva said, winking.

At ten o'clock, Eva headed down the hallway for her meeting, but Yardley's door was closed. She wandered into Dottie's office.

"Need any help?"

"Oh, my dear girl, I would love it. Look at my desk. Most stations have a receptionist, a traffic and continuity director, *and* a bookkeeper. I'm all three." Dottie found two carts in the rubble on her desk. "Here. Can you transcribe these ads, please? I need the scripts for co-op."

Taking a pen from Dottie's gold spray-painted macaroni pencil holder, Eva added "transcribe ads" to her list of abilities. When Yardley's door opened, she picked up the tapes and met him in the hall.

"I was just coming to find you," he said.

He stopped and held a finger in the air. Their new promo was playing over the speaker in the ceiling. His lips moved involuntarily, like a puppet, as he listened to his own voice.

> YARDLEY: Tune in this Friday when Tanya and I will feature a boy band from Botswana!
> TANYA: Botswanan rock? Cool!
> TOGETHER: Don't miss it!

They listened to the rest of the promo, which segued into "We Are the World" by the super-group USA for Africa.

"Wait a minute. Do we have enough mics for the band?" she asked.

"That's a good question. We'll have to put the boys in production and pipe them through. Or maybe the engineer can move some mics into the studio. Good thinking, Tanya."

See, I am valuable.

"What's up, kiddo?" Yardley swept his arm through the open doorway, gesturing for Eva to sit.

Heat rose from her chest to her cheeks. She handed him the pay stub and blurted, "Was this a mistake? Will my new salary show up on the next check?"

Yardley adjusted his reading glasses. When he handed the stub back, he didn't say a word but bent down and tugged on a desk drawer. It wouldn't open. He popped it with his fist. Eva recoiled. While he perused her file, she fidgeted with the tassels on her white embroidered tunic.

"Hmm." He snapped the folder closed and wagged a pencil-thin finger. "'You git what you git and you don't throw a fit.'"

"But you said the morning show personifies the station. And Donn got a nice bump when he moved from overnights to evenings."

"Is that what this is about? Donn has a wife and children to support."

So shocked by the revelation Donn was married, Eva missed the implication of what Yardley had said. She sat dumbfounded.

"Let's wait to see the numbers—it's nothing for you to worry your pretty little head about." Leaning sideways, he pulled a tangle of keys from his pocket and unlocked the top drawer. He rifled through a wad of envelopes. "Make friends with the AEs. They can hustle up remotes. I've asked Merv to get talent fees for you guys. In the meantime, trade for a stereo, a bike, clothes, whatever you want."

Eva jammed the sweat-smeared list back in her pocket. Trade didn't pay the bills. She didn't want a stereo, she needed cash.

Yardley checked his watch for the umpteenth time.

"But I've never missed a shift." She tried to think while sniffing back tears. "What if I picked up some overtime transcribing co-op ads, or writing commercials, or answering the phones?"

"Darlin', you can always help Dottie. But no overtime." He shoved an envelope across his desktop. "Take this."

Glowering, she ignored the envelope.

"C'mon now. Have a nice time with Artie." He leaned forward, sliding the envelope across the desk, right up to the edge.

She stared at it for a second before opening the flap. "Harlem Globe Trotters?" She huffed. Yardley must have felt guilty because he dove into his drawer for another bribe.

"Make a night of it." He slid a second envelope labeled *Cracker Barrel* in Dottie's neat cursive writing. "Beggars can't be choosers."

Eva pulled herself together. Tanya Starr wasn't going to beg. She'd try harder.

"Thank you, Yardley."

Head hanging with defeat, Eva walked across the mall parking lot to the bus stop. What had happened? Having started as a starry-eyed radio debutante, she'd paid her dues working overnights. She got in early every weekday, did a solo show every Saturday morning, and worked on holidays. *I'm a brown-nosed toady. A doormat.*

The bus jerked forward. Eva plopped into a seat. She leaned her flushed cheek into the cool, soothing glass. Below, in a car traveling alongside the bus, a couple held hands across the front seat. The man reached over to squeeze the woman's bare thigh. She pushed it away. Radio was like a bad boyfriend, Eva thought, one who sweet-talks a girl until he gets his way. Suddenly, the image of Artie reading his paper while she was walking through the apartment naked came back to her.

19. STAND BACK ~ STEVIE NICKS

After her shift on an idyllic June day, Eva settled on a stool at the station's breakfast bar. With no production to do, she began editing a pile of public service requests. Peony-scented air wafted in through the screen on the patio door. Crows cawed the song of summer. Distracted by the beautiful day, she doodled in the margins on a plea from the Red Cross.

Dottie approached and took a stool. The bright daylight accentuated the deep lines around her lips. She unsnapped a quilted cigarette case and with her mauve nails clawed out a Virginia Slims. "Want one?"

"Sure." Eva lit it using Dottie's lighter, picturing the brand's sponsorship of women's professional tennis during the 1970s.

Dottie snapped shut the case. "You guys were funny this morning. That bagpipers bit?"

"Bonkers! I thought Yardley was going to pee his pants."

Eva took a puff. The cigarette tasted rich. Maybe she should switch. *I've come a long way, baby.* She took another drag. *For all your lung cancer needs. . .*

"There's a letter for you in today's mail," Dottie said.

Eva blew smoke out in a stream. "Really? For me and Yardley?"

"Nope. For Tanya." Dottie dropped a bombshell. "So, did you hear? Donn is leaving."

"What?" She wondered if it was because of the tapes she'd sent. It didn't matter now. Maybe Yardley would hire Sunny Sommers.

"The station he worked at in North Dakota asked him to come back. He starts in two weeks. Schmidty's taking evenings."

"Good for both of them." Eva inhaled her cigarette and, with practiced skill from her boring hours on overnights, blew out consecutively concentric smoke rings.

Jack came bursting out of the studio and sprinted toward the bathroom. "I've got fifty-five seconds!" he exclaimed.

The women consulted their watches.

"He reminds me of my son. The goofy one." Dottie laughed, swatting his rear as he rushed by.

"Why doesn't he wait for a long song?" One of the emergency carts, like Harry Chapin's "Taxi" which was 6:29, or the Moody Blues' "Nights in White Satin" at 7:10.

"It's a competition. For some godforsaken reason, they do it during commercials." Dottie checked her watch. "Forty seconds."

Eva crinkled her nose. *Did the contest include hand washing?* She didn't allow herself to think about the germs crawling on the microphone and all over the board.

Dottie tapped her nails on a stack of paperwork. "Anyways, Yardley asked me to train you on commercial logs. He said you'd be a good backup 'cause you're organized." Her wrinkled lips pressed into a tight mauve line. "If I'm out sick, it's a bear to reschedule the ads."

Eva found satisfaction upon completing office tasks, as opposed to being an announcer who felt compelled to spend all hours with an ear to news and culture.

They looked up to see Jack flying through. He swung into the studio just as Merv appeared from the hallway carrying a cardboard box with a lamp sticking out.

"Dottie. Tanya." Merv nodded at the women, wrestling an arm free to open the basement door.

"Something's up," Dottie said. "He's moving to the sales pit."

"Why?"

"They don't tell me nothin'." Dottie stubbed out her cigarette and stood. "Stay here. I'll go get your fan mail."

Yardley entered the kitchen. He used an oven mitt to open the refrigerator—the handle sometimes gave out shocks—and retrieved a carton of cream. When he poured coffee into his mug, its steam rose, backlit against the bright window. He took a sip.

"Looks like you could use a desk, Tanya. There's an extra one downstairs."

"I'm okay." She'd rather work from the parking lot than the basement.

"You deserve it. Nothing's too good for my little partner. Ask Dottie to scrounge up an extra typewriter." He set down his mug. "While we're alone, there's been something I wanted to propose. A chance for you to earn some extra cash."

Eva's eyes lit up.

"You've heard of Ayds, the diet candy, right? Well, there's a local startup doing something similar. They want you to be their spokesman, er, woman."

Eva's eyes narrowed. "You want me to go on a diet? I'm not overweight."

"I thought all women wanted to lose a few." He scrunched his brow, looking truly confused.

Is that what he thought? Unbelievable.

"Regardless, as Tanya, you have a certain image to keep up. This is a huge opportunity."

"I don't think I'm comfortable telling people they can take a shortcut to a magazine body. The fitness membership is one thing, Yardley. I'm not taking diet pills."

He sneered. "Don't we trust each other? Look. Where do you want to be in five years? If you don't want to play the game, then boom," he smacked his palm, "suddenly you're on the outs and that's it for you in La Crosse. Come on, now. All you need to do is to talk about your progress for a minute each day. It's a lucrative account. Think about it."

Eva stared at him, stupefied. Could Yardley have her blacklisted? He turned toward his office, spilling coffee on the counter. It dripped down the cabinet. Dottie returned, waving the fan mail. She set it down before wiping up Yardley's mess. Eva tore open the letter.

Dear Tanya (formerly Lizzy),

Congrats on getting promoted to mornings. Cool beans!
I know it's been a while, but I wanted to apologize for
my behavior. I thought you liked talking that way, but
I guess I took it too far. You have such a sexy voice—I
couldn't help it.

Yours truly,
Mystery Man

Eva frowned. How dare he blame her. *Fucking men.* And the phrase he used, "promoted to mornings," was something someone in the business would say. She wanted to burn the letter with her lighter but instead gave it to Dottie for the Public File, where— according to the Federal Communications Commission—all correspondence to the radio station must be saved. She shook her head. At least he hadn't addressed the letter to "Eva."

A few weeks later, she finished a sandwich while confined to her new desk in the airless basement which smelled of stale cigarettes. To enhance a creative atmosphere, she lit a gooseneck lamp, then went over to shut off the stark overhead lighting.

It seemed too quiet. The AEs were out meeting with clients, golfing, or getting their nails done. The DJs often speculated on what they did all day. According to Dottie, what mattered was if— not how—they met their monthly sales goals.

At the cold metal desk, Eva's attention wandered to a bright window well where a patch of blue sky shone. It was a glorious day, but Eva felt trapped like a rat in a cage.

A thick stack of papers sat in her in-box, mostly PSAs, but surprisingly, there were trade requests for Tanya. *Nice perks.* The salon at the mall was offering a facial in exchange for an on-air report of the experience, plus a full line of cleansers and lotions. And there was the paperwork for the free fitness studio membership. That would be fun to talk about on the air. She'd

113

always wanted to try the Jane Fonda workout. As she hummed "Let's Get Physical" by Olivia Newton-John, she considered the neon sweatbands, high-cut spandex thongs over leggings, and matching leg warmers everyone was wearing. Maybe she'd rip up an old concert T-shirt a la *Flashdance*. Being Tanya Starr was starting to feel cool.

The basement door creaked open, and the lights flickered on. Two men bumbled down the stairs, laughing and joshing each other. Eva held her breath. She hadn't learned their names because, like many new AEs, they wouldn't last a month.

"I could have bagged that bartender chick. She was all over me."

"My man. Because you had a fifty-dollar bill laying on the bar."

"Did you see her lean in when I asked for a light? She was into me!"

"Until you gave her that cheesy line."

"What's wrong with saying I believe in love at first sight?"

Wasn't he the one who had just gotten married?

There was a loud thud.

"Ow!"

"Whoa, buddy, be careful. You had one too many Gibsons."

Martinis? It wasn't even noon.

"I fell in love with her décolletage."

"Her what?"

"Her chest, numb nuts."

"Oh, my god, she was stacked. It makes me want to get my wife a boob job. In the bra department, she's a straight-A student. Like our morning show girl, what's-her-face."

Eva flinched.

"Otherwise, that bartender chick is a brown-bagger."

"I'd still do her."

They burst into dirty laughter.

"Let's go back to the bar. I've got that big contract coming. My budget is made."

"Yeah, thanks to your uncle's tire store."

"Hey, it all counts."

The rowdy guys rustled around in their cubicles, then tromped up the stairs, cracking each other up with more juvenile drivel. Undiscovered, Eva let out a breath. They must be the two buffoons Yardley had spoken to Barry about. That's who represented the station in the community? Immature pinheads?

It wasn't worth getting upset about; they'd be gone soon. Once a week, it seemed, Merv Harms made the rounds introducing the "latest addition to Sales." A revolving door of often good-looking recent grads. They were cast onto the streets without training, like how Eva's father had taught her to swim: toss her off the pier and shout "Dog paddle!" Abruptly, the new salespeople disappeared. Many got pink slips. Some went on a call and never returned.

It dawned on her why local business owners, like Mr. Pfister the realtor, seemed hostile. They had to endure a continuous stream of salespeople, not only from radio, but television, the Yellow Pages, newspapers, direct mail, magazines, and billboard advertising reps. Over and over, new AEs got thrown off the pier. Many drowned. It cheapened the station. Feeling disappointed and disillusioned, she wondered what her role was in all of this, from Donn's girlie magazines and randy behavior to the sales guys drinking on the job, driving around town drunk. Was it time to say something?

Curious about the "big contract," Eva snuck over to Merv's desk and, right on top, found the Master Account List. She ran a finger down the AE column. *Rolf Markham.* Yardley had accounts? He had never mentioned doing sales. *Candace Koehne.* Eva took a sharp breath. The girl in the complaint about Merv was Candi Kane!

Water rushed through the pipes from a toilet flush upstairs. Eva froze. Footsteps sounded across the ceiling. She placed the master account list on Merv's desk exactly how she'd found it. Even though it wasn't noon, she got her purse and left.

20. I KNOW I'M LOSING YOU ~ ROD STEWART

Months later, Eva relaxed in the sunny window seat at the front of their apartment. B93 played low, as Artie was still in bed. She stifled a yawn, wishing she could have slept in late, but it was too beautiful a Saturday to waste. Trees up and down the street blazed in brilliant gold, vivid red, raging orange. She set her self-help book down and took in the autumn light. A commercial came on the radio. "The leaves are falling and so are our prices." *How original.*

Eva laughed when Ludwig bumped his head against the book, which recommended wearing a rubber band to snap negative or angry thoughts. Was her exhaustion due to her early hours or was it emotional, from pent-up frustration?

She had put up with Donn's magazines, drugs, and womanizing without complaining to management. But enough was enough. Empowered by Candi's brave complaint, she'd gone to Yardley, telling him the salesmen were drinking during the workday and were talking crudely about her and other women.

"What do you expect? You're a pretty brunette," he'd said, adding, "You're the talent; stay in your lane."

He insinuated she needed to grow up, then gave her another gift certificate. No one had taught her how to deal with these situations. Snapping a rubber band on her wrist seemed too flimsy a way to alleviate the aggravations at work or at home, frankly.

A Todd Rundgren song came on, Artie's favorite. Funny how some songs were identifiable with their first notes. She'd be a whiz on *Name That Tune*, as would most DJs. In music, she mused, a note by itself is just a note; it takes relationships with other notes to deem it major or minor. Why couldn't her dissonant relationship with Artie resolve itself harmoniously? Just once, she wished he would stand up for her and be nurturing. Her mind reviewed his faults and slights. She caught herself and snapped the wristband.

Wanting to get high, she stood. The book, blanket, and cat spilled to the floor in a tangle. Ludwig jumped onto the coffee table and batted at a stray bead. Eva had been repairing the first choker she'd made for Artie many years ago. Recently she'd found it—unraveled and stashed in a drawer with his old baseball cards. Shaking her head, she sat on the couch and lit a half-smoked joint. Within seconds, her lungs expanded, her head became woozy with a surge of loving emotions.

"Oh, Luddy, I wuv you so much," she said, squeezing the cat, making kissy sounds against his striped head. "*Mwah. Mwah.*"

Artie came into the room, eyes stuck together, a big crease on the side of his face. "Wakin' and bakin', I see."

He sat next to her and yawned, scratching his stubble. She passed the joint. He talked while holding in smoke.

"I'm telling you, Eva. You're more affectionate with Ludwig than me." He blew out the smoke, leaning in for the obligatory morning kiss.

"Ugh. Your beard is stinky." She pulled away. She had just read a news story about beards, how they harbored more bacteria and fungus than dogs. Artie's habit of constant whisker-stroking made her want to slap his hand. "I wish you'd shave it off."

"Why are you so crabby lately?" he retorted.

"Artie, I finally have a day off. I'm beat and I need to relax. It's draining to be Tanya all the time."

She fled into the kitchen, not wanting to hear him tell her to go back to a normal job. He didn't respect her feelings. *Did he even see me? Or am I just someone who makes food and cleans the house—a warm body?* Artie never wanted to talk about the relationship or express how he felt. Work seemed to be his number one focus, his only focus. Was she even number two, or were his precious sports? Why couldn't they be more like Faye and Dwayne, who were still lovey-dovey. Faye made lunch for Dwayne every day. He left sweet notes all over the house and surprised her with flowers. Eva removed the rubber band from her wrist and shot it at the back of Artie's head. It fell short.

117

Perhaps a hot shower would wash away her frustrations. Twenty minutes later, she left the bathroom wearing her terrycloth robe and a bulky towel around her head. She found a note on the counter. *"Out for a jog. Back in 45."* No *Love, Arthur,* or *xoxox.*

When the mailman came up the steps, Eva tightened her robe and retrieved the mail. Bills and more bills, then a letter from: Coco Nix, 452 Montezuma Ave., Phoenix, AZ. She tore it open.

LaVette,

Big news! I'm rockin' out at Desert Rock 105 in Phoenix. It's a top 15 market! You won't believe how it happened. First, I got hired at a Florida station looking for a neutral, Midwestern voice. I packed my shit, hit the highway, and drove to Tampa. (Sorry for not calling. I left town in a hurry.) When I got there, no one knew who I was—the PD who'd hired me had left. I lost it! But they had nothing for me. I applied for a position in Phoenix and here I am, although I had to borrow money from my parents for the second move. It all worked out. Just gotta Keep On Truckin'!

I just re-read your letter. (Glad the mail was forwarded properly.) You shouldn't have to put up with that crap at work. That's partly why I left Z100. Lurch, my PD, had all this time to hang out with me in the studio yet never went over my airchecks. He wished he was on the air. The kicker? He showed up at every single one of our tailgate parties with a new girl on his arm—his "friend" Suzanne, or Keiko, or Melissa. Barf me out! The creep was married. He made me give the grand prize—an authentic Badgers letter jacket with leather sleeves—to one of his bimbos. I hate to call them that; maybe they're intelligent, but they dress sleazy. When I told the GM, he tried to bribe me with gift certificates. That was the last straw.

It's like what you said about Artie ignoring you, so you've given up trying to talk to him. (Side note—no one has a beard anymore.) My parental units say when you hide your feelings, it invalidates your sense of self, which can prevent you from achieving your goals. Speak up, girl! Stand up for yourself! I'm one to talk, though. Instead of expressing my feelings, I stuff them (and my face). But overall, things are good. I like being on middays a lot.

I had The Dream last night. The turntables were replaced with coin-operated table-top jukeboxes, like the ones you see at diners. I searched high and low but couldn't find a quarter to save my life! Meanwhile, dead air!

You should visit. I'll take you to the Sonoran Desert. No snowstorms—here we have dust storms. I'd better sign off. Call or write soon, okay?

P.S. I got a new bumper sticker. "A good segue is better than sex!"

Eva laughed, but Coco's news knocked her down a peg: her friend was on middays at one of the top markets in the country. Being single, Coco could go anywhere at the drop of a hat.

Damn Artie. She grabbed the wall phone. The long cord, when uncoiled to its max, reached the couch. She unwound the towel from her damp head, settled into the pillows, and dialed Coco's new number. The phone rang and rang.

When Coco didn't answer, Eva wrote back to her at the kitchen table, emphasizing the good news. How a lady in line at the grocery store heard her talking and asked if she was Tanya Starr, the new clothes she was getting on trade, and how Dottie was teaching her office stuff.

Someday, we'll do an all-girl show in Minneapolis . . . Mornings with Eva the Diva and Coco Puffs!

119

21. CHAIN OF FOOLS ~ ARETHA FRANKLIN

At South Towne Mall, adoring women stood in long lines to meet the infamous Yardley St. Martins, who thrived on sticking a microphone in their lovesick faces. One middle-aged lady held her hand to her heart, hyperventilating, as if she was about to meet Paul McCartney. Wearing a Santa hat, Yardley greeted the ladies with open arms. It wasn't even Thanksgiving, and here they were pushing Christmas.

Eva stood behind a table at the compact remote board, glad to let him do his thing. It had been a long week; she couldn't wait to spend a quiet weekend at home. She was planning to ask Artie to see a marriage counselor, one thing she could do to stand up for herself, as prescribed in the self-help book.

When it was time for their next live break, Eva clapped her hands and addressed the crowd. "Quiet, everyone! We're going on the air."

Yardley waved to a woman at the edge of the crowd, weighed down by shopping bags. She squealed and ran up, dropping her bags at his feet.

> YARDLEY: B93 with Yardley and Tanya live from the mall, where Friday is Fan Appreciation Day! Here's a gorgeous lady. What do you want for Christmas? Say it into my mic, hon.
> FAN: Oh, golly. A new car? A vacation?
> YARDLEY: What are the magic words?
> FAN: Wrap Me in the Arms of Love!
> YARDLEY: Close enough, my dear. You've won a pair of shoes from Thom McAn, or maybe you'll pick out some boots for the snow that's coming. One more winner, on B93 FM.

That was the cue to throw it to Jack, who ran the board back at the station. Eva handed the woman her $20 gift certificate. Yardley came behind the table and leaned in close.

"Tanya. Why are you hiding?" he hissed. "We're entertainers."

Eva's really screwing up. She became her alter-ego, smiling broadly as she modeled her new clothes from the County Seat, a store that was all the rage for women on a budget. Tanya then breathlessly described them on the air as per the trade agreement. A steady stream of fans kept them busy throughout the morning. After a break, as she tugged on the flouncy skirt, someone familiar caught her eye. Artie approached the throng with a determined stride and clenched jaw.

"What a surprise!" she gave him a peck. "You took the bus out here just to see me at my remote?" Was this a romantic gesture for once?

"It's Ma," he said, looking distraught.

"Was she in an accident?" The mall faded away as Eva flashed to a vision of a doctor stitching her wrist at the hospital, her mother holding her hand, whispering that everything would be all right. It never was. Tears filled her eyes.

"She collapsed at the grocery store. From coughing really hard." Artie's fingers fumbled behind his glasses. He hadn't taken the time to put in his contacts. "She bashed her head on some shelving."

"When did this happen?"

"Early this morning. My brother called . . . I could hardly understand him. After some tests, the doctors did a CT scan. Ma has tumors in her lungs."

"Oh, no." Eva threw her arms around Artie's neck.

"I don't know what to do," he said with a sob.

Yardley was waving. Reality snapped into place.

"Can I have the car keys?" Artie asked, his face red and blotchy.

"I should go, too." She wiped her eyes. Her mind raced. "Damn. I've got a remote tonight at the disco, and I'm on the air tomorrow morning."

"It's okay," he whispered.

"Just be careful driving. Oh, Artie, what about the tires? There's a snowstorm on the way."

Their mechanic had said the threads were so thin the tires were border-line illegal. She pictured his winter driving, his nose above the frozen steering wheel of the Chrysler, peering through a snowball-sized peephole he'd scratched into the ice until the defroster melted the rest. She got the keys from her purse under the broadcast table.

"I'll be careful." His head hung; his shoulders drooped.

There had to be a million things to say, but all she could think of were clichés. "Don't forget to take your gloves. And make sure to check the oil. That car leaks like a sieve. And watch out for deer!"

"I will."

Artie hurried away. Eva watched until the poor guy rounded the corner at the brilliantly mirrored jewelry store. This was a time when she needed to be there for him, despite her frustrations with his behavior. Maybe Yardley would let her take time off.

"Tanya!" Yardley brayed. "Your fan wants to meet Bart Starr's daughter."

She ran up, aware of what an odd couple she and Yardley made: the skinny yet distinguished six-foot-two old man towering over his petite, junior sidekick.

"Tanya Starr. You're true Wisconsin royalty," the fan gushed.

"Hi there," she said, flashing her best smile.

He shook her hand until it almost fell off. Yardley shot her a look. Was he jealous?

###

Later that morning, a cheer erupted from the kitchen. Eva ran in to see what was happening. The entire sales department was clustered at the counter celebrating that Candi landed an annual contract with a car dealer. After high-fives and much backslapping, everyone dispersed.

"I'm on fire, Tanya," she said.

"Congratulations. Who did you sign?"

"The Volkswagen dealer on the north side. Merv says automotive accounts build the foundation for a successful sales career. Let's celebrate tonight at the remote." Candi eyeballed the colorful selection of pastries on the counter. "Smells so yummy."

"I know. Say, can you get me a Punch Bug on trade?" Eva asked, picking out her favorite doughnut, a chocolate cream with chocolate frosting.

"Hilarious." Candi bit into a cruller, talking with her mouth full. "I'll get right on that."

"Seriously, I'm happy for you."

"It's huge. After I told them about your *La Crosse Magazine* nomination, it was a slam dunk. They're going to sponsor your show!"

"Excellent." Eva wiped her mouth on a slippery station-logo napkin. Yardley said not to get her hopes up about winning Best Morning Show. The Morning Zoo at Z100 always won. Maybe now was the time to ask Candi about her complaint. "I heard something about Merv harassing you."

"Yeah. Don't ever be alone with him."

"I keep my distance from him *and* Yardley. During my job interview, they both creeped me out." Eva cringed when she remembered the way Yardley's hand had brushed her backside.

She touched Candi's elbow. "Are you okay?"

"You know, I thought it would be the clients I had to worry about—the lunch meetings, the happy hour planning sessions. But no, it's my fucking boss."

She leaned close to Eva's ear, "Beware the smiling tigers—they're inside."

In production, Eva found it hard to concentrate. Artie was driving with bald tires. Surely, he'd have the music cranked up, heedless of the first snowstorm of the season on the way. What happened to his mother was serious. Eva hoped the doctors caught it early enough.

Yardley poked his head in the door, a concerned look on his long face. "I want to express my sympathy for the situation with your mother-in-law. Is there anything you need?"

"Can I use my vacation time? Artie is taking a week off. I should be there."

"Sure. You can do the disco gig this afternoon and your shift tomorrow, right?"

She looked at the clock, her head spinning like a disco ball. By the time she stopped for a can of Aqua Net at the mall, took the bus home, packed for the trip, got dressed—black parachute pants, lacy fingerless gloves, an oversized white blouse with the collar turned up, chunky plastic earrings—then did her hair, it would be time for the gig. Eva had never been able to pull off the straight, long locks of the '70s, however, she rocked big hair. She would wave it out in a pyramid shape, spray it high to one side, and fix it with a bejeweled comb.

"Next week, I'll do the morning show by myself." He placed a finger on his lips. "Or maybe Sunny Sommers can sub."

"Who would saddle their child with that name?"

"Actually, I think it's cute. It's better than Winter Sommers, although she told me her sister's name is Autumn." He laid a hand on her shoulder. "Go ahead and take your vacation time."

Eva called her mom, who agreed to feed Ludwig and let Eva use her car. After they hung up, she melted into tears. Regardless of her mother-in-law's situation, the relief of having an entire week off felt titanic. Thanksgiving and Christmas were coming, and since Yardley kept bankers' hours, there was no doubt she'd be paying him back, working the holidays by herself.

I'll take a break from everything next week. No Yardley, no Merv the Perv. No radio, television, or newspapers. It would be heaven.

At the end of Eva's shift on Saturday morning, Artie called to say his mom was being released from the hospital and Eva should go to her house. She steered her mom's Yugo onto the interstate, relaxing for the first time in ages. The sun had melted any remaining snow from the roads. Away from La Crosse and being Tanya, in a week, she'd go back to work refreshed and ready for the hectic holidays.

One of her commercials came on. She turned it up. "*Hey, kids! It's cold out! Time to put on your toasty down coats from Ley's.*" She remembered cutting the ad shortly after she'd started at B93. Besides "motherly sounding woman calling out the back door," the writer of the script specified sound effects of "softly falling snow." When she'd shared the story with Coco, her friend laughed so hard she cried, and said, "Sales should not write copy."

Eva turned off the interstate at Mauston onto Highway 23. The further she got from La Crosse, the more clearly she was able to assess her trajectory at the station. At first, it had felt like whiplash: she'd pivoted from the doldrums of overnights to being a celebrity on a whirlwind morning show. Awards, trophies, and gold records were all in her future. As she sped past red barns and snow-blown fields, the scope of her accomplishments sharpened. Despite the music format, landing a spot on the morning team had met her wildest dreams. Still, working six days a week, month after month, wasn't easy. She'd sacrificed her personal life, missing countless birthday parties, weddings, even her high school reunion—all because of radio.

Overheated, she wriggled out of her coat, careful to stay on the road. She craved a cigarette, but her mother had explicitly forbidden smoking in the car. Eva popped a piece of nicotine gum into her mouth and turned up the radio, harmonizing with Neil Young on "Only Love Can Break Your Heart."

Hours later, Highway 23 led Eva straight into downtown Sheboygan. A tradition, she took a quick detour to the lakefront. The magnificent Lake Michigan glowed turquoise, looking like the Caribbean, but as still as a pond. The red lighthouse at Deland Park blushed from the golden hour sun. She remembered a time during a storm when the lake was so churned up, giant waves smashed against the pier and wetsuit-clad surfers rode longboards on the swells, something she'd never expected to see in the Midwest. Artie's mom lived up the hill and a few blocks to the west within the massive lake's influence, which kept temperatures cool in the summer and moderate in the winter.

That afternoon, steeped in nostalgia, Artie's mother sat surrounded by musty photo albums. The gash on her temple was covered by a thick square of white gauze. She coughed into a dish towel while she paged through pictures from the sixties, when Artie and his brothers were children. In most of the photographs, a lit cigarette hung from her mouth and a silver whistle encircled her neck. She talked about everything but cancer while Artie sat on the floor, lapping up stories of bygone days. After a few attempts to turn the conversation, he got serious.

"Ma," he implored. "You need to call first thing on Monday to get that operation scheduled."

Her pulmonologist strongly recommended surgery followed by radiation.

"Yah, yah," she said, waving her hand. "I feel fine."

"The sooner you get those tumors out, the better."

"God will take me when He deems it so."

"Ma!" Artie took her freckled hands in his, an unusually tender gesture. "There are other things we should talk about." He hesitated. "Are your affairs in order?"

"There's nothing to know. Besides a little cash, I have no assets except what you see here." She swept her arm toward an antique hutch, filled with vintage cut glass. "My car is old. I owe more on the house than it's worth."

"Will your insurance cover the surgery? Do you have a will?"

"Artie, let her take her time," Eva interjected.

"His name is Arthur!" his mom barked.

Eva's head snapped to the side as if she'd been slapped. There had been animosity between the women since Eva's refusal to be married in the Catholic church. His mother had frowned throughout their small civil ceremony and the dinner afterward. And then they lost the baby, another reason Eva felt shunned by his "ma." Maybe *she* had turned Artie against Eva. He had been ecstatic over their accidental pregnancy. All he talked about for months was having a son with whom to play catch, teach guitar, take fishing, build model airplanes . . . *Does he blame me?* That would explain the change in his behavior after they married. She went into the kitchen for a glass of water, eavesdropping while she leaned against the counter. A cherubic picture of Jesus—blue-eyed and blonde-haired—watched her from above the kitchen table. In a gentle voice, Artie offered to chip ice from his mom's sidewalk and take care of a fallen tree limb. She pressed money into his hand, saying he was a good boy, but too skinny.

"Is that wife of yours cooking?" she asked.

He mumbled something about their different hours. She started in about grandchildren again.

"Don't you want to be around to see your grandkids? You'll have them organized into teams in no time."

"I'm not holding my breath with you two." She croaked out a tight, painful-sounding cough.

That evening, sitting on swiveling stools at Lakeside Lanes over the crash of bowling balls hitting pins, Eva shared some exciting news.

"When I picked up Mom's car, she said we can take Pop's piano."

"That'd be nice but there's nowhere to put it," Artie said.

Eva wanted that upright with every fiber of her being.

"If we move the couch real close to the TV cabinet, we can squeeze it in."

A group of Artie's high school friends came up to say hello, and everyone seemed impressed to hear about Eva's cool job. A guy came around encouraging them to try karaoke, handing Artie a list of songs. After doing a shot of brandy, they jumped onto the tiny stage at the front of the bar and dug through the sheets of lyrics, selecting "Love Shack." The guy cued the B-52s song on a cassette deck. Eva and Artie sang their lungs out, a welcome way for both to relieve stress.

Back at the bar, breathless, Eva noticed the reflection of a smiling, middle-aged couple in the smokey distorted mirror. *Holy shit. That's us someday.* Life was rolling by like a bowling ball down a greased alley. Artie ordered shots of Schnapps. The alcohol loosened Eva's tongue and the story about Candi's complaint against Merv tumbled out.

"I don't like it, Eva. Keep away from him. And that Yardley guy? He's a wacko. Always flying by the seat of his pants."

"It's true. I never know what's going to happen when I get to work, whether it's a breaking news story, Sales springing something on me, or what."

"At Penzle's, each department has a strategic plan. For a month, a year, even five years out." He took a drink and wiped his beard with his sleeve. His brows knit. "That radio station is crazy. And now I find out there's a pig who's grabbing women?"

Artie lifted his arm to wave at the bartender, almost knocking over Eva's drink. He ordered another shot. She switched to cranberry juice. They stared at *Sportscenter* on the TV above the bar. When a commercial for Fleet Farm's toy department played, Artie began to blather about children. Out of the blue, he asked her to stop using birth control.

"Let's try for a baby before Ma is gone," he said.

"Sheesh. You think your mom is that sick?"

"Yeah, I do." He swiveled toward her on his stool. "Don't you want kids, Eva? I don't want to be an old dad."

"We can't raise children in an apartment. And who will take care of them when I'm at work?"

Not Tanya Starr. The odd hours, mandatory holidays, and an unpredictable future were part of radio, none of them conducive to a stable family home. Besides, unbeknownst to Artie, her doctor had said she may never conceive again.

At four-thirty Monday morning, Eva arrived for work, newspapers in hand, ready to re-enter the rat race and be Tanya again. In retrospect, the week off seemed like only a couple of days, but she felt reinvigorated. She sprinted up the stairs into the bullpen, raring to go. Yardley stood at the Teletype, reading. He shuffled through the news, his head down.

In the studio, Schmidty bounced in the air chair with his headphones on, singing along to "Raspberry Beret." Eva took off her coat and hung it on the rack, looking around. She had missed the place.

"Any good stories?"

"VHS rentals are up twenty percent over last year and are cutting into box office receipts," Yardley read. "A new study shows AIDS patients die about fifteen months after being diagnosed."

"That's heartbreaking. Just awful." She gave him the once-over. "Are you going to a funeral in that fancy suit?"

"We need to talk," he said.

"Are we changing the format?" she asked, laughing nervously.

"No, but we are making a change." Eva's knees went weak. "Sunny is taking your spot."

Her eyelids blinked like wipers on a foggy windshield. "The sub?" she said weakly, trying to meet his eyes.

He looked away.

"Am I moving to a different shift?"

But she knew the answer. In one moment, the bottom of her world collapsed. A black pall gripped her heart, the same visceral reaction she'd had after her father died. All the stories of being fired spun in her mind. She couldn't find her equilibrium, like riding The Rotor at the county fair when the floor drops away. *Nothing will be the same.*

Yardley's words made it through the thunder in her ears. ". . . very sorry, but we have to let you go," he said, his face gravely serious, his long chin pointing to the floor.

Letting her go. Indignation smashed through her haze of denial. So that's why he was in early. Wearing that damn black suit.

"Yardley, I don't understand."

He withdrew an envelope from inside his jacket. "Here's your paycheck, plus some severance to tide you over."

"But we've been having so much fun."

"You're young, Eva. You'll bounce back."

He called me Eva. She took the check, stupefied. Over the monitors, The Carpenters sang the happy, sappy "(I'm on the) Top of the World."

The *La Crosse Magazine* "Best of" edition lay on the counter. Although they hadn't won best morning show, they had made the cover. The two of them wearing headphones, facing another, Eva looking stupid with her mouth twisted mid-word. She stabbed her finger into his paper face.

"We're supposed to be the Grand Marshals for the Christmas parade. We've already recorded the promos. Why, Yardley?"

"Look. I spent years building this show. You're just the sidekick. You think you can tell me how to run Sales?"

Her complaint about the crude, drunken AEs?

"You whine about your pay. Working here is a privilege—we don't have to pay well. You were lucky to be here, and you know it. And besides, *you're* the one who took a vacation during a ratings period. And Sunny was dynamite. The phones went bananas."

Stunned, Eva collapsed onto a stool at the breakfast counter. The darkness of early morning only added to her disorientation. He took her by the elbow, steering into the lobby, where a cardboard box held items from her desk. When she imagined him pawing through her stuff, anger plowed away her confusion.

"You were the one who granted me the time off. It's not like I jaunted to Florida. I was visiting a sick family member. You should have paid me sick time. You're an asshole!" She glared. "*Rolf.*"

Without opening the severance envelope in her damp hand, she tore it to pieces and tossed it into the air. Check confetti littered the shag carpet.

His face and ears reddened and his voice became cruel. "I'm not *doing* anything to you. It's the nature of the industry, kiddo. Look. I've been waiting for you to be authentic, but you haven't grown into the role I envisioned. I mean, where's the beef, Eva? The success of this show is all me."

She wanted to punch his smug face but instead teared up. She had changed her name and her clothes and her attitude for him and it still wasn't good enough. Every time she'd tried to assert herself, he shot her ideas down. Her cheeks burned.

"You never gave me a chance. You can cut me down all you want, but I'm a professional. You should treat me like one."

He flipped a finger toward the basement. "Go check your desk, see if I missed anything."

She hurtled down the stairs, her fury pinned like VU meters in the red. Nothing she could say mattered. Everything she had worked for was gone. All the sacrifices and frustrations of finding a radio job, working overnights, the Lite music, the low pay, having to clean, dealing with the guys and their grossness, the important moments she'd missed with family and friends.

"What the hell?" she said, slamming a desk drawer. "I got out of bed for this?"

She dropped a stapler. It split open, spilling shiny silver spikes onto the concrete floor. She left them lie and stood, pinching the bridge of her nose with her fingers.

Schmidty came poking down the stairs. "What's going on?"

"Yardley let me go."

"Before Christmas? Wow. That doesn't compute. You guys are great together."

"I bet he knew last week. Why the hell didn't he tell me before I came in today?"

"Gosh, Tanya, I'm sorry."

"Well, it's over. I'm not Tanya anymore."

133

The realization sent another jolt of anguish through her body. With shaking hands, in a daze, she scooped up her magic markers, boom box, and tissues, and for good measure, threw in a few office supplies. *If he wanted me to be authentic, why did he make me into someone else: a perky, stylish, and complemental sidekick.*

Eva rushed out the front door, carrying her box and sniveling. There would be no going-away party. No "good luck" card signed by her coworkers. She'd never step inside the station again and wouldn't get to say goodbye to Dottie and Candi and the rest of the gang. As she took a last look back, she slipped on the icy sidewalk, landing on her shoulder. Her box went flying.

"Damn it!" she bawled as she fished Ludwig's photo and her headphones from the snowbank.

In the parking lot, next to her car, the blithe Sunny Sommers stared.

"What are you beaking at?" Eva screamed. Snot dripped from her nose. "You stole my job. What did you do? Give him a frickin' hand job? Well, here's what you can look forward to when he tires of you."

The poor girl had no comeback, just stood there with her pouty mouth hanging open.

Eva got into the car and drove off, swearing like a sailor. On the day of her interview, Yardley said everyone started out with an A—which meant the only direction was down. She had failed. When Yardley assigned her the name, he'd taken away her autonomy. He never gave her the chance to make Tanya her own. Now Tanya was dead. This was the second worst day of her life, almost worse than her father's death because of the humiliation.

"*Ugghhhh!*" she shouted, pounding the wheel, barely able to concentrate on driving. She knew what Artie would say. "I told you to be a teacher."

She fumbled for a cigarette. What did the fresh-faced Sunny Sommers have that she didn't? And what the hell was she going to do now?

PART THREE

24. TELL MAMA ~ SAVOY BROWN

Many months later, Eva sat in the kitchen, tapping a pen on the Formica tabletop. It was a gorgeous September afternoon, and, in a favorable configuration of the planets, she had the entire day free. She decided to write a letter to Coco in Phoenix, then take advantage of the weather and tackle a long put-off project. She put her pen to paper and winced as the radio withdrawal pains resurfaced.

> Sorry I haven't responded to your letters. I hit a rough patch and I'm trying to regroup. I got fired.
> It made no sense. Things were going so well. I feel clueless, not to mention ashamed of how big my head had gotten. Everything changed in an instant.
> How do radio people do it, Coco? I wish I could shrug it off like everyone else. No one outside the business would understand why being fired is a routine thing—an occupational hazard like hearing loss or dead-air nightmares.

The cute stories about getting fired hadn't prepared her for the trauma of losing her identity and the public disgrace of being fired. Tanya Starr wasn't just a mask she could toss in the trash. Eva had spent forty hours a week *being* Tanya.

After the firing, she self-flagellated, trying to figure out what happened as she listened to Sunny titter at Yardley's jokes. Missing him and comparing herself to Sunny only fueled her misery. Then one day she'd tuned in and Yardley was on the air by himself. According to an article in the paper, Sunny had become the sidekick on the Z100 Morning Zoo. The burn gave Eva more satisfaction than anything. She laughed. Yardley would be pissed he had to be on until ten o'clock again.

Artie goes on as if nothing has changed. I feel so alone. He works during the week and drives the four hours to Sheboygan every weekend to help his mom. He hasn't even tried to comfort me through this. Now he's pushing me to get my teaching degree. Maybe he's right, and radio isn't for me anymore.

But I don't know who I am without radio—when I listen, I feel like a nobody, like I'm on the outside looking in. I'm SO jealous of those announcers. Could I put myself through that again? Although it's somewhat of a relief to not have to act like someone else, all I need to do is be myself, if I can figure out who that is. I guess I'll just Keep On Truckin'.

She described the three part-time jobs she'd pieced into a chaotic schedule. Four mornings a week, she waitressed at a truck stop off the Interstate on Highway 16. The early hours were like being on the morning show, and with the ever-changing cast of characters who came into the diner, just as entertaining. Weekday afternoons, she answered phones at Action Insurance, a one-man shop in West Salem. Hugo Acción, the friendly agent, wanted her to work for him full-time so she could sell from the office while he concentrated on procuring lucrative commercial accounts. On weekends, she made cold calls for Derby Vacuum from the back of a dilapidated warehouse in a windowless room, oddly lined with mirrors. The leads came directly from the phone book: make a call, read a script (*Get a free gift valued at over fifty dollars, just for allowing us to demonstrate our wonder vacuum, the Elite Model V!*), get rejected, move the ruler to the next name. People on the other end of the line routinely cussed at her or hung up—also like radio. Her odd jobs were like three dissonant notes that never came together as a chord.

Her life was like a spliced-together master tape: her happy childhood, the bleak time after Pop died, living in the dorms and meeting Faye, her marriage to Artie, being Billie, Lizzy, Tanya, and now, three part-time jobs. Tails out, waiting for the next segment to be recorded.

Eva licked a twenty-two-cent stamp and placed it on the letter. She stared out the window, barely noticing the fall colors. On the radio earlier that day, she'd heard a football player say, "I'm not going to let the moment define me" regarding a dropped pass that cost the game. *Wow.* For months, she had wallowed in guilt and shame. The hardest part to accept? Yardley may have been seeking the opportunity to let her go. Sunny waiting in the wings made it easy.

She got up from the table and searched under the sink for her rubber gloves, her brows furrowed. Before heading to the garage, she donned an apron to protect her clothing from the dirty job ahead: stripping paint from her old piano bench. It was painted a hideous mint green, the color of asylums and school cafeterias. When Eva commented on how ugly it was, her mother had replied, "If you can read, you can learn to do anything. Go to the library and get a book on refinishing furniture."

In the garage, Eva pressed the automatic opener. The door *ka-chunked* as each section folded around the rails. She breathed deeply, savoring the fragrant autumn air. A fresh breeze flung in crisp leaves. She dragged the bench into the light near the door and, using a scraper, scratched at the paint. Underneath the mint, she found a layer of white paint, and under that, a coat of black. She set out newspapers, turpentine, and rags, and pulled the yellow rubber gloves up to her elbows. An old Playtex ad popped into her head. *So flexible, I can pick up a dime!* She laughed. *For all your stripping needs . . .*

The can glugged as she tipped paint stripper onto her rag. She rubbed the liquid on, waited for the paint to bubble up, and scraped harder and harder, imagining Yardley's smug face under the paint.

Writing to Coco had dredged up the old anger. After getting fired, she'd gone a little crazy, plotting all kinds of revenge, from

141

slashing Yardley's tires to punching him in his wrinkled, hangdog face or kicking him in the nuts. Hadn't they been friends?

After a few hours of scraping and wiping, she had cleaned most of the paint from the bench's surface. It would be worth the work. Through streaks of paint, the tawny wood grain looked beautiful. With the perfect stain, it would match the piano from her mom, which they had crammed into their crowded living room.

She wiped her sweaty forehead with the back of a glove, wanting to finish so Artie could park his car in the garage after work. Since having the lung lobectomy, his mother's condition had only deteriorated, and his mood also tanked.

The stench of turpentine overwhelmed her. On the way into the apartment for a glass of water, just as she took off her gloves, the phone rang. She sprinted to answer it before it went to the machine.

"Is this Tanya Starr?" a man asked.

Hearing the name felt like a stab at the heart. Painful, yet a gush of excitement followed. She switched to her radio voice. "Well, it was. I'm Eva."

"I'm Reid Rogers, calling from River Country, an AM/FM combo in Winona," he said. His voice sounded confident, soothing. "A little birdie told me you're looking for a job. We have an opening. Can you meet, say, Wednesday?"

It took a second for her to absorb his words. She scrounged in the junk drawer for a pen. Ludwig rubbed against her legs.

"Wednesday?" She vaguely remembered Yardley talking about a Q106 regarding ratings. Otherwise, Winona was nothing but a green highway sign on the way to Minneapolis.

"Yes," Reid said. "Our FM is one-hundred-thousand watts."

"That's an impressive signal. Is this full time?"

"Well, not at first. Right now, I need a weekend announcer."

"Oh." She dropped the pen. "I'm already working weekends."

"In radio?"

She didn't want to tell him about her shitty job at Derby Vacuum. She kicked at the kitchen cabinet with her toe, scaring off the cat. "It's country?"

"Yes, the FM is."

She finally gets a call, and it's frickin' shit-kicking music.

Reid stepped up his pitch and dangled a carrot. "I regularly need backup for people on vacation and whatnot. I'll have something full time soon, I promise. Possibly on the morning show."

That piqued her interest. Thinking, she tucked the phone between her shoulder and chin while peeling mint green paint from her cuticles. Who was the birdie?

"Anyway, I remember hearing you on the air. You were outstanding."

"Really? Thank you," she said.

The praise fueled her courage, lighting a fire from scattered twigs of hope. People talked excitedly in the background. Reid's voice became muffled. She had already formed a picture of him; tall and fatherly, wearing a fringed powder-blue western-style suit and Stetson hat. He came back on the line.

"Sorry. We're having a staff meeting in a few minutes. I'm unveiling a big contest. So, have you done any copywriting?"

"Yes. PSAs and ad copy. I also helped with commercial logs."

"Sounds like you can do everything. Can you make coffee?" he said with a hearty laugh.

"Of course!" She laughed along, then abruptly stopped. "Does this job involve cleaning?"

"I've never been asked that, but no, dear, we have a service."

"I guess I could talk with you."

"Alrighty," he said, sounding pleased to seal the deal. "We're on Water Street, smack dab in the middle of town. Look for the big sign. Can you start next weekend?"

Her eyebrows scrunched together. "It's not an interview?"

"If you want the job, it's yours. Listen, Dottie is an old friend. She spoke highly of you. Weekends can be your audition for our next full-time spot."

After hanging up, she stood with her mouth hanging open. Like her pop always said, *you never know what's around the corner.*

She bounced back to the garage and put away her refinishing supplies, rehashing the flattering conversation while trying to get her feelings about radio straight—every positive situation tinged with something bad. But Reid's call refreshed the good: the camaraderie, exciting contests, interviewing bands, free tickets. She dragged the bench into the corner, having had enough of the fumes for one day. *It would be cool to say I'm on the air again.*

Later that afternoon, Eva put a load of laundry in the dryer, made a cup of tea, and plopped into a comfy chair. Goldfinches flitted around the tube feeder hanging in front of the window. A brilliant red cardinal took a sunflower seed and flew off to feed his lifelong mate who waited in a bush. Eva's heart melted at the sweetness of the doting gesture. Artie complained about money spent on seeds, but birds were the best entertainment in the world.

Ludwig meowed to go outside. Eva reached down to stroke his fur. "No, kitty. It's dark."

She sipped her tea. Her thoughts wandered back to Q106. Years ago, she wondered if her voice was good enough for radio. What if radio wasn't good enough for her?

That blew her mind. She picked up a pen.

PROS: Better than crummy vacuum sales. Reid seemed nice. Meet new people. CONS: Weekend shifts. Country music. A long drive. More miles on the car.

With Artie gone on weekends, more time spent on the road wouldn't matter. But if she did become full time, would it lead to getting fired? Why should she have to start on the bottom rung? Still, it was better than telemarketing. *Country or not—here I come! Yeehaw!*

25. PHOENIX ~ DAN FOGELBERG

A quaint Mississippi river town, Winona, Minnesota had a population of 25,075 according to the city limits sign. It was half the size of La Crosse. After Eva passed Sugar Loaf Bluff—topped by a surprising rock pinnacle—she turned off Highway 14 toward downtown, passing a park along Lake Winona where the trees sported every shade of red, gold, and orange. She turned up the radio, expecting to hear a corny morning guy who talked in puns, but instead, found Spike Owens to be clever and engaging. When he played "The Devil Went Down to Georgia," she whistled with the fiddle.

At a red light, Eva leaned out the window. The tall façades on the old buildings snuggled wall-to-wall with their neighbors. Fancy cornices revealed the original names. Farmers Insurance, Est. 1901. J.R. Watkins, 1868. When the light changed, she made the turn, spying a vintage Q106 River Country Radio sign on a two-story, fortress-like red sandstone building. She parked her used 1983 VW Golf Mk2 across the street. A string of bells jangled when she entered the sunshiny room.

"Hi, my name is Eva LaVette. I have an appointment," she said to the slim woman with henna-colored hair at the front desk.

"For the secretarial position?" the woman asked.

"Ah, no. I'm meeting with Mr. Rogers."

"I'm sorry, it's been crazy." She took a closer look. "Oh! You're Tanya. Have a seat. I'm Betty."

Eva sat on a hard wooden bench and while she waited, observed the handsome office. Up front, there were two large department-store-sized windows filled with vintage broadcast equipment, including a collection of colorful antique radios. With its brass light fixtures and fancy doorknobs, the place reminded her of a grand state capital or an old bank. Polished granite panels extended part way up the walls hung with Minnesota Broadcasters

Association award plaques. Sunlight warmed the wide-plank floors. She smelled pine and linseed oil as she squirmed on the uncomfortable seat.

At the back, a wide staircase led, she assumed, to the studios. A dapper man with sparkling eyes wearing brown corduroys and an argyle sweater vest came rushing down.

"Tanya? Hi, I'm Reid Rogers. Come on up."

"Call me Eva."

No Stetson hat? Henna Betty waved her through a swinging half-door. Reid put a finger to his temple.

"Wasn't it Little Eva who had a hit called 'The Loco-motion?'"

Eva smiled and nodded. Reid knew his music.

He ushered her into his office at the top of the stairs, pushing aside a pile of papers on a brown and orange plaid couch—colors which matched his sweater vest. Gold records lined the wall behind his desk. Cut crystal trophies lined his shelves. Reid's transistor radio played the country station on low. When Eva sat, a life-sized cutout of Kenny Rogers startled her from the corner.

Reid explained Q106 FM boomed out over a hundred miles in any direction, its sole focus was country music. The AM, established in 1948, served the city of Winona and surrounding agricultural communities and was renowned for its in-depth local news.

"Not an afterthought like many are these days."

"Real reporting?" she asked. No more "rip and read," like B93.

"You bet. The Minneapolis and La Crosse stations don't bother to cover this area."

"What's on the AM the rest of the day?"

"Shows like Paul Harvey mixed in with easy-listening music—Frank Sinatra, Henry Mancini, and whatnot. Unless there's a game. We have rights to the Gophers, Twins, and Vikings."

"Is the FM automated?"

"Not at all. The announcers program their own music," he replied. "Spike Owens is our morning guy. He's followed by Lena Kenworth on mid-days." Reid turned up the radio.

LENA KENWORTH: River Country Radio, Q106, with "Smoky Mountain Rain" from Ronnie Milsap. Did you hear? Quincy Jones and Peggy Lipton have split up. The music producer and his *Mod Squad* wife cited irreconcilable differences. Sources say Lipton's interest in Hatha yoga caused the rift.

Eva smirked. Artie always said the lead singer for Canned Heat sounded like he had a hot potato crammed down his throat. Lena's voice had the same mashed, adenoidal quality.

Reid turned down the radio. "Dusty Miles is on afternoon drive and Danny Davies fills out the daily schedule on evenings."

No overnights! "You're not on the air?"

"No. I fill in, but as GM, I'm both program director and sales manager."

"How do you know Dottie?"

"We go way back," he said. "I worked at B93 in the '70s. It was one of the first FM rock stations."

"I didn't realize Dottie's been there that long."

"Was. She just retired. Emphysema. I told her to quit smoking."

Poor Dottie. Eva glanced at the beckoning pack of Virginia Slims tucked into her purse and vowed not to smoke around Reid. She made a mental note to send Dottie a thank-you card, not just for tipping Reid, but for issuing a new severance check.

"So, what do you think?" he asked, his gray-green eyes twinkling.

Eva gathered her thoughts. "What's the pay?"

"We start out at $5.25."

Same as Derby Vacuum.

"Take your time. I realize what happened at B93 was rough."

"They fired me out of the blue. It felt horrible." Her voice caught. The partially healed wound in her chest became unstitched.

"We're not like that here. We think highly of your experience," Reid said gently. He stood. "Come on. Dusty will show you around."

Dusty Miles was in production and Reid had to make a call, so he sent her to wait in the lobby where the phones were keeping Betty busy. As Eva sat with nothing to do, she craved a smoke. Reid's kindness regarding the situation at B93 had been impressive, but dredging up being fired released bad memories. Here she was, a shiny starlet once again being wooed by the bad boyfriend.

Betty walked over, holding a clipboard.

"Here's an application. I'll need your FCC operator's permit."

Eva had searched everywhere for it that morning. The tan-colored rectangle of shame probably remained tacked to the cork board at B93. She started on the paperwork. Name, address, former supervisor's name . . . *Ugh!* She hated to even think of Yardley St. Martins.

If she accepted the position, she'd need a country name. Tanya Starr was actually perfect. And she did want Yardley to know she was back in the game. He may have bestowed the name, but he couldn't prevent her from using it. She smirked; the taste of revenge sweetened her lips. *I need a new story, though, something of my own creation.*

Eva finished the paperwork. She tapped her pencil on the form. The new Tanya Starr: *Formerly Tanya Montana, the daughter of a roper and a rodeo clown, Tanya set fashion on its head in the mid-70s with her cowboy glam style. Briefly married to Ringo Starr, she now runs Starr Bright Equine Sanctuary.*

"Billie Soul?"

Eva blinked, not believing her eyes. It couldn't be him. No glasses—he must have gotten contacts. His tawny feathered hair had been transformed into a permed mullet. The last she'd heard, Dustin worked at an NPR station in Minneapolis.

"*You're* Dusty Miles? What a fun surprise!"

He came over and gave her a gigantic hug. "My god. You're Tanya Starr? Or should I say, Tanya Starr is *you*? I never would have guessed—you changed your voice. Wait, I'm confused. I thought Tanya was Bart Starr's daughter."

"That was a joke."

"A good one. Wow, you look great!"

He stepped back, smiling like he'd nailed the perfect intro to his favorite song. Dustin, or Dusty, had acquired a twang, a slight southern drawl which suited him. He took her by the hand and escorted her up the stairs into the broadcast area before she had time to ask questions. Upstairs, the wooden floor creaked as they walked into the center of the massive room.

"In its previous life the building was a Masonic Hall," he said.

In the middle, six mismatched desks sat in two rows. The alley side was brightened by high windows. On the other side, a kitchenette sported vending machines and two small tables. Bumper stickers and music posters covered the walls, one featuring Reba McEntire in a low-cut emerald gown with a revealing leg slit. At the back, the transmitter and other broadcast equipment formed a wall. The production, AM, and FM studios were located behind it. Dusty took her hands and held them out.

"I can't believe it's you," they said at the same time.

He dropped her hands as a balding gentleman in a trench coat dashed in from a side door. The man hung his jacket on a chair, sat, and started banging on a typewriter.

"That's Sanders. Always on the trail of some hot story."

When the bathroom door burst open, Eva and Dusty turned to see a man with wild, gray, wiry hair sticking out like question marks from his round head. Small in stature, he looked more like a horse racing jockey than a disc jockey. He stepped out, waving his fingers in front of his nose. "Whew, don't go in there for a while!"

"Tanya Starr, Spike Owens." Dusty shot the man a triumphant look. "Tanya and I went to college together. We were partners in production class."

Spike stepped back and bowed, greeting her with a velvety, inflective voice. Eva laughed before curtsying to avoid shaking his hand.

"Well, I'll be. Welcome to our humble radio station, my dear lady. Bart Starr's daughter."

"Oh, no. That was just a rumor Yardley St. Martins made up."

"You're not here to take my job, are you?" He laughed before whispering behind his hand. "Beware of this guy. He'll steal your M&Ms."

"Hey, now." Dusty punched him in the arm. "You're the candy swiper."

"Anyway, I hope you'll join us, Tanya," Spike said. "You had quite the popular morning show. My biggest competition."

Eva couldn't hide her look of surprise. Spike turned and ambled over to his desk, digging into the breast pocket of his army-style, camouflage shirt for a cigarette.

"Let's check out production," Dusty said.

They entered the studio nearest to the kitchen area. The tapes were as well-organized as the production studio in college. Through the window, a deeply tanned, skinny woman with bleached hair around the age of fifty leaned on the counter in front of the board, picking at her fingernails.

"That's Lena. So, what have you been doing since B93?"

"Since they 'let me go?' Waitressing and working in an office."

"Really? That's tragic. You are so funny and smart."

Her hand covered a coy smile.

"I didn't tune in the rest of the day," he said. "But your morning show? You guys cracked me up." He leaned toward her and whispered. "I had a crush on you."

How many other men liked Tanya Starr? She reveled in a sense of well-being that had eluded her for ages.

150

Next door in the FM studio, Lena rolled up to the microphone. They watched her talk.

"I never expected Lena to look like *that*."

Dusty touched Eva's arm. "Don't get me wrong. Maybe that's why I didn't know it was you. I thought Tanya was big and tall—like your father, Bart." He grinned.

"Very funny." She smiled. "But I get it. Your cousin Coco and I have talked about that. When you only hear a voice, it's like being blind—your imagination kicks in and you get a visual impression."

"Yeah." Dusty stroked his jaw. "When I hear someone who can sing—like, sing beautifully—it makes me wonder if we really are connected to angels. It gives me hope for humanity."

Dusty wasn't just a pretty boy. Eva inspected his now-mature face. The dimple in his chin had deepened. Crinkles had formed at the corners of his eyes which matched his faded denim shirt, blue and sparkling like the ocean. Bedroom eyes. He pointed to a rack laden with albums.

"Here's our generic jingle collection."

"Generic? I thought all jingles were custom."

"These are industry-based. They have tag lines that rhyme." He sang. "*We're your hometown bank. We've got you to thank. Or We're your friendly hardware store. Tools, supplies and so much more.*"

She laughed at his singing. "Is there one 'For all your roast beef needs?'"

"I don't think so," he said with a perplexed look.

"I'm joking. You seem to love this place."

"Yeah, I dig it. Reid is great. We're involved in everything—from county fairs and parades to the Great Mississippi Mosquito Festival."

She put a hand to her mouth and giggled.

Reid burst in, waving a script. "Sorry, guys, I need to cut a new intro for the market report. The cart broke."

Eva and Dusty hurried out of production and into the now-smoky office. Every desk held an ashtray; smoke ribboned up to join a thick cloud trapped at the ceiling.

Under the bright windows, a beefy guy wearing a checkered jacket sat at a cluttered desk. He gestured excitedly while talking on the phone. Near the transmitter, an older fellow holding a pipe between his teeth tinkered with equipment. Spike sat at his desk, feet up, staring off into space, blowing smoke rings, most likely thinking of bits for his morning show. At a desk close to the studios, the trench-coat man typed intently while chewing a yellow pencil.

"Sanders, this is Tanya Starr," Dusty said.

The newsman nodded, but his eyes never left the story. "Good to meet you," he said, talking around the pencil, his voice clipped. "Sorry. There was a fire at the foundry."

"Was anyone hurt? My friend works there." Dusty leaned in to see what Sanders had typed.

"A fireman was treated for smoke inhalation. Everyone else is safe," Sanders said, pecking at keys.

"Thanks, Sanders. Let's leave him to it."

Dusty led Eva to the sports desk where the muscle-bound guy in the loud coat was now reading the paper, his sleeves too short for his hairy arms. *Trevor Travis*, according to his brushed-nickel desk plate which sat next to an overflowing ashtray.

"Hey there," Trevor said as he reached out a beefy hand. "Reid told me we might be graced with the famous Tanya Starr. I hope you decide to join us. We all saw your nomination in *La Crosse Magazine* last year."

His rough voice rasped like sandpaper.

"That's nice of you to say." She pulled her shoulders back as she shook his hand. It seemed like everyone had listened to her at B93.

"I know it seems hokey, small-town radio and that, but we have fun. You'll have to join our softball team. We only have three girls." Trevor counted on his fingers. "Betty, Lena, and my sister-in-law Annabelle." He shoved Dusty, laughing. "He's the home-run king."

"Yeah, right, Trevor." Dusty bumped Eva's arm with his. "Honestly, I'm happy if I get to first base."

Her face got hot.

Trevor's phone extension lit. He had to take the call.

"Let's check out the studios," Dusty said, whisking her past the broadcast equipment and into the bright FM studio.

Dusty shut the door to block out the office noise. His tone became reserved, a lot less friendly than how he acted with everyone else.

"Hey, Lena. This is Tanya Starr."

Obviously taken aback, Lena sat up straight, said hello, and quickly put on her headphones. She eyed Eva suspiciously as she held a finger to her lips. "*Shh* . . ."

She opened the mic and talked. They held their breath until she finished the break. Eva noticed a small poster and read it out loud. "*LOST: Wedding Ring. Somewhere in the station. Call Danny.*"

"Oh, my, that's a peculiar story," Lena said, perking up. She crossed spots off the log as they played. "Danny, our evening guy, lost his wedding ring. He's frantic. I heard his wife's divorcing him."

Behind her back, Dusty rolled his eyes. "Ahh, no. Not true, Lena."

"Where are all the records?" Eva asked.

"The top songs are recorded onto cart because we play them so much. The record library is behind you."

Under a window with a view of the parking lot, a few thousand albums were stored in custom-built wooden bins.

Lena spun around and started lecturing in her nasal voice. "Always return them to the right spot. Artists are filed by their last name. For example, Ronnie Milsap is under 'M.' Obviously, if the band name starts with 'The,' we ignore the 'The.'"

Eva stifled an urge to snicker. Dusty waved the remark away. She followed him out. When the door swung shut, they burst out laughing.

"I know. She's a trip," he said.

Lena had worked at Q106 for over a decade, he explained. She and her husband were cranberry farmers. The midday shift allowed her to do morning and evening chores. Her nephew Wes, whom she had gotten started in the radio business and was very proud of, also worked at the station. He was a regular on Saturday night.

They entered the AM studio. Its control board faced into the FM and had similar rotating cart racks, but no records. Through the window, Lena picked up a magazine.

"Sanders will be in soon," Dusty said, pointing at the clock on the board. "The midday report spans the entire noon hour."

"Is there really that much news in Winona?"

"We report every fender-bender, kitchen fire, lost pet, and obituary."

"Obituaries?"

"Right out of the local paper. We have an arrangement." He pretended to read, *"John Doe went to heaven on Tuesday. He's survived by his wife Jane, his twelve children, and Rex, his dog."*

"Oh, the dog has a name, but the kids don't?"

"We only name survivors on a slow news day." Dusty smiled.

Sanders came rushing into the studio. He arranged his stories on the counter, and as they left, donned his headphones.

Eva followed Dusty to his desk.

"Pull up a chair," he said, lighting a cigarette with a fancy silver monogrammed lighter. As he flipped the lid, it made a satisfying clink. Eva's fingers twitched. "Want one?"

"Oh, no, thanks. I'll wait." She'd had her first cigarette with Dusty on the roof of the J. Wayne Communications building.

He rocked playfully in his chair, lifted his chin, and blew a plume of smoke toward the nicotine-stained ceiling.

"I can't believe you're here," he said, his marine-blue eyes shining.

A sudden wave of pleasure surged through her.

Just then, an old man in a proper suit carrying a briefcase came in from the back and clomped up the stairs. He sped to his desk, picking up the phone before he even sat.

"Our sales department. Reuben is seventy—he's been here more than forty years." He looked at his watch. "Well, Tanya, I need to grab some lunch. Call me if you need help deciding on the job."

This was the moment of commitment. Would she step through the radio portal? Q106 gave off good vibes. Would the third time be charmed? Everything Reid and Dusty had said enticed her to say yes. And no one had called her "darlin'" or "kiddo." Yes, she wanted in on the radio club. *But this time, I need to be myself. I will not get lost in Tanya. Although, I'll need to pretend to like country music.*

Eva tapped on Reid's door. After reminding him of his promise for the next full-time position, she agreed to start the following weekend. Knowing Dustin—Dusty—was there made it feel right.

At home, Eva checked the answering machine. Only one message, Faye teasing that she and Dwayne had big news. They wanted to meet for a fish fry on Friday night. Eva scribbled a note to Artie, asking if he could wait until Saturday to go and see his mom. She called Derby Vacuum to resign—at least she extended the courtesy of a phone call. Most people simply failed to show.

26. TOO LATE FOR GOODBYES ~ JULIAN LENNON

On Friday night, Faye waved Eva and Artie to a corner booth at the Bodega Deli in downtown La Crosse. "Over here," Faye yelled above the clamor of customers chatting and dishes clattering.

The girls hugged and the guys clasped hands while leaning in for a shoulder bump. Artie did a double take at Dwayne's closely shorn head. "I haven't seen your hair that short since first grade," he said.

Dwayne pretended to primp.

"Wow, Eva, your hair grows so fast," Faye said.

"I know. It so frizzy, it's back in the braid." Eva tried to see Faye's stomach. "What's the big news? A baby?"

Faye doubled over, laughing. Dwayne slapped the table.

"No," he said. "I got this spiffy haircut for an interview. We're moving to San Jose for my new job: a UNIX system admin."

Artie stopped with his beer in midair. Eva almost choked on her drink. California was two thousand miles away. Her mind flashed to grade school when the teacher said the Golden State could break off and be swallowed by the Pacific, but she refrained from commenting about earthquakes and fault lines. "What'll we do without you?" she asked quietly.

"It's not like we'll never see each other again." Dwayne summoned the waiter and ordered another pitcher of Old Style.

Artie hadn't uttered a word since the announcement. He had taken the news about Eva's new job cooly, agreeing it was better than doing vacuum sales for Derby. For a moment, all four of them sat in silence, surrounded by the din of the restaurant. "Tell me about the job," he said flatly.

"I'll be installing software and hardware, maintaining servers, troubleshooting. . . They're paying for our move."

"Can you believe it?" Faye said. "There's just one thing—"

The waiter appeared, pulling a pen and pad from his apron.

"We haven't looked at the menu," Faye said. She sipped her beer. He left, looking peeved. "We need a favor."

Eva reached across the table to grab her hand. "Anything. You know that."

"Will you take Ditzy?" Their sleek black tuxedo kitty with white paws, nose, and bib.

"How old is he?" Artie asked. "I'm just thinking about the costs."

"He's five," Faye said. "We'll pay his bills, and we'll leave a big bag of food."

Eva gave Artie a questioning look. At least they'd have a piece of their friends to hold. He nodded his approval.

Faye sighed. "I am so relieved. I know you guys will take good care of him. With the uncertainty of where we'll live, and what'll happen if we have children—"

"You can't have kids and cats?" Eva asked, leaning on the table.

"Dwayne's grandma says cats steal the breath from babies."

"That's an old wives' tale."

Faye rolled her eyes. She reached into her purse and presented Eva with a hand-drawn invitation on orange paper. "Tell me you guys can come to our Halloween party. It'll be the last big bash before we move. I know it's your favorite holiday, Eva. You could roll your hair up like Princess Leia. I'm going as a cat—a sexy one."

"I'll be a jazz cat." Eva wondered what happened to her mom's granny glasses, the pair she wore during her Billie Soul days. They'd make a good costume along with her dad's ruby beret and the electric blue velvet jacket she'd found at Goodwill.

Faye chattered about the fantastic weather in California. Eva sat back and took in the noisy restaurant, Faye's crazy laugh, Dwayne's bristly hair, and Artie raising his glass in yet another toast. Swept up in feelings of nostalgia, like a reverse déjà vu or a time warp, she saw their youth through the eyes of an old woman and tried to grasp the moment. But it was futile. The night slipped away.

Faye and Dwayne's Halloween party should have been a joyous farewell. As most of their furniture was on its way to California, Eva sat on a pillow on the floor, nursing an apple cider margarita with Ditzy in her lap. Through rose-tinted glasses, she watched her friends hug everyone goodbye. An empty, hollow feeling gnawed at her insides. How would she and Artie survive without the glue of their best friends? Artie's relationship with Dwayne alone spanned twenty years, from Little League to varsity baseball at Sheboygan South. Eva and Faye hadn't found each other until college, where they'd been inseparable since freshman year.

The drink tasted funny; she set it down.

Later, while helping clean up plates and beer bottles, she asked Faye how she could give up her daycare center and just up and move because of Dwayne's job. A painful look crossed Faye's lovely face for a moment before she smiled and said, "When you love someone, their dreams become yours."

That should be a two-way street, Eva thought.

A few weeks later, in the car on the way home from work, Eva sang along with the radio. The drive from Winona to her apartment in La Crosse was longer than Reid had said, but the ride gave her a chance to wind down. That morning, he'd called to see if she'd sub for Dusty, who had laryngitis. She saved the day, but after the high-energy afternoon drive shift, couldn't wait to get through the door to kick off her new cowboy boots.

As she navigated the winding roads along the Mississippi, she pressed the high beams off with her foot to see through the thickening fog. Closer to home, Eva swerved to miss a dead skunk. Unlike most people, Eva liked the smell of skunk, not that she wanted them to get hit. Rain must have washed the smell away.

She steered into the alley as sleet began to hit the windshield, feeling lucky to have gotten home before the roads got slick.

Eva's heart swelled with affection for the station and her new coworkers. Once inside the apartment, she dropped her keys on the hall table where Artie had left the mail. A postcard picturing high-rises and palm trees sat on top. Ludwig rubbed her legs as she read.

> *I made it to KIIS-FM, LaVette! Livin' the dream–it's totally tubular. Come visit me in LA.*

"Oh my gosh! Coco made it!"

Across the room, the answering machine blinked. The message was from Artie. He'd picked up bread, lettuce, and bananas. He forgot to get cat food. Again. In the kitchen, she shook the nearly empty bag.

"Din-din!"

Ludwig came tearing into the kitchen. He crunched away.

"Ditzy!"

She flipped on the light in the bedroom where he liked to nestle in the pillows. Had Artie let him out? She checked outdoors.

"He'll come when he gets hungry," she said as she emptied the last of the food into their bowls.

Later, during *L.A. Law*, she fell sound asleep on the couch.

Artie came in at midnight. "Eva, it's late," he said, as he sat on the edge. "You should go to bed."

"You're home? Sheesh, I've been asleep a while." She pushed the hair off her forehead and sat. "How was work?"

"The same. I'm starving."

"I made a mushroom omelet."

Artie went into the kitchen. He heated his food in the microwave while Eva shook off her grogginess.

"Artie, did you put Ditzy outside?"

"Yeah. Why?"

"How many times did we talk about this? He's not used to it here," she scolded. "Poor baby is probably starving."

"Here, kitty-kitty!" he called out the door.

Despite her irritation, she snickered at hearing him use his high, pet-friendly voice.

"Can you keep checking? I've got to hit the hay."

"I will. I'll be up for a while."

On Friday morning, Ditzy was still missing. They went door to door. The upstairs neighbor said he'd seen something furry squashed on the street. Dread spilled over Eva like a dark stain. She thought back to her drive home from work earlier in the week. What if it hadn't been a skunk? They thanked the neighbor and hurried out to the road. Thick clouds hung low as a winter storm gathered.

"It was over here," Eva shouted.

They searched through the gutter of both sides of the street while cars raced by. Icy sleet bounced off the road. She pulled up her hood. Car lights flashed in her eyes, blinding her.

"Nothing on this side but trash," Artie yelled across the road.

A delivery truck rumbled past, showering them in a cloud of mist. Abruptly, the unmistakable stench of decomposition hit. Her throat constricted. Matted black fur and white paws. She moaned.

"Oh, no. Sweet little kitty."

Tears rolled down her face, mixing with the sleet. She found a stick and turned a flattened Ditzy over. White maggots squirmed. Artie waited for a car to pass. He loped across the street.

"He's roadkill."

"You think, Artie?" *What a numbskull.* "Poor Ditzy. Why did you let him out?" she asked, blubbering. With no tissue at hand, she wiped her nose on the sleeve of her parka.

"I don't know. We let Ludwig go outside."

"Ditzy has always been an indoor cat. Faye trusted us. How many times did we talk about this?"

"Geez, Eva." He held out his hands. "I made a mistake."

"Damn it, Artie. You're such an idiot."

She pushed him away, wanting to strangle him, and walked home in a huff through the stinging sleet. *He can't even keep a cat alive or make his own dinner.* No way would she consider bringing a baby into their lives.

27. MORE THAN THIS ~ ROXY MUSIC

Eva stood in the parking lot at the Red Owl, microphone in hand. A gust of wind kicked up as the River Country news helicopter approached. She adjusted her horn-rimmed glasses and smoothed her long, glossy hair as her coworkers, Johnny Fever and Venus Flytrap, handed coupons to the clamoring crowd. Overhead, Sanders leaned out of the chopper, chucking frozen turkeys. A bird missile hit Reuben, the old salesman, square on the head. He collapsed into a heap. Eva screamed to Dustin back at the station, "Abort! Abort!"

Loud yelling woke Eva from her dream. The couple upstairs was having a row. Doors slammed. A car squealed away. All became quiet. She dragged herself out of the empty bed. Her shift started in a few hours, and she had a lot of laundry to do, plus she wanted to practice and memorize "Clair de Lune," the piece her father loved.

Artie was in Sheboygan, celebrating Thanksgiving with his family. She was still mad at him for sending Ditzy to the happy hunting grounds. He said if Faye and Dwayne stayed in California, there was no reason to tell them and make them sad. Reluctantly, she agreed, yet when he had reached out for her, she pulled away.

Later, Eva dressed for work—a fringed suede jacket from Faye added a chic layer to her denim skirt and red plaid western shirt. The weird WKRP in Cincinnati-infused dream flashed through her mind. Without a doubt, she preferred Q106 over doing phone sales for Derby Vacuum, but there was nothing she could do to force a full-time opportunity . . . unless she did something underhanded, like sending Lena's audition tapes to other stations. She chuckled at the thought as she put on her boots.

At work, a memo from the National Association of Broadcasters addressed Headphone Creep, the tendency for announcers to keep turning up the volume. They should have addressed it to Donn; his cans were always maxed out. He'd be deaf before he was forty.

After her first break, Reid called. When he mentioned Dusty would be taking a week-long vacation, she volunteered.

He hesitated. "Danny or I will do it."

Eva frowned. "Reid, you said I did a good job when he was out with laryngitis. I even talked sports with Trevor."

"You did." He cleared his throat. "But you can't follow Lena."

"Because she'd be threatened?" According to Wes, Lena's nephew, she thought Eva was gunning for the midday slot.

Reid laughed. "We don't position women DJs back-to-back."

"I don't understand. Hold on." As she segued into her next record, she remembered Yardley's dumb rule about not playing two female artists in a row. *Stupid. It was the '80s, not the '50s.*

"I'm not sure what the logic is," he explained. "There are certain traditions passed down from generations of programmers and whatnot. Perhaps we should revisit the policy."

She grasped for another way to be helpful. "Well, if Danny fills in for Dusty, I could do evenings."

"That'll work."

After hanging up, Eva took note of the positive things he'd said. Taking compliments to heart was an assignment from the self-help book she'd been reading. After becoming more mindful, she'd noticed how often she felt afraid to express her truth.

Reality struck: if a daypart adjacent to Lena's was forbidden, the only full-time shift available to Eva was nights. Reid had hosed her; there were few options for advancement after all. The yoke of being female fell on her narrow shoulders. She slapped her fist on the counter. Motivated to create a new audition tape, she threaded a blank reel onto the Akai deck. Maybe it was time to quit working three jobs and try for something full-time in La Crosse. If Yardley had blacklisted her, she would have heard about it.

She used her toes to wheel the chair over to the bins and found Nancy Sinatra's "These Boots Are Made for Walkin'."

163

###

The next day, Eva settled onto the couch with a basket of fresh laundry. She dialed Coco in Los Angeles. They made small talk about the weather—winter approaching in Wisconsin, beach weather by day and sweater weather by night in California.

"I'm totally wired," Coco said. "We hung out at this club in Pasadena called Vermie's last night and saw this incredible singer named Melissa Etheridge. Mark my words, she's gonna be big."

"That's so cool! I'm jealous. But I have some news. You'll never guess who I'm working with." After they discussed the incredible coincidence of Eva discovering Coco's cousin at Q106, she told her friend about Reid and his no women back-to-back rule.

"It's bogus, but it happened to me, too," Coco said. "I got called out for playing Heart followed by Stevie Nicks."

Eva let out an exasperated sigh. "Hello?!? Equal rights for women."

"Right? Heart's a band. I asked where the line was, how many female members in a group made it count as a female artist. He couldn't answer that."

"It's like going back in time. I just learned that in the '70s, Ms. magazine published a story about sexual harassment in the workplace, and it got banned in supermarkets."

"That figures."

Eva tucked a warm towel around her cold feet. "So, what should I do? My first inclination was to burn Reid's stupid Kenny Rogers cutout in effigy on the front sidewalk."

"Don't get caught," Coco said.

"It's a rhetorical blaze. I'm not going to burn bridges." Like how she'd ditched Gateguard. Or called Yardley an asshole to his face.

"Put them on the spot at the next staff meeting. Suggest an all-girl artist weekend."

164

"Good one. I will, just to see their faces." There was a pause in the conversation while their gears turned.

"What's that midday chick's story?" Coco asked.

"Lena? She's got an awful voice. She's lazy and paranoid. She accused me of using her headphones. I never touched them."

"Can you slip some cyanide into her Jolly Good?"

"Hard core, Coco!" Eva sipped her tea, imagining gossipy Lena with dead XX's for eyes. Ludwig jumped into the laundry basket, purring and kneading. Eva shooed him out and began to fold towels with the phone tucked into her neck.

"You can go anywhere, LaVette. You've got experience."

Eva sighed at the thought of starting over. "I could mention to Wes or Lena that I've got tapes and résumés out. They'll spread it like wildfire."

A doorbell rang on Coco's end. "That's my pizza. Hold on a minute."

The receiver clunked. Eva picked cat hair from a washcloth.

"I'm back."

"What kind did you get, Coco?"

"A sausage and pepperoni with double cheese and a Hawaiian pizza." Coco talked with her mouth full. "Oh, this is funny. Call me Raquel."

"What? Like Raquel Welch?"

"Yes. Before me, they'd been promoting a new DJ named Raquel Rockwell, but she never showed up. This all started after they fired a different chick—the PD said he'd rather listen to dead air than her."

"That's so mean! This business is flippin' nuts."

"Right? So don't get worked up. Keep your head down. Do your best." Exactly what Eva's pop would say. "You'll have the last laugh when you're on a morning show in Chicago."

"Or middays in Minneapolis."

"That's right. I forgot about that," Coco said. "In radio, things change on a dime. At Desert Rock in Phoenix, the day they canned me—"

"You were fired?" Eva sat up in her chair, knocking over the stack of towels at her feet.

"I didn't mention that? Yeah, everyone was. Format change. The GM escorted the morning guy out of the building during his shift. He'd been with the station for twelve years and they didn't even let him get the stuff from his desk. Some schmuck just out of school took his place. For half as much, I bet. I mean, gag me."

"How do you deal with everything, Coco?"

"It's hard. I have learned to put my foot down and ask for what I want. You're a bit of a pushover, LaVette."

"I guess I am," Eva said. "Maybe I should start lifting weights."

"There you go. So, what else is new? How's your old man?"

"I am so fed up with him. We took in Faye's cat after they moved. He let it outside and it got run over. Dead." Eva's eyes welled up.

"Oh, shit."

"I am so mad. Honestly, I hate him right now. But I'm stuck with him. Speaking of, he's going to be pissed when he sees this phone bill. I better let you go."

"Hang in there LaVette," Coco said.

Eva grabbed Artie's clean Wisconsin sweatshirt from the laundry basket and chucked it toward his guitar collecting dust in the corner.

Eva arrived at work on a mild March Saturday morning and found Dusty Miles smoking on the back steps. Icicles melted in the noonday sun on either side of the stairs. His eyes were puffy.

"Did you get locked out?" she asked.

"No, I had to get some air."

She removed her mittens and looked at her watch.

"It's okay, Tanya, I'm playing 'My Home's in Alabama.' Six minutes, twenty-seven seconds." He snuffed his cigarette on the concrete.

When the two of them were in the studio, she dragged a stool over to the bins and began to pull records. Facing the board with his headphones on, Dusty let out a long, miserable sigh.

"We loved with a love that was more than love," he said, before turning on the mic.

After his break, he turned to face Eva and confessed. Jasmine, his girlfriend of two years, had called—while he was on the air—to say she'd "met someone." Eva wondered what was wrong with the woman, besides being cruel, as he was a catch.

"I'm so sorry, Dusty. I can tell you're wrecked."

"Yeah." He gathered his things and turned the chair over to Eva. He sat at the guest mic with his chin in his hands, looking dejected. "At least I found out she's a cheater now, not later."

"That must feel awful."

Eva wished she could console him. Give him a hug or rub his back. She decided to bake him a batch of M&M cookies.

When she took the air chair, he sat at the guest mic. She flipped to the P section in her country music notebook. While she talked over the ending of a song, she gave him a sidelong glance.

TANYA: That's Charley Pride, "Roll On Mississippi" on Q106. Did you know Charley pitched for a farm team in Fond du Lac? He wanted to be a professional baseball player but became a musician instead. Now, he has fifty Top Ten hits! I'm Tanya Starr. Coming up next, it's Rosanne Cash on River Country Radio.

Eva started a commercial. She slid the headphones off and moved her braid to one side.

"You know your stuff, Tanya."

She handed him her notebook labeled Tanya's Country Book of Bits, hand-doodled with colored markers. Over the winter, she'd begun to compile flavorful artist facts and stories.

"I can tell you the name of Freddy Fender's pet poodle or how Bill Monroe got started on the mandolin." She'd leave it to the lazy DJs to blather on about celebrity gossip. Music was her shtick; she would stick to it. She dropped the needle on a record. Doubting its placement, re-cued it.

"Careful, there. You're going to burn the record," he said.

"But I don't want it to *wow*."

"The last thing the listeners want to hear is cue burn."

After she segued from a promo into the song, they listened. "Hmm," he said. "This one's a little punk. It doesn't fit the format."

"But it's Rosanne Cash."

"I'm serious, Tanya. I don't think we should play that track."

After listening for a few seconds, Eva agreed. "Pink Bedroom" wasn't country. She faded it down and segued into a song by Marty Stuart.

"Hand it over. I'll make a note." He stuck a small piece of masking tape on the back of the album cover and wrote, DO NOT PLAY next to the track, his writing neat and distinctive.

"In college, I found an album with a stripe of nail polish blocking a track," Eva said.

"To permanently damage a record? That's outrageous."

"It's blasphemous!" she riffed, roaring with laughter.

"Did you just snort, Tanya?" He bent forward, laughing, holding his stomach. The twinkle came back into his eye.

"I'm happy to see you smile, Dusty Miles." *And forget about Jasmine.* She smiled back. Was she flirting? She'd forgotten how delicious it felt. A wave of guilt crashed over her.

He gathered his things. "I've gotta book. If you want the afternoon to go fast, ask for requests."

It worked. The calls poured in. She dedicated songs to folks in all directions, in the process, learning how to pronounce names of the surrounding towns: Nodine, Donehower, Eyota, and Minneiska.

It was a great afternoon. Until a more sinister call came in. "This is the operator," said a mechanical voice. "You have a collect call from an inmate at New Lisbon Correctional Facility. The prisoner will now state his name."

A man's voice dropped in. "Hiram Tenny."

"This call may be monitored. To accept this call. . ." the recording droned.

Eva slammed the receiver, pushing away so fast the chair jetted out under her. She spilled forward, bashing her jaw on the counter. After picking herself up, she brushed off her jeans and called Reid. She steadied her voice.

"An inmate called. Collect. I hung up."

"Good girl. Don't accept collect calls. What prison?"

"New Lisbon."

"Really? That's quite a distance!" he said. "I had no idea our signal reached that far. Between the bluffs and coulees, why, there must be a direct funnel from us to them."

"What if he calls back?" When she felt her chin, blood wet her fingers.

"Just hang up."

"Yeah, but—"

"There's nothing to worry about, Tanya. Only the good ones get radio privileges." Reid laughed. "Seriously, we've never had an incident. But you've given me an idea. I'm going to send Reuben down there. Maybe he can pick up some new advertisers in New Lisbon."

29. THE RAIN SONG ~ LED ZEPPELIN

Eva stood at the studio window while Gary Morris sang "Leave Me Lonely." Layers of heavy fog obscured the dwindling snowbanks at the edge of the parking lot. The mist glommed onto the backs of old buildings and funneled into puddles in the alley. For her, St. Patrick's Day was just another day.

Eva hadn't seen her husband all week. Over the winter, and especially since the Ditzy incident, their marriage had slid further downhill like a toboggan careening toward a cliff. During their last argument, he'd accused her of wanting their relationship to be perfect, an impossible goal. What was wrong with striving for excellence?

"Ahem."

Eva almost jumped out of her boots. The station engineer stood in the doorway holding a cart machine, an unlit pipe in his mouth.

"Geez. You scared the crap out of me," she said.

"I'm heading home."

She hadn't known he was there in the first place. Usually, the smell of cherry tobacco wafting up from his workshop gave him away. He turned and left.

At the top of the hour, she played a legal ID and segued into "Broken Lady" by the Gatlin Brothers. It was only two o'clock. Four more hours. She cued the next record.

Looking for answers in her marriage, Eva had started listening to an advice show on the AM. The kindhearted Dr. Adore preached action: be brave, take initiative, and behave the way you want to be treated. So, she had done something she knew Artie wouldn't. She gave him a cute card (UR2Good2BTrue) and invited him out for a romantic Valentine's dinner, hinting strongly he needed to step it up in the love department. Despite having picked up convenience store flowers, he'd acted sullen and aloof the entire evening. On the way home, she'd lost it. The night ended with her Valentine shredded to bits in the trash.

After that disaster, she needed a change. Too chicken to shave her hair or dye it purple, she purchased a jumbo curling iron and coconut oil conditioner that promised *From Frizz to Fabulous!* To her surprise, it worked. Her long hair flowed in silky waves instead of its usual mess.

Eva stroked her tresses at the record bins. The night before, she had tried calling both Coco and Faye, leaving cheery messages on their answering machines. Feeling sorry for herself, she ate a family-sized bag of generic potato chips while watching a rerun of *Don Kirshner's Midnight Special* which featured a smoking performance of "Can I Tell You" by Kansas. Now, her stomach felt queasy.

She flipped through albums. *Hmm.* No country artists started with Q, U, or Z, a tidbit for her notebook.

"Whoops." Someone had filed Steve Earle's *Guitar Town* under S. Lena would flip. "You naughty boy, Steve. Get back in your spot."

Using a noisy hand vac, Eva sucked stubborn dust balls from between the albums. She turned it off just in time to hear her song ending. Nimbly, she jumped into the air chair, avoiding dead air by a second. The fake smile dropped off her face as soon as she finished talking. While commercials played, she cued up a Randy Travis song and wrinkled her nose. "Here's a little ditty for those of you with a low music IQ," she said in a judgmental voice. But the facts were undeniable; people liked music they could sing mindlessly to, and the guy did sell millions of records.

The side door slammed. The engineer? She couldn't see past the equipment. She ran into the hallway, crashing into Dusty chest-to-chest as he turned the corner.

"Sheesh. You scared the hell out of me," she said.

"Sorry. Have you seen my yellow raincoat? I'm heading over to Schott's to rake the courts."

"Volleyball? It's still technically winter."

"The Spring Thaw Tourney. It's early this year. It'll be nippy."

"There's a slicker on the coat rack." Dusty had mentioned Schott's Tavern before. "Do you work there as well?"

"No, no," he said, laughing. "The owner is an old friend." Taking Eva by surprise, he grabbed her arms, holding them out. "You changed your hair, Tanya. I dig it!"

"Thanks," she said. She could only hold his gaze for a second.

He smiled. "You look so pretty. It floats around your face like a cloud."

Eva pivoted. Heat rushed into her cheeks.

"Come to the bar and have a green beer. The gang will be there."

"Maybe," she said, stepping back, wondering if she should go. Artie was at his mom's again. Ludwig wouldn't miss her.

While he looked for his coat, Eva sped back to the oasis of the studio. During the break, she stuttered, a rarity. A few minutes later, he appeared at the door, holding his raincoat. With her foot, Eva moved albums she'd brought from home from his field of view.

"How do you like the new Randy Travis song?" he asked.

"It's so cheesy. Such forced rhyming and the pun is lame." Eva glanced at Dusty's slim body and long legs. She got the urge to reach out and touch the dimple in his cleft chin.

"I prefer the classics," he said, leaning casually on the frame. "You played 'My Tennessee Mountain Home' earlier, I love Dolly. Say, if you need a good song for your Oldies selection, check out 'Takin' Me Too Soon' by Blake Hale."

She jotted the title on scratch paper. "When did that come out?"

"Sixty-nine, I think?" He sang, affecting a southern drawl. "*I went to jail for life, for somethin' that I done. I left behind my wife, a daughter, and a son. Forgive me, dear, for dying, death row's takin' me too soon. I assailed, and I failed. Life's takin' me too soon.*"

172

Eva burst out laughing as his vocals were significantly higher than his rumbly radio voice. "That's impressive. You stayed in tune. Sit. I'll put you on the guest mic."

"No, no, I'm leaving." His eyes locked onto hers. "We'd have fun together on a morning show." He said goodbye and hurried off.

Eva took a request for "Rednecks, White Socks and Blue Ribbon Beer." Dangerous as it was, she worked ahead and pulled commercials for the next two hours, patting the plastic carts into neat towers. It seemed like eons ago when she'd knocked Donn's carts to the floor. Before Artie's mother fell sick and their friends moved to California. Before Artie let Ditzy outside to meet his maker. Before their marriage had gone from disappointing to depressing. These days, when they did cross paths, it was all business—updates on his mom or discussions about their finances.

The record ended. She forced a smile and went on the air. After the break, she lifted the record from the turntable and flipped it like a gunslinger, deftly sliding it into the sleeve inside the jacket. Hard rain began to drum against the window. She lit a cigarette and returned to alphabetizing and her thoughts.

On the other hand, working weekends kept her from having to sit around Artie's mom's sick room and make stilted conversation with his family. She enjoyed having the apartment to herself; she could bang on the piano, chat on the phone with Coco or Faye, eat popcorn, watch movies. And she slept a lot better without Artie's eruptive snoring which sometimes quaked the bed. How was his mother getting any rest?

When her song wound down, Eva cued up an album from her personal collection. A cheap thrill and a no-no, but in her opinion, it fit perfectly into the format. This time she smiled a genuine smile, announcing "Fire on the Mountain" from The Marshall Tucker Band.

Just as the chorus kicked in, the hotline blinked red. "Oh, shit."

"Hi. It's Reid."

Eva's heart dropped.

"I know you're working two jobs—"

"Three," she interjected.

"Three? Anyway, Reuben has been asking for a copywriter."

Reid finally had a full-time position for her. She bounced in the chair.

"I'll need you here weekdays from ten until five to write copy and assist Sanders with the news. You can keep the Saturday afternoon air shift."

"When can I start?"

"As soon as you get out of those other jobs. And Tanya, don't bring in albums from home. It alienates the listeners when you break the format."

"But they're country."

"I like Marshall Tucker—and the Eagles, and John Denver, and Pure Prairie League, too, but we need to stay in our lane. So, knock it off."

She could tell he was grinning.

After they hung up, it dawned on her: no more job juggling. She whipped her fist into the air. A triumphant smile on her face, she rolled the chair over to the bins. As she lifted out the Blake Hale album Dusty recommended, gold sparkled from the depths. Danny's wedding ring! She tore the employee phone list off the bulletin board and called Danny.

At ten minutes to six, thirsty for a beer, she emptied the ashtray and gathered her things. Wes would be there soon. Another gossipy busybody like his aunt Lena, Wes owned a handyman business and had a high opinion of himself. During their shift change the prior week, he'd bragged about how he never had to buy a drink at any bar in Winona County. Eva didn't get it. Yes, he had a decent voice, but on the air, he sounded like a robot. *It's 6:15. Here's Conway Twitty. It's 6:22. Here's Tanya Tucker.*

174

The side door slammed.

She consulted her artist notebook for Wynonna Judd's real name. *Christina Claire Ciminella.* When she looked up, Wes stood in the doorway watching her, his craggy round face streaked with rain. He reeked of greasy bar food.

"It's freakin' pouring out there." He shook the rain from his coat. "Sooo . . . I was fixing a clogged drain over on Evergreen, and I heard something quite interesting about Spike and his wife."

"I don't want to hear it."

"It's juicy," he taunted.

"I don't care, Wes." He collected dirty secrets from the good folks in Winona like a loaded bee spreading pollen from flower to flower. She signed the log and turned the page, then pushed the microphone away on its boom arm. It let out a squeal.

"Do you ever think the mic looks like a big dick?" he asked, leering, the booze on his breath detectable from across the counter.

"Why would you say that?" Her shoulders tensed. Eva slid her headphones into their pouch, avoiding his red-rimmed eyes.

He slung his coat over his arm and looked her up and down. "You're looking fine. Big plans tonight?"

"I'm going out for dinner," she improvised, "with Yardley, my morning show partner from B93." We'll see if he spreads this around the station, she thought. Stupid blabbermouth jerk.

"Didn't you get fired from there?" he asked.

"Yeah. But we're still friends. Guess he misses me." Toying with him, she piled on. "It wasn't his decision, you know."

"Cool beans. Well, have fun."

Something about his voice seemed familiar. He gave her the willies.

She left the studio in a hurry. Before leaving the station, she grabbed a note from her cubby and jammed it into her pocket.

###

At Schott's Tavern, cars overflowed from the parking lot onto the shoulder of the highway. In the smoky bar, Eva pushed through the boisterous crowd. At the jukebox, she slipped a quarter into the coin slot. It jingled down the chute. 3 PLAYS QUARTER, 1 PLAY DIME. After making her selections—"Long Train Running" from the Doobie Brothers first—she went to the corner of the bar, where Dusty stood with Trevor Travis and a group of people she didn't recognize.

The bartender, Dusty's friend from high school, was a giant man in bib overalls with meaty forearms. He filled a glass with green beer and handed it across the bar. "On the house, little lady."

"Thank you!"

She clinked glasses with Dusty and Trevor.

Dusty shouted over the song on the jukebox, leaning in. "You sounded great today. Did you get my note?"

"Oh, yes." She pulled the paper from her snug back pocket and squinted to read it in the dim bar. *"Dear Tanya, daughter of Bart. Haha. Here's another oldies suggestion. 'Daddy Sang Bass' by Johnny Cash, written by Carl Perkins in 1968. You'll like it—there are lines from 'Will the Circle Be Unbroken.'"*

"It's about a family band and all their instruments," Dusty said. "It sat at number one on the Billboard country charts for weeks."

"Sounds good," Eva said and smiled, catching his contagious enthusiasm. "Oh, big news. I'm going full-time. Copywriter and assistant reporter."

"That's great! I know you've been wanting to get back into news, and you're good at writing ads."

He touched her arm and started to say something else when a diminutive woman appeared from the crowd holding an orange-colored drink.

"Eva, this is Annabelle, my sister-in-law," Trevor said.

In her low-cut angora sweater, Annabelle looked like a brunette Dolly Parton. A crystal pendant hung from a chain in the

176

middle of her cleavage. At five-foot-two, she stood even with Eva. "We finally meet."

Eva took a swig of her green beer, drinking it faster than she should have.

"Hey you guys!" Dusty turned around. "I propose a toast to Eva. She's going full-time at the station!"

"Here's to Tanya!" Annabelle raised her glass; the guys eyeballed her curvy body. "Let's do shots."

The bartender poured brandy into a row of shot glasses. Eva debated whether to drink one, feeling guilty for being a married woman in a bar alone. But Artie was probably out with his friends back home. She slammed it. The aromatic liquid coated her stomach with warmth. Her self-restraint loosened; it tasted so good she wanted more.

"So, Tanya," Annabelle said. "Tell me a crazy story about radio, something behind the scenes. You ever have sex in the studio?"

"No, not me," Eva said, raising her brows. Donn's hussy in the teetering heels came to mind. "But I know people who have."

The bartender poured another round. She slammed another shot. Dusty bought a pitcher of green Stroh's and began to fill glasses. Eva decided not to drink any more, but then Annabelle offered up her couch for the night. When "I Like Beer" from Tom T. Hall played on the jukebox, Eva held tight to her new friends, drunkenly singing along.

After her shift at the diner, soon to be one of her last ones, Eva found an urgent message from Reid Rogers on her answering machine. He apologized for having forgotten to invite her to the Monday morning staff meeting. With no time to spare and still in her soiled uniform, she jumped into the car and drove to Winona.

Sitting near the kitchenette on a cold, metal, folding chair, she looked up as Trevor approached, wearing an outdated tan leisure suit with a busy blue-and-gold polyester shirt. He made his way through the crowded, noisy office and sat next to her. "I sure had fun at Schott's on Saturday." He lightly pinched her arm.

"Me too." She tugged at her rumpled uniform which reeked of hash browns.

The group quieted when Reid emerged from his office, patting his breast pocket. The hubbub dwindled to a murmur.

Trevor leaned close to her shoulder, whispering in his scratchy voice. "I'm so glad Reid brought you on full time. Sometimes I get the dumbest scripts—Reuben lets his clients write ads."

Reid hustled into the center of the room and clapped his hands. "Listen up, people. I've got exciting news. But first, a side note for the on-air folks. We've installed a professional compact disc player in the studio. We're in the process of building a CD library. Dusty will issue a memo, so stay tuned." He reached inside his jacket, taking out a thick envelope. "I know summer is a way's out, but as usual, Q106 will have a major presence at the Winona County Fair. We'll also have a booth at the Houston County Fair down in Caledonia, and the La Crosse County Fair across the Mississippi. As the official sponsor of the fair here, we've landed a monumental act. Maybe the biggest name ever to headline."

He built up more suspense by pausing. In concert, everyone took a sharp breath.

"The artist is . . . You know him, you love him . . . The red-headed stranger, Willie Nelson!"

Eva joined her fellow employees as they shouted and applauded. Reid waved a mitt full of tickets above his head.

"Settle down! Listen. It's not for a few months, but you'll need to be on your best behavior—no drinking. Wear your station T-shirts."

He made his way around the room, handing tickets to the elated employees. When he got to Eva, he said, "One for your spouse."

She got up to check the date on the Action Insurance calendar hanging in the bullpen. The night of the concert, July 24, landed on a Thursday. A circle symbol meant there'd be a full moon. She prayed for clear skies. Artie would have to ask off, because nothing was more romantic than a summer concert by moonlight, and they could sorely use some passion.

###

When July 24 arrived, Eva sat on the stairs behind the station, alone. She brushed dirt off her sandals while she waited for Dusty, the gang's chauffeur. Although she'd reminded him, Artie had forgotten to ask for the night off until it was too late. She'd accused him of not making her—them—a priority. He said he didn't feel like seeing Willie Nelson.

Artie the spoilsport. Eva pulled her knees into her chest. Being away from him, she felt free and a little giddy. There was nothing like going to a good concert on a fine summer evening with your friends.

At six-thirty, Dusty's steel blue 1975 Buick Electra four-door sedan—a literal land yacht—pulled into the lot. Trevor and his wife Tracy were already sitting up front. As the car engine ticked down, a dusty pickup came roaring up. It was the husky bartender from Schott's. As he approached, Trevor hooted at his T-shirt: *Chicks Should be Obscene and Not Heard.* Eva rolled her eyes and got into the back. The big man slid in, taking up half the seat. Annabelle arrived with her new boyfriend and had to sit on his lap. Eva got shoved onto the bump in the middle.

Barreling down the highway, Dusty cranked up Q106's Willie Nelson marathon. Her hips pinched, Eva scooted forward and peeked into the front. The bench seat reminded her of making out at drive-in movies in high school. But nobody was kissy-huggy on this road trip. Beer cans popped with a *shrrtt!*

"What happened to the Barracuda you had in college?"

"It's in storage. My dad realized it'll be a classic someday."

At the fairgrounds, a teenager with an orange flag directed Dusty to park at the far end of the field turned parking lot. Thunderheads towered in the distance, but they were far to the north and not a threat. They walked in loose groups to the outdoor venue, the couples holding hands. Eva sighed as she thought of Artie and their declining marriage. She inhaled the fresh air, sweetened with the scent of fast-growing alfalfa in the surrounding verdant farmland. Once inside the grounds, Dusty ran off to find the stage manager. The rest of the gang headed for the beer stand.

At the front of the crowd, Eva swayed to the pre-concert music piped through gigantic black speakers stacked high. The bass notes thrummed in her chest cavity. Artie was going to be so jealous. It was the ultimate summer concert experience. She chugged her beer.

"Nice outfit! You look like Daisy Duke," Annabelle said, tapping her can on Eva's.

Suddenly, the floodlights went dark. The exuberant audience cheered as Dusty ran onto the stage.

"Alright, music fans! I'm Dusty Miles from Q106."

From the crowd, a woman screamed. Someone behind Eva whistled with their fingers, right in her ear.

"On behalf of the Fair Committee, we thank you all for coming. It's the event of the year . . . The show you've been waiting for . . . Willie Nelson!"

Everyone whooped and cheered as Willie came out holding Trigger, his guitar. The band jumped into "Mammas Don't Let Your Babies Grow Up to Be Cowboys." Minutes later, Dusty joined the gang, who sang, smoked, danced, and slammed their beers. Eva bounced up and down in the pressing crowd. Adding to their euphoria, as it got dark, a coral moon rose behind the stage. As the night wore on, she became acutely aware of Dusty behind her, his knees knocking into the back of her legs.

At one point, he put his hands on her hips and moved in close to her ear. "Settle down, lady. You're stepping on my foot."

When his late-day stubble tickled her neck, a frisson of excitement passed through her entire body. A clear, strong message struck her, the way an unexpected bolt of lightning announces a fast-moving thunderstorm.

I don't want to be married.

She gulped her beer and stood her ground, letting the crowd push her toward him, her body vibrating like a tuning fork. He didn't budge. A bold longing she'd never known before ignited an internal tug-of-war: Eva pulled the rope from one side; Tanya tugged on the other. The desire to turn around and kiss Dusty became unbearable.

31. HONEY BEE ~ TOM PETTY & THE HEARTBREAKERS

The following morning, Eva woke alongside Artie with a whopping headache. With difficulty, she pieced together the events of the previous night. After the show, the radio group had walked in circles as no one could recall where they'd parked. But after that? Dusty had dropped everyone at the station in Winona. How had she made it back to La Crosse? She could have driven off the road, not to mention hurt someone. *Stupid.*

Her feet ached and her head throbbed as if squashed in a vise. Sleeping in a bra had made her ribs hurt. *Ugh.* She was sweating. No wonder, there was a Willie shirt layered over her station T. She peeled it off. *How much did I spend on that?* Her cutoff shorts lay crumpled on the floor next to the bed. *Where are my sandals?*

She got out of bed and dragged herself to the bathroom where the mirror reflected mascara-blackened, bloodshot eyes. In the bedroom, Artie let out a loud snore. With a start, the switch-flipping moment hit her.

I don't want to be married.

Thinking of Dusty's smooth, rumbly voice in her ear, she swooned and grabbed onto the sink, overwhelmed with the ecstasy of falling in love on a balmy summer night. *Falling in love, or lust?* Like a pendulum, a wave of nausea hit. She leaned against the counter massaging her aching temples. Before the situation with Dusty escalated, she needed to separate from Artie. She was done. The fragility of their bond had been evident from the start. Pressured into marriage, she felt little obligation to uphold her commitment. Artie's increasingly bad moods only deepened her belief that he blamed her for the loss of their child. They were doomed from Day One.

The phone rang. She hobbled into the kitchen. "Hello-o."

"It's me, Dusty. I wanted to make sure you got home okay. You were pretty trashed."

"Thanks, but I'm fine," she whispered. "I've got to go."

"See you at work, Tanya."

In the bedroom, Artie snorted and turned over. Why did people think getting married was like a fairy tale? And what happened when marriages broke up after seven years? Did they have to return the wedding gifts? The emotional pain exacerbated her headache. After taking two aspirins, she stepped into a steamy shower, hoping the tormenting thoughts would wash down the drain with the foamy rosemary shampoo.

At work that afternoon, Eva peeked over the top of her typewriter at Dusty, who was engrossed in conversation with Travis. They high-fived, perhaps making another wager, like back in June when the Celtics lost in the NBA playoffs. Trevor had to eat habanero peppers while doing his sportscast—a bad idea with all the spitting and coughing.

She paged through the mess in her overflowing in-box where Reuben regularly dumped fodder for writing copy: newspaper ads paper-clipped with client notes, rewrites of old scripts, co-op guidelines, and a request for her to compose a custom jingle. *Cool!* She read over a client's prior ad.

"For all your roast beef needs," she said.

"What?" asked Sanders, at his desk next to hers. He held a cheese and butter Wonder bread sandwich in one hand and poked at his typewriter with the other.

"These scripts are so boring." Eva flipped to another page. "It's one cliché after another. For all your staffing needs, for all your heating and cooling needs, for all your mashed potato needs, et cetera."

"Huh," he said, shrugging.

Reuben came over, well-groomed and smelling wonderful. Eva loved his textured face, a sea of freckles embedded in a mass of wrinkles, as if he'd been in the sun every day of his life. He wore a dazzling ruby ring. She took his hand.

"That's magnificent, Reuben."

"Why, thank you, Tanya. It is showy," he said, raising the ring to the light, "but my clients want me to be prosperous. It gives them confidence in the radio station." He lifted his eyebrows. "Did you type up the travel ad?"

"It's way too long."

He pretended to sigh and shuffled through her in-box, locating the script he had written in longhand on the back of a travel brochure. He good-naturedly shook the paper. "When I read it, it was precisely sixty seconds."

"Did you read it out loud? I can only talk so fast, Reuben, and this ad has to be exactly sixty seconds because it's airing in the Twins game."

"Time me." His eyes flashed. His smirk said, *I dare you.* "Go!"

She clicked the stopwatch. His read clocked in at seventy-two seconds. Eva struggled to not look smug.

"When you read it in your head, you can cram a lot more in."

"Well," he huffed, playing up his role. "Talk faster."

"It's a disservice to the advertiser if no one can understand it."

"Alright, Miss Smarty-pants. *I'll* rewrite it."

With a wry smile, Eva smacked her palm to her forehead. From experience, she figured he'd come back with even more copy, maybe add the phone number—an age-old tug of war between copywriters and sales.

As Reuben started to walk away, she said, "Say. What do you know about Wagner & Thomas, your family law client? I heard their ads and, uh, my friend is looking for a divorce lawyer."

"They're top notch. They drew up my will."

She opened her phone book to the Yellow Pages and found the number, but an ad for an employment agency needed to be written before the end of the day. While reviving memories from her own job search, concentrating as hard as she could through the hangover, she wandered into the kitchen for a cup of coffee. The ad could feature a cantankerous matchmaker. She heard footsteps and turned to see Dusty.

"Hey, Dimples," he said.

Their eyes locked before he surreptitiously looked up and down her body. Did he notice the flush on her chest? Could he tell she had dreamed about him all night?

"You look cute."

"Thank you." She held his gaze as long as she dared and winked. "Are you pitching tonight at softball?"

The last time Dusty had filled in, he walked four batters in a row, scoring a run for the other team.

"Very funny. I think I'll stick to shortstop. Someone has to block the balls before they roll past you."

She put a finger to her lips. "*Ssst.* Burn. Maybe I should be the catcher."

"That's hard on your knees," he said, his eyes surveying her legs.

"Maybe I'll just sit in the stands and be a fan."

"No matter how sucky you are, we need you, Tanya. Hey, you left your shoes in my car. I'll bring them in later."

Now she remembered. Bare feet on gravel as they searched for his car. She smiled at him and returned to her desk.

What if she wrote an ad within an ad for the staffing agency? It could feature an office worker and an announcer. *Me and Dusty.* She rested her hand on her chin and grinned. They'd have fun recording it, plus she'd get a talent fee. Eva loaded a fresh form, releasing and turning the platen knob to line it up. She typed at top speed.

Eva looked up from her typing to see Sanders looming. The motion of raising her head caused her headache to rebound.

"I'm going to a ribbon-cutting at the new hospital," he said. "You're doing the noon news. The stories are ready on my desk."

An hour of news, all by herself, hungover. Great. She chewed another aspirin.

###

At the end of the workday, after setting up a free, no-obligation consultation with the law firm, Eva changed into her softball uniform in the tiny bathroom. Hurrying, she pulled striped athletic socks up to her knees, then slipped on her beat-up tennis shoes. The headache was gone but her stomach ached from all the aspirin.

When she arrived at the ball diamond, her teammates were already batting. Dusty waved from the bench. Spike had managed to get into the announcer's booth and was calling the game.

"That's two outs for Trevor's Error Terrors. Next at bat, River Country DJ and copywriter extraordinaire, Tanya Starr!"

Each week, the radio team drew a small but loyal crowd of supporters. They clapped and cheered. "Tanya" tossed her gym bag onto the bleachers and ran out to home plate, where, distracted by the thought of Dusty watching, she whiffed every pitch.

The radio station team didn't score a single run that night. After the game, as the sun entered its golden hour near the horizon, Eva sat in the stands rubbing her thigh where she'd been hit by a line drive. Dusty noticed the nasty bruise and offered an ice pack which was in his car. She followed him past the popcorn stand and players warming up on the sidelines, balls smacking into gloves. They hopped into the back seat, leaving the doors open to let in the balmy night air. From a shabby Styrofoam cooler, he handed her an ice pack and popped the tops on chilled cans of Old Style.

"That's one heck of a bruise, Tanya."

Dusty reached over the seat and finagled a joint from the car's front ash tray. She ogled his back side.

"This will help reduce the inflammation."

Eva hadn't been stoned since Faye and Dwayne left town. She held the joint under her nose and sniffed. "Mm. Thanks."

186

He lit it with his monogrammed lighter. After taking a puff, she handed it back. A mellow rush hit her brain. The sensation buzzed down the back of her neck and tingled in her arms.

"I really need to quit smoking," she said. "Cigarettes, that is. You know it's your fault I started!"

"From what I recall, I didn't force a cigarette into your mouth." He nudged her with his elbow before passing the joint. She took another hit followed by a sip of beer.

"My mother-in-law has lung cancer."

"That's awful. Every time I try to quit, I do okay for a few days. Then I think I can have just one and that's all she wrote." He burped and wiped his mouth. "Pardon me. I will quit, someday."

"When you're young, it seems like you have time to do everything."

Cheers erupted from the crowd. The sun had set. In the dark, through Eva's expanded mind and dazed eyes, the brilliant lights surrounding the field became glittery pinpoint stars. Colors intensified; the grass seemed greener. Dusty's nearness aroused a deep longing. He took another hit.

"I had a radio nightmare last night."

"I have those, too!" Eva said. "They're stressful, like it's the last day of class and you forgot to study for finals."

"Everyone has those. My dad hasn't been on the air for ages, and he still does," Dusty said, draining his can. He held out the joint. "'Ere."

"No, thanks. I've got cottonmouth."

Eva smacked her sticky, dry lips. Dusty dug two more beers from the cooler. They popped them open and sipped, sharing a moment of silence.

"Ah, refreshing. How's that bruise?" he asked.

She lifted the bag from her leg. The swelling had gone down. But Eva didn't reach for the door handle. "It's better. Speaking of dreams, do you want to be a DJ forever?"

"Actually, I want to be an announcer for the Minnesota Twins or your Milwaukee Brewers. Play-by-play or color, I don't care."

"You have the voice. Did you collect baseball cards when you were little?"

"You bet. I was obsessed. I kept stats for every game."

"Well, I commend you for shooting high. How long do you think Bob Uecker will stick around with the Brewers?"

"He's been there since 1971—sixteen years, now. Who knows how long he'll stay? I really dig talking sports with Trevor during my show, but I should be calling games to get experience. Even high school."

Eva slammed the rest of her beer and was about to say she should go when Dusty said, "What a great concert last night. I really had fun. But I was wondering, what's the situation with your husband?"

A kick in the guts. She pursed her mouth, searching for the right words. "Things have been rough. We never see each other because Artie works second shift. He goes home every weekend to help his mom." She sniffed back a tear. "My marriage is dead."

"I thought something was off," he said, and took a long drink.

"Remember that time we recorded the sound of a toilet flushing over Coco's news sounder?" Eva asked.

"That was so funny! She kept her cool and potted up the news right on time."

"Before falling off the chair laughing," she said.

"We'd get fired for doing that now."

A cool breeze kicked up, bringing the sweet summer smell of cut grass into the car. Without warning, Dusty leaned in and planted a kiss on her lips. Taken aback, excitement mixed with guilt, she pulled away.

A group of ball players walked past the car, talking excitedly about their big win. Eva watched Dusty's handsome face as he looked out the open door. He brushed ashes from the front of his shirt.

"Tanya, last night at the show, I was wishing you were single."

She paused for a beat.

"I have to admit, I did too."

32. WILL THE WOLF SURVIVE ~ LOS LOBOS

On Saturday morning, Eva tuned in to Dusty's show at home. While she cleaned and did laundry, she invented a game: the songs he announced would be meant for her.

> DUSTY: River Country Radio, Q106 with Rodney Crowell and "I Couldn't Leave You if I Tried," the story of a man who tells his lady that no matter what, he'll always be there. Very romantic. Up next, "You Look So Good in Love" from George Strait.

The run of love songs continued during her drive to work along the winding Mississippi. What were the odds?

Dusty hung around after his shift, going on the air with Eva during the noon hour—just like a morning team. They talked about Crystal Gayle's hair, Barbara Mandrell's prowess on the steel guitar, and T. Graham Brown's many nicknames. Off the air, they discussed radio, cars, and softball. They discovered a shared love for cribbage. She hoped he'd invite her to his place that evening to play.

But he didn't. After he left, she wondered what she had got herself into. She slouched in the air chair, feeling so alone. Out in her cubby, she found a note from Dusty listing a dozen "kick-ass" country songs. Finding the records occupied her for an hour, but still, time dragged. She couldn't wait for Wes to take over.

At ten minutes before six, she cued a CD, which always made her nervous. The CD player's digital display indicated Track 03, but it wasn't like a record where she could visually verify it; the disc sat hidden inside the machine. She double-checked the song order on the CD cover.

The odor of fried food wafting in made her look up. Wes stood in the open studio door, watching her with glassy eyes. Something about him made her nerves jangle. She needed to request a shift change from Reid. Maybe Sunday afternoons. He stared.

"You have ten minutes, Wes."

"Do you put your lips around the mic when you talk?"

The vulgar remark dredged up a memory. *Winona. Mystery Man had been from Winona.*

She tried to hide her distress. "No. Do you? Geez, Wes, you smell like a deep-fried beer."

He belched. "Yup, I jus' had a burger and fries."

"And a few beers?"

"Just one. Sue me. I look handsomer on the air when I drink." He set his grimy baseball cap on the counter next to a jumbo soda. His tone changed. "Does your husband know you were in Dusty's car after the game?"

Uh-oh. She scrambled to quash his accusation. "I had an injury. Dusty gave me an ice pack. End of story."

"I saw you all cuddled up. Were you making out?" He coughed: it sounded like "slut."

Son of a bitch. Even though she hadn't done anything wrong— Dusty had kissed her. If Wes was gossiping around town, her reputation as a married woman was at stake. She furrowed her brow.

"You're imagining things."

"Whatever you say-ay."

Wes pulled albums from the bins at the back of the studio. Eva shifted in the air chair, waiting for her record to end and her chance to get away. She waved an arm around her head.

"There has been a pesky fly in here all day. Bug off, fly!"

After starting the happy song "Fishin' in the Dark" by the Nitty Gritty Dirt Band, she unplugged her headphones. The fly landed in her hair. She brushed it away, only to catch Wes's hand. She froze as he stroked the back of her head.

"Your hair is nice," he said, bending to sniff it.

"Stop it, Wes."

She sprung up and ducked under his arm, but as she tried to get around the counter, he blocked her.

"C'mon, Tanya. Give me some of the sugar you've been spreading around town, first with your old morning show partner, now with Dusty. Why don't you let *me* sample the merchandise?"

"Damn it, let me out! My *husband* is waiting."

She twisted away. Why had she lied to him about meeting Yardley for dinner? In Wes's twisted mind, she had led him on. And letting Dusty kiss her in public? A huge lapse in judgment.

She pushed past, but he caught her arm. He spun her around and thrust her with his chest. She tripped backward. Her head hit the studio window with a loud, resounding bang. The sill bit into the small of her back. *That's going to leave another nasty bruise.* The next thing she knew, Wes was grabbing her face with his smelly hands. Was he trying to kiss her? Acid rose from her stomach. She turned and raised her fist to strike his shoulder, but he caught it and interlocked his doughy fingers in hers. When she tried to pull away, he pushed her hand against the wall, scraping her knuckles.

Over the monitors, The Dirt Band sang about falling in love under a bright, full moon.

"Why don't you go out with me, Lizzy-Tanya? I'll buy you a nice ribeye, a baked potato, we'll have a glass of wine, the whole deal."

Wes's sour breath made Eva gag. She turned her head away, trying to get her wits about her. By calling her Lizzy, he revealed he was Mystery Man. Letting him know she'd made the connection might flatter him. No. She wouldn't do it.

"Let me go, Wes. You're drunk."

She struggled to get away. Why, oh, why, had she laid bare her soul during their long chats? Because he asked questions and listened? He'd had the most soothing voice. He remembered the things she told him. How could she have been so gullible? Maybe she could talk him down.

"You're not thinking straight."

He stepped back, still gripping her scarred wrist.

"You're hurting me!"

He sneered in her face. "You're so ambitious. I know how you shot from overnights to the morning show at B93—and you won't even give me a kiss. Tanya, the daughter of Bart Starr. Lying to everyone about your dead father. You come off all cute and brainy, but deep-down, you're a cheap hustler. You probably don't even like country music."

Eva caught her reflection in the window: her western plaid shirt, fitted leather vest, turquoise earrings. "Let me go. Now!"

"You're a sell-out, touting your perks—the free clothes, the VCR on trade." All the things she'd told Mystery Man. "You're a girl who sleeps her way to the top."

Despite her fear, his remark struck her funny bone. "To the top of the Winona country radio market? Get a grip, Wes. For the record, I had a business-only relationship with Yardley."

Using his hips, he pushed her against the wall, with more force this time. "C'mon, Lizzy-Tanya. Give me a kiss." One hand slithered under her shirt.

"Stop it!" she screamed, jerking her knee toward his crotch.

Wriggling her arm free, she punched hard into his soft gut but couldn't get enough inertia behind it to hurt him. As they wrestled, she knocked Wes's soda off the counter. Cubes of ice scattered across the carpet. His song ended; the needle scratched into the record's staticky inner groove.

Eva shouted, "Wes! Dead air!"

"You can't blame a guy for trying," he said, as if he'd done nothing wrong. He let her go.

With rubbery legs, she dashed out of the studio, forgetting her headphones. She grabbed her purse from her cubby and locked herself in the bathroom. While digging for a cigarette, she noticed the scrape on her hand. With her heart booming like a bass drum, she put a bandage from the medicine cabinet over her bloody knuckles, all the while deliberating whether to call Reid, or maybe the police. She peeked her head out the bathroom door. Through the studio windows, she could see Wes at the board taking a nip from a silver flask. With her purse slung over one shoulder, she tiptoed to the phone sitting on Spike's desk and started to dial Reid's number.

Wes appeared. He ripped the phone away.

"If you tattle, I'll tell everyone about you and Dusty. You'll get fired for fraternizing with staff."

Eva stepped back. He kept his position at the desk, phone in hand, no longer in a state of physical aggression.

She shook her finger. "You bastard. I'll tell Reid to come down here and smell your breath. Drinking on the job is against FCC rules. You'll lose your broadcast license."

"You wouldn't dare," he said, glaring. "I'll call your husband right now. I'm not bluffing."

A stalemate.

She turned on her heel and ran for the exit, her shoulders practically touching her ears. At the door, she yelled, "If you ever touch me again, I'll kill you!"

"I'm not even attracted to you," he hollered.

As she drove home, the lump on her back began to throb. Indignation burned in her chest. She pulled over and parked at a picnic wayside along the Mississippi, locking the doors, cracking the window an inch. Candi's words floated back: *Beware the smiling tigers.* The monster was on the inside. And to think, all those times she'd worried about a stalker outside the station.

Her bloodied hand shook as she lit a cigarette. The deep inhale and exhale of nicotine helped settle her nerves.

Wes wouldn't dare tell anyone about her and Dusty. If he did, she'd make sure he lost his precious Saturday night gig. Over the years, plenty of people would have witnessed him drinking at the bar before his shift. She wanted to forget the whole thing, but her body kept shuddering at the thought of his grimy hands on her, his putrid breath in her face.

If Wes told people about the kiss, they'd make the same assumptions he did. Winona was a small town—if she got fired, it would be nothing short of scandalous. Eva stubbed her cigarette in the flip-out ashtray. *I need to get my act together.* The thought of Artie finding out this way filled her with dread; he'd be humiliated. When she leaned forward to turn the key in the ignition, pain shot across her lower back. If she had to work adjacent to Wes next week, she'd bring pepper spray or Artie's hunting knife.

As she navigated the hilly coulees on the way home, Wes's words ricocheted in her head. The idea that someone could see her through such a cynical lens struck her with sharp pangs of shame and despair. Was he right? Had she sold out? Had hiding behind the masks of Billie and Lizzy and Tanya rendered her a fraud?

Besides the fact that Wes had no right to touch her, what would Coco say? Eva sighed. Perhaps she had turned to radio in search of the adoration she missed from her father. The thought released her shock, allowing the tears to flow.

In her heart, she knew she wasn't a sell-out. What about all the country musicians who changed their names and slapped on a rhinestone-studded cowboy hat? Or the hair bands—those guys didn't go to the grocery store wearing eyeliner and torn T-shirts with their nipples exposed. There were plenty of things she had turned down: the diet pills deal, voicing a political ad from the politician who'd had questionable relationships with young girls. Even if she hadn't appreciated country music at first, she liked it now. Yes, she had made mistakes—she hadn't planned on falling for Dusty. But Wes's accusations made her feel so dirty.

The annual Schott's Inn tug-of-war competition ended late in the afternoon under a glorious deep blue sky. It had been a hot day, perfect for a slip in the mud. The Q106 co-ed station team, The Earnest Tuggs, made it to the final match, losing to the bar-sponsored team, The Wankers. Afterward, they partied at a picnic table, the sun drying their soaked shorts and tank tops. The strenuous exercise had made Eva hungry.

Inside the bar, the sun streamed in from open doors that led to the volleyball courts. Shouting over the jukebox, she placed an order for deep-fried cheese curds, then lit a cigarette. In the back booth, people shot pool or played darts, some with streaks of mud on their faces. She rubbed the knot on her lower back. All that rope pulling had aggravated the injury inflicted by Wes. *Thank God he isn't here today.* A spike of rage shot through her. There had to be a way to get rid of him. Eva took a deep puff of her cigarette. If Reid found out about Wes drinking on the job, he'd surely fire him. *Sweet revenge.* She blew smoke out of her nose so hard it burned. A warm hand touched her back.

"Can I join you, Tanya?"

Dusty's barstool made a loud scraping noise as he pulled it closer. The bartender poured two shots of Jägermeister and set them on the bar. They clinked glasses and downed their shots. The Bellamy Brothers "Feelin' the Feelin'" played on the juke box and they sang along to the song that seemed to have been written just for them.

At home, as she walked through the front door, Eva stumbled over the threshold. The greasy cheese curds weren't enough to soak up the alcohol she'd imbibed.

"Dang," she muttered, catching herself with a hand to the door.

"Eva, is that you? Did you drive like that? You gotta stop hanging with those country losers."

"What're you doin' home, Artie?" She belched.

"There were too many people at Ma's," he said, rising from a prone position on the couch.

He sat partway up, his chin turtlenecked under a blanket. On the TV, an accordionist swung his instrument in front of an orchestra on the Lawrence Welk show.

"How is your mom feeling?"

"Honestly, she's getting worse. She's in a lot of pain."

"Oh, I'm sorry to hear that." Eva tried to think straight. "Your aunt and uncle were there?"

"You mean the meddlers? Yeah. I couldn't take it anymore. I'm telling you, Eva, they came barging in, saying Ma should go to something called a hospice. When I said she doesn't have the funds, they asked to see her accounts and insurance papers. I had to sleep on the floor." He yawned. "I was so beat, I left."

"Why do you have the AC turned on so high? It's freezing."

Eva went to the laundry closet in the hallway between the living room and bedrooms and yanked the bi-fold panels. The damn doors were stuck again. She wished he would fix them.

"How was the tug-of-war?" he asked.

"We made it to the finals then lost by an inch. My arms are sore."

Eva stripped off her damp, muddy shorts. She set her cowboy hat on the dryer and bent into the washing machine.

"What the hell? Artie, how long have your clothes been in here? They stink."

She removed a pair of mildewed jeans. Alcohol bile rose in her esophagus. She dumped his clothes onto the tile floor.

"Gross. Why didn't you put them in the dryer?"

"I forgot," he yelled from the couch.

"Just like you forgot to feed the cats before you left. And forgot to write in another ATM withdrawal. And forgot our anniversary."

He finally got up from the couch and approached her in the hall where she stood in mud-stained underwear.

"Geez, Eva. When was it?" Artie screwed up his face.

"It's the same day every year."

Was he that mindless? Leading up to their anniversary, she had waited for him to mention it. When he didn't, she assumed he'd surprise her with flowers or something. Was it her job to remind him? Had she set him up?

"Gol' darn it, Eva, why didn't you tell me?"

He put a hand on her shoulder. She threw it off. The booze in her system exaggerated her emotions, yet her head was clear enough to know she was agitating the situation, creating a reason to reject him.

"Why is it my responsibility? Have you even noticed how tough it's been for me over the last few years? Losing the morning show? Working three jobs? Starting over? I'm emotionally drained. My tank is empty. If you cared, you would have done something to cheer me up. You would have remembered our anniversary."

He stepped back, looking flabbergasted. As she staggered toward the bathroom to get her robe, she tripped on his wet jeans, releasing a cry of exasperation. He followed her to the door.

"How many times have I asked for a date night?" she demanded.

"Eva, we're hardly ever home at the same time."

"Would it kill you to be creative? Plan a picnic lunch. Make some effort for once." She punched her arm through the sleeve of her robe. "Just forget it."

"Cripes, Eva. You're being a bitch."

"Fuck you, Artie. Finish your damn laundry."

Artie grabbed her arm, like Wes had. She flinched.

"Hey. Why are you so mad?" he asked. "You're out partying with your radio friends every night while I'm doing right by my family."

"Your family? What about me?" Tears began to roll down her face. As his wife, wasn't she supposed to be the most important person in the world? "Aren't I your family? What if we had kids? Would you be running off to your mom's all the time?"

"Well, excu-u-use me." He said, hands out, imitating Steve Martin.

"Was that an apology?" She wiped her eyes with the sleeve of her robe. "Why did you even marry me?"

He stood in the bathroom doorway, his face forlorn, his arms limp at his sides.

"You can't think of one reason besides the pregnancy?"

"Man, oh, man, Eva. Where is this going?"

"God, Artie, you don't care about me at all, do you? I'm just here, cooking and cleaning, making everything nice. You take me for granted. Well, guess what? I'm done."

Eva stormed past him into the bedroom, collapsing onto the bed. In the fetal position, she buried her face in the pillow, not quite believing she had said the words aloud. Ludwig jumped up and snuggled into her belly. She pulled the blanket over them both, a baby-sized bump. As she strained to think, her head began to ache, the hangover kicking in. Her heart said leave, pursue Dusty. Just the thought of him, how he listened, how he constantly touched her; it made her insides warm and sweet, like pudding. But could she afford to live on her own? What would their families think? Would she make the same mistakes with Dusty?

Artie cranked up the TV. The upstairs neighbor stomped on the floor.

Now, thoroughly embarrassed, Eva cried for her marriage. How could a marriage license, a dry, inanimate piece of paper, cause so much anguish? She stroked Ludwig's soft head while he purred. Artie wasn't a bad guy. His father had left when he was young, so he'd had no example of a loving husband. She had to admit, he was a dutiful son, the way he took care of his mom. Wouldn't she want a husband who'd support her when she was old and ailing? They had taken vows, in sickness and health, for better or worse. *Oh no, what if the marriage got worse.*

Sheesh. She held the cat too tightly. The best thing for both of them would be to end it. She would move out.

With more than an hour to kill before work on Wednesday morning, Eva made her way to an empty booth at Daisy's Diner. She spread the *Winona Daily News* classified ads across the table, leaning one page against the window. Outside, a cedar waxwing fluttered in a crab apple, filling up on berries, oblivious to the downtown traffic. She switched her attention back to the ads. No new rentals. A tear of frustration and guilt splotched onto the dry newsprint. A waitress appeared and without asking, flipped her cup and filled it to the brim.

Eva kept her head down and said, "Just coffee, thanks."

The apartments she'd toured the day before were still listed. The first had been a filthy dump above a biker bar with squished cockroaches in the sink and, according to the people moving out, throbbed with music every night until two a.m. The second place was clean, affordable, and had a nice yard for her cat, but was too far from Winona.

At this point, there'd be no going back. Eva had declared their marriage was over.

According to what Hugo, her boss at Action Insurance, preached, rent should amount to no more than thirty percent of one's income. Any more meant supremely frugal living. She stared into the steaming cup, thinking of alternatives. A double-wide trailer might be cheap. And there were jobs in other cities. No, not an option because of Dusty. Eva set the cup down. Was this what she really wanted? Who was running the show? Herself or Tanya, a carefree single DJ?

She sipped her coffee. The least combative way to move out would be while Artie was gone, like sneaking out of a terrible party.

She'd leave a note saying she was sorry, that he deserved to be with someone who wants children—and that she was taking Ludwig.

She wanted to be a career woman, not a homemaker baking pies and wiping snot from the noses of sniveling brats. The perfect life would be hosting a morning show with Dusty, followed by lazy afternoons making love, riding his motorcycle, cooking dinner, steamy showers, cuddling . . .

Lena walked into the diner followed by Wes the Molester, who wore a scowl on his face and a dingy jean jacket despite the warm fall day.

Eva quickly angled her back to the entrance. The coffee in her mouth tasted metallic, the back of her neck went cold.

She raised the newspaper in front of her face which led her eyes to a different heading: Houses for Rent, under which there was listed a two-bedroom bungalow on Main Street. It included heat, electricity, and water. Pets were allowed. But it was a hundred dollars over her budget. Eva circled the ad. She might starve to death, but at least she wouldn't freeze.

"Hi, Tanya. Whatcha doing?" Lena peered around the edge of the paper.

"Hi, Lena. Just leaving." She folded the newspaper.

"Wes bought me a doughnut. I'm on the air soon."

Behind his aunt, Wes made a lewd finger-in-hole motion with his hands and ran his tongue around his lips. Eva shot daggers at him and scratched her cheek with her middle finger.

"Did you hear that someone died from mad cow disease down in Mankato?" Lena asked.

Eva would check the wire when she got to work even though she was sure the sickness affected only Great Britain. Typical Lena, plugged into every nutty conspiracy network. She folded the paper and slung her backpack over her shoulder.

"See you at work." *Get me the hell away from these pinheads.*

She left, bells jingling in her wake.

After the last softball game of the season, the team celebrated their winless season under twinkly party lights on the outside patio at Schott's. Sitting next to each other at the picnic table, Dusty leaned close and asked Eva to go for a walk.

She followed him to the shadowy side of the volleyball court where they sat on the grassy edge, shoulders touching. Her heart raced. She dug a pit in the cool sand for her beer and observed the star-freckled sky.

"Thanks for all the notes, Dusty—I've discovered some great artists. Never in a million years did I think I'd like country music."

"You're welcome. I sure love listening to you on the air—your delivery is so musical. That little crack in your voice kills me." He caressed her thigh. "Mm. Your skin is silky."

She wished he'd never stop. "I made something for you." She took a beaded choker from her bag. "I used three different blues. It matches your eyes."

He stretched it over his head. "No one's ever made something for me before." Just as she had imagined, he leaned in for a kiss. "Thanks, Tanya."

Laughing, she turned her face, "Please, Dusty, call me Eva."

"Those dimples make me crazy."

He took her face in his hands and rubbed her cheeks with playful thumbs. Euphoria rose from her core with an intensity that stirred her soul. Is this how falling in love felt? She wanted to tackle him.

"Did you get this in the car accident with your dad?" Dusty asked, touching the raised scar on her wrist.

"Yes. At first it was all red and jagged. The mean kids at school said I should wear a glove. Every so often, tiny pieces of glass work their way out."

The wound had healed quickly, however her broken pinky mended in a bent position—quite a disadvantage for a concert pianist.

"It's a part of you. That makes it beautiful."

A million butterflies fluttered into her heart. She couldn't take it. "Can I have a smoke?"

Dusty lit two cigarettes using his fancy Zippo. Eva eased back, exhaling clouds into the night sky. He followed suit. A slivered moon shone through silhouetted branches. One by one, the lights above the volleyball court blinked off. They reclined in the sweet grass, taking in the astronomical night sky. *From their 1974 album* Secret Treaties, Blue Öyster Cult *with "Astronomy."* The ground felt damp beneath her back. She stroked his thumb.

"What's the dumbest thing you ever said on the air, besides the time you said 'shit' on a live mic back in college?" she asked.

"Skunny sighs. How about you?" He squeezed her hand.

"Breast bread."

"Noooo."

"Yup. And another time, I was reading a story about a professor emeritus, and I said 'emer-EYE-tis' like he had a disease."

They lay there, laughing, smoking, and telling stories.

Abruptly, Dusty sat up. He flicked his lighter. Sparks flew, strobing his face. "I've got to be honest, Tanya. Something my dad said is bugging me."

"What?" Eva asked. She placed her hand on his forearm.

"He says I shouldn't see a married woman."

Ouch. But Dusty had mentioned her to his dad. In the dark, she smiled. "You never told me what happened to him at the station."

"Yeah. Well. He had an affair with Betty years ago. It caused a huge scandal because she was young—only eighteen. She had just started as our receptionist. But you're changing the subject. Are you staying with your husband? I don't know what to think."

"Think fast," she replied.

They no longer touched. She drained her cup.

"I'm serious. Please don't be cagey. I hate lying. Jasmine lied to me and—" He sniffed.

Her head felt muddied. When she thought of her grumpy, non-romantic, cat-killing husband who used to be in a band but was now either gone all the time or sitting on the couch, her anger stirred. She put a hand to her head and rubbed her temple. Unraveling the marriage would be as tricky as untangling a fine, knotted necklace.

"I'm not lying. I've been looking for an apartment. First, I need to save for a security deposit."

"I could give you a few hundred."

"That's generous, but I'll figure it out."

"Look at me," he said as he turned her face to his. "I'm right here. I can help."

When she leaned into his shoulder, he slid an arm around her. They sat in silence. If only she could step out of her life into a parallel universe, to leave Eva behind and just be Tanya. Artie needed a traditional wife. She'd be doing him a favor, giving him the freedom to remarry and start a family while he was still young. With no kids, ending the marriage would be simple: divide the assets, move out, move on. She chuckled to herself—between the two of them, they would've had short kids.

"Everything will work out," Dusty said.

He hummed a slow melody and rocked to the rhythm. An owl joined in with a low hoot. They laughed.

"I don't know how long it'll take," she whispered.

"I will wait for you, Tanya."

Eva tapped her fingers on her thighs, reminding herself to breathe as she waited for the lawyer. Over the phone, he said she could file for a no-fault divorce as there was no longer the necessity to prove cruel and inhumane treatment. Through the thin, bland walls in the waiting room, she heard voices escalating, one high and one low. The receptionist gave her an apologetic smile and offered a cup of coffee, which Eva declined. She did not need to be more wired. Just being there behind Artie's back felt rotten enough.

They made a mistake. They were young and would be better in their next relationships. No regrets, no grudges, no fuss. A clean break. *That's what I'll say to Artie.*

Fifteen minutes after her scheduled time, the office door opened. A couple stepped out, smiling. They shook hands with the pudgy, middle-aged lawyer and left. *See, this can be cordial.*

"Mrs. LaVette? Have a seat."

They settled into beige chairs in a dull room. The ugly pinkish border trim at the top of the walls needed to be taken down. A dusty plastic palm sat in the corner.

She explained her situation and asked how much it would cost.

"The filing fee is seventy-five dollars. You'll submit that at the courthouse when you file the petition. Our fee is a hundred twenty an hour, so the cost depends on how much negotiation there is. You mentioned you don't have children. What are your assets?"

She shifted in her chair. "Two cars. A piano. A few hundred dollars between checking and savings. That's it."

"What is your debt? Home loans, credit cards, et cetera . . ."

"We rent. We owe a thousand on my car. No credit cards."

He shuffled papers on his desk. "Should be a cinch. You won't need a lawyer. I'm happy to act as a mediator to make sure you're crossing your Ts and dotting your Is. Four hours at the most."

Eva winced as she did the math in her head.

"Talk to your husband. First, go to the courthouse in La Crosse for the forms. Once you file, there's a six-month waiting period."

When she got into the elevator, Eva let out a sigh of frustration and defeat. Saving up enough for a security deposit on an apartment was hard enough. Now she'd have to come up with hundreds for the divorce. Her mother would most likely lend it, but Eva hated to ask. Maybe Hugo at Action Insurance would let her come back part time.

She leaned her head against the cold steel elevator wall.

At the Houston County Fair in Caledonia on Labor Day weekend, Eva made her way from the parking lot past exhibitors re-staking their wet tents. Heavy thunderstorms had blown through the area overnight. Despite the puddles, it was the kind of September summer day a Midwesterner dreamed of all year—hot sun, the breeze, fragrant and cool, clouds forming fluffy animal shapes. "Tanya" had gone all-in on her country persona: not-too-short cutoffs, a white sleeveless shirt with a ruffle down the front, her shit kickers, and a cowboy hat tied with a red bandana over her braids. With a spring in her step, she hurried to the broadcast booth.

Dusty grinned when he saw her coming. She was thrilled to see he wore the blue choker she'd made. It did match his eyes. All morning, they interviewed fairgoers and doled out swag, the speakers boomed country tunes. Their choice location on the midway made for great radio, within earshot of mooing cows and honking poultry. Hundreds of listeners came by to see the personalities they'd heard on the air. She enjoyed watching their faces when they registered the disconnect between what they expected and real life.

"I thought you were blonde," more than one said.

"You sound much taller on the radio," said another.

"I am much taller on the radio," became her standard retort.

Dusty used every opportunity to touch her waist or arm while they moved about the booth. A crowd cheered when they two-stepped in the midway to "Louisiana Saturday Night" by Mel McDaniel. Like Pepé Le Pew, love flooded her eyes, her heart beat out of her chest.

Just before noon, Lena and Wes arrived to take the afternoon shift. Eva tried to steer clear of Wes, but he managed to get close.

"Having fun with your boyfriend?"

"Shut up, Wes," she hissed.

He wobbled off to the back of the tent where he stood in a dip in the rain-softened ground and poured liquid from a flask into his paper coffee cup. She wished he'd crawl into a hole and die.

"Who's taking over at four?" she asked.

"Spike and Reid," Lena said, eager to spill her inside knowledge. "I talked to Reid this morning. He's bringing his wife and kids early so they can go on all the rides. It's his littlest one's birthday today."

"I hope he brings more swag," Eva said. *Hmm, the boss is coming.* If Reid caught Wes drinking, the creep would be in big trouble.

"Hey, Wes. Watcha got in there?"

"A little Brandy. Want a nip?"

"No, thanks. But you'd better pace yourself. Don't drink it all at once."

"I've got more." He bent to unzip his duffle and exposed a quart bottle. He looked around before sneaking a sip from the silver flask.

Reid needed to see him sloshed. "I bet you five bucks you can't drink that whole thing," she cajoled.

Like she knew he would, Wes guzzled the contents of the flask. He wiped his mouth with his sleeve and bent down to quickly refill it.

"Good job, Wes." *You slob.* She pulled a five from her pocket and slapped it into his hand. When she turned away, Dusty was smiling, his magnetism the opposite of Wes's repulsiveness. Her heart sang as she went to Dusty.

"Let me buy you some lunch, Tanya."

The mingled aromas of cotton candy, corn dogs, and funnel cakes had whetted her appetite. Happy to be finished with her obligation to the station, she followed him down the crowded midway. They made their way to a bright white canvas tent surrounded by food vendors and discovered they both had a tradition of eating grilled cheese at the fair. Eva sat at a freshly painted picnic table in the shade and people watched while he ordered their food. The scenario brought up fond memories of going to the fair with her pop.

Back at the table, Dusty unwrapped his grilled cheese. He broke the cheesy sandwich apart, taking a bite.

"We work well together," he said. "I'll ask Reid if we can get paired up for Oktoberfest in La Crosse. We could emcee the Festmaster's Ball together. We'd get to present the award to the winner of the Oktoberfest medallion hunt."

"You know, I can see us working together on a morning team." Eva smiled. It wasn't too much of a stretch. They got each other's humor, loved music, and their sexual tension would heighten the banter. She tried her sandwich.

"I could use some mustard."

"Stay there."

When he jumped up to fetch a yellow bottle from the counter, she admired the view as he walked away. Artie never offered to do anything for her. Since she had declared their marriage over after the tug-of-war, they'd barely spoken. True to form, he'd done nothing to fight for her. His silence did the talking.

She sipped her beer and watched a mom let her toddler gnaw on a corn dog. Man, she could not wait to move out. After moving, she'd have to save seventy-five dollars for the no-contest divorce plus a few hundred for the lawyer. Until then, she would not waste another minute of her life thinking about Artie.

Dusty sauntered back to the table. He bowed.

"Grey Poupon, madame?"

She laughed. "Silly man."

"So, Tanya. Have you found an apartment yet?"

"I found a house for rent that looks promising." The listing she'd found was already taken, though. "And I met with a lawyer."

After they finished eating, she got up and put her plate in the trash. It was too nice of a day to waste talking about heavy stuff. "Do you like going on rides?"

"I do. Looky here." Dusty pulled an accordion string of tickets from his pocket. "Complimentary tickets. Let's hit the Zipper."

Artie hated going on rides.

"I'm game," Dusty said. "We can make it if we run."

"You Shook Me All Night Long" from AC/DC blared and grew louder as they approached the carnival. He held tight to her hand as they sprinted. At the line, her braids swung when he picked her up and twirled. For a split second, she worried someone might see them, her in her little country outfit, acting single. But the fair was in Caledonia, nearly an hour's drive from the station in Winona and thirty miles from Artie in La Crosse. After a quick delicious hug, Eva kicked at the wet piney mulch under her boots, looking for spare change from the upside-down Zipper riders.

Eva and Dusty plopped onto duct-taped cushions in the tippy cage. A wiry tattooed carnie slammed the safety bar tight across their waists with a bang. He pressed a button which quickly raised them twenty feet. Preoccupied by the view of contoured fields to the east and the city to the west, she didn't notice Dusty's passionate gaze until he turned her face to his and kissed her.

The car jolted them apart as it moved up a stop. Eva gripped the welded handles and rocked with all her might. Dusty joined in; they couldn't flip it. The ride finally started, catapulting them from the throes of laughter to wild shrieking as the car somersaulted with neck-snapping momentum. Delirious, they stumbled off, ecstatic from the loud music, the spinning, and their attempts to make out. The ride ended too soon.

"My heart is about to jump out of my chest and roll down the midway," he said, grabbing her hand.

"Hey, are you Dusty?

A guy pushing a kid in a stroller approached. When the men began talking football, Eva kept walking, whistling along to Aerosmith's "Back in the Saddle."

As she neared the station's booth, she noticed a commotion. Red lights spun and flashed. What was going on? The loud music must have masked the sirens. She sprinted through the crowd, holding on to her hat, almost tripping over her boots. An ambulance blocked the view. She pushed in closer. A stranger was giving details to an officer taking notes.

"I saw him stumble into the equipment back there. His body just spasmed and his eyes bugged out, then his hair started smoking."

Paramedics were bent over a blue-tinged Wes who lay on a gurney with a lacerated forehead. Behind them, the Marti unit antenna was tipped. She looked up. It had hit a high-voltage power line above the booth. Horrified, she remembered laughing with Donn over Yardley's remote safety memo and her thoughts about Wes from earlier.

"Stay clear!"

A utility worker in a neon vest and hard hat shoved her out of the way. Lena appeared from the crowd and clutched at her.

"He wasn't drunk. He slipped in a puddle," she blubbered.

She clawed her way back to the ambulance. When the paramedics stopped giving CPR to her nephew, Lena began to wail. They covered his face with a white station logo golf towel. Lena fell to the ground.

Wes the Molester was dead. After the ambulance left, Reid arrived and shuttered their booth for the day.

Wes's death made the national news, spit out of the Teletype, a cautionary tale for radio DJs across the country. Many memos were issued at work and more than one meeting was held to address equipment safety, the behavior of staff during remote broadcasts, drinking on the job, and how to handle outside media inquiries. Because Wes had brought this on himself—admittedly, she had encouraged him to drink more—Eva harbored no guilt.

In the middle of a dead-air nightmare about a tsunami inundating the studio, Eva flailed her arms, reaching for Wes, whose swollen face receded into the deep. She woke to a hard rain hammering the window. Relieved that it was only a dream, she snuggled under the sheets, lulled by the rhythmless percussion. *I don't have to work today.* Falling into a light sleep, she dreamt of kissing Dusty at the fair. Thunder startled her awake. She rolled over to look at the clock on her bedside table. Artie wouldn't be home from his mother's until after lunch. The plan? Take him to dinner at a neutral location for the big breakup. Ludwig jumped on the bed, head-butting Eva's chin until she got up.

Later, out in the garage, she tuned the boombox to the public station. Her half-finished piano bench sat in the corner where she'd left it, newspapers still stuck to its feet from the day Reid first called. For the past year, she'd been using a chair at the piano which made it hard to reach the higher and lower notes. How could an entire year have passed? Time compressed into a flash of images: driving to Winona on that first day, the station tour with Dusty, becoming a country music lover, the Willie Nelson concert, the promotion to copywriter, all the notes Dusty had left in her cubby. She stirred the paint thinner with a stick. Organic vapors filled the air.

When the classical host played Vivaldi's "Four Seasons," the piece transported her back to music theory class. The beginning notes matched her melancholy mood. As the tempo increased, a lilting melody blossomed, winter melting into spring. A burst of vibrating strings like bees on flowers interrupted as the violinists agitated their bows.

With an old toothbrush, she scrubbed at the table leg where a line of stubborn paint clung to a carved groove. Although she and Artie had grown apart, marriage kept them stuck together. In the beginning, she had glossed over Artie's complacency, his lack of participation in the marriage, and, since his mother's illness, his foul moods. By wanting him to be different, a romantic suitor, she'd stripped him of his true self. To cope, they pretended to be a happy couple, presenting a false veneer to the world.

She stepped back to assess the wood grain, clean of paint. The piano bench would gleam under a fresh coat of shellac. It went on fast. After securing the lid with a few taps of a hammer, she dragged the piece into the corner to dry.

Eva practiced having various conversations with Artie. The words "I want a divorce" had been in her mouth for weeks, but there hadn't been an opportunity to say them. And now it was out in the universe: she promised Dusty and had told Coco in a letter. It was now or never.

But asking for a divorce seemed too abrupt. She needed to ease into it, maybe start by saying she didn't want to have children and, for that reason alone, they should separate.

Would she have to go back to living with roommates? What if Artie wanted to stay living together during the mandatory six-month waiting period that Wisconsin required between filing and finalizing a divorce? Or maybe *he* would move out. But she was getting ahead of herself. She would remain calm, not dwell on past insults, keep the conversation moving forward. The first step was to say the words. There'd be a minute of extreme discomfort while he reacted, then days or weeks of avoiding each other until she moved out, followed by the unbearable shame of telling their families, friends, coworkers, classmates.

The delicious memory of Dusty's kisses rippled through her core. Shame overcame pleasure. Artie didn't deserve this. The longer she waited, the worse it would be. Especially if she got caught.

###

That night, at a sports bar in Onalaska, where drinks were cheap and strong, a waitress guided Eva and Artie to the only available booth. Eva noted the location of the nearest TV and sat with her back to it so Artie could watch the game. They slurped old-fashioneds while they perused the menu and talked about football.

Artie switched to beer when they ordered. Already tipsy, Eva asked for a glass of red wine. The alcohol fueled her courage. She reached over to grab his hand and knocked over his water glass. They sopped the liquid with napkins. She spilled the beans.

"Artie. I'm going to move out."

"What?" He stopped wiping the water.

"You don't love me. You never have."

His mouth twitched. "What are you talking about?"

"You don't care about me. You're always gone. Since we got married, you've ignored me, you never . . ." Hating herself, she started to cry.

"That's crazy, Eva. I've been helping my mom. I know you were pissed that night you came home drunk, but why haven't you said anything before then?" He rubbed the back of his neck.

"Why haven't you asked? You always avoid talking about us. 'Now's not a good time.' That's what you say when I try."

The waitress set down their fish fry dinners and extra napkins. A family near them erupted in laughter. All around the restaurant, people were smiling, making toasts, cheering for the Packers.

Artie glared, his fries getting cold.

"I knew you'd be mad," she said.

"I'm—speechless. What do you want from me?"

"I want to feel like I'm special, Artie. I need you to be romantic. You haven't done anything to pursue me, let alone say you love me. I want to be nurtured."

Artie went silent. His own father had run off, leaving his ma to raise three young boys alone. "I don't take care of you?" he asked in a small voice.

"You go to work and come home. Eat, watch TV, sleep. The same thing you'd be doing if I wasn't in the picture. It'd be nice, just once, if I'd get home and there'd be dinner waiting. I do that for you all the time. But no. You leave every weekend. You forget important dates. You borrow my car and leave the tank empty. That one time you spilled a thermos of coffee on the back seat and never cleaned it up."

She paused, taking note of his shocked face. A baby at the table next to them babbled and banged a spoon. Eva sat forward. The volume of her voice escalated as she carried on.

"I do all the housework. I pay the bills and balance the checkbook. I feed the cat, clean the litter, and take him to the vet. You never even ask how I'm doing. When I cut my finger last week, you just sat there watching TV. When I had a cold, you didn't make me a cup of tea!"

"Keep it down, Eva. I make tea for you," Artie said, his voice low.

"When? When have you ever brought me tea?"

He glared. "When's the last time you gave me a blowjob? Huh?"

So that's what he wants. They weren't remotely on the same page. *What a numbskull.*

Artie's jaw tightened and his inner Scorpio came out. He loved a good debate and now he defended himself.

"While I'm at work, you're going to concerts and playing softball. You've got all those new friends, people who don't use their real names even when they're off the air. I mean, who *are* you?"

He shoved his plate so hard, fries spilled onto the table.

Eva slid farther down into the booth each time he flung an accusation. She resolved to move things forward.

"We made a mistake. We got married too young. Then you stopped trying to catch me."

"Catch you? I committed to you forever. That's what you wanted, a ring on your finger." His nostrils flared.

214

She slapped the table. Her wedding ring clacked. "Me? That's what your mother wanted! Her and the church. She couldn't bear the shame of her son having a bastard."

"Ma told me to do the right thing."

"The right thing to do would be to love me."

She wanted the old Artie, the guitarist who sang to her in the crowd and pushed her against the wall backstage, kissing her with a burning desire. That time in their lives had lasted only a few months but had held so much promise. She started to cry.

"You never even put your arm around me or ask me to sit by you or compliment me or anything anymore. You act like I don't exist."

"Well, I'm lonely, too. Do you think I like all the driving, shoveling Ma's sidewalks, paying her bills, sleeping on the couch?"

The waitress asked if they needed anything.

"We're fine," Artie said emphatically, scaring her off.

"Why doesn't your mom hire someone?"

He huffed. "Eva, she's barely scraping by."

"What about our money? You're spending a fortune on gas, driving across the state all the time. Not to mention all the oil for the car."

"Oh, yeah? What about your shopping? You spend plenty on cigarettes and stuff we don't need."

She ran her hand down her braid. "I know. I need to quit. But the rest are necessities."

"Baskets. Candles. Makeup? All junk."

"Why don't you get a better job? Do you want to work for Penzle's School Supply your entire life? You're not even using your degree. That's stupid and lazy."

He got up abruptly and walked toward the men's room, his hands holding his head. By insulting him, Eva had gone too far. She tried to eat, but tears fell into her mouth as she chewed. Her nose became too stuffed to breathe. She blew it into her napkin.

When Artie returned, he seemed recomposed.

215

"This whole discussion started with you saying you wanted to move. Why?"

"The truth is, I don't think I want kids, Artie. We never should've gotten married."

"Are you saying you want a divorce?" He squeezed his eyes shut. "There's someone else, isn't there?"

She froze. "No."

"You're lying. One of those radio guys? Come on, Eva, fess up. Look me in the eye."

Not able to do that, she locked in on a freckle on his forehead and managed to twist the truth. "I swear, I'm not sleeping with anyone. This has been coming for a long time. I can't pretend anymore."

"Then stop being 'Tanya' or 'Lizzy' or 'Billie' or whoever." He scrunched his forehead. Could he see the secrets in her eyes? "How long have you felt this way?"

The waitress slipped their bill under a plate and dodged away.

"Since you started leaving me alone. Since you murdered Ditzy."

"It's that again. For cripes sake, Eva, it was an accident." He glowered at her. "We can work this out. Let me try and fix it."

So, he wanted to stay married. But anger took over. She crossed her arms. By hardening her heart, she justified his hurt.

"I have no more energy for this marriage, Artie. It's over."

She gathered her purse and coat from the seat of the booth. They paid their bill and left through the busy bar, Artie sullen, Eva hiding her distraught face under the collar of her jacket.

Several weeks later, on a perfect October afternoon, Eva paced in the lot behind the radio station, jacket in hand, waiting for her date. Her heart flip-flopped with anticipation and the recklessness of her intentions. Announced with a rumble that echoed from the street and down the alley, Dusty steered his motorcycle into the parking lot, his face beaming under his weathered leather cowboy hat. He looked like an outlaw. It turned her on.

"Hey, Tanya," he said, handing her a helmet. "Be careful. Pipes are hot." He steadied the bike. She scanned for witnesses before mounting it. When he brought the motorcycle to life with a twist of the throttle, the roar of the engine—and the thrill of putting her life in the hands of another—turned the butterflies inside her belly into a nest of buzzing bees. There was no backrest, forcing her to hold tight to his waist.

Her helmet knocked into the back of Dusty's head as he steered the bike out of the alley and thundered through Winona toward Boyer Lake and his secret place. At the main stoplight, Dusty put his feet on the ground. A car approached, an old Chrysler, exactly like Artie's. She turned her face in the opposite direction, shutting her eyes. It couldn't be him; he was at work. They hadn't spoken to each other since their squabble at the restaurant. Thanks to their opposite schedules, they could avoid each other most days. He had not actively tried to fix the marriage since then—or been involved in getting the divorce. It would be up to her. Should she save money to move out or pay the lawyer?

Once in the countryside, Eva relaxed. She slid her hands farther around Dusty's waist, resting her head on his leather-clad shoulder. The low vibration of tires rolling across the rough road heightened her senses.

When he geared down and turned onto a gravel lane, their weight shifted perfectly in tune. She became acutely aware of the firm muscles in his back and thighs. He rolled on the throttle. The colorful autumn woods became a blur. She had never seen the world so clearly. Even the air tasted different. It was exhilarating.

"Here we are," Dusty shouted, parking in a spot near the lake.

He switched off the engine. In the quiet, waves broke at the shoreline, a gentle, rhythmic sound. The sky blushed pink, its colors mirrored onto the water's surface in tones of mauve, teal, and steel grey. Once off the bike, Dusty hugged her so completely it seemed as if his arms were wrapped around her twice. Any remaining reticence drained away.

"Oh, Tanya. I've been waiting for this all day."

Eva slipped her hands under his soft denim shirt, pressing her small palms to his warm skin. She glanced over her shoulder before kissing him. He lifted her off her feet and bent back so far that she could feel every part of his body, including his pounding heart. Separating, he retrieved a bottle and a flashlight from the saddlebag. He undid a bungee holding a tightly rolled sleeping bag to a rack. *For all your love-making needs . . .* She breathed in the lake-scented air.

"It'll be dark soon," Dusty said softly.

He pulled her into the crook of his arm. Joined at the hip, they walked to a path just off the sandy beach. A flock of ducks caused a commotion from the shallows, splashing and quacking as they flew off. Holding hands, the couple laughed as they plunked over a wooden footbridge and ran around a bend into a cathedral of cedars.

"This is it." He led her off the main trail.

"Wow, it's beautiful," she said, stopping to take in the view.

Ahead, a smooth outcropping of rock shone in the fading light, surrounded by a thick grove of trees. *Artie would like this place.* She pushed the instinctual thought away as Dusty brushed cedar berries and pine needles from the rock. He spread the plaid flannel sleeping bag onto the concave surface. After they scrambled up, he twisted the top off a pint of brandy and sipped. He passed it to Eva. She tasted the sweet, biting liquid.

"Kiss me," he whispered, pushing off her coat.

They lay back in the shallow nest, the stone warm from the sun's heat. He rubbed her arms with long, comforting strokes, a lesson in erogenous zones. Lying there alone with him at last, she closed her eyes and nestled against his chest. *I've died and gone to heaven.* He lifted her chin, kissing her again, deeper, not letting up. Clothing flew into the cedars; her racy new bra hung from a branch. As they moved together, her entire being buzzed with excitement. With expert fingers, he touched her, a vibration below her navel grew into a galaxy of sensation, spinning into a swirling tempest, getting darker and hotter until it spread like a supernova. The call of loons masked their exclamations.

When Eva finally opened her eyes to twilight, a bright star shone through the branches above. Her wrists tingled as if she had hyperventilated. She listened to Dusty breathing, replaying the afternoon from the moment she'd jumped on his motorcycle to the present. Emotion welled up and out as tears. Her heart burst from its rusty chains. Love flowed in.

"Are you crying, Tanya?" he asked.

"No, my nose is a little runny." Had he just made love to her, or Tanya? "Dusty, you can call me Eva."

"You got it, Eva."

A gust of wind rustled the tops of the trees. Letting out a heavy sigh, he drew the sleeping bag around them and hugged her close. The temperature had dropped. She shivered and breathed in his skin.

"You're a very, very beautiful woman."

Wow. Artie had never said anything like that to her. She grinned. In a way, she liked it when Dusty called her "Tanya." It boosted her self-esteem, as if she were part of the radio insiders club.

They gathered their things and walked back to the lot, stopping every few feet to embrace. The night had been perfect. Eva would never forget it; she had fallen completely and thoroughly in love.

39. SPARE ME A LITTLE ~ FLEETWOOD MAC

At six o'clock on Friday night, Eva "just happened" to be at her desk, catching up on copy. She looked up and smiled when she saw Dusty walking over carrying headphones and hoped he had the evening free. He flashed a devious smile her way and asked if she'd ever seen the engineer's workshop. She hadn't. He led her into the basement, where their voices echoed off the cold concrete walls. They peeked into the engineer's shop. The workbench was piled with spare audio equipment, parts, and tools. A blackened pipe sat in a dented metal ashtray.

Dusty ushered her into a room next door, unlit and empty except for a bare mattress which she eyed with suspicion. Desire overcame any aversion when he took her in his arms and whispered that he needed her. She took hold of his belt and brought him close. They embraced in the blue-green fluorescent light streaming in from the workshop. He threw her down on the lumpy mattress, covering her body with his. After kissing her lips, his burning mouth moved to her neck. A jolt of desire coursed through her body. She marveled at their chemistry. There in the raw basement of the radio station, they dare not be naked. When he unzipped his Levi's, she helped him wriggle the tight jeans down over his thighs. She caressed his strong back and muscular arms through the fabric of his denim shirt. He lifted her skirt.

Kindled by a state of arousal still burning from the night before, their bodies married. His talented hands seemed to touch her everywhere at once. Just as he let out a groan, heavy footsteps above loosened dust from the beams over their heads. Breathing hard, Eva was left wanting more. Instead, they hurriedly dressed and ran up the stairs, laughing and undiscovered. Perhaps they could continue at his place?

But Dusty was going to his friend's farm to help restore an old Farmall tractor. Outside in the parking lot, he put his hands on her shoulders, giving her a chaste kiss. Empty and unsatisfied, Eva headed home to Ludwig. She really needed a place of her own.

###

The next morning, the glittery world outside Eva's front window took her breath away. Grass, cars, and branches sparkled with frost. It would burn off quickly, as the forecast called for a day as warm and golden as the previous. She ate breakfast, paid bills, tidied the house, packed a lunch. When her shift ended, the sun would be down, "along with the temperatures" said the copywriter in her, so she pulled a heavy sweater over her Mike + the Mechanics T-shirt and grabbed the chic suede jacket that Faye had outgrown long ago. She let her hair down—how Dusty liked it—brushed it smooth and applied a coat of strawberry gloss to her lips. Thinking of him day and night had worn a groove into her gray matter. The needle was stuck on the same track. *Cue burn of the brain.*

After arriving at the station, she popped her head into the studio. Dusty's grin stretched wide when he saw her, but he had to do a break, so she went to make coffee.

While her beau finished his Saturday Morning Classics show, she hunkered by the bins to pull records. Someday, they'd run the place, a husband-and-wife dynamic duo, a powerhouse of love and radio. They'd change the format to rock, possibly rockin' country, and live in a big house on a bluff overlooking the Mississippi, filled with cats, a dog, maybe even goats, a donkey, and chickens.

"I wish I could stay," he said, wistfully. "But the weather could turn any time. I've got to help my dad build his new garage."

Eva's insides scraped out when she realized she wouldn't see him until Monday. Another weekend alone. She mumbled something about finding her headphones and ran into the bathroom. Tears dribbled down her cheeks as she sat, head in hands. *I can't be in this boat six months from now.* If she filed for divorce right away, instead of using the money for moving out, her new life could be in place by the following summer. Maybe she should file before her mother-in-law died. People would think she was terrible if she did it after.

She glanced at her watch. It was almost noon; time to put on her game face. She wiped her eyes using a square of toilet paper.

Outside the studio, she heard Dusty singing along with George Strait through the open door. She stopped in her tracks when the on-air sign lit up.

DUSTY: "All My Exes Live in Texas," George Strait on Q106, where the heart of country lives. Up next, it's our very own star, the lovely and talented Tanya Starr. Here's the old possum, George Jones, and "I Always Get Lucky with You."

His words gave her a thrill.

"Yes!" he said, off-mic. "Hit the post."

"You nailed it," she exclaimed as she entered the studio.

"Want to watch the country music awards with me next week?" he asked. "The results will be the talk of the airwaves."

"Are you asking me for a date?"

Joy filled her heart. She went behind him and nuzzled his warm neck. He smelled so good she wanted to burrow inside his shirt. Her body hummed.

"Yes, but why don't I come over to your place?" he asked, raising his brows. "You could play the piano for me."

Eva weighed the risk. There'd be plenty of time to watch the show; Artie worked until midnight. "Sure. You can meet Ludwig."

She jotted her address on an index card. Dusty tucked it into his pocket.

After he left, she settled into the air chair, still toasty from his body. Before he came over, she'd have to finish "Hunk of My Heart," the song she'd been inspired to write after they'd first made love.

The record he had left cued up was "Baby's Got a New Baby" by Schuyler Knobloch and Overstreet. Eva dropped the needle and

222

listened to the lyrics in preview. "Baby" was coming home late, buying new clothes, talking about a place of her own. The other song he'd set up was an oldie, "Your Cheatin' Heart" by Hank Williams. Had he done this on purpose? He would have made a joke if he'd noticed. But the message hit loud and clear. Every song she played that afternoon accused her. "If Loving You Is Wrong, I Don't Want to Be Right," "She's Actin' Single, I'm Drinkin' Doubles," and "Ring on Her Finger, Time on Her Hands."

Eva lit a cigarette. In country music, a cheatin' woman is older, perhaps a bit weary. A cheatin' woman has needs, because her trucker, businessman, or barfly husband was never home. A cheatin' woman cries herself to sleep or has one-night stands with men from the local watering hole.

A blinking phone line broke Eva's strange train of thought.

"Q106, this is Tanya. Who's calling?"

"Horace from Galesville. Say, who did that song, 'Tulsa Time?'"

"That was Don Williams. Maybe you remember the version by Eric Clapton? It was written by Dana Flowers and—"

"You should play more songs like that."

The feeling of being cut off by a man aroused her ire. "Thanks for your input. I'll pass that on to our programmers."

Horace was the last caller that day. When the phones were dead, announcers had to work harder to envision the audience in their minds. It wasn't the same as a comedian or singer receiving instant feedback from a live crowd. Eva no longer brought the photo of her dad but still talked to him. Sometimes she pictured her Grandma Chastine sitting across from the mic wearing a floral chintz robe, a cigarette burning between her polished fingernails, bristled curlers slathered with Dippity-Do in her hair. Other times, Eva imagined Faye listening while she drove through the hills of Santa Cruz in a convertible. Too bad radio airwaves only traveled so far.

It occurred to her; Dusty might be listening with his dad. She could talk to them—a covert introduction to her possible future father-in-law. After the next break, she segued into the song "Let Me Introduce You to My New Love."

Out in the office, Eva found a note in her cubby. Her breath caught as she read it.

A Haiku for You, by Dusty
We are a love song
Instrumental fingers strum
Hearts falling like leaves

She pressed the paper to her heart and ran back into the studio.

A few hours later, with the *New York Times* crossword puzzle partially finished, Eva stood up to stretch. There was a decent aisle behind the counter to do calisthenics. She did fifty jumping jacks, then tried a few yoga moves, occasionally dipping to the board to cue up a record or announce a song. Stretched out, she sat in the air chair and lit a cigarette before her break.

TANYA: River Country Radio with John Anderson and "She Just Started Liking Cheatin' Songs." He's not sure if it's the cheatin' she likes or maybe just the melody. I'm Tanya Starr. A significant change in the weather is coming tomorrow—it'll be cold with showers, only 44 degrees. Stay tuned for the Oak Ridge Boys on Q106, the best in country music today.

Eva turned off the mic and listened while the spot set played. There were ads for bowling leagues, chimney cleaning, and car winterization. She shuddered. Summer was her favorite season— shorts, flip-flops, swimsuits, and long hot days.

She picked up the newspaper and debated whether to put more effort into the crossword. From the opposite page, a headline jumped out: "Infidelity and Women: Shifting Patterns." The article reported that up to fifty percent of men had affairs, and since the sexual revolution, just as many married women cheated.

Up to half was a lot. If so, people certainly kept it a secret.

When "Elvira" faded out, she segued into "Guitars, Cadillacs" by Dwight Yoakam, one of the best songs she'd ever played at River Country. While bopping in the chair and singing along, she loaded the cart machines with spots for the next commercial break.

She picked up the paper again. *Only eight percent of spouses suspect their partner of cheating.* What if she confessed? The answer resounded in her heart. Absolutely not, it would devastate Artie. She'd rather carry the weight of her wrongdoings for the rest of her life. A cumbersome burden that, hopefully, would lighten over time.

Line 1 flashed.

"Eva, it's me." It sounded like Artie was calling from a racetrack. "I'm at a filling station. My car broke down."

"What happened?"

"The engine blew. The mechanic is looking for a rebuilt one."

"Are you okay?" she asked. *Damn, more money down the drain.*

"Yeah. Ma needed furnace filters, so I was driving to Fleet Farm when the car started knocking super loud. Then it went *bang!* Scared the living crap out of me. Luckily, I coasted to the side of the road."

"I'm glad you didn't get hurt. Hold on a minute."

She prepared herself for a break while wondering how much a new engine would cost. The car leaked like a faulty faucet; dollars to doughnuts he hadn't bothered to check the oil. He was such a dipshit. Forcing a smile, she announced a song and came back to the phone.

"How much?"

"Eight hundred."

She almost dropped the receiver. "Where are we going to get that kind of money?"

All her plans went out the window.

40. WHAT'S ON MY MIND ~ KANSAS

An hour before the awards ceremony was to begin, Dusty arrived at Eva's apartment in La Crosse. He wore a dopey grin and carried chips and a twelve-pack. Seeing him at the door—he'd come so far just to see her—seemed to fill a gaping hole in the center of her being.

Once inside, she threw her arms around him, crushing his snacks, clinging to him, overjoyed that he didn't let go. They rocked together, her head on his chest, her ear on his heart. He set the goodies down on the coffee table. After hanging up his coat, he lifted her hand above her head and twirled her in a circle.

"Let's two-step."

Light-footed, he danced her around the room and over to the couch where they plopped down. He leaned forward and popped two cans of beer.

"Your cheeks are rosy," she said, cuddling into him, tucking her legs.

"The wind is supposed to die down later. We can go for a ride."

"Yes. *Vroom, vroom.*"

Delighted, she imagined holding him tight, watching the city fly by from the back of his bike. As they snuggled close, his fingers tangled with hers.

"Is this your high school ring?" she asked.

"Yes," he said, holding out his hand. "I didn't know what color to get, so I picked sapphire. It's my birthstone."

"It's blue, just like your eyes."

"Aw, you're sweet. Don't you have a class ring?"

Eva slid her left hand under her leg even though she had removed her wedding ring before Dusty arrived. A hot new country song kicked up inside her head, "Love Knot," by Amanda

Stacks: *On the way to the bar, she takes off her ring, and drops it inside the glove box. Her lover slips in, shares shots of dark rum. She's well on her way to a love knot.*

The love knot ended with a gunshot.

"I had a class ring," she said, "but in college—after you coerced me to start smoking—I was so broke, I sold it at a pawnshop for cigarettes. Got seven bucks. My mom would kill me if she knew."

When was the last time she'd talked to her mom? September? The woman had been so busy with her new boyfriend, they rarely connected with each other.

"What a bad girl." Dusty said, picking up his beer. He held it high. "Here's a toast to your buddy Randy Travis. Do you think he'll win album of the year?"

"Spike conducted an informal poll this morning. George Strait and The Judds were tied." Eva touched her can to his. The cold beer hit the spot. She licked foam from her lips. "I'll bet on The Judds."

He got up and went over to Eva and Artie's stereo stand, where he flipped through their assortment of records, cassettes, and CDs. She wondered what he thought of Artie's punk and heavy metal collection. There was not a country album in the mix.

"When I was a kid, radio stations played everything," Eva said. "Johnny Cash followed by The Kinks or Chubby Checker and the Supremes. They'd throw in some Andy Williams or a song like 'The Girl from Ipanema,' maybe even some bluegrass from Flatt and Scruggs. It was all over the place. The soundtrack of my childhood was mostly Motown, though."

"Everyone loves Motown," Dusty said. He flipped through her albums. "You don't have any disco, but I see a bunch of stolen jazz records from the campus station."

"They were duplicates!"

"I'll admit, I have a few work records at home."

"What's your favorite song, Dusty?"

"*Too good to be true, that's why I like you,*" he sang.

"That's not a song. You made that up."

"It's true. I dig you, Tanya. I always have, even in college. You're so smart and talented, and I must say, incredibly cute. Compared to—well, I've never met anyone like you."

Dusty looked away. When Ludwig jumped into his lap, he petted the cat. "After my breakup with Jasmine, I was in a dry spell. You've been—I'm attempting to be poetic here—you're like fresh rain watering my soul. We just click."

Eva's heart danced; love rushed into the spaces between beats. No one had expressed such sweet sentiments to her. While she was pregnant Artie commented her ass was getting bigger, but that was the extent of him noticing her. *Damn.* Why hadn't he put oil in the car? She owed Dusty honesty about her situation.

"Dusty?"

"Yes?" He took her hand. "Did I say too much?"

But she couldn't find the words. This attentive man was right here, and he wanted her.

"Never mind." She pecked his cheek.

"Alright," he said, reaching for the remote.

The awards show had just begun. They settled into the davenport as Kenny Rogers took the stage. Imagining an ordinary life with Dusty made her catch her breath and when he started nibbling her earlobe, her stomach tightened like a spring wound too tight.

"Give me those sexy lips, woman."

He leaned in to kiss her. Ludwig jumped away.

"I might be getting a cold," she mumbled.

"Give it to me."

His smooth radio voice made her quiver. He pushed her onto the cushions, kissing her hungrily. They missed most of the program.

By the time Ronnie Milsap came on stage for the final act, Dusty was asleep, his head in her lap. Like a young Paul Newman, he had a strong jaw. The line of his nose was as straight as a Greek statue's. A work of art. His brow flickered as she touched a faint scar above his eye. The relationship had the potential to be a masterpiece. Or a catastrophe.

She smoothed his hair, marveling at the silkiness between her fingers, and became overwhelmed with wanting him again. *I will love him even if he becomes baldheaded.* She'd been dreaming of him, lucid dreams so deep with unconditional love it felt like being cradled by the universe. Did he dream of her?

When the pins and needles in her arm grew unbearable, she slid it out. He woke.

"What time is it?"

"Almost ten. The show is ending." They had a good hour before he'd have to leave. Eva turned his face so she could see into his loving eyes. She leaned in to kiss him. "We should have gotten together way back in school. Think of all the years we missed."

"I guess it wasn't the right time." He pulled her close, gently rocking while he hummed. "I was going to bring you flowers, but they didn't have enough in the store to show how much I adore you and your torrid voice."

This couldn't be real. What had she done to deserve such a sweet man? If Coco was there, she would say something about ego boundaries collapsing and lovers believing they can take on the world. She would warn that it takes a year to truly know someone.

"Can I stay over?" he asked.

Eva froze. What if Artie came home early? He never had, and they'd been avoiding each other so it hadn't crossed her mind. She drew a strained breath from under the landslide of guilt on her chest. *I am so foolish. I've done everything out of order.* She brought Dusty's hand to her heart.

"There's something I need to tell you. I met with a lawyer. I'm filing for divorce. Soon, I promise. But Artie hasn't moved out yet."

"At the fair, you said you'd found a house for rent. I thought you moved already." He sat up and stroked his dimpled chin as the credits rolled. "You lied?"

"It wasn't a lie. The house didn't work out because I couldn't afford it. I'm still looking." Her eyes pleaded with him to say he understood. "I swear. My marriage is over. I'm crazy about you. I only want to be with you."

He tucked in his shirt and walked stiffly to the coat rack, punching his arms through the sleeves of his motorcycle jacket.

"I don't know what to say, Tanya. I'm dumbfounded," he said, grimacing. "Hold on. Is he coming home tonight?"

"Not until after midnight," she said, barely a whisper.

Seeing the look of hurt and disbelief on his face made her stomach clench, a fist in the gut. He glared with eyes as hard as marble.

"Oh my god! Are you trying to get me killed?"

When he turned to leave, she flew to the door. He pushed past. Hanging on the jam, she shouted as he mounted his bike under the streetlight.

"Dusty! Come back!"

He stomped on the kick starter. The bike roared to life. She ran into the yard. After revving the engine a few times, he peeled out, leaving a black stripe of evidence in the street. The lights blinked on in the upstairs apartment as his taillights faded into the distance.

Eva stood, disheveled, bawling uncontrollably like a child. What if the neighbor spied them? She ran inside and threw herself on the couch, burying her face in the scratchy fabric. Ludwig climbed on her back, kneading his paws.

"Oh, Luddy, what the hell am I going to do?"

Hollowed out, she cried until nothing remained but a dull ache in her temples.

Dusty would come to his senses. They'd talk it out. If he cared as much as he said, he'd understand. Someday they'd laugh about the time he could've gotten beaten up by Artie.

41. A DREAM GOES ON FOREVER ~ TODD RUNDGREN

The Midwest experienced a major snowfall: fourteen inches in La Crosse, eighteen in Winona. An Arctic high-pressure system followed, bringing with it dazzling blue skies and bitter cold temperatures. Stiff winds created wind chills below zero and whipped up drifts, rendering the roads treacherous.

After a white-knuckle drive, Eva made it to work. She laughed at Spike, dressed in a snowmobile suit with his buckled boots propped on his desk as he smoked. She removed her own layers and sat at the typewriter, relieved to have made it to work in one piece. The nerves from driving were soon overtaken by her apprehension over confronting Dusty. He'd brushed her off the last few weeks when she'd tried to take him aside. She couldn't wait any longer to know what he was thinking.

Her in-box contained two scripts. She pulled a stopwatch from the desk and did a dry read, out loud but quietly.

NOW THAT THE GRASS-CUTTING SEASON IS OVER ARE YOU GOING TO PUT YOUR LAWNMOWER AWAY FOR THE WINTER WITHOUT DEFENDING IT FROM THE GASOLINE THAT CAN ERODE YOUR ENGINE WITH HARMFUL GUM AND VARNISH DEPOSITS AND MAKE YOUR MOWER DIFFICULT TO START IN THE SPRING?

Eva gasped for air. "What idiot wrote this horseshit?"

"A jockey?" Spike quipped.

"This is the longest sentence in history! And I can't alter it, it's co-op. With all the snow out there, it's irrelevant."

"It's only November. The weather changes so fast around here, people forget to winterize their lawn mowers." He reached for the script. "I can talk fast."

"Thank you." He could have the production money.

"At your service anytime, m'lady."

Sanders was out covering storm damage and had left Eva in charge of the noon news. The stories and carts were stacked neatly in the AM studio on the counter. Before sitting at the board, she checked the wire for any late-breaking news. An accident was clogging the interstate. She'd lead with that. While she waited at the mic for the network news to end, she observed pictures pinned to the walls. Paul Harvey, David Brinkley, Edward R. Murrow, Eric Sevareid, Larry King . . . Sanders' heroes? Eva said a silent prayer of gratitude to the founding mothers who'd help pave the way for her: Cokie Roberts, Susan Stamberg, Jessica Savitch, Nina Totenberg, Diane Sawyer, Linda Wertheimer, Christiane Amanpour . . .

She wrapped up the hour with obituaries and, after hitting the network news sounder at one o'clock, gathered her stories, tapping the papers on the counter. Out in the office, Dusty, Reid, and Trevor had returned from their lunch meeting. They all wore dour looks. What was going on?

As Eva walked past the FM studio, Lena poked her head out the door and said, "Dusty took a job with the Brewers. I heard him on the phone this morning."

Eva blanched. Dusty had never mentioned applying for a job in Milwaukee. He disappeared into Reid's office.

"You don't look so good, Tanya," Lena said.

Eva walked unsteadily to her desk. Fifteen minutes later, Dusty exited Reid's office and walked straight to his desk. He put on his coat and made a beeline for the door. On his way out, he glanced at her without smiling or saying a word. His cold shoulder chilled Eva to the core. She was about to run after him when her extension lit up. She took the call, all the while glancing over her shoulder toward the side door.

Sanders blew in, trench coat billowing.

"I was just at Daisy's Diner. Someone vandalized the high school locker rooms. Go get an interview with the principal."

"Me? What'd they do?"

"Find that out," he said.

Eva inserted fresh batteries into a portable cassette recorder, put on her heavy parka, and hurried out into the white world where the roads were still snow-covered and slippery. She hadn't been in a school since having to cover the Teacher in Space Project, and, unwittingly, ended up reporting on the horrified reactions of children in the aftermath of the space shuttle Challenger disaster.

When she interviewed the livid principal, he allowed her to view the profane graffiti, none of which could be said on the air. A group of girls huddled outside the locker room, watching. She readied her tape recorder. Within minutes, they divulged the names of the vandals, which she gave to the principal. Excited to have gotten a scoop, she drove back to the station. Dusty's car was gone.

In the production studio, Eva went to her desk and typed the story. It was almost three o' clock. Dusty would be back any minute for his show. She went to her desk and typed up the story.

Suddenly, Reid came storming out of his office, headphones in hand. She jumped up.

Noticing her bewildered look as he passed, he said, "I'm doing afternoon drive. Dusty up and quit. He's moving to Milwaukee."

She took in a sharp breath, clutching the cart to her heart, which had just cleaved in half.

As the days passed, Eva went through the motions of life. Day after day, at work, ghosts of Dusty haunted her everywhere she turned. Night after night, she sat on the couch alone, ears eager for the phone to ring or the growl of a motorcycle that would never come. Taking things into her own hands, she snuck into Reid's office while he was doing afternoon drive. The staff list sat next to his phone. She copied Dusty's new contact information.

At home that night, she stared at his phone number. The digits swam in her eyes. She mustered the courage to call; 414, an unfamiliar area code. After two rings, he answered.

"Dusty? It's Eva."

Silence.

"So. What are you doing for the Brewers?" she asked, nonchalant, biting her nails.

"Well. I'm the network director, the point of contact for broadcast affiliates around the state. I send out team schedules, I coordinate the advertising, that kind of stuff." He talked faster, sounding excited. "And I've found a high school that wants me to call football games." He paused. "Yeah. That's it. Why are you calling, Tanya?"

"To see where we stand."

"Where we stand? I moved over two hundred miles away from you. I'm over it."

That hurt; her whole body winced. She bit the inside of her lip.

"Dusty, you said you were crazy about me. That you'd wait. I'm not an old shoe you can just toss out. Sometimes after you throw something away, that's when you realize you need it."

"You did make me crazy. But I don't want a relationship based on lies." He flicked his lighter. His voice hitched. "You weren't honest with me—that's what I can't get over. I can't be with a schemer and a manipulator. I've got to go."

The line clicked. Eva stood stock-still, listening to the dial tone. Finally, she hung the wall phone on its handset. The cord swung around, twisting over itself, hanging like a noose. How could he be so callous? Hearing his devastating words had been worse than not knowing what he thought. That night on the volleyball court, he had said that he would wait for her. Such a sweet talker—how could she resist? The cord came to stillness.

And he had called her "Tanya" again. Perhaps she had fallen for the suave radio guy Dusty Miles, and not the real person. *Dustin Nixon.* Her jaw tightened. She knew people lashed out when they were hurt, but he had pointed his finger at her. What about the fingers pointing back at him?

Eva dialed again. While she listened to the phone ring, her lips trembled. After five rings, he answered. She gave him hell.

"You act so innocent, like I hurt *you*. Well, Dustin, *you* seduced *me*. *You* got involved with a married woman. You manipulated me with your bedroom eyes and your poetry and your pretty singing. You called me Tanya, even after I asked you to call me Eva."

She slammed down the phone.

"Take that, you bastard!"

She sat at the kitchen table, head in her shaking hands. What a mess. Just as she had feared, she'd lost both of her men. And her father, too, only forty-one years old the day he died. She massaged her temples, thinking of the accident: the ice, the broken glass, the blood. How could her pop have left her? A tear slid down her face. She reached over to the junk drawer for a pen. Forty-one minus twenty-seven. What if *she* only had fourteen years left to live? Would she be like Coco, focused on her career, depending only on herself? That would be a lonely life. Would she stay with Artie, maybe adopt children, stay at Q106, or leave him and start over with someone new? *Someone at the station, Tanya?* she thought, mocking herself. By examining her life, it suddenly felt unrecognizable, like a word she had stared at too long.

Ludwig padded up and put his paws on the chair.

"You love me, don't you Luddy?"

The cat meowed. She scratched his head.

"You're the only one who loves me unconditionally. No matter how I look or what I do."

Something had to change—either her marriage, her job, or herself. She'd read that risking change pushes a person out of their comfort zone toward self-confrontation, the reason why most people don't want to. Bravely, she looked at herself.

Cheating on Artie had splintered her, even more than pretending to be her various on-air personalities. Regardless of the changes to come, her soul wanted to do the right thing, to bend toward the light and be whole.

Eva made her way through the sea of desks and clouds of cigarette smoke to Reid's office, her aircheck in hand. She hoped for a positive critique. Writing copy and composing jingles had been the bright spots in her life over the long winter; she'd put all her focus on work.

"Wow, it's so clean," she said as she entered his office.

He wore his usual corduroy pants and a sweater vest. Eva looked to the corner, where a life-sized promotional cutout had stood.

"Where's Kenny Rogers?"

"In the prize closet."

"Is that the top of your desk? Can I see wood?"

"You're funny, Tanya. In fact, I need to talk to you about something after we listen to your aircheck."

Alarm bells rang in her ears while her mind raced. Did it finally get around about her and Dusty? What if the engineer had seen them in the basement?

With his thick fingers, Reid took her precious reel and wound it onto the deck sitting on the counter behind his desk. He pressed play. Eva studied his face while he listened. No reaction. After a minute, he fast-forwarded. After a few seconds, he forwarded again. *Ugh, he's bored.* She tugged on her lip as she flashed back to college and her aircheck sessions with Professor Holt, who had minutely and harshly scrutinized every phrase, inflection, and word.

Reid hit pause and turned to her, meeting her eyes.

"Very nice, Tanya. Your commercial voiceovers sound good. The scripts you write are crisp *and* they tell a story. That's hard to do. You sound great on the air. You're knowledgeable about the music—"

"It was all new to me when I started."

"I know, you little rock-and-roller. The only criticism I have is that you're saying your name a lot. Probably a carryover from being on mornings. Once or twice an hour is plenty."

Eva frowned. She had mocked Wes for using the time as a crutch. Wes the Molester, may he rot in pieces.

"I'll do better," she said, waiting for a shoe to drop.

"So," Reid said, leaning forward.

She braced.

"I found an eager young guy for Dusty's shift. He graduated from Brown. He's new—but he sounds mature. And since we're revamping afternoon drive, I thought the rest of the day could use a refresh."

Crap. He found another "guy" to take her place.

"How would you like to join Spike on the morning show?"

As if poked with a sharp pin, the air she'd been holding escaped all at once. She could hardly believe it. "Really? We do have good chemistry."

"He thinks so."

"He knows?"

"It was his idea."

Eva fell back in the chair, bowled over.

"I want you guys to get more involved in the community. With two people on the show, you can interview the mayor, artists, council members, teachers, bikers out on the Elroy-Sparta trail, whatnot. Just remember, with the repeal of the Fairness Doctrine, you no longer need to worry about equal time for conflicting viewpoints."

Reid put her reel back in its box. He returned it, sliding it across the desk.

"I want you to consider moving here, Eva. We take pride in the longevity of our air staff—most of us call Winona home."

He was asking for a commitment. She'd have to get a Minnesota driver's license, find a new doctor, veterinarian, hair stylist . . .

"After the Spike and Tanya Show, continue to write copy and help Sanders with the news. As for your weekend shift, Dusty recommended you as his replacement on the Saturday Morning Classics before he left."

Dusty respected her work. She squeezed her eyes shut. Maybe he *had* been hiding his feelings for her when she called. Taking over his show and the tradition, she'd feel closer to him, like in a parallel universe.

"Are you okay?" Reid asked

"Can I think about it?"

"Of course."

Reid's line lit up. He took the call, talking low.

Eva shook off mixed emotions. *Where do my commitments lie?* Good question. In her heart, she had never truly committed to Artie, having been bum-rushed into marriage with him. Was she ready to commit to Reid and the station? What about committing to herself? Being on a morning show was the ultimate. Yet Spike liked to tease her—Bart Starr's daughter. Did she want to continue the Tanya charade? Maybe she should start fresh, take her chances in La Crosse, or Madison, even use her real name. But what if she moved to Winona? Spike would retire someday; he had gray hair and had served in Vietnam. Perhaps her dream of doing a show with Dusty could come true. He might tire of living in a big city like Milwaukee and move back home.

Reid hung up the phone. He gave her a questioning look.

"If I accept, I'll need a raise."

"Oh, yes, of course. I've approved a dollar an hour."

"I need more than that, Reid." It was the morning show, after all.

He crossed his arms while he thought. "Okay. A buck-fifty. And you'll get one Saturday off each month."

She sat back, tugging on her lip. What would *Eva* do? The offer exceeded her expectations, which amped up the stakes. On the one hand, a small-town morning show and the certainty of divorce. On the other hand, greener pastures?

Eva ran the board while Spike made funny faces at her from across the counter. Ashes fell onto the log as the cigarette dangling from his lips bobbed.

> SPIKE: Thank god it's Friday! So, what's in the forecast?
> TANYA: Cold! Sunny skies with a high of eighteen tomorrow.
> SPIKE: Yikes! Here's some freaky news. Seismographs in St. Paul registered an earthquake yesterday. Did you feel it?
> TANYA: I wish! It registered 2.2 on the Richter scale. At 2.5 and under, earthquakes can't be felt.
> SPIKE: An imperceptible earthquake, an excellent name for a band. Say, what did one earthquake say to the other?
> TANYA: Shake it, baby?
> SPIKE: I was gonna say, it's your fault!
> SPIKE & TANYA: *Hahaha!*
> TANYA: Coming up, the latest state and local news after this song from Jerry Jeff Walker.

When Eva arrived home at 1:30 p.m., she found Artie holding the phone, his head hanging. He looked up briefly when she came into the apartment, but his eyes were remote.

"What's going on?" she whispered.

He didn't acknowledge her. Finally, he hung up. He rushed to the closet, yanking out a duffle bag.

"That was my brother."

"Did something happen?"

"Ma's in the hospital."

"Oh, no."

"She's on a ventilator."

From the floor below, Ludwig looked back and forth as if at a tennis match. A kitty metronome.

"I took the night off. Where's my bomber jacket?" Artie asked, running a hand through his hair.

"In the closet. I'm so sorry about your mom, Artie."

Eva held her arms out for a hug. He turned his back. She went into the kitchen while he looked for his coat.

"I'll make you a sandwich for the ride."

The front door opened and closed. When he came back in, he held something blue, his eyes questioning.

"I found one of your chokers outside, lying in the mud."

A broken elastic string hung from one end. Several beads had fallen off.

"Really?" *Shit.* Dusty must have torn it off the night of the music awards.

"Who was here, Eva?"

He furrowed his brows. Had he suspected something all this time? Surely, he had noticed the skid marks in the street.

"I must have dropped it," she said, improvising. "I've been beading during my Saturday morning shift. It's pretty boring."

"I feel like you're lying. Or maybe 'Tanya' is."

She wrapped his peanut butter and blackberry jam sandwich in wax paper and handed it to him. He tucked the sandwich in his bag and stood in the doorway, defiant, tears in his eyes.

"Call with an update, okay?" she said.

"For cripes sake, Eva. Quit pretending you care. I don't anymore."

Desolation gripped her heart. With the tables turned—him rejecting her—she felt a sense of loss bigger than herself. The bottom of her world dropped away, out of her control, like getting fired. A pleading urge for love and acceptance surged in her chest. She felt weak and ragged, a torn-up Valentine lying in the trash.

Yet this is what she'd wanted. To end the relationship. Why didn't she feel free?

"I do care about you, Artie," she said quietly.

"What am I going to do if she doesn't make it?"

He let out a sob and hurriedly gathered his things, scanning the room as if he'd forgotten something. Eva ran to the window as he left, wishing she could have comforted him. He backed the car out of the garage and drove off.

She collapsed onto the couch, holding Ludwig tight to her chest.

Later that evening, she sat on the floor with a shoebox full of old letters between her outstretched legs. Ludwig sauntered up and sat on the papers, crinkling her precious notes from Dusty. In shoving the cat off, she bumped her highball glass, spilling her sixth 7&7 on the carpet. After wiping feebly at the mess, she got up to mix another, more fortification to confront her memories.

Back in the living room, underneath a letter from Coco, she found a note written on the backside of paper torn from the Teletype.

> Hey Dimples,
> You're sounding great! We get a lot of truckers tuning in and they love getting a shout. "East Bound and Down" by Jerry Reed or "Convoy" by C.W. McCall. You can reference the movie Smokey and the Bandit with Burt Reynolds. XOXOX, Dusty

She flipped the paper to the other side.

DATELINE: AUGUST 1987–MOLLY YARD ELECTED PRESIDENT OF NOW, THE NATIONAL ORGANIZATION FOR WOMEN.

Dusty had left the trucker songs note in her cubby around the time of their first kiss in the back of his car. His stylish masculine penmanship lilted like his voice, the words angled slightly to the future, fit into the center of the page as if in a frame. Her tear smudged the signature. XOXOX wasn't hugs and kisses, he'd said, but kisses and hugs—the Os go around you and the Xs are puckered lips.

Her head knocked on her heart: *Wake up, Eva. It's over.* She slammed her drink. The reckless way she'd gone after Dusty had caused so much pain. For her, for him, and now Artie, even though he was unaware of the source. She thought about his reaction when he found the choker. For once, he'd looked her in the eyes and seemed jealous, possessive even. If only he cared enough to look at her like that every day. To really see her.

It takes two to two-step. They couldn't just glide through life focused on their careers, taking each other for granted. There was more to life than work. Eva experienced a sudden moment of clarity, a revelation. Had she been copycatting Coco's script for life?

Ludwig jumped into her lap and lifted his head while she scratched his little white chin. She was in control, not Artie, not her job. Honoring her pop's legacy was one thing: she'd gotten a taste of success. Her fifteen minutes of fame with Yardley was fun while it lasted, yet unsatisfying. *It wasn't me.* Like the horrifying lines that had been forming around her mouth from smoking, the passage of time etched her own personal history.

Now came the moment to stop ad-libbing her way through life. So, what lay ahead? Why stay at a country station? The musical landscape of the '80s was unexplored terrain, a vibrant mosaic, from U2 to Bon Jovi and Guns N' Roses, to the beats of Run-D.M.C. and the Beastie Boys. As much as she liked the variety in her job and the people, the answer was no, Eva did not want to be at Q106 in five years. A big wave of change could wash the past clean. It was time to get the hell out of River Country.

The next morning, nothing helped ease Eva's wicked hangover. Not aspirin, nor the acetaminophen she'd swallowed with cold coffee in the car on the way in. At work, she went through the motions like a ghoul, her mouth dry and her head drooping. The songs mocked her pain. "Wasted Days and Wasted Nights," "Whiskey Bent and Hell Bound," and now, "Sunday Morning Coming Down," by Kris Kristofferson, who, Eva recalled from her notebook, had been married to Rita Coolidge. Artie was still AWOL; he hadn't called with an update on his mom. While keeping an eye on the phone, she jotted the Kristofferson fact on a piece of scratch paper.

When she opened the mic to speak, her adrenaline took over. When she turned it off, her energy crashed. She listened to the lyrics with her headphones still on. Something about country music wasn't sitting well. All the cheatin' and drinkin'. *I'm Tanya Starr—a country cliché?* When did she become a binge drinker?

Eva drained a glass of water while waiting for the last commercial in the break to end. She smiled when she noticed the cart label:

#102   FRANKLIN JEWELERS   :60
". . . for all your jewelry needs."

TANYA: This one's going out to Vinnie in LaCrescent, who's girlfriend left him for another guy. Have a good cry while you listen to the next song, buddy, then put yourself back out there. Originally released as the B side of a blues record, here's "I'm So Lonesome I Could Cry" from Bocephus's dad, Hank Williams. On Q106.

There was no Vinnie.

Some upbeat, rockin' country, that's what she needed. In between songs, she perused the albums at the back of the studio, all the while wondering about Artie's mom. At the board, she jotted interesting bits from the album covers.

After draining her coffee mug, she bellied up to the microphone to announce Willie Nelson's "Blue Eyes Cryin' in the Rain." The song carried her right back to the county fairgrounds.

Stab me in the heart. Needing to get up and move, Eva left the studio.

With her hands on her hips, she surveyed the untidy office. It looked like everyone had left during a fire alarm. She stuffed trash into the bin and closed the bathroom door. A stray chair had made its way into the kitchenette. She guided the chair to Dusty's old desk. Lingering behind it, she squeezed the cushiony shoulders. The woven blue fabric reminded her of his faded denim shirt, the one with the mother-of-pearl snaps. On the desk phone, two lines blinked at once.

She lifted her hands. Her life hadn't ended since he left.

Eva ran into the studio.

"Q106, this is Tanya. Can you hold?"

"Yes." It sounded like Artie. She pressed hold, then Line 2.

"This is Vinnie," the man said. "You just dedicated a song to me?"

"Are you in LaCrescent?"

"I am. And now my wife is accusing me of having a girlfriend. Who put you up to that?"

"Well, I got a call from Vinnie himself," she quipped. Her husband was on hold. "Whoops. My song is ending. Thanks for calling."

She hung up, putting Artie on speaker as she changed records.

"I'm back. How's it going?"

"I have bad news," he said, his voice strangled. "Ma died this morning."

Eva had known this moment was coming but hadn't expected to feel shocked. There she was, hours away, chained to the air chair.

"Oh, Artie. I'm so sorry. Were you with her?"

He began to sob. While waiting for him to regain his composure, something palpable shifted. The depth of his grief wrenched at her heart, weakening the wall of resentment she had built. As she gave him the space to cry, she felt an unexpected longing. To start over and go back to when they first met, to do everything right this time. Years and years of Eva's tightly held anger unwound into compassion.

"I was with her, by her bed most of the night. I fell asleep and when I woke up it was so quiet. I'll miss her, alright." He sniffled. "The doctor says it's a blessing. She'd been in so much pain. The cancer was everywhere."

"It's a horrible disease." Eva grimaced. *I should be crying, too.*

"Promise me you'll quit smoking, Eva."

He still cared.

"I want to, but it's hard. Everyone in radio smokes."

"Another reason to move on."

She huffed, then got it together. Now was not the time.

"Please tell your family they have my deepest sympathy. I'm so very sorry, Artie. About everything."

He heaved a long, ragged sigh, speaking in a colorless voice, flat as if he'd been run over. "I wanted to give her a grandchild. It's all she talked about at the end."

"Oh, Artie. I've got to do a break."

She grabbed a PSA without having time to pre-read it.

TANYA: Tammy Wynette with "D-I-V-O-R-C-E." She came up with the hit after spelling out the word in front of her young son. Say, if you or a loved one are living with cancer, don't miss the "Coping with Cancer" talk at the Hyatt in Rochester next Saturday. Call the county health department for information. From the '86 studio album *Storms of Life*, here's Randy Travis and "Reasons I Cheat" on Q106, the best in country today.

"You still there?"

"Yup," he said, recovered, his voice normal. "The mass will be on Tuesday. Where did I write the time? Hang on." The phone clunked. She put the line on speaker and readied a single on Turntable 2.

The funeral. Eva envisioned Artie and his brothers looking somber at the monolithic Catholic church in Sheboygan, uncomfortable in black suits, nodding their heads, murmuring with relatives on the steps while the priest shook everyone's hands. She wondered if Artie's father would come out of the woodwork.

Suddenly, the tears came. Her chest heaved, the way people sob when death triggers a reminder of their own loved ones: her father, Grandma Chastine, the baby. *I would have named him George.* Someday she would lose her mom, her friends, her cat, Artie. How had this escaped her? After a few moments of self-pity, she settled down and blew her nose with a honk. The cheatin' song ended; she took it off the turntable and cued up a CD, Kathy Mattea's "Love at the Five and Dime."

At her pop's funeral, people had walked around like zombies, in total shock. He had been so full of life, then he was gone. Her mom had shuffled from group to group with little Eva pressed close to her body, a mama bird protecting a wounded chick. Eva touched the scar on her wrist. Her world, the studio, everything seemed to go white for a few seconds. As Kathy sang about getting married and losing a child, Eva envisioned a church, people crying.

Someday it would be her mother in the coffin. Her mom—her biggest supporter. Who would stand by her side then? She had no siblings. Coco and Faye and Dwayne were in California. Dusty was never coming back. Trevor and Spike and Annabelle and everybody were friendly—working and drinking friends—but not real ones.

Her eyes welled. She reached for a tissue. Despite his flaws, Artie wouldn't stand her up. He *would* stand by her side. Is this what unconditional love meant? Someone who is there all the time? Her heart softened. The poor guy was trying to get along in the world just like every other human. Had she held on to stubborn anger like a mask, to hide herself from the pain of potentially losing another loved one?

When the song ended, Eva segued to another without giving a station ID. She flipped to the next hour's page in the log. Carts and records needed to be pulled.

247

"I found the obituary," Artie said, startling her from the speaker phone. "Visitation is at one, the funeral after. I was just talking to my brother. He asked if you would play a song on the piano."

"Sure. I could play a canon by Pachelbel or 'Ave Maria.'"

"How about 'Over the Rainbow?' It's her favorite. You do it well."

"Of course. I wish I was there to hug you."

"We're meeting at the Pine Lake Supper Club tonight. I'll wait for you," he said, hesitating." I still love you, Eva."

He did? Finally, the words she longed to hear. Maybe it was time to flip the record of their marriage, to play the B side.

"Me, too, Artie."

After they hung up, her mind reeled. She chewed another aspirin while she made a list: *Call Mom, Reid, Sanders.* Tucking the phone between her ear and shoulder, she dialed her boss. The line rang and rang. It seemed wrong to feel relief over her mother-in-law's passing, but honestly, without the woman's influence, perhaps now she and Artie could start fresh. There had to be something worth salvaging. They weren't kids anymore. Since the devastating end to her affair, Eva had begun to desire stability and commitment. *How ironic. For all your matrimonial needs . . .*

The call finally went to Reid's answering machine. She left a message and added *Make appointment with OB-GYN* to her list. It had been many months since she'd made love with Artie, long before her tryst with Dusty at Boyer Lake. What if she'd caught VD?

Eva sat in the window seat reading *Rolling Stone* with Ludwig on her lap. Artie plunked on his guitar in the bedroom—a good sign. For weeks after his mother's funeral, he'd been too quiet. Perhaps he grieved his father, too—the bum never showed. Eva lifted the cat from her lap and went to the piano bench where she'd hidden Artie's birthday present. She sat at the piano.

"Hey, Artie. Come here. I want to show you something."

He came out of the bedroom looking bedraggled in his faded Badgers sweatshirt, the guitar still strapped around his neck.

"Happy birthday, a little early." She handed him a flat bag.

"*50 Duets for Piano and Guitar* and *The Greatest Songs of the '70s.*" He turned the music books over, scanning the titles. "This is very cool, Eva. Thank you. Let's try one."

He scooted her over on the bench, his arm over the guitar. She opened the songbook to "Let it Be." They struggled through it at first, picking up speed on the second run-through. Soon they were laughing and harmonizing like the old days. When he made up silly lyrics, she knew they'd turned a corner. He stopped strumming and put his hand over hers on the keys.

"I don't know how things got so bad between us, Eva. I mean, things became worse because of our messed-up work hours and Ma's cancer, but we also got started on the wrong foot. I'm sorry."

"Me too. But you know what? I'm tired of rehashing the past." She put a hand on his knee and squeezed. "Although—"

"What? You can say stuff to me."

"I need more from you. Nothing big. Just little things. Like when we're out with friends, or at the movies, or on the couch, I wish you'd put your arm around me. Tell me you think I'm pretty. Say you love me. I'll try harder, too. I want this marriage to work, which means we can't slide back to how things were."

Artie held out his pinky finger and hooked it with hers. "I promise I will do these things for you. I want this to work, too."

With his trademark strumming and slapping method, he played the opening chords to "I Can See Clearly Now" by Johnny Nash, rocking them back and forth. This was the guy who had stood on stage and excited her.

###

The next afternoon at work, Eva opened *Radio & Records* to Opportunities/Midwest. Seemingly preordained, the first listing was for a reporter in Madison. She called Artie's direct line.

"Accounting department. This is Arthur."

"How's work?" she asked.

"It sucks. But I'm looking forward to lunch and the treat you made for me. How'd you know I like key lime pie?"

"From our very first date. You said it was your favorite."

"Wow. I completely forgot. That's sweet, Eva."

Reuben ambled up waving a script. Most likely a last-minute commercial. She gave him a thumbs up. He slapped it into her inbox and headed for the door.

"The reason I'm calling is . . . What if we made a fresh start and moved to Madison? You always wanted to live there. Coco is from Madison; she might move back someday. I should leave Q106 on a high note, you know? Not wait for something dreadful to happen. The time is now, Artie."

She circled the job listing using a wax editing pen. Her decisive manner must have jolted him.

"After the shitty day I've had, it sounds tempting. Will you help me update my résumé? You're better at that stuff than me."

"Of course."

"I suppose I'll have to get a haircut before I start interviewing."

And get rid of that yucky beard.

"And I should probably shave off my beard," Artie said.

250

PART FOUR

Fired, again. Eva hung up the phone and sat at the kitchen table, head in hands. The Madison News/Talk station had been sold to a national corporation, the air staff replaced by syndicated programming. Only management and sales would remain.

Ludwig sauntered up. "Oh, kitty. I can't win. Radio bites."

From the trash, Eva dug out the pack of cigarettes she'd thrown away that morning. At the table, she lit one, taking a deep puff. It wasn't her fault this time, which should have stung less. If she'd been fired for a poor performance, well, she could've dealt with that.

Intoxicating at first, being a reporter in the capitol city had given her access to Madison's epicenter of action. For almost two years, she'd sat through government meetings, running back to the station late at night to type up the stories. And how many times had she been called to cover an emergency press conference, jostling for a spot among a sea of big, pushy men? It had taken a year for her to master the one-way streets around the Isthmus without a map. She gritted her teeth. News was a tough gig.

And here she was at another crossroads, jilted by the bad boyfriend once again. Like marriage, radio looked good on paper, but in reality. . .

The other prominent news station in Madison had cut people, too, a trend, it seemed. At this rate, radio would cannibalize itself and become irrelevant, all for bottom-line corporate profits. To heck with serving the community. It wasn't fair and it wasn't right.

She stubbed out her cigarette.

"You know what? I'm done! Screw radio. Tanya Starr, signing off for good."

Determined to find a normal job, Eva unfolded the *Wisconsin State Journal* to the classifieds. She sighed with relief. The General section filled an entire page, Office/Clerical two pages. Tracing down the paper, her finger landed on a listing for an office manager—at a radio station. The sparsely worded ad left a lot out. Where was it located? A single station or a group? She rested her chin on her hands. Format changes wouldn't affect an office position. She had skills, thanks to helping Dottie and working at Action Insurance. And she knew the lingo: bits, spots, pots, carts, bumpers, sweepers, kickers, liners, programming, promotions, production, remotes. *They'd be lucky to have me.* This could be the best of both worlds. She could still work in radio, but without the pressure of having to be a personality. It was worth a shot.

She smiled, surprised by how calmly she was handling being fired.

Artie ambled out of the bedroom; his eyes half closed. Seeing him without a beard always caught her off guard. That, and how he'd started picking up his clothes and hanging up wet towels. He paused on his way to the bathroom.

"Mornin'."

"Good morning. Wish me luck. I'm looking for a new job."

"What?"

"I'll tell you after you wake up."

He stepped into the bathroom. She dialed the number. After one ring, a man answered.

UNCLE ANDY: Radio Rummage-A-Rama. You're on the air. What have you got to buy, sell, or trade?
EVA: Uh, I'm inquiring about the office manager position?
UNCLE ANDY: Oh! Fantastic! Stay on the line. More Radio Rummage-A-Rama is coming up, folks. In the meantime, I'll find out whether they're thirty-year-old chickens for sale or thirty, year-old chickens. Haha! It's fifty degrees with sunshine high atop Radio Hill. Stay tuned for the Six Fat Dutchmen after these messages.

Was this a prank? He put her on hold. Commercials blared. Eva held the handset away from her ear. A used car spot played, followed by a per inquiry ad for a smokeless ashtray. After having oompah music forced on her for a few minutes, he came back on the line.

"Sorry about that. I'm Mason Andrews, the general manager. Also, Uncle Andy, star of Radio Rummage-A-Rama. We really need someone to answer the phones."

Even off the air, he spoke with a polished announcer's voice. His delivery reminded her of Gary Owens, the prim and silly announcer on *Rowan & Martin's Laugh-In*, the way he talked into the classic gimbaled boom microphone, a finger on the earpiece.

Frickin' old folks' music.

He had two minutes to talk. She gave him her background and stated she had no intention of going on the air. They had agreed to meet on Thursday in Madison.

Working at a polka station would be quirky at least. Hands down, it would beat working at an insurance agency. If she could stand listening to polkas all day.

On the morning of the interview, Eva took a walk along the northern edge of Lake Mendota, the largest of Madison's five lakes. Having a beach within walking distance was like owning lakefront property. While strolling near the marina, she weighed the pros and cons of the new position. If she didn't like it, she could search for something else while gaining office experience. A great blue heron took off from the shallows, wings moving to a slow beat. A sign? She picked up her pace on the way home, cutting under a railroad trestle and through Warner Park.

At Troy Drive she took the sidewalk, where on a billboard, a man in a tux hooked a diamond necklace around a woman's neck. *Show your love with diamonds,* it proclaimed. Eva pondered the image. She would rather have someone cook dinner for her.

Shortly after she arrived home, the doorbell rang. A package? She tore it open to find a gift from her mother. Pepper spray in a pink case with faux gold trim. Laughing at the absurdity, she practiced spraying it out the back door. Even though her mom had expressed concern about her meeting Mason at a motel, Eva wasn't worried. From his rich bass voice alone, it was apparent he was a radio guy.

But just in case, when she arrived, she patted her pocket to make sure the pepper spray was upright. Waiting in the hall outside the room, while the ice machine clunked, she leaned against the damask wallpaper and reviewed her skills, one for each finger: team player, self-starter, experience, communication, trainability. TSECT. If they asked a question that stumped her, she could look at her fingers and concoct a story around the prompt.

Finally, Mason Andrews, a clean-cut man in his mid-thirties, opened the door and introduced himself. He was not the "good ol' Uncle Andy" Eva had expected. Mason wore a bold navy pin-striped suit which fit impeccably. The magnetism of his smile overcame a certain mournfulness in his eyes.

He introduced her to a silver-haired man. "This is Barry Snow, my business partner." The name rang a bell. He reached across the table to shake her hand.

"Mr. Snow, did you own B93 in La Crosse?" Eva asked. She sat.

"Indeed, I did, young lady. How did you know that?"

"I worked there. We never officially met. I was Tanya Starr."

"Oh, yes," he said, eyeing her up and down. "I wasn't aware your real name was," Barry paused as he referred to her résumé, "Eva. Why did you leave B93?" he asked, not recalling.

"Uh, I was let go," she said. "Remember Yardley St. Martins? He said it was because I took time off during a ratings period, but he was the one who approved my vacation. He always told me I shouldn't worry about ratings."

Eva's face became hot. *He said I wasn't authentic.* She squirmed in the chair.

"Oh. That guy."

The men exchanged glances.

"Sorry. He was good on the air, but . . ." Barry shook his head.

Eva's breath came easier. She had expected to be grilled about being fired. "The woman he hired to take my place, Sunny, quit after a few months."

"Sounds like him," Barry said, smoothing his silver hair. "He treated his sidekicks like he was dating them. He wanted them to be special, but then his ego got in the way. We think you're a splendid candidate. The fact you have radio experience alone is great."

Mason described how they'd been working for months to replace the transmitter and tower, rebuild the studios, and restore the building.

Eva felt inspired by his passion. It could be stimulating to help start a new business from scratch. But there were other things to discuss. "Does the station have a cleaning service?" she asked.

"Er, we will," Barry said. "We don't expect you to clean."

"With your skills and background," Mason said, "you could help us get up to speed even more quickly than we'd hoped. We need a self-starter and a team player. The big question is, are you interested?"

"I can do 'The Chicken Dance.'" She lifted her hands in the air, mimicking a clucking chicken and wiggling her elbows.

Mason smacked the table. Even Barry laughed. Eva thought of all the weddings she'd been to, never imagining the dance would come in handy at a job interview. "Are you in?" he asked.

The past decade rolled up and over her like a wave. The many faces of Eva swam past: Billie, Lizzy, Tanya. *Jump in. The water is fine*, they clamored. But this wasn't about radio as much as job security. Like Dottie and Betty, secretaries weathered format changes. She sat up straight, brushing her hair off her shoulder. These people seemed desperate.

"Make it seven dollars to cover gas and two weeks of vacation. If I never have to go on the air, I'm game."

Mason showed her his Colgate smile. "When can you start?"

46. ROAD TO NOWHERE ~ TALKING HEADS

On Saturday morning, Artie came home after swimming at the Y. He gave Eva a chlorine-scented hug and pulled out his wallet, surprising her with a fifty-dollar bill.

"Go to the mall and pick out something nice—we're going to celebrate your new job tonight," he said.

Blown away by his thoughtfulness, she drove out to Fashion Bug and found a black knit dress with an off-the-shoulder cowl and a wide belt.

At six o'clock, all dressed up, Eva paced around the apartment in the strappy heels from Faye and Dwayne's wedding. *What's taking him so long and where are we going?* With the move to Madison, as she had hoped, a new chapter had begun for her and Artie. The past seemed far away, dark and small, as if compressed down a tunnel.

He came out of the bedroom wearing a blue dress shirt, open at the throat. The white beaded choker she'd made for him accentuated his tanned skin. He whistled in appreciation of her new dress.

"I've got something to tell you." He took her hand and led her to the couch. "You know I've been seeing a grief counselor."

"I still can't believe it."

"Well, it's covered by my health insurance." A pained look flickered over his face. He squeezed her hand. "It's been good, but—we were talking about my parents, and something came up. The counselor said it might help you understand me better. When we were kids, my Pa never played catch or interacted with me and my brothers, at all. We were dirt-poor after he left. Ma never threw birthday parties. No cake, no presents, not even a card. It hurt so much that I never wanted to revisit those memories."

It suddenly became clear why Artie wanted children: he wanted to fix things. Eva scoffed at the thought of his loser father and his mother and her shrill whistle.

"My parents threw parties every year," she said. "All my friends came over. Mom made a confetti cake with pink candles. Pop sang songs and invented clever games where every kid won a prize."

"Yeah. Never had that." He socked the pillow, another coping mechanism suggested by his counselor.

"Wow, Artie," she said softly. "Why didn't your mom do anything for you?"

"She always said stuff like 'spare the rod, spoil the child,' or she'd call me and my brothers ingrates. One time on my birthday, she said I should be honoring *her*, because she's the one who gave birth." He wrapped his arms around a throw pillow. "I guess it had to do with my father leaving. She was probably depressed."

"That makes sense. She always seemed so downtrodden. I thought it was the church." Eva leaned toward him, touching him on the arm. "Artie, you did everything for her."

"When she was sick. But I was a smart-mouthed kid. Always fighting with my brothers."

"You can't dwell on that. All kids are naughty."

"I know. My counselor thinks I have unresolved grief from when Pa left, like when a pet runs away and you never find out what happened, there's no resolution. Which has affected my adult life; I never get my hopes up for anything, because, well, people leave, and it hurts. So, we're working through that now."

"Artie, I'm so proud of you. It can't be easy."

They had both lost fathers, just in different ways. Tears welled in her eyes.

"Don't cry, Eva."

"It's okay. Tears are love. Love that I've—*we've*—missed all these years. If we have kids, Artie, please don't tell them not to cry."

"I get it. Anyway, I want to be better than Pa. I want to be a good husband." He put the pillow behind his back.

261

How brave. He was seeing the counselor for her. For them. Eva's heart flooded with empathy. The little boy who was never celebrated hadn't learned how to give. To have something he'd never had, he was trying something new.

"Thank you, Artie," she whispered.

He spoke faster, talking with his hands. "I know we're celebrating your job tonight, but I've got some exciting news. Remember Kevin, the drummer from the Inverted Paradiddles? He moved to Madison, too, and he wants to start a band! He knows a guy who plays bass, and that guy's brother knows the manager of the Café Palms, and—we're in!"

Eva jumped across the couch and threw her arms around his neck. She gave him a kiss.

"I'm so happy for you. The Palms is a good-sized club. Do you still have those sexy bell-bottoms?"

"I'll look." He winked and put his arm around her. "We want to do some originals. Do you have anything?"

"I've been working on something, actually."

"What's it about?"

"The song is called 'Have It All.' It's about realizing that—even when you can't get what you want, what you have is pretty good. I've only got the chorus." She sang, "*And if you want it all, it's time to smash that wall.*" Her natural vibrato faded into silence. "The verses could be a metaphor for swimming—churning through life, racing for the wall, spinning around, propelling forward."

Artie nodded slowly. "I like it." He got up and kneeled on the window seat, grinning like a mischievous cat. "It's here!"

She jumped up and stood next to him, her hand on his back. A shiny stretch limousine pulled up to the curb.

As Eva chugged up and over hilly roads lined with spring-green farm fields in her VW Golf, she scanned the rural route numbers assigned to posts along the way, looking for the polka station. At the top of the highest hill sat an odd, two-story building, an unkempt Bauhaus palace that needed a coat of paint. The stucco sagged. A large vertical sign spelling out the call letters hung from a rounded upper balcony. She pulled into the parking lot, spotting a person wearing headphones through a window next to the weather-beaten stoop.

The studio was just inside the employee entrance. Mason sat at the board wearing pajamas. He must have noticed her face questioning his appearance.

"I live upstairs," he said. "Usually, I get dressed before coming down."

After doing a break, he tightened the belt on his navy chenille robe and whisked Eva into the lobby at the other side of the building. A splendid view of Sauk County provided the backdrop: outside, cows grazed in a dandelion-studded pasture under the broadcast tower. They could see for miles.

Clipboards with forms attached lay on top of the tall reception desk, one for her and one for the new midday guy. Mason ran back to the studio and his show. Eva filled out her W-4, then created a form for scheduling commercials like Dottie's at B93. As she picked her way around stacks of drywall and two-by-fours, looking for a copy machine, the lack of AEs running around seemed eerie. Earlier, Mason had said their lone salesman was temporarily working from his car, covering a lot of territory each day. After the remodel, Otto would work out of the office adjacent to the lobby.

An hour later, with the Tuesday commercial log finished, Eva felt energized and in control. The midday guy was due to arrive soon. Not her concern, as her job was to run the office.

A carpenter arrived and introduced himself as Charlie. The strong young man dressed in cut-off painter shorts and a holey Kool-Aid Man T-shirt made numerous trips in and out of the future master control studio, hauling tools and equipment, each time giving her a friendly smile. A delivery woman appeared with a splendid bouquet of sunflowers, lilies, and snapdragons. Expecting it to be from Artie, Eva tore open the card.

> *Congrats on the new job, Eva! Wish we could be there to celebrate. Love, Faye & Dwayne.*

Astonishing. Artie must have spread the news. They really needed to tell their friends the truth about Ditzy.

Eva set the sweet-smelling flowers on the tall reception desk. She turned up the radio and started labeling file folders with the names of their limited advertising clients. She found herself tapping her toes. The upbeat music was reminiscent of her childhood, when she'd danced at family weddings with her parents, grandparents, aunts, and uncles to polkas, waltzes, and Schottisches under a glowing tent or in a dance hall.

In the main studio, Charlie the carpenter turned on a blaring boombox. He quickly turned it down, but then his air compressor engaged with a loud whirr. Even at the other end of the building, the noises would get picked up on the microphone.

Eva went down the hallway to the makeshift auxiliary studio to check in with Mason. He sat surrounded by chock-a-block office furniture and web-covered equipment. Over the polka music, he described how he'd cobbled the studio together. In addition to being the morning DJ and the general manager, he was a mechanical genius.

"Spit and bubble gum is all that's holding this board together." He wheeled over to the window to smash a fly with a flyswatter and wheeled back, waving his hand toward the board. "Wait until the new master control is finished. This will be just a bad dream."

Despite her satisfaction being the office manager, jealousy twinged in her throat at seeing him in the air chair. *I can do that. I'm good at that.*

Eva went back to the lobby to work on creating the master logs, one for each day of the week. While she typed, she tolerated the pop and hiss of the air compressor. Another florist appeared, this time with an exquisite bouquet of red roses arranged with pine boughs and baby's breath. From Artie. She pictured him excitedly ordering the flowers and anticipating her response. The roses smelled heavenly; she stuck her nose in and breathed deeply. Each soft petal spoke of his affection, each bloom evidence of the forethought he'd put into this surprise. She softened, sad over the pain they'd inflicted on each other in their efforts to protect themselves. Another layer of her wall crumbled, and with its collapse arose the fear of losing him. She had to call him. She dialed his direct line at the UW-Madison computer science department.

"The flowers are beautiful. How did you know I love baby's breath?"

"I remembered it from when you were in the hospital." His voice carried a wide smile.

"Oh, that's right. You brought pink roses," she said.

When the baby was still on a breathing tube. When she was kept in the hospital for a week—from psychological anguish rather than physical issues, which was why she'd missed the rest of the semester. She made a mental note to look up the date of the baby's death and celebrate it every year. It was likely Artie carried the pain with him too.

"Artie, I've been reflecting on what you said about your parents. How when you love someone deeply, if you lose them, you lose yourself? I was afraid, too. I put up a wall to protect myself."

"Maybe everyone does. Avoidance of pain and all that."

"Yeah. Anyway, I'm sorry. If we took the good pieces of your childhood and spliced them with mine, we might piece together a good life. A 'master' piece."

"I like that."

She stepped into the bright sunshine spilling from the tall windows, highlighting her flowers. With the phone under her ear, she rearranged the stunning bouquet. "I made the right decision to take this job. All the crap I've been through has led me to this. I love it—I'm working in radio, but I don't have to be someone else."

At nine-thirty, Mason poked his head out of the studio saying more flies had crawled out of the walls. She wondered how he could stand it in the dirty room. Before she could stop herself, she donned an apron and yellow rubber gloves and dragged the heavy shop vac down the hall, happy to help.

When Mason opened the door, using the same deep voice he used on the radio, he said, "Full disclosure, the midday guy just called on the studio line, and, well, he's changed his mind. I need you to cover the shift."

Standing there in the doorway, dressed like a maid, she bristled. *Was this a trick?*

"Please. I'm in a bind." He checked his watch. "I need to get showered. There's an implement dealer in Lodi who's interested in sponsoring the farm news. It could be our first major account."

"Mason," she said, raking her hands down the sides of her face. "You and Barry said . . . Ugh! I should have asked for a contract." She removed the rubber gloves and threw them on the floor, fuming.

"I'll do everything in my power to get someone in here ASAP." His voice sounded firm although he looked pathetic sitting there in his robe. He gave her puppy dog eyes, daring to smile despite knowing she was furious. The guy had balls.

In a huff, she sped down the hall and into the lobby in seconds. He stepped out of the studio, calling after her, but his song ended. The needle scratched around the record. *Dead air!* He darted back in. She punched her arms through the sleeves of her new lilac-colored spring coat and took her car keys from her purse. She turned off the radio, gathering her thoughts. The reason she had taken the job was to avoid the pressure of being on the air. She didn't even have a name.

On the other hand, during the interview, she'd promoted herself as a team player. She'd already completed the logs; what would she do for the rest of the day besides answering the phone? She had the skills. So, what was the big deal? It might be fun.

New feelings rushed in, of being open, of taking control, of saying yes and not being so stubborn. The past didn't have to repeat.

Mason came down the hall. "Look. There's no pressure. It doesn't matter if you screw up. What listeners we have are deaf or senile."

"I'm sorry I reacted that way. I can fill in. It's no problem." Eva unbuttoned her jacket.

Mason put his palms together, bowing and backing toward the studio. "Thank you, thank you. You saved my life."

"Holy crap!" she said, looking at her watch. She tore off her coat.

In the filthy studio, Eva watched as Mason segued into the legal ID. He potted up the network news with meticulous timing. Eva sneezed as he offered her the air chair. The board was labeled clearly with red embossed sticky labels, the white letters slightly askew. She chose a record from a flimsy shoebox full of 45s. On a piece of scratch paper, she scribbled "Everybody Polka," by Florian Chmielewski and the Fun Time Band.

Play the sounder. Go to Weather Central. Say 'Thanks, Ray.' Introduce myself. (The Polka Princess?) Announce the song.

After cueing a record, Eva wiped the cruddy counter, hoping she wouldn't get nauseated. *So many flies.* Dozens crawled on the window. With her jaw clenched, she picked up the fly swatter and smashed a cluster of the little buzzing bastards. They landed on their backs along the sill and *zzrrpd* as they slowly lost their lives. She scraped the bodies into a coffee can with the others, grimacing. No doubt this would come back as a gross dead-air nightmare. She put on a pair of headphones as the song faded.

I do have a name.

Maybe this was the opportunity she'd been waiting for to honor her father, Dean "Pop" Chastine.

A scene popped into her mind: not the typical out-of-body experience, but its mirror opposite. She envisioned herself snapping *into* her body, as if she'd spent years hovering above her own life watching herself play the roles that she believed she should. Never really plugged in to who *she* wanted to be. Acting as if her pop was up there at the ceiling, watching. "He'll be an angel on your shoulder, Little Eva." What good-intentioned adult had said that? She had interpreted it the wrong way. Her funky father would want her to find her own groove.

Eva clutched her notes and drew the corners of her mouth into a smile. When she spoke into the microphone: the daddy's girl, the fatherless teen, the wife, and now the woman, came together as one.

> EVA: Romy Gosz and the "Gaytime Polka." Before that, "Everybody Polka," by Florian Chim-ah—oh geez, and the Funtime Band.

She giggled on the air.

> EVA: Thanks for listening to the new polka station. I'm Eva Chastine. We're glad to have you with us on Polka Power Radio.

Messing up by flubbing the band's name and using the name she was born with had pushed her past her normal comfort zone. She'd goofed. The universe hadn't collapsed. The fake personalities had never protected her. The burden of pretending dropped like autumn leaves. *The leaves are falling and so are our prices.* Eva laughed as she removed a record from the turntable and got to work.

When the studio line blinked, a helpful listener corrected the pronunciation of Chmielewski. *People were listening!* The records turned. The happy music played. The flies buzzed. A string of callers welcomed her to the airwaves.

During a song, Eva dug Candi's Avon mirror from her purse and checked her makeup. Despite a bit of smudged mascara, her eyes were the same eyes that reflected in the mirror that morning. After all her failures, she'd become an office manager at a radio station. One who would pull an occasional air shift to help the boss. Thousands of students graduated from broadcast school every year. How many took weekend positions while holding down a day job, waiting for their big break—and eventually got married and raised children while their radio dreams faded? By taking the air chair and using her given name, Eva achieved what her old boss Yardley said was missing: authenticity. She felt an incredible release, like removing layers of winter clothes in the springtime.

During a commercial break, she flipped through the shoebox of 45s, counting a grand total of seventy records, of which the average length was two minutes. They'd be worn through the grooves in days. Ridiculous. They needed more music.

At one-thirty, she ate her peanut butter sandwich while playing four short polkas back-to-back, all the while wondering who would take over at two. The odds of it being someone she knew were slim. Probably some lame-ass has-been with a nasal voice who couldn't get a job in Madison to save his life.

As she finished eating, Mason came in carrying an armload of records.

"Albums?" she said. "Each with dozens of songs!" More overjoyed than she wanted to admit, Eva chucked her sandwich bag in the can with the flies and snatched the records.

"We made the sale," he said, smiling from ear to ear, "and the client donated these from his own collection."

"Fantastic!" She flipped through the polka albums.

Mason cleared his throat. Someone tagged behind him.

Eva's eyes widened as she took in the striking baby-faced young man with spiky bleached hair. He wore a watermelon-pink-and-white-striped rugby shirt and skin-tight black jeans tucked into ankle boots adorned with chains.

"This is Dana Elliott. Show him the ropes. He made an audition tape in his bedroom. This will be his first gig."

Dana grinned, obviously brimming with excitement over being hired as "the afternoon drive guy." A self-proclaimed radio geek, he oozed charisma like Yardley St. Martins yet seemed unaware of his own charm.

"There's a rest stop outside of Red Wing," Dana gushed. "I drive up there and listen to the Minneapolis rock stations. Have you ever heard Bubba G at K-Rock? He's the *best*."

Dana's enthusiasm made Eva realize how cynical she'd become, a way of thinking that went all the way back to Donn and her training at B93. Donn despised the callers, disparaged the AEs, banged the fan girls. Cynicism was a DJ's shared language, fueled by all the shitty, seedy parts of the business. The kid was too fresh to know. She fed on his exuberance.

"What does Bubba G sound like?" Eva asked, solicitously.

Dana ruffled his hand through his spiked hair. Out poured a super-hype DJ.

"ZZ Top with 'I'm Bad, I'm Nationwide.' *Rawrr!* I'm Dana Elliott with you on K-Rock! Yeah! No one else has your ticket to rock! *Rawrr!* And we're doin' it with Ozzy! Rock on, Minneapolis!"

He air-guitared, mimicking with his mouth the opening riffs to "Crazy Train," stomping his boot.

Mason stood in the background like a proud papa, beaming, his arms crossed. "Do yourself a favor, kid. Keep the energy up but tone down the puking."

"The what?" Dana asked.

Mason brought his hand to his neck. "*Blahhh!* Puking your words out. Sound natural."

This was Eva's new family. She didn't mind being on the air so much. Seriously, what else would she do all day? Wait, was she the mom or the sister?

"Mason," she interrupted. "I don't mind doing middays, but I'm not working weekends. Ever." Dana could be her witness.

"It's a deal," he said, smiling, and slipped out of the studio.

That was easy.

Dana took a seat behind Eva to observe. She gave him the flyswatter. They cracked up over funny songs like "Who Stole the Keeshka," "Free Beer Today Polka," and "I'm My Own Grandpa."

She imagined what Artie would say when she told him about her day. "I'm telling you, Eva. Admit it, you really wanted to be on the air again."

48. SLOW TURNING ~ JOHN HIATT

After "The Eva Chastine Oompah Midday Show," she stepped out for a cigarette break. Mason had banned smoking in the office. As the months wore on, more advertisers created more work leaving Eva with little time to smoke. She hurried out to the parking lot, bracing the collar of her parka against the wind. The frozen seats crackled as she got into the Golf. She started the engine and cracked the window before lighting her cigarette. Maybe it was time to try the patch. In their latest letter, Faye said it had helped her and Dwayne quit because no one smoked in California. Eva decided to drop her on-the-drive-home-from-work cigarette.

When she turned on the radio, the opening guitar riffs of "Don't Dream It's Over" rang out. Madison's new station, MAD96 FM, played fresh music called Alternative Rock. The DJs sounded very cool. She sang along for a bit, then sat in awe, listening to Neil Finn's glorious high notes during the chorus. It was the perfect antidote to the last song she had played, the frantic "Clarinet Polka" which, now that she thought about it, reminded her of "Flight of the Bumblebee" by Rimsky-Korsakov. She took a deep drag and leaned back. The four-hour shift always sapped her energy. One song had been only one-minute and twenty-seconds, barely enough time to cue the next.

I should apply at MAD96. Closing her eyes, she imagined herself behind the mic in a dimly lit posh studio with an espresso machine and patchouli incense filling the air. The royal-blue velvet air chair would be super-comfortable . . .

The wind howled, blowing through her drafty car. She shivered. The phones had been ringing all day, and she didn't want Dana to get annoyed. Everyone was truly amazed he hadn't moved on. She set her cigarette in the ashtray. Just as she reached to turn off the radio, an intriguing song came on. The singer lamented how love was both sweet and bitter. Although her feet were cold, she listened to the entire song.

"'Bittersweet,' Big Head Todd and the Monsters," the DJ said.

The past hit her like a ton of tubas. Falling in love with Dusty had been sweet; swallowing the pill of their breakup, bitter. She seized the steering wheel. *Stop it! He didn't care about me. I've got a second chance with the new Artie, an attentive, caring husband.* She felt so proud of him.

Eva made a vow to leave Dusty where he belonged, in the past along with Tanya and the rest of her personalities. She reached forward and turned off the radio. Making a leap, she imagined a jumbo-sized knob on her chest. Using both hands, she twisted the imaginary dial to OFF.

Running across the lot made her cheeks sting with cold. Inside, she finished producing a restaurant ad. Soon it was five o'clock.

At home that evening, the answering machine blinked. While leaning against the hallway table, she lit a long-awaited cigarette and pressed play. Ludwig ran up meowing. Eva gave him a scratch on the head.

"LaVette! You won't believe it. I'm coming home to work at MAD96 FM."

49. DON'T CHANGE ~ INXS

Eva stood at the spotless picture window in the auxiliary studio, watching for Coco. A cherry-red VW Beetle surfaced over the top of the hill and pulled into the lot.

"Welcome to the Polka Palace!" Eva yelled from the stoop.

Coco wore a black satin MAD96 jacket. The bumper sticker on her car read *DJs Do It With Frequency.*

"Whew, it's blustery up here," Coco shouted. The icy wind whipped her dark bangs. As usual, her high tops were untied.

"Come on in. I've got a Volkswagen, too. It's the white Golf," Eva said, gesturing to her car in the lot. "Although mine's not new like yours."

'I custom-ordered it, hot off the assembly line."

"Nice. I like your jacket."

Coco's brunette hair was still short, but she'd spiked it with hair gel. In her ears there were daring new piercings; a silver lightning bolt on one side and a series of studs up the other.

They hugged.

"It's good to see you," they both said at once.

Coco paused inside the front door, taking in the old and new. "Guess what, LaVette? I'm renting a high-rise apartment with a view of Lake Monona. You'll have to sit out on the balcony with me, have a beer."

"Groovy. I can't wait." Eva checked her watch. "It's time."

She waved Coco into the studio. Eva sat in the air chair and Coco took a position at the guest mic.

"So, what's your big news, LaVette?"

"I quit smoking!" She rolled up her sleeve, revealing a plastic patch on her deltoid.

"A transdermal nicotine patch. Way to go. I'm proud of you."

"And me of you. From the campus station to a big star in LA, and now you're the hometown rock chick at MAD96. I've been listening. You sound great. I love the music."

"Thanks, LaVette. Or should I call you Chastine now?"

"LaVette's fine." Eva swapped out a record. "Can you believe it's been a decade since you taught me the ropes? What a roller coaster!"

"And now you're the polka queen."

"Polka Princess, thanks to a feature article in The Polka News, where they also said I was forty-two and played the accordion." A realization hit her: all along, she'd been comparing her career to Coco's. "And now I'm not just a DJ, I'm an office manager."

"I'm glad you let go of your imposter syndrome. Man-a-ger. Own it." Coco drained her bottle of Polka Cola.

"That's right. I like this job. I'm a big fish in a tiny pond."

"You're a lutefisk." From across the counter, Coco grinned. "I'm proud of you."

Eva had been a fish out of water for most of her career: jazz, Lite Hits, country, polka. It had taken a lowly AM polka station to bring out her true self, not a rock station in Chicago or LA.

"The only downsides are the long drive and besides homemade gifts from fans—you should see the rolling pin a woodworker sent to me—we don't get any swag."

"Well, aren't you lucky to know someone who can get you concert tickets?" Coco said, pretending to fan herself with her nose turned up. "Traveling the country was fun while it lasted. But to be home? I feel sane, and grounded."

"The grass is greener in Wisconsin."

"That's for sure."

"What was it was like in LA?"

"Beautiful. Palm trees, spectacular weather—when it's not smoggy. Everything's super expensive. You spend lots of time in your car. Oh, and I'm obsessed with avocados now."

"What was it like at the station?"

"A whirlwind. Actors, comedians, musicians coming in and out—I met *everyone*. We were on the thirty-ninth floor. I could see Dodger Stadium, the San Gabriel Mountains, and the Hollywood sign from the studios. On a clear day—which was rare—we could see all the way to the Pacific." She leaned forward. "There's a new music trend. It's hardcore."

"What's it like?"

"You know how disco evolved into electronic dance music? Well, this is the opposite. It's rock, but raw and less produced than the slick music of the '80s. Kind of grungy. I'm predicting it's a new evolution of rock."

"That's exciting. I'm so sick of synthesizers," Eva said.

Coco laid her hands on the counter. Her eyes sparkled. "I have big news, too."

"You met someone?" Eva asked. The way it sounded, in California, Coco got propositioned by men every day. *Why is she still single?* Eva returned an album to its jacket.

"No, LaVette. I'm the new MAD96 music director!" She hooked her fingers in her suspenders.

"Far out! Just like we talked about in college. Do you get to preview all the new songs?"

"Yes. And talk to record labels and do a weekly show. I'm interviewing a new group called Soundgarden next week."

"Nice." Eva smiled at her friend. "I can't believe you're back."

Coco told more stories, bowling Eva over. While the serene Mississippi meandered through the Midwest, it seemed cocaine and pay-to-play schemes had flowed in LA. But Coco did not do drugs, at least not coke.

After Coco left, Eva pondered the adage. It was true, the grass wasn't always greener—in work or marriage. Wanting to be famous or to be with someone else, none of it had worked. But the years continued to stack one upon the other and build her life. Kind of like a backbone. She could finally stand up. For herself.

After Coco left, Mason whooshed through the door.

"Eva, I need someone to catalog the record library. How would you like to add music director to your title?"

She whipped around, catching herself from tipping over with a hand on the counter. "Really? Does that come with a raise?"

"It comes with an expense account. Just don't overdo it."

She put a hand on her hip. "I'll do it for an extra dollar an hour."

He blinked. "That's a little steep."

Eva waited, a deal-closing trick she'd learned from Candi at B93.

"Okay," he said, shaking her hand.

"Music director, huh?" Eva grinned. She recognized the synchronicity with Coco and the plans they made years ago.

"Put out a memo. Order whatever supplies you need."

Eva collected the previous day's log from a wire bin on the shelf above the albums. It was wavy and stiff, stained with spilled coffee.

Office manager, DJ, and music director. Perfect.

50. RIGHT HERE RIGHT NOW ~ JESUS JONES

Two weeks before Christmas on a Saturday night, Eva sat at the guest mic next to a decorated table-top tree while Coco worked the board in the cozy MAD96 studio. Next door in production, a guy wearing a Green Bay Packers cap bulk-erased carts. Over in the AM, an announcer read the paper while he board-opped a game.

Coco lit a stick of incense. "This is my first time subbing on the night shift. I'm glad you could come."

"Are you sure it's okay?" Eva asked. Artie was at band practice, so she had jumped at Coco's invitation to sit in.

"No one cares, LaVette. I visited you at the Polka Palace. Man, that place is a trip. A throwback to the old days of radio. Not only the building, but the whole feel. It's a bona fide, stand-alone community AM station. Doing anything you want creatively—I can't get that investment firm ad out of my head."

Eva wolf whistled. "*Nice assets!* Mason wrote that one."

Coco pushed a stack of CDs toward Eva. "Here. Take these. My PD says they're not mainstream enough for us."

Eva shuffled through the CDs. "Hole? That's a weird name for a band. It's got so many meanings."

"Right? Black hole. Hole in the ground. Butt hole."

They laughed.

While Coco got ready for a break, Eva regarded the MAD96 studio with its shiny, faux-wood-trimmed console. "Wicked Game" played over the monitors.

COCO NIX: Chris Isaak on MAD96 FM. So much vulnerability in that song, reminding us how powerful falling in love and how tragic losing that love can be. I'm sure you felt it, too. Before that, we heard the English band The Sundays with "Here's Where the Story Ends." I'm Coco Nix, the Rock Chick. Smithereens are coming up next and they'll do anything to win over "A Girl Like You."

While commercials played, Coco ejected the Chris Isaak CD, snapping it into its case. "I saw him in concert at the Oakland-Alameda Coliseum. He's funny."

"I went to see Tuba Dan and the Polkalanders at the Essen Haus last week," Eva joshed.

"That sounds like a blast, actually," Coco said. "I can't believe we're both on middays and we're both music directors. I've had some high-profile gigs, but this is better 'cause I'm home. I missed Wisconsin and, I hate to admit it, but I missed my parents." She started a new song. "Here in Madison, I don't feel like a name on a billboard or just another voice on the radio. I can make a real difference."

Eva felt the same way. She didn't need a flashy morning show or tens of thousands of listeners anymore. *Stars shine the brightest when no one's looking.*

When the phone line blinked, Coco put the caller on speaker. He wanted to know the name of a song she played an hour ago, saying it was about love and started with guitars, like half of their playlist. She asked if he could remember any of the lyrics and he sang, off-key. Coco paged through the music log, offering a half dozen options. Finally, she sang a bit of "Lovesong" from The Cure.

"That's it!" he said.

She gave him the address for B-Side Records on State Street.

While her friend pulled carts, Eva wandered around the studio. At a bulletin board in the back, she scanned FCC licenses. "Where's yours, Coco?"

"It's there. Collette Marie Nixon. That's my real name."

"Collette? Why didn't I know that?"

"Nobody does. If we used two first names like the guys do, I'd be Coco Maries and you'd be Eva Jeans." She chuckled as she changed out a CD.

279

Back at the guest mic, Eva examined tiny ornaments on the countertop Christmas tree, thinking about all the people she'd met in radio and all their various names.

"Hey, do you and Artie like Bonnie Raitt?" Coco asked. "She's at the Civic Center next week. I have front-row seats and backstage passes."

"Cool! Yes! The perks of being the rock chick's best friend. I can live vicariously through you."

After crossing off spots and flipping to the next page of the log, Coco turned to Eva with a serious face. "Say, I haven't asked how you guys are doing. I know the move was hard."

"It's been good. I'm not the same girl who got married at nineteen, the one you met on campus."

Her mind went back to sitting in Dusty's car after the softball game, looking out at the glittering stadium lights and the green ball diamond. And to think, here she was, sitting with Coco again—a bookend in time. So much had changed, yet much had stayed the same: they were still in radio and Eva was still married to Artie.

"The grass is greener where you water it and pull weeds. After you told me about having a fling with my country cousin, I wondered—Baby Shrink talking here—maybe you wanted to distance yourself from Artie before he abandoned you. Because of what happened with your dad."

"Pop didn't leave. He died."

"It may have felt like abandonment to your inner child."

"Possibly." Eva twirled her braid. "After he passed away, I lost myself. I went from role to role—the small kid everyone felt sorry for, a neglected teenager with a basket-case mom, and suddenly I'm a wife with Artie's last name. Being Billie, Lizzy, and Tanya made me feel like somebody."

"I hated pretending to be Raquel Rockwell," Coco said. "In relationships, it's hard enough to maintain your own identity. Then layer on the fake radio personas?"

"Sheesh. There's an excuse—*Tanya* was the unfaithful one." Eva winced. "I've always wanted that head-over-heels, in-love feeling."

"Me, too."

The guy engineering the game in the AM jumped out of his chair and waved his hands in the air, cheering. He gave them a thumbs up through the window before sitting back at the board. Eva returned the thumbs up.

"I guess someone scored," Coco said.

"You always say you're married to radio," Eva said. "Did you have a boyfriend in LA?"

"No, I'm—" Coco glanced at the commercial log. "I haven't been in one place long enough to meet someone special, let alone fall in love."

"Well, I fell hard for Dusty. All it took was for him to say he liked my hair. But the question is, did I really know him?" Deep down, though, she believed Dusty had been falling in love with her. "We never discussed religion or politics, or even if he wanted children."

Coco shook her head while reading the back of a R.E.M. CD.

"I hope time changes the way he thinks of me." Eva buried her face in her hands. "He said I was pretty."

"You're stuck like a skipping record. Be present. Each new moment deserves its own song." Coco loaded the CD into the player. "Did you confess to Artie?"

"Oh, no! Why upend his life for my mistake? It was stupid and I regret it." Eva chewed on her lip. "Telling Artie would only humiliate him. It would erode his ability to trust people—not hurting each other is a form of trust, too. I'll never cheat again."

"Then the only person who needs to forgive you is you."

Eva sat up straight, scrunching her forehead. "You know, Artie's changed since his mom died. He's really trying. That night he got the limo for our anniversary? After dinner, the waiter brought out a lemon poppy seed cake, the same kind we had at our wedding. Artie had it shipped from a bakery in Sheboygan. And last week, he changed the oil in my car. I didn't even ask."

"So manly," Coco said, filing carts.

"The big news is he and his bandmates reunited. We're writing songs together again. The vibe we had when we first met is back."

"Music increases levels of dopamine and oxytocin, the love chemicals in your brain," Coco said, sitting back. "I'm happy for you, Eva. Long ago, you told me you just wanted to play beautiful music with someone."

"I remember. Maybe I'm falling in love with Artie."

"For the first time?"

"Feels like the first time," Eva said, smiling.

Coco slipped headphones around her neck.

"How long are you staying at the polka station, LaVette?"

Eva had a wicked thought. She pictured herself taking Coco's place behind the mic in the posh velvet chair, knowing only one woman could be on the air at any station.

"I don't know, Coco. How long are you staying at MAD96?"

###

Thank you for reading RADIO STARR!

Like radio and listeners, books and readers are inseparable. One amplifies the other. If you enjoyed the novel, it would rock my world if you could tell others about it and leave a short review on Goodreads or Amazon, helping Eva reach more readers.

There were a number of chapters cut from the story during the final edit. If you'd like to read them, send an email to radiobook@lisalehmann.com with "Cut Chapters" in the subject line.

In addition, I have created a soundtrack for you based on Eva's Top 50 Countdown. Scan the QR codes below for links to the playlist on YouTube and Spotify.

Enjoy!
—Lisa

SPOTIFY

YOUTUBE

For more on Lisa's books and photography, and links to her social media, visit lisalehmann.com.

Acknowledgements

First, I send heartfelt gratitude to the phenomenal musicians whose songs instantly bring back memories of the past. Thank you! Hats off to the talented radio people who mentored and/or inspired me along the way and made work fun—there are so many of you. I'm glad our paths crossed. And I love reading posts about the crazy days of spinning vinyl. Rock on social media radio friends!

As for writing, I couldn't have written this novel without UW-Madison's Writers' Institute, Write-by-the-Lake, and Literary Writing programs. I would like to recognize my writing instructor, Christopher Chambers, who edited the novel in 2020, and editor Dana Boyer for her excellent literary eye.

I am blown away by the benevolence of friends who took the time to read early versions of the manuscript. Words cannot express how grateful I am for the optimism of Gabby Parsons, who coined the phrase "For all your roast beef needs" and the retort "I am much taller on the radio." Thank you to John Ehmann, my partner, for his invaluable feedback and devotion (and for reading the book twice!); to my dear, lifelong friend Anita Odekirk who I trusted as my first reader and who helped me get the motorcycle scenes right; Lee Harris, the super-creative and dynamic radio boss who was an early beta reader; Journalist and personality Liane Hansen, for her positive feedback and enthusiasm. Thank you to Jean Tobin, the late Jim Tobin, Gary Shea, Rebecca Eyer, and Tom Swaya for their input, and to family members: Marion Lehmann (my high school English teacher and beloved stepmom), my sweet sisters Lori Gebler and Liz Higgins, and the Ehmanns. I wish my mom was here to read the book; she'd be especially delighted about the music.

Thank you, Tara Huck, Tracey Koach, Peggy Turnbull, and Sophia Dramm with Fresh Water Press for taking a chance on RADIO STARR! Thank you, Vagabond Creative Studio for the wonderful cover. Special recognition goes to Tara Huck for her contagious enthusiasm, brilliant writing brain, hard work, flexibility, and spot-on feedback.

Mastermind Group, thanks for your support through the years: Pam Kachelmeier, Barbara Techel, and Monica Garbisch—my walking partner and a great listener. I appreciate the Mead Library Writer's Club, the Writers Circle at WordHaven BookHouse, and authors Mary T. Wagner and Lisa Hewitt. Sherry Lynch, thanks for massaging out my writing kinks.

A nod goes out to the DJs at WLHA The Big 64, WORT-FM in Madison, 88.9 Radio Milwaukee, and Sirius XM's Deep Tracks DJs for providing the soundtrack to my writing.

Thank you to Fresh Air, produced at WHYY in Philadelphia and distributed by NPR for permission to use the Bob Edwards quote. Along with Cokie Roberts, Bob inspired me very early in my career.

Thank you to everyone who made this book possible.

The Fresh Water Press was founded February 2024 in Two Rivers, Wisconsin, and specializes in books by writers who live in or write about the northeastern Wisconsin lakeshore.

The Press publishes in several genres and welcomes submissions from underrepresented authors and unique voices.

Titles from Fresh Water Press:

Opening Nights: A Collection of Theater Stories

Ghost(ed) Woman & the Electric Purple Pants by Emilie Lindemann

Dial Down: Holistic Strategies to Move from Chaos to Calm by Raquel Durden

Radio Starr by Lisa Lehmann